Just Plain Bad

Greg,

Better than Bad-Ass!

D1504840

Edited by Danielle Ackley-McPhail,
L. Jagi Lamplighter, Lee C. Hillman, and Jeff Lyman

Mundania Press

This Book is Dedicated to
Overturning Preconceptions Everywhere

Published in a earlier edition by Marietta Publishing ©2008
The Series title Bad-Ass Faeries™ is a Trademark of Sidhe na Daire Multimedia.

A Mundania Press Production
Mundania Press LLC
6470A Glenway Avenue, #109
Cincinnati, Ohio 45211-5222

To order additional copies of this book, contact
books@mundania.com
www.mundania.com

Cover Art by Thomas Nackid, www.tomnackidart.com
Book Design by Danielle McPhail, Sidhe na Daire Multimedia,
    www.sidhenadaire.com
Page Border by Ruth Lampi
Edited by Danielle Ackley-McPhail, L. Jagi Lamplighter,
    Lee C. Hillman, and Jeff Lyman

ISBN (trade paper): 978-1-60659-206-9
ISBN (eBook): 978-1-60659-205-2
ISBN (limited edition hardcover): 978-1-60659-210-6

Praise for *Bad-Ass Faeries* ™ 2: *Just Plain Bad*
Winner of the 2009 EPPIE Award for Best Anthology

"Just Plain Bad . . . twenty faerie stories ready to rip all of your
preconceived notions of faeries apart."
—Becky, Bitten By Books Reviews

"Another wonderful collection of stories about Faeries the way they
were meant to be, just plain bad. I loved the peek into the real world of
Faeries who would have Tinkerbell for lunch."
—Penny Ash Rites of Romance Reviews

"*Just Plain Bad* is a wonderful collection well worth your time . . .
I highly recommend this anthology!"
—Jim Stanton, The Fix Short Fiction Reviews

"The stories just keep getting better and better . . .
One read and you're hooked. These authors reign supreme!"
—Shannon Raley, Amazon Review

Praise for *Bad-Ass Faeries* ™
Finalist for the 2007 Dream Realm Award for Best Anthology

Nineteen Faerie tales which in no way resemble the cute little faeries of our
childhood...all of them have a serious twist that I could not help but be
fascinated by. A terrific anthology that I am proud to recommend!
—Detra Fitch, Huntress Reviews (Starred Review)

Bad-Ass Faeries offers a fresh look at a pervasive denizen of our
mythological subconscious. Much as in *Peter Pan*, the collection will
leave the readers applauding, cheering, "I believe in bad-ass faeries."
—Alyce Wilson, Wild Violet | Mortal Coil Reviews (Starred Review)

Bad-Ass Faeries is bound to charm and amuse you
with at least one of its creatively mischievous tales.
—Tom Powers, Small Press Reviews

If the title brings to mind Tinkerbell with twice as much 'tude and
heavy armaments, [then] you've got this anthology in a nutshell.
—Daniel Robichaud, Horror Reader.com

A fine summer read for anyone looking for
a large dose of faerie magic of all stripes.
—Jim Stratton, Tangent Online

Other Mundania Titles by Bad-Ass Faeries Authors

Danielle Ackley-McPhail
Yesterday's Dreams
Tomorrow's Memories

Elaine Corvidae
Daughter of Snow (2010)

Tyrant Moon
Heretic Sun
Sorceress Star

Winter's Orphan
Prince Of Ash
The Sundered Stone

Wolfkin
Crow Queen
Dragon's Son

James Daniel Ross
Radiation Angels: The Chimerium Gambit
Radiation Angels: The Key To Damocles

Skyla Dawn Cameron
Bloodlines
Hunter (2010)

River
Wolfe (2009)

Contents

Shadow Fae ....(Art by Matt Hawk)

Enforcer Fae ....(Art by Ruth Lampi)

Rebel Fae

Way of the Bone

James Chambers

AMONG NEW YORK'S GRIMY BUILDINGS AND THEIR PATCHWORK OF rooftops spread the telltale flickers and momentary distortions of light that signaled the presence of Gorge's enemies. They gathered in the shadows and quiet places of the city's high perches, forsaking the beauty of the Faerie Kingdoms for this world of coarse landscapes and ugliness. No doubt their spies had spread word that Gorge was gathering magic in the mortal world, and though they couldn't know what he planned when he took the stage tonight, they couldn't let whatever it might be go unanswered. In less than eight hours, Red Gorge would perform the biggest show of their long career.

The most important of Gorge's life since his exile.

And there's still much to do, thought Gorge.

He turned from the window to where half a dozen unconscious people lay scattered like wilted flowers. Dev, his drummer, was dead to the world, still dressed in his immutable costume of denim and motorcycle boots, entangled with three sleeping women on one of the couches. Empty bottles and mounds of pills peppered the room. Someone had smashed a torchiere lamp through the widescreen television. Gorge opened the first adjoining room. Inside, Roald, his guitarist, sat meditating on the balcony, his bed empty, his room clean.

Gorge retreated. Next door, his bass player, who looked like he hadn't yet slept, entertained a handful of women in bed. Three of them stared at Gorge's naked body with open lust.

"Sound check at four o'clock. If you're late, I'll have your balls," Gorge said. "I fucking mean it, Tank. Don't screw this gig up."

The bass player nodded over the soft arc of a perfect buttock, and Gorge shut the doors.

He cherished the chaos and abandon these people brought to their celebrations, sweetened so much by their mortality and the very real possibility of dying for a good time. Gorge had known excess before his exile, but it had been bland in comparison, without consequence and therefore cheapened. Here, life was lived on the hard edge of a genuine abyss, and he found it addictive. He'd participated fully for many years, but drugs and alcohol didn't affect him the same way they did the others, and anyway it was the atmosphere of risk and the sense of blind defiance that got him off. This was the way to live: with one's ego and libido unchecked, forever ready to flip the bird at convention.

Back in his room, Gorge opened the curtains and let his skin drink in the midday heat. An old melody from the Faerie Kingdoms flashed through his thoughts, and he sat on the edge of the bed, picked up his guitar, and strummed while he sang the tune in a whisper. He felt a sense of falling into his past, when every day had been a thousand times more glorious than this one, and he had been worshipped, and lived among kings. But the melody Gorge heard perfectly in his mind could not be played as intended here. He put down his guitar and chose that moment to tell himself, as he had every day for more than half a century: *Now I am free.*

Behind him, Delilah uncoiled from the sheets and cupped herself against Gorge's back, wrapping her legs around his waist. Her skin, still damp with sweat from a morning spent in passion, plastered to Gorge. The gnarled knobs of flesh over his scapulae tingled as she cleansed their weeping scar tissue with a moist washcloth from a bowl on the nightstand, and then caressed them with her fingertips and her lips. Electrified with anticipation of tonight's concert, she and Gorge felt more playful and intimate than they had in years.

Delilah hugged him tight, so that her words reached Gorge on the palanquin of her honeyed breath, as she said, "Tell me again about how it was in the Faerie Kingdoms."

Gorge settled against her, caressing the silky tops of her thighs. "Which version do you want today? The paradise I sacrificed for my life here with you, or the gilded cage from which I broke free to save my soul?"

"How do *you* see it today?"

"Today, I see through new eyes. Today it's a delicate fruit rotten at its core, and I will destroy it before it spreads its taint."

"How will you do it?"

"I will find the way, the Way of the Bone."

Delilah glided her tongue over Gorge's neck and slid her hands downward along his chest and abdomen, but he stopped her with a gentle touch.

"You'll keep me here all day if I let you," he said, with a wicked grin. "I've got interviews and a sound check."

Flashing Gorge a luscious pout, Delilah rose and moved to the bathroom. Gorge watched, captivated by her deep, blue-black hair, the shapes and textures of her body, and the sublime way her curves and muscles shifted when she walked. She hadn't aged since he met her more than five decades ago; he'd brought enough magic with him for that, at least, when he'd been banished here, much more in fact than any of those who'd exiled him had ever suspected.

While Delilah sang in the shower, Gorge dressed in black leather pants, a faded orange Killing Joke T-shirt, and a black jacket. On his way out of the suite, he dialed up the Motörhead playlist on Dev's iPod, cranked the stereo volume to full, and then let the door swing shut as the feverish opening riff of "Ace of Spades" kicked in. Guitars screeched, bass and drums thundered, and then came the shouts of sleeping people blasted awake.

Glancing at himself in the elevator wall mirror, Gorge noticed that he'd forgotten his make-up, and he spent a touch of glamour to get his appearance right. The public never saw Gorge absent black lipstick, eyes circled with kohl, and wild spikes of black hair rising from his hawkish face. His transformation to a human body had dampened his native faerie features, but Gorge emphasized their remnants for an exotic appearance. Today of all days, he needed to be the dangerous rock god to perfection; he wanted the undivided attention of millions. When Red Gorge played Madison Square Garden tonight, their performance would be televised live via satellite around the world, opening a tour that would take them to five continents. It was the first step in the last leg of the journey Gorge had begun before he'd been cast out of the Kingdoms.

Snow, a black man with the build of a professional wrestler, greeted Gorge on the twelfth floor. For ten years, Snow had been Gorge's personal assistant and bodyguard, and he'd also become an excellent sound engineer, helping the band plan their performances.

"They're gathering," said Snow, leading Gorge toward the concierge suite.

"I know. I saw them from the window."

"I counted a couple of dozen. Different types, but mostly blackjack sprites."

"Vicious little attack dogs." Gorge grimaced as he remembered the bloodthirsty blackjack sprites that had chewed his fiery, gossamer wings from his body before they'd left him in iron chains in the desert.

"You've trained me to see them, even when they keep themselves mostly invisible, but there are some I still don't recognize," Snow said.

"A handful from the Choruses are here," Gorge said. "As if they could turn song against *me*. And I sensed a trio of elementals, probably the Winds of Change, but I couldn't get a good fix on them."

"So, how do we play it?"

Gorge held back the wise-ass comment that rose to his lips and placed a reassuring hand on Snow's back. "We stay alert. Take down anyone of them that comes within ten feet, and we do what we've always done—play the fucking show. Let them come. They think I'm weak, that if they punish me long enough, I'll repent, or give up, or die. They have no idea how close I am to destroying them."

Snow opened the concierge suite door, and said, "Just keep your guard up, boss, 'cause me, I got bills to pay."

Gorge laughed then turned his attention to a young man inside, whose face glinted with silver piercings. The man was nervous; Gorge played on it, sizing him up with a stony glare, before he flopped onto an easy chair and said, "So, what the fuck do you want to know?"

The man jumped at the sound of Gorge's voice, then introduced himself as Kenny Choi, editor for *Guitar Gun* magazine. The next thirty minutes passed with a series of questions about everything from Gorge's early underground recordings to his influences to what he thought about illegal music downloading, and Gorge delivered every rude, indifferent answer he could think of, grinding hard on his punk-inflected image.

"So, uh, *Way of the Bone*, your new album, out last month. The singles, especially the title song, have been burning up the charts, but there's more to it. It's kind of a concept album, right?" Kenny said. "What's the inspiration behind that?"

Gorge grimaced, counted silently to ten, then said, "It's my fucking life story."

"Wow. So, like, it's a metaphor?"

"Yeah, a metaphor." Gorge slid into his stage voice, and its effect on Kenny was immediate. "About a musician who was the greatest musician who ever lived. I mean, he had, like, headphones plugged directly into the music of the spheres, right? And the music he composed brought tears to the eyes of the dead. His music made virgins tremble. It made royalty melt. And even though he lived in a place where musical talent was a natural gift to nearly everyone, there was no one better than him. So, this guy, he becomes friend to kings and queens, the confidante of emperors and empresses. They even initiate him into the Flock of Eternity, the 1,000 entrusted with all the secrets of the great Kingdoms."

Gorge kicked his feet up on the coffee table in front of him and sneered. "Except it all turns out to be a steaming load of dog shit."

He dragged out a pause to let his story breathe in Kenny's mind before he continued: "Because it was all just a way for these uptight pussies to break him, to keep him in an invisible prison, and make sure he did what they wanted him to do. And when he'd finally had enough, when he spurned their laws and castrating traditions, and pursued the music they'd forbidden, they took him down hard and fast, mutilated him, and cast him off to what they considered Hell. But he only got stronger there. He rose again. He reclaimed his music, and with it came serious fucking magic, and now he's going to bring darkness down on all Creation."

"The Way of the Bone?"

"The dark way, the music that makes gods of men."

"Fucking giving me chills here, man. Tonight's so gonna rock."

"I know," Gorge said, satisfied with the light he'd fired in Kenny's eyes.

Gorge wanted everyone who heard his story to believe in its meaning if not its facts, even if only subconsciously, so that when they later retold it or wrote it down, they imparted some of their belief to others. Gorge's tale resonated powerfully with the band's fans, especially the young, because so many of them sensed that better worlds existed beyond this one, although there was no way for them to ever reach or even perceive them. They were left grappling with anger they couldn't understand, with rage born of soul-deep frustration and the primal knowledge that they were unjustly cut off from great glory. They were left only to dream, and Gorge was happy to inspire them. It had taken years to gather so many fans, and tonight, as Red Gorge played *Way of the Bone* live in its entirety, millions would be enrapt in Gorge's story, focused on *his* life, *his* desires. He would gather the power he needed to wedge open the Way of the Bone. His gain would seem small for the effort spent to obtain it, but the power would be of a special type that would enable Gorge to collect more from around the world, until he became unstoppable and could finally, fully open the Way, and bring all the wild, dark, slavering things in the universe right to the fucking doorstep of the Faerie Kingdoms.

Kenny stood. "Thanks for the interview. It was awesome to meet you. I've been a fan for practically my whole life. Your music is the real fucking deal, man."

"No shit. Keep dreaming, Kenny."

"Count on it."

As Kenny pocketed his digital recorder and his notepad and turned toward the door, Gorge spied it: a faint, bronze shimmer along his spine, like a shirt-seam dusted with glitter. Gorge recognized it at once and flew from his chair, shoved Kenny to the floor, and wrenched free the glimmering, semi-invisible thing that had grafted itself to the editor's back. Kenny screamed. The door flew open and Snow barreled in, just as Gorge rose, wrestling a winged lightning bolt. The creature whipped around, trying to fly free, dragging Gorge against the coffee table, but Gorge held tight, squeezing so hard, his knuckles turned white, until the thing gave up, flickered, and became fully visible. The slender creature had a snake's body topped by the miniature torso, arms, and face of a man. Its wings were like white crow's wings, and at the end of its tail dangled a knobby, spiral stinger.

"Holy . . . shit," Kenny said from the floor.

Snow wrapped a hand around the gun holstered under his jacket. "You okay, boss?"

Gorge nodded. "Look what I've caught."

"A dragon pixie."

"Correct."

"Then we're compromised."

"No, don't you get it? They really don't know what's coming. They sent this pathetic little thing to find out. They're as fucking clueless now as ever. Isn't that right?" Gorge said, looking closer at the dragon pixie. "Don't you know who I am? What I am?"

The pixie trembled, and in a hissing, surprisingly deep voice, it said, "They call you the Death-Singer, black-hearted from the day you were spawned."

"Yes." Gorge smiled, pleased. "And well they should."

"Holy . . . *shit*," said Kenny. "It's all fucking real? The magic shit? That's so mind-blowing!"

"Snow?" Gorge said.

Snow yanked Kenny to his feet, maneuvered him into the corridor, and said, "See you at the show tonight, kid," before he slammed the door shut. Turning back to Gorge, he asked, "So, what do we do with it?"

"Do you know, little pixie," asked Gorge, "what I'm about to accomplish?"

"You think you can open the Way of the Bone from this world, but they'll stop you," said the pixie. "She'll stop you."

"She? Who?" said Gorge.

Realizing it had said too much, the pixie clamped its lips tight.

"Is it Soniella? I don't fear Soniella," said Gorge. "The Flock doesn't know what's coming, else they wouldn't have sent you here to find out. They'd just have killed me outright. But the law is the law, and they sentenced me to exile, not execution."

The pixie said nothing.

"I know them better than you, little wyrm. There's nothing more revealing of someone's nature than being the object of their hatred and subjected to their torture. You're about to learn that, because I'm only going to let you go after I've blinded you, sliced out your tongue, and cut off your hands, so that you can share nothing of what you know with my enemies. You'll be my message to them, because I'll leave you your ears, so that when the great destruction arrives on a crashing wave of sound, you may witness it."

The pixie squealed and thrashed, but Gorge pressed it against the table. It lashed out with its tail, landing its stinger deep in Gorge's arms several times, but Gorge ignored the wounds, and when Snow handed him a knife, the first thing he sliced away was the pixie's tail, chopping off its sting with a single blow. The rest went quickly, and soon Gorge released the decimated creature out the window, cleaned up the room, and called for his next interviewer.

They ended the sound check with "Soniella," Gorge's ballad for the woman who'd been his lover in the Faerie Kingdoms. Soniella had tricked him into surrendering himself for exile, and the song told of a man betrayed by his true love, who then laments that he can't find enough hatred in his heart for her. Only Delilah knew the story, so when she stormed backstage during the song, her fury seemed inexplicable to all but Gorge.

Her reaction pained him. He and Delilah were each other's sanctuary, each the only one the other trusted with their life and soul. In his old existence, Gorge had never known such devotion, but in this world of cruelty and filth, it was essential.

He had been cosmically lucky the day Delilah found him chained to rocky ground in Death Valley. He had terrified her, especially when he attacked her friend after mistaking his camera for a weapon, but he'd fascinated her, too. She freed him, gave him water, brought him home to her city, nursed him, and taught him how to *be* in the flesh of dust and ashes, and he took it as a sign that his way was good, and he must continue. If not for Delilah, he'd have shriveled up and dried in the desert sun until he rotted away to dander, blown across the sand.

He found her in his dressing room, drinking beer and scratching a charcoal stick across one of her countless sketchpads.

"I'm sorry," he said.

"Forget it. It's fine. It's just that you promised me you'd never play that fucking song again."

"I need to prepare myself. I think she's here."

"How can that be?"

"Agents of the Kingdoms will attack tonight, probably during the concert," said Gorge. "I caught a spy this afternoon, and he said, 'She'll stop you.' He couldn't mean anyone else."

"Shit," said Delilah. "Why her?"

"Because they think I won't be able to stand against her. Or maybe they think I still love her."

"Do you?"

Gorge met Delilah's dark stare and said, "I love only you," feeling the nearly palpable truth of the words as he spoke them.

"Will she try to kill you?"

"No, she's of the Flock, and so, supposedly, above such things. But she knows my music better than anyone else, and she might be able to disrupt it. There are faeries from the Choruses and elementals that control the wind. Everything must be played perfectly for the Way to open. If they distort the sound or stop us from playing our full set, it could exhaust what magic I've gathered in this world and leave the Way closed."

"Will you die?"

"No," said Gorge "But you might, if they wipe me out and I can't replenish my magic soon enough. Last time, I had an edge, having brought some with me from the Kingdoms. This time I'll have spent everything I have to crack open the Way. I'd be starting at empty. It could take a century for me to recover."

"Find her and kill her now."

"There's no time. Besides, I'll be the strongest I've ever been as a mortal during the concert. Better to face her then. Soniella will only show herself when the balance of my spell is most exposed. I'll be ready. I won't let her harm you. I won't let her destroy what you and I have." Gorge took Delilah's chin in his hand and turned her face toward his. "I promise. You're my night-haired beauty. You saved me, and I'll save you. We're meant to be together for all time."

He kissed her, stirring to the heat of her lips. He folded himself against her on the couch, feeling how she trembled and clutched at him, and then they slid out of their clothes, moved together, and afterward lay there until it was time to dress and for the show to go on.

Four songs into their set, Red Gorge had already driven the crowd to frenzy. People in the audience danced and slammed against each other, screamed lyrics from raw throats, and surrendered to the deep rhythms rising from the band. Their faces resembled ghost buoys bobbing on a dark sea. Dev, Roald, and Tank played like never before, the best Gorge had ever heard them: tight, fast, and with a will that would've left entire cities dead in their wake had they been an army on the march. They thrived on the excitement of the crowd, on the fulfillment of their deepest wishes of greatness; it flowed through them into the music. And Gorge worked his voice to its limits, ascending scales in rapid succession as he wove ethereal song over the hard terrain of the instruments. That was Red Gorge's signature sound: the grinding, irresistible progress of guitar, bass, and drums, elevated by transcendent melodies and Gorge's unearthly voice. In the Kingdoms, where many more notes and musical scales existed, their music would've sounded crude, but in this world, it surpassed anything people had ever before heard.

As Roald bit into a guitar solo, Gorge raised his microphone stand and slammed it against the stage like a spear. He drifted from the spotlight while guitar notes blistered the air, and he glanced offstage at Delilah and Snow, who looked worried by what Gorge's enemies might bring. To Gorge they seemed immeasurably fragile, like toys of paper and wax vibrating in the barrage of sound blasting out of the arena's speakers. Part of him wanted to grasp Delilah's hand and comfort her, but another part wondered why he bothered with such a trivial creature as a human woman who should've been dead ten years ago—and the moment that thought formed, he knew his enemies stood nearby. He hadn't even noticed their attack beginning, so subtle had it been; but now that he'd sensed the arrogant taint of the Kingdoms creeping into him, he couldn't miss it.

It knocked him off balance and he almost lost his cue, but then he launched back into the song with a roar that shook the walls. The audience responded with thousands of voices that together barely measured up to the power of Gorge's amplified singing. The band tore into the end of the song with terrifying force, and didn't skip a beat launching into the next one. The others sensed Gorge's urgency and played with fantastic speed, as the lyrics emerged from Gorge like a cyclone slamming cars together along a rain-slashed highway. The arena rumbled, and the full force of the audience's energy connected with Gorge; a feedback loop opened as he absorbed it, skimmed away what he wanted, and kicked it back to them through the music. It was the moment he'd been working toward; the opening had begun.

The people nearest the stage thrashed to the beat, writhing like panicked animals. Security guards struggled to contain the melee from the rest of the crowd. Gorge watched the sea of people shoving, dancing, fighting, some of them even fucking in the dark, and he swelled with pride at what he'd wrought. Like a living thing, the song grew around them in the shadows, stretched itself in the flashing stage-lights, reached its thunderous crescendo, and then Red Gorge segued straight into the next number: the title song from *Way of the Bone*.

Dev assaulted his drums and Tank's fingers ripped along the bass. Rhythm ruled for two measures and then Roald's hands moved over his guitar strings, creating a riff that filled the arena like a jet of something molten. The world wavered, as if the walls and roof, the advertising posters, and the overhead jumbo television screens were peeling back from reality, so that the audience existed only within the music. Gorge rose at the edge of the stage like a crane about to dive into the air and sang:

> *Born in a moment*
> *Born in pain*
> *Nothing's ever the*
> *same again*
>
> *Chained in the desert*
> *Chains in my mind*
> *Wings bit off by*
> *my own kind*
>
> *Once, lord of lyrics*
> *Once, prince of peace*
> *Now a demon let*
> *off his leash*
>
> *And I will find the way*
> *the Dark way, the way home*
> *the way to Hell*
> *the Way of the Bone*

His voice soared, hounding the melody along a gouging assembly of sound that lifted and enhanced it, and then a hundred voices joined in, then a thousand, then ten thousand, and more as the crowd sang, and the seal on the Way of the Bone loosened. The arena faded away. Power flowed into Gorge, and he sensed the universe trembling at his hubris, for the Way of the Bone would bring only death, would stir only the carrion eaters and the blind things that stood hungry in the night. It was the forbidden Way, submerged inside the deepest pockets of reality, and Gorge was slipping his filthy fingernails in around the edges to pry it loose for his pleasure.

Empress loved me
King smiled down
Until I stepped upon
hallowed ground

Music surrendered
Love became dread
Cast away, scarred, and
left for dead

But I will find the way
the Dark way, the way home
the way to Hell
the Way of the Bone

The blackjack sprites came first, swarming across the darkness like oversized wasps, but Gorge swept his gaze in their direction as he repeated the chorus and vaporized them on a burst of sound, hurling them back to the Kingdoms. Next came the Winds, howling, driving down on the band, forcing Roald and Tank to the stage floor, rattling Dev's drums like dice, but Red Gorge kept playing, kept the rhythm, and hit every note with practiced precision and the smoldering passion of fifteen years of hunting a dream. The Winds clutched at the sounds. Gorge watched the whirling elementals as they lashed out with airy tendrils, trying to grasp individual notes, to warp and change them, but the music was too powerful. It carried on. His enemies hadn't had half a century to become acclimated to this world like Gorge had, and as he started into the song's final verse, he funneled some of his power upward to create a countervailing gale that sent the Winds of Change home.

Sing to me of shadows
Of stars gone dark
Of death and lies,
the hideous art

Now a light glowed across the arena, and as Roald and Tank drove into a synchronized barrage of notes, a new sound rose over the music, although only Gorge heard it at first. It came in harmony, three voices singing a gentle tune ill-conceived for the way sound worked in this world, yet effective nonetheless, especially when joined by a fourth singer with a much more powerful voice.

A voice Gorge knew.

Soniella.

She flashed across the black expanse.

She'd brought three of her best from the Choruses. They were singing, but not to disrupt Gorge's song, as he'd anticipated. Like him, they were singing to open a way. The light that glowed around them became brilliant, almost blinding, at least to Gorge, who could perceive it fully, and perhaps to Snow and Delilah, whom he'd trained to see as he did. The audience would glimpse only enough to think it was part of the light show. Notes flowed outward from Soniella and her singers, rising from their lips like delicate snowflakes etched from candle flames. They amassed to form a ragged, swirling oval. Through its heart, Gorge saw the place he'd once called home: his conservatory in the Kingdoms, untouched from the day he'd left it. The half-finished composition he'd been writing still sat propped up beside his instruments. The faeries' magic slowed time, so that each single note Red Gorge pumped out lasted what seemed like minutes, while Gorge stared at the indescribable beauty beyond the opening, astonished by how much it exceeded his memories, how much sweeter the air flowing out of it wasthan the air of this dingy gutter world, how much more sublime were the sounds.

Soniella descended to the stage with open arms. Gorgeous beyond Gorge's capacity to describe with a human mind, she stood bathed in light and clothed in transparent, iridescent cloth that revealed every measure of her perfection. Her hair moved like liquid gold, and from her back sprouted glorious double wings of blue and yellow. Once their beauty had been equaled only by that of Gorge's wings, and when they'd flown together over the Kingdoms, entire villages had stopped to watch them pass. Gorge met her eyes, dizzying in their depths, and watched her lips move as she sang out, working hard to form the right sounds in the unfamiliar environment. Then her singers held a long, trilling note, and reality seemed to freeze.

"Come back, Gorge," Soniella said. "We wronged you greatly. We see that now. Return and be restored. My guilt has never faded, and I miss you, my love."

Gorge's eyes wandered over Soniella, over the view of the Kingdoms, and then he looked at Delilah, who, in comparison, appeared crudely formed, like a statue fashioned of cinder and silt. He looked at Soniella's wings and felt an ache in his shoulders as a sensation of phantom wings emerged from his ruined joints.

Seeing where Gorge's gaze led, Soniella said, "We can heal you. You'll fly again, and you and I can be as we once were."

Gorge had never considered that the Flock might offer him reconciliation; that all he had forsaken might be restored to him, and his lost glory renewed. The entire arena was awash in magical energy, barely contained by his efforts and those of Soniella. It made him tremble. He felt cold. Here was a choice he'd never anticipated. The anger he'd nursed for so long now seemed like surf breaking over an eternally rocky shore. It would be madness to refuse, but there was so much behind him that he felt the pull of this world strongly. He stared into his conservatory, remembering his days there, letting his eyes move over the wonders he'd once possessed, until he spotted a small, crystal square, engraved with musical notations, and carved to act like a prism, always surrounded by color. A gift from Soniella. Once he'd cherished it. The memories it held were the most potent Gorge possessed—and the most painful.

Gorge peered into Soniella's flickering eyes. Her magic strained her here, but she'd accumulated a great deal of power since he'd last seen her. She welcomed Gorge into her arms, and he whispered, "I have a gift for you, love." Then Gorge kissed her and stroked her dusty, silken wings, holding Soniella close enough to feel some of the tension leave her as she decided she'd won him over. She let down her guard. Gorge pressed his lips to hers and inhaled, sucking a blast of magic out of her body and into his. His power surged as Soniella's withered. He made a claw of his hand and ripped away the top quarter of her left wing, before he shoved her aside and released a burst of energy, almost everything he'd accumulated that night. Soniella's spell shattered and the brilliant opening vanished, taking with it the three singers, and Gorge's last glimpse of the Kingdoms. The music thundered back to full life and Gorge sang:

> *My gift to you*
> *My gift to them*
> *Nothing's ever the*
> *same again*

> *And I will find the way*
> *the Dark way, the way home*
> *the way to Hell*
> *the Way of the Bone*

The song rumbled toward its ending, as Soniella—shocked, confused, and wounded—ghosted to nothingness and faded back to the Faerie Kingdoms. Roald led the band to a crashing conclusion, and when the music ended, Gorge alone sang out:

> *And I will find the way*
> *The Way of the Bone*

The crowd exploded with applause, and Gorge collapsed to the stage. He struggled with what magic was left in him to keep the Way open, but there was not enough, and everything around him snapped back to substance as the Way slammed closed. He would gather no more power tonight. The band rushed to his side, but he couldn't move, couldn't stand. Delilah shoved past Tank, knelt down, and took Gorge's hand. Before she could speak, he grabbed the back of her neck and pulled him to her, kissing her, and as he did, he released all the magic left inside him, delivering it to her body, recharging the magic already there. He watched for a moment as Delilah quivered with shock, and then Gorge's eyes shut, and there was only darkness.

Gorge ached when he awoke, but Delilah's face at his side eased the pain. There was sunlight. Gorge lay in a hospital bed.

"Shhh," Delilah said. "It's okay. You collapsed, but the doctors don't think there's any permanent damage."

"She came to take me home," Gorge whispered. "And I said no."

Tears welled in Delilah's eyes. She took Gorge's hand, pressed it against her cheek. "You feel so cold. You sent all your magic into me. It filled me up the moment the Way closed. Why, when you were so close?"

Gorge shut his eyes and pictured Soniella as she'd appeared last night: glorious and vibrant, rippling with power, and yet deep in her eyes there had dwelled black terror curling like venom in a place where he only ever saw warmth and love from Delilah.

"In the Kingdoms, they fear me. That's enough for now. And what would opening the Way mean without you beside me? What would anything mean without you? The magic is my gift to you."

Gorge took Delilah's hand and pulled her into bed beside him. It was only in the halo of Delilah's warmth that this life felt right and his way felt good. Delilah nestled her head against Gorge's chest, hearing his heartbeat, and they lay there, listening to each other's breath, to the indifferent rhythms of the city outside, to the breeze humming past the half-opened window. Gorge chose that moment to remind himself, as he did everyday: *Now I am free.*

Moonshine

Bernie Mojzes

I N THIS ROOM, PROHIBITION WAS SUSPENDED. BOOZE FLOWED LIKE
the music at Pogo & Bud's: hot and sultry, drums and bass laying down
the groove as the piano tinkled like ice on glass, saxophone splashing
across the bar and into darkened corners. Bryn Mawr debs in feathers and
fringe danced with nattily dressed negroes from the city. Tobacco and
marijuana mingled in the hot June air, blown around by lazy fans.

Tom Marich leaned back against the bar with closed eyes, letting the
music wash over him, fingers tapping echoes of the melody against his
whiskey glass. He wasn't the only regular attracted more by the music
than the speakeasy's other offerings. Young musicians who pushed the
boundaries wouldn't find work at respectable venues like the Dunbar.
Bud McGarritty made a point of booking some of the most innovative
jazzmen in the country.

"It's what makes having *that*," McGarritty had said to Tom
once, glancing toward an unmarked door at the back of the room,
"bearable."

Through that door and down a corridor was another world, one of
men with haunted eyes, and sometimes girls in giggling pairs or three-
somes. Tom had been there once, enticed by a pale slip of a girl whose
name he'd never known. He'd paid a man for passage to a place where
something akin to heaven awaited. The opium was sweet as nectar,
the sex sweeter, but one look at the wasted men, too lost in dream
and decay to appreciate the willing flesh around them, made him
swear to stick to jazz and whiskey.

Tom chain-smoked through the set, watching the flappers
dance as he sipped his drink. When his last smoke threatened to burn his lips, he caught the attention of

the tantalizing redhead with the cigarette tray. He tossed three nickels on the tray and tapped a cigarette out of the pack of Lucky Strikes, smiling as the girl leaned forward with a lighter. She grinned and winked at him.

"My name's Mary," she tossed over her shoulder as she walked away.

After the set, Tom waved his empty glass at McGarritty, but the bartender was down at the end of the bar in distracted conversation with a small man that Tom had never seen before. Tom reassessed—there wasn't even a hint of stubble on the boy's face as he looked up innocently at McGarritty's scowl. His oversized jacket and pants made him seem even skinnier than he probably was. Tom drew his bar stool closer for a listen . . . and for a place at the front of the queue once McGarritty was pouring again.

"That ain't the way things're done," McGarritty was saying. "In this world there's rules; even a punk like you knows it's bad for your health to go making side deals."

The kid took off his hat. Fine brown hair fell to his shoulder.

Tom blinked in surprise. All thoughts of the Lucky Strikes girl vanished.

"Mr. McGarritty," the kid said in a woman's low alto, the words falling like music from his—her—lips, "I'm not asking you to do anything on any side at all. I'd simply like you to sample my wares. I believe that with the endorsement of a fine businessman such as yourself, and perhaps some of your more discriminating customers, I shall be able make the arrangements necessary for a long and lucrative partnership for all those concerned."

There was something slightly alien in her voice: the accent of a girl who had come to America in early childhood. Tom struggled to place it. A first-generation Serb growing up in a neighborhood of immigrants, he had experience with accents, but this one eluded him with a familiarity that lingered just out of reach.

McGarritty hesitated. "I dunno . . . ."

Tom set his empty glass on the bar between McGarritty and the girl. She jumped, just slightly, surprised by the sudden intrusion.

"I'll try it," he said with a playful smile, "if you'll join me. Hell, right about now, seems like it's the only way to get a drink around here." The last he directed to McGarritty, though his eyes never left her face.

"Excellent," she said, pulling a tall, thin bottle from inside her jacket. The liquor that poured from the dark green glass was a translucent, milky white that glowed in the dimly lit bar.

"Is that Absinthe?" Tom asked.

She smiled. "Not quite, though it's quite potent in its own way. We call it Moonshine. That's what gives it that glow. I'm told that it's also a pun. This recipe has been in my family for a long time, and it's time to share it with the world. So, here I am." She raised her glass and clinked it against Tom's. "To world domination," she said, and her eyes glittered.

There was a mild burn, the licorice-gummy anise almost masking the bitter bite of wormwood that gave Absinthe its distinctive properties. Tom smiled knowingly, then his eyes widened in surprise. A secondary flavor washed the anise from his mouth with a harsh burn reminiscent of *Slivovics*, the strong plum brandy his father used to distill in his basement. But there was something else, something he couldn't pinpoint. Like the girl's accent, it was almost familiar, hovering at the tip of recognition, but when he thought too hard it slipped away.

"That's amazing," he said, as the warmth burned slowly through his limbs.

"Amazing how?" McGarritty demanded. "What's it taste like?"

"It's . . . ." Words failed him. "Just try it, you'll see."

"Fine." McGarritty grumbled as he set out a third glass.

"Another?" The girl smiled as she tipped a bit more into Tom's glass, then poured for McGarritty and herself.

"Sure." It was good. Better than good. He felt warm and strong and sexy. Every sight was more vivid, every sound more tactile, every touch more flavorful.

A look of wonder crossed McGarritty's face. "How much?"

"This bottle? It's free. The rest? Well, that's going to depend on how big a piece your, uh, acquaintance is going to require. I think that we can find a price that will keep all of us happy. Maybe we could talk again on Tuesday? You'll arrange that with the relevant parties." It wasn't a question.

"Tuesday? Yeah, I'll see what I can do."

"You do that," she said, pushing the bottle across the bar toward him. "Or Wednesday I'll be talking to some Italians."

McGarritty nodded sharply. "Yes, ma'am. I understand. We got one shot."

"Good boy." She tucked up her hair and fit it back under her fedora. Tom wondered how he could have ever mistaken her for a boy. Maybe it was the puckish grin, accentuated as it was by her angular features.

"For the record," Tom said, "wherever this stuff ends up, that's where I'll be." He smiled at the girl. "I'm Tom, by the way. Tom Marich."

She held out a hand. "You may call me Evelyn." She pronounced it with a long 'e,' and Tom thought of apples and gardens and snakes, of the original Eve, standing up naked and unafraid to pluck the Fruit of Knowledge away from God. He bent to kiss her hand, then surprised himself by leaning forward boldly and whispering in her ear. A smile played across her lips.

"An interesting proposal, Tom Marich." She fingered the collar of his shirt thoughtfully, slid her hand down his chest, then pulled back abruptly. Something burned fiercely on Tom's chest. Her eyes narrowed warily. "Or not," she said. She pushed her hat down firmly, tucked in a stray strand, and turned to leave. "Tuesday," she said, over her shoulder. "Three o' clock."

Tom blinked, suddenly clearheaded. He caught the Lucky Strikes girl's eye as she worked her way across the floor. She smiled as he rose to meet her.

"Would you like to come upstairs with me?" he asked, setting a glass of Moonshine on her tray.

Mary bit her lip. "I don't know. I've never . . . ." She gestured helplessly. "And I'm working till ten."

He smiled, nodding toward the stage, where the band had started tuning up. "I'll be here."

Brogan O'Connor checked himself in the mirror of the car before he got out. One of the boys handed him his hat, and he set it carefully on his head, then straightened his suit.

Evelyn watched this display from her seat outside the lunch counter two doors down from Pogo & Bud's. She sipped her coffee, determined it tepid, and warmed it discreetly. O'Connor adjusted his cuffs and his bow tie. Only then did he walk through the door one of his boys patiently held open for him. He was on time.

How conscientious.

She waved for another cup of coffee.

O'Connor was properly agitated by the time Evelyn slipped past the man at the door. He'd taken a corner table against the wall, where he sat with his legs crossed, sipping a Manhattan. He checked his pocket watch, polishing it before putting it away. Compared to the men who flanked him on either side, he looked harmless. Evelyn appreciated the illusion, even as she perpetrated her own. She walked up to the table without introduction, and without a word, set a bottle of Moonshine in front of the man.

"What the hell's this?" O'Conner stared at her as if she was a bug.

Evelyn kicked a chair back and sat, not waiting for an invitation. "This is Moonshine, Mr. O'Connor," she said, putting one foot up on the table and hooking a thumb under a suspender. "I've got a shipment coming in Thursday, and I'm bringing it here, but Mr. McGarritty was insistent that I speak with you."

O'Connor turned to the thug on his left. "Remind me to have a little chat with Bud."

"Yes, sir." He chuckled.

Evelyn nodded. "Yes, I think it's only right that you thank him personally."

"Yeah. Y'know what I'm thinking, Miss . . . ?" O'Connor paused expectantly.

"Evelyn."

"What I'm thinking, Miss Evelyn, is . . . ."

"Just Evelyn. I don't give out my full name to anyone."

"Just Evelyn. Fine. The clientele at our fine establishments expect only the best, and we take great pains to procure the finest spirits available from reputable manufacturers. There is no market for backwoods corn squeezings in this city."

Evelyn kicked suddenly, shoving the table back and spilling O'Connor's drink in his lap. Both of his men reached for their guns. She put her hands on the table and leaned forward. "Moonshine is not corn squeezings, and it is infinitely better than that crap you're wearing."

"I think you'll want to take your 'Moonshine,' *Miss* Evelyn, and shove it up your ass." O'Connor spoke coldly, then smiled easily and leaned back in his chair.

"Pardon my French. And please, if you have any problems making it fit, let me know. I'll have one of the boys help you out."

Evelyn laughed. "These boys?"

"Gentlemen!" McGarritty set an armload of empty glasses on the table with shaking hands. "And lady. This ain't the way to start out a business relationship." He fussed nervously, mopping the table with a towel, then hesitating as he contemplated the wet spot on O'Connor's pants. He'd rushed over as soon as he saw Evelyn. How she'd gotten in without his notice he didn't know. He uncapped the bottle. "Let's just calm down and share a drink. And, uh, calm down." He poured three trembling shots of soft, white light, knocked one back without waiting. Tension uncoiled visibly as he exhaled and he refilled his glass. He held it up and looked at Evelyn and O'Connor expectantly. "To future friends?"

"That seems unlikely."

"Please, sir, just try it."

O'Connor looked at the glass suspiciously. "Her first."

"To future friends," she said, draining her glass.

O'Connor scowled, sipped tentatively. He licked his lips. "It's . . . ."

"A hundred dollars a case," Evelyn said. "That's what I want. Anything else is purely between the two of you."

"A hundred for a drink nobody's heard of?" O'Connor made a small gesture. One of his associates refilled his glass. "Eighty would be generous."

"I'm not asking you to be generous. A hundred will do."

Mid-September, but it felt like August. There was no relief from the heat. The ceiling fans merely blew the thick, humid air around the oven that was Pogo & Bud's, mixing the smoke into a dense, uniform haze that stuck shirts to skin, beaded up and ran in thin, greasy rivulets down faces and throats. Even the most fastidious of the Negro gentlemen had shed jackets and loosened ties. Tom had lost the tie entirely, and unbuttoned both his collar and his cuffs, something that would have been unthinkable only a month ago.

Tom sipped his Moonshine and listened to the band. They weren't very good: an insipid swing reminiscent of gumdrops. Mary leaned her head against his arm, her hair clinging damply to her face. It was hot, oppressive, and only guilt kept him from telling her not to touch him.

"Do you want to dance?" she asked, looking up at him with disinterested eyes. She was shivering, despite the heat.

Tom looked out at the dance floor, where bodies moved in time to the music with frantic exhaustion. There was something almost desperate there—souls seeking something elusive, something they had once held, but somehow lost. It had been said that Heaven's greatest pleasure was to see clearly into Hell and watch the torment of one's former oppressors. But perhaps the reverse held more truth: that Hell's greatest torment was to see clearly into Heaven and know, but never quite believe, that those pleasures would be forever just beyond one's reach.

"No," he said.

Mary laid her head back against his shoulder. There may have been relief in her eyes.

On the dance floor, two men bumped and scuffled. Punches were thrown and a knife was pulled. There was blood, but not much, before bouncers pulled the men apart. A week-long heat wave was bound to make tempers flare, and all the extra ice McGarritty put in the drinks wasn't going to change that. Tom reached for his cigarettes. The whole town was a tinderbox. There'd been daily murders for the past month. People were on edge, angry, rude. It had to be the heat. But it felt like something more. It felt like the whole world was slowly going mad.

"Take me upstairs." Mary ran trembling fingers across his arm.

Tom closed his eyes and pulled hard on his cigarette, letting the smoke out through his nostrils.

"C'mon, baby," she said. "It's been days."

What might have been years or minutes later, Tom woke to the smell of vomit. All he could taste was ash. Mary lay next to him, her long, matted hair wrapped around his left arm. He untangled himself carefully. The breath caught in his throat as he brushed against her cold skin, and the memories flooded back: Mary pushing the needle into his vein—his first time, though apparently not hers—the pleasure flooding his body as she'd loosened the belt around his arm. He'd watched with detachment as she refilled the syringe for herself, watched her fall back against the cushions with a sigh before losing himself in dream.

She was breathing, shallow but steady, and fear eased its grip on his throat. But she didn't wake up when he shook her. He decided to wash up a bit and collect his wits. Time was meaningless here, but apart from a few passed out junkies, the room was empty. It had to be sometime in the morning.

Tom stumbled his way downstairs and stopped short. The door to the men's lavatory had been ripped off its hinges. Inside, porcelain shards lay in a pool of bloody water. Sinks had been ripped off the walls, urinals shattered. A half-dozen bullets had splintered the wooden toilet stall, and blood seeped under the door.

He'd slept through this?

He rubbed his eyes and considered his bladder, and then pushed open the door to the ladies' lavatory, and he tried not to think of the sounds he'd heard coming from inside the splintered stall. The sounds of something feeding.

Pogo was the first one in. He burst through the door and ran around the room, checking behind the bar and sniffing under the tables, stopping briefly to scratch behind his ear, then with a grunt he set off in the direction of the men's lavatory. He stood in the doorway with the stub of his tail lowered, ears back, growling his confusion.

"Pogo, boy! Never mind that." Bud McGarritty followed slowly, slapping his thigh with his good hand to quiet the old rottweiler. The dog whined once, still bristling. His eyes darted from McGarritty's face to the lavatory. Something was upsetting him. Probably the blood.

McGarritty shook his head. "Good goddamn, Pogo. Look at the state of this place." Cigarette butts and broken glass littered the floor. Empty glasses and overflowing ashtrays covered the bar and tables. "They call this cleaning up?"

Pogo nuzzled his knee. There'd been bodies the night before. McGarritty didn't know what had happened to them, didn't want to know. 'Cleaned up,' he supposed. Hell, he didn't even know if the guy who'd shot him was alive or dead. He'd fallen and woken in the hospital with his arm in a sling, and now he had to deal with this. And with company coming, at that.

With a sigh, McGarritty collected glasses and stacked them on the bar, pushing trash onto the floor as he cleared the tables. He'd get it with the broom.

"Gentlemen," said Brogan O'Connor with a smile. "I'm glad you could make time to visit the City of Brotherly Love." He looked around at the assembled East Coast mob bosses and their entourages. "Apologies for the mess. There was a small incident here last night. But our business here is important enough to put up with a little discomfort. Seems we're missing only one person, our perpetually tardy guest of honor."

"Oh, I'm here," Evelyn said, tipping her hat with a half-smile. She was leaning against the bar. "I've been here."

Pogo jumped, hackles raised, and started barking. "Hush," McGarritty said, to no avail. The morphine dulled more than the pain—he didn't remember letting Evelyn in. She smiled at him and took the empty seat across from O'Connor.

O'Connor tapped his fingers on the table. "Bud," he said, "you look like you're about to fall over. Why don't you go upstairs and take a load off your feet? Keep the junkies out of trouble. And take the damned pooch with you."

Business was long and complex, and Evelyn found her mind wandering. She had little interest in how these people distributed Moonshine around the country. They'd done a fine job throughout the Northeast with minimal infighting, and she was pleased with the results. Demand was outstripping supply, and that only fed the frenzy of orders. The drink had become popular with stockbrokers in New York, and some of the shipments to the capital had found their way to both the White House and Congress. Demand was building in Los Angeles and Chicago. The meeting today was to carve up the rest of the country between them, and to figure out how to best leverage the demand for Moonshine into national power.

None of that was her concern. She was only there to guarantee that whatever scheme they came up with, the supply of Moonshine would be there to support it.

"Capone's the real problem," one of them was saying. Evelyn had smiled politely through introductions, but hadn't bothered to learn their names. As far as she was concerned they were interchangeable. "He's gonna do everything in his power to get at the source. He won't take to playing second fiddle without a fight."

"That, gentlemen, is the crux of the problem." O'Connor leaned back, hands behind his head. "We're completely dependent on one single person. If something, God forbid, happened to her, where would we be? I think that it's time that that changes." He smiled. "Miss Evelyn, it's time to renegotiate the terms of our agreement. It's time for you to step aside and let the men handle things. We are, of course, extremely grateful for the opportunity you have presented us, and we've got an extremely generous offer for you."

"Oh. Really?"

"We're about to go to war with Chicago over something that could up and walk out on us one day. That just ain't good business sense. All you've got to do is put us in contact with your supplier. We'll pay you enough to make sure you never have to work again."

Evelyn smiled. "No, I don't think so."

O'Connor shot a look at one of his men, a large Swede. "I'm going to ask you once more to reconsider, before we're forced to resort to alternative methods. Trust me. A suitcase full of hard cash is by far the more attractive option. Though Anderson here might disagree." The Swede grinned stupidly through broken teeth.

She shook her head sadly, though the smile never faded. O'Connor sighed, and then gestured with his chin.

Anderson grabbed her by the hair, pulling her roughly to her feet. He ripped her white button-down shirt open with the other hand, then threw her on the table.

"Not here, idiot!" O'Connor's eyes flashed. "Take her, I dunno, in there." He pointed at the ladies' lavatory. "Bring her back when she's ready to talk."

Anderson dragged Evelyn out of the room. She bit his wrist as he pushed her against the wall, but his slap took her to her knees.

"Is that all you've got?" she asked, as she got back up. With a sudden movement she raked out with her hand, fingernails gouging deeply into cheek and lip and chin. She grinned.

"Bitch." The punch bounced her head off the wall and she collapsed, bleeding from her mouth and nose. Anderson laughed, an innocent, boyish noise that made Tom's blood run cold where he huddled, perched on a toilet seat in one of the stalls, not ten feet away. He heard the sound of fabric tearing.

Anderson knelt between Evelyn's legs and readied himself. In a fluid motion, Evelyn pulled herself up and kissed him. His mouth opened to her tongue.

"Blood to blood I bind thee," she said softly, "and seal it with a kiss." She pushed him away. "I think we're done here."

Evelyn made her way unsteadily to her seat at the table, belt and suspenders holding her torn slacks in place, her shirt left tattered and open. Anderson took his position behind O'Connor.

"I guess that makes this a tittie bar," someone said. People laughed.

O'Connor glared at them with displeasure. He took a deep breath. "Apologies, Evelyn, for these unpleasantries. Are you ready to give us what we asked for?"

"I've already told Anderson my answer. Perhaps he'd be so good as to deliver it?"

Anderson's gun roared. O'Connor's face dissolved, his blood splattering across the table and over Evelyn's face and chest. Brogan O'Connor slumped face-down on the table with a rustle of silk and a soft thump. There were more shots then, from a half-dozen guns—almost inconsequential, they seemed nearly silent after the first shot tore the air. Anderson danced erratically before he dropped.

Evelyn ran a finger between her breasts, licked the blood off it and smiled, ignoring the guns aimed at her head, ignoring the grim faces. "Not bad," she said with approval, then: "I'm willing to honor the existing agreements at the existing terms. I will continue to leave the details of distribution to you and to you exclusively, for as long as your organizations continue to operate smoothly and efficiently. Unless there is someone else who would like to renegotiate? No? I thought not. Negotiations are such messy things." She wiped some more of O'Connor's blood from over her eye and suckled her finger once more.

"Actually," she said, "he's not bad at all."

Pogo & Bud's grew quiet at last. Tom gave it a few minutes to be sure, and then took a tentative step off the toilet seat. His legs were cramped and he nearly fell. He resisted the urge for a cigarette. Get out while he could, that was the important thing. There would be plenty of time for cigarettes later. Once out of the stall, he tried to ease the cramping, alternately stretching and massaging his calves. He'd need to move quickly and quietly if he wanted to get out of this alive.

The door opened abruptly and Tom found himself staring straight at Evelyn. She looked around the room, seeming not to see him, then stripped off the remains of her shirt. Every time her eyes slid across him, something on his chest burned. It was the pendant, the old iron amulet his grandmother had given him. That, he suddenly realized, was what she'd touched the first day he'd seen her, when she abruptly pushed him away. Maybe she hadn't simply been rudely pretending she hadn't seen him these past months. Maybe she really hadn't.

She washed her face and body briskly over the sink, and Tom watched, heart pounding in his throat. Evelyn was a monster, he reminded himself, who had cold-heartedly gotten two people killed. But that didn't dull the longing that burned suddenly in him, longing that he'd barely remembered from the first time he'd met her. She dried herself with a towel and then looked closely at her face in the mirror.

Tom gasped, and she spun around wildly. Her gaze seemed to slide right off him. Again, the pendant burned against his skin. He held his breath. He must have been wrong. Her face was bruised, her lip split, her nose crooked and probably broken, but she was still heart-stoppingly beautiful, in her harsh, boyish way.

Her reflection, on the other hand? The green, wrinkled thing in the mirror that mimicked her as she gingerly prodded her lip and nose bore only the faintest resemblance to Evelyn. It licked its lips as she did, wincing at the pain. "They died too quickly," she muttered.

Evelyn turned on the tap and threw water on the mirror in front of her, spreading it over the glass with her hands. As the water ran in thin rivulets, the image behind it changed. The woman reflected shared some of Evelyn's features, the same thin, sardonic lips, the slightly angled eyes, but she had long, raven-black hair that matched the silk evening gown hugging her slight curves. Red-gloved fingers brought a long-stemmed cigarette holder to her lips.

"Little sister," said the woman in the mirror, each word a delicate puff of smoke, "you look a frightful mess."

"We all make our sacrifices, yes?" Evelyn touched her lip. "How are things in Germany?"

A slow smile. "The Germans love their *Bier*, but they seem to have found something they like even better. *Geistwasser* is now served in every bar in the country, and also in Austria. We have been exporting to Italy, but I think we need a new strategy. The Italians' capacity for self-absorption is defeating our best efforts."

Evelyn snorted. "Call it *Mente del Luna* and put it in a weird looking bottle."

"That might work. How go things in America? It looks like you've had some difficulties."

"No, no difficulties. Today we simply explained the hierarchy. It's understood now. Tonight's the full moon harvest, and by next week we'll have national distribution. The way this is going, things may happen much faster than we expected. These animals take very little prodding to start tearing each other apart."

"The Queen has no suspicions?"

"The Queen is an idiot who can't see past her own teats. Everything is fine."

"Still, the quicker this world falls apart, the better. Until we are established here, she remains a danger."

Evelyn nodded. "You shall make an excellent Queen, big sister."

"As shall you, little sister. I must run. I'm meeting with a French entrepreneur in a few minutes."

Evelyn left the tattered remains of her shirt on the floor and slipped back into the main room of Pogo & Bud's. Tom followed her quietly, then stopped dead in his tracks. The mob bosses had gone, but their minions remained. Two were frozen, bent over in the act of rolling a body into a carpet. Bud McGarritty had been scrubbing blood off the table with a wet rag while Pogo sniffed a second carpet that lay rolled against the wall. Another mobster had frozen while drinking a beer. The bottle had emptied, its contents running down his face and suit jacket. Tom looked at his watch, and then at the clock on the wall. The second hands on both ticked normally. The fans still turned. A fly settled on the sticky table. Another buzzed around it. Only the people, including Pogo, were frozen.

Evelyn poured herself a tall glass of Moonshine, tipped it back and downed it in three long swallows. "Lightweights," she said, and headed for the door.

Tom glanced toward the back of the room. Mary was still upstairs, but there was nothing he could do for her. He scurried after Evelyn. He didn't want to be anywhere close when those guys came unstuck.

Chico Borenko looked suspiciously through the narrow gap, then grinned widely as he slipped the chain and threw the door open.

"Tomislav!" He grabbed Tom and kissed him three times on the cheeks, left, right, left again, clapped him solidly on the shoulder, then dragged him inside. "Betty," he yelled, "your worthless, long-lost nephew is here! Put on some coffee!" He turned to Tom. "Come in, sit, please. You want coffee, yes?"

Tom couldn't help but smile. His uncle lived a grandiosely jolly life, evident in the dense belly that stretched his food-stained undershirt to its limits. His generosity never failed to leave his guests heavier in body but lighter in spirit. Tetka Betty was almost his opposite. She was soft and sensual, so small she seemed almost frail next to her husband, and in contrast to her dark skin, his ruddy features practically glowed with chubby pink cheerfulness.

"Hi, honey," she said, bringing a plate of cakes into the room. "Coffee's brewing." She kissed him on both cheeks in Balkan fashion.

"Thanks, Betty," he said. "Actually, I'm here to see Baba. I've run into some trouble, and I thought maybe she could help."

Betty looked at him with soft eyes. "I see. On the other hand, you could marry the girl. You're twenty-six now. Maybe this is God's way of telling you it's time to settle down and start a family."

Tom blinked. It took him a few seconds to understand what she meant. "Oh. No, not that kind of trouble. It's really a lot more complicated, and I don't know where else to turn."

"Ana's in the back. She likes the tree."

The back yard was a small plot the width of the house, surrounded on three sides by cinderblock walls. Raised beds with herbs lined the walls. Another raised bed in the center of the yard offered lettuce and cabbage and peppers and tomatoes. A dogwood tree raised its branches in one corner, and Tom's grandmother sat in her rocker, knitting in the tree's shade. She squinted at him with milky eyes.

"Baba Ana? It's me, Tomislav."

She smiled. "Ah, *mali Tomice. Sedi.*" She patted a chair next to her rocker. "And tell me what is wrong. Betty, *Tursku kafu, molim.*"

"You will think I'm crazy."

"Whole world is crazy. I see when I go to market. So tell me."

"I came to you because of the locket. The one you gave me." His hand went to his chest. "I think it protected me. I felt it burn."

Ana nodded gravely. "*Vodonoj* kind of crazy. Yes. So, tell." She listened without judgment as he told her about Moonshine, about Evelyn and what he'd seen in the mirror. The tale was garbled and incoherent: the details were slippery in Tom's mind, but Baba Ana just sipped her Turkish coffee, speaking only to prod him now and again when he fell into confused and sheepish silence.

She rocked slowly, eyes closed, for some time after Tom finally rambled to a halt. He wondered if she were asleep.

"Your uncle, he is a good man," she said. "He is a good son, and a good husband. There is never any trouble with him and Betty." She gazed at Tom. "Then one day he goes out, and when he comes home in the morning he smells *ko javna kucha*, like a whorehouse, and he hits poor Betty so hard when she says something, I think he maybe breaks her neck. It is this Moonshine he was drinking. He does not drink anymore, only coffee. Take off your shirt."

"What?"

"I show you something. Please." Tom stripped off his shirt. Ana held the old iron pendant in withered fingers. "This protects. While you wear, they will turn away from you, not noticing. It guards against their charms, and fights their poison. I make for you when you were born."

"That explains a lot."

Ana dropped the pendant and poked at an old scar on the left side of his chest. "This is other part. When you were a baby, I take," she paused, held two fingers apart just a hair, "very, very small part of your heart, and hide it." She laughed. "Your mother, she almost kill me, she is so angry."

"That's insane! What were you thinking?"

"When your heart is in two places, the *vodonoj* cannot find you. You slip from their heads just like they slip from yours. When you first met this Evelyn, she does not see you until you introduce yourself, yes? This is because of the pendant. And she forgets you before she leaves the room. This is because of your heart."

"Oh." Tom rubbed his temples. "So what do I do?"

Ana frowned. "The *vodonoj*, the English call them faeries, usually it is enough to protect yourself and they go find somewhere else to play. This Evelyn of yours, maybe this is not enough."

"I know, I know. They want to start a war. I think they mean to break us and take over."

Ana pressed her lips together. "A man who fights the *vodonoj*, maybe he loses." She placed a wrinkled hand on his face. "Even if he wins."

"Yes. I understand."

"With your head you understand. Not yet with your heart." She shook her head. "With all things, there is balance. Where there is power, there is weakness. Everything they can do to us . . . ." She hesitated, held both hands up equally with fingertips pressed together. *"Kako se kazhe?* Where is here, can also happen here same way?"

"Reciprocal?"

Ana shrugged. "If the *vodonoj* can bind, then they also can be bound. With the right knowledge." She smiled. "Tonight is bingo. I talk to my friends. You come back tomorrow and we talk again."

Tom stalked Pogo & Bud's from open to close for three days before he saw Evelyn again. His lungs felt like an ashtray and his kidneys ached.

Evelyn slipped past the doorman, making her way through the crowd without notice. She waved at McGarritty. He pulled out a pint glass and poured her a glowing drink. His smile was easy, but the muscles in his neck twitched.

Tom checked his pockets. The pouch his grandmother had given him felt cool under his fingers. He rehearsed everything in his mind. Handing Mary some cash, he murmured, "Why don't you go upstairs? Wait for me, I'll be right up."

Mary looked at the cash. "Okay."

He pulled the pendant over his head and set it around her neck. "Hold on to this for me, okay?" He watched as Mary made her way to the back of the room, then pulled a stool up next to Evelyn. "Now that's how to drink," he said with a nod to Evelyn's glass. "Bud, can ya set me up with one like that?"

"I'm not sure that's a good idea, Tom." McGarritty gave him a warning look.

Evelyn laughed. "Oh, go on. Give the man a proper drink, on me." McGarritty shook his head as he poured the pint. Evelyn clinked her glass against Tom's. "So tell me, how is it Bud knows your name, but I've never met you?"

"Incredibly bad luck on my part, apparently." Bolstered by Moonshine, he reached out and touched her face, running a finger along her healing lip. "Tell me who did this, and I'll make sure he never touches you again." He was surprised to realize that he meant it.

"Don't worry, he won't." She held out her hand. "I'm Evelyn, and I believe I'm pleased to make your acquaintance."

"I'm . . . ."

"Tom. Yes, I know."

Tom kissed her hand, then, heart racing, leaned forward and whispered in her ear. He tried to make it sound unrehearsed.

"That's a very interesting proposal," she said. "If you can finish that drink without falling over, I'll take you up on it."

They'd kissed in the taxi, long and sweet, and it was not difficult to forget the image of the hideous green creature. It would have been harder to keep hold of it—it slipped around the edges of consciousness at the best of times. He felt dizzy as he led her up the stairs to his bedroom, and as he walked her into the circle cast by his *baba* and her friends from bingo, he felt a twinge of guilt. But even that was hard to maintain. Her fingers were like fire as they tugged at his belt, as they sought the skin beneath his shirt.

He didn't want to do this. He ached to give himself to her, body and soul. With one hand he dug in his pocket and pulled out the small pouch of salts and spices and whatever else Baba had put in there, tugged at the strings until it loosened. His other hand gripped her hair as he kissed her throat.

The first time he bit down on his tongue it wasn't hard enough. He bit harder and the sharp, metallic taste of his own blood filled his mouth. Then he pressed his mouth against hers and bit hard on her split lip. She gasped and tried to pull away as their blood mingled in each other's mouths.

"*Sa krvi ti si moj*," he said. "With blood you are mine."

She looked at him with shock. "You can't." His heart ached with the betrayal.

His fingers shook as he poured the contents of the pouch into her mouth. She stiffened, fingers tensing with rigor. Her breathing slowed. "I'm sorry," he said, wondering if she could hear him. He kissed her rigid lips, and then turned away from her accusing eyes.

Baba Ana brought her friends, Ethel Berkowicz and Gwen Bythell, and Ethel's grandson Elijah. Evelyn's skin was rough under Tom's hands as he lay her tenderly in the trunk of Elijah's Packard, taking care not to break any of the new growth. He kissed her one last time, then watched Elijah and the old women drive away.

The next day, a truck drove up to Tom's house and delivered three cords of green firewood. The men stacked it in the small back yard to dry. "You might want to put a tarp up over it," one of them said, "so it doesn't get wet in the rain."

Tom stared at the stacks of firewood for a long time after the men left, chain-smoking and chewing on his lip. It was impossible that he felt this way. He barely knew her, but she seemed more real to him than Mary did. After some time, he locked the back door and pushed the icebox in front of it.

The snow lay thin on the tombstones, but the sharp, grey air promised more. Tom laid his hand on the pine box and remembered holding her, but it was an empty memory, devoid of joy or grief or even love. Two days before Christmas he was burying his fiancée, and not even her parents had come to the funeral.

Bud McGarritty put a hand on Tom's shoulder. "Mary was a hell of a gal," he said. "I'm sorry."

"Yeah." Mary had died alone with a needle in her arm, at the end of the path Tom had set for her. He still felt nothing, not even guilt. Just emptiness. Everything had gone to hell, even with the flow of Moonshine cut off. Maybe it was too late. Or maybe it would have been worse. It didn't matter. October of 1929 had brought the Crash and the world was spiraling toward disaster. This was just one more thing.

"I've been thinking about shutting down," McGarritty said. "Even before this. But where's a guy like me gonna get a job now that everyone's getting laid off? I got kids, you know."

"I know."

Tom walked home from the cemetery, stepping over the bums wrapped in newspaper for warmth. Some of these men had been successful, just a few months back. He ignored their pleas for money. There was nothing left to give.

Baba Ana had cooked for him and left the house warm, a fire burning in the hearth. Tom left the food untouched, reaching instead for his last bottle of Moonshine. It was a night for drinking, and he took a swig from the bottle.

Tom watched the dying flames until the chill began to creep in. Then, with a sigh, he threw another log of Evelyn on the fire and listened to her hiss.

Party Crashers

Trisha Wooldridge & Christy Tohara

Y OU'RE DRESSED *NOW?*" LCPL CAMERON FAIREWEATHER ARCHED
a blond eyebrow as an evening gown-clad Monica arrived in the
helicopter bay.

"Well, we'll be arriving in San Diego just short of the party . . . ."
Monica protested, glancing at the uniformed Cameron with the rest of
Shadow Guard Alpha 2 before the chopper. "What are you going to do,
dress in the helicopter?"

"That was the plan." He tapped a dry-cleaner bag.

"Oh." Her face reddened at the thought of the lance corporal changing
in front of her, more so when she considered herself dressing in
front of him.

LCPL Michaela Tyler glared at Cameron. "You try putting on panty-
hose and a strapless gown in a moving chopper!" Her dark skin and
uniform stood out against Monica's bare, porcelain shoulders as she
helped her friend into the helicopter.

"Thanks, Mike," Monica replied. "I would prefer uniform—"

Private 1ˢᵗ Class Roy Fletcher, a strapping male doppelganger of
Monica's fairness, piped, "I would prefer my little sister not going on this
mission at all."

Monica huffed past her brother. "Really, Royal—"

"You've only been on a few missions," Roy argued. "In the background, on a mic!"

"I'll be fine!"

"Fine? You certainly aren't wearing armor under that gown! What
if this monster goes all blazing guns? He's a Dark One! Unpre-
dictable!"

Monica peeked at Cam, catching his worried

glance at her unprotected torso even as it lingered a moment on her bosom.

She looked away, seeing her older brother glare electric blue daggers at their commanding officer. Her heart pounded, but she spoke up, "I'm the one with-with the information. I HAVE to be undercover . . . right, Cam—I mean . . . sir?"

"Right," Cameron replied firmly, face growing harder. "Everything stands as is. Now, lock yourselves in." Roy scowled silently as Cam adjusted his headset and ad-dressed the team, "Okay, ETA 20:10. Police are on-call for possible disturbance, but it's our job to make sure it doesn't come to that."

"The cops are involved?" Roy asked, temper cooled with business.

Cameron replied, "This guy's been on their radar for a while."

"Greeeat. Nutter Dark One with a fuzz stake out." Roy rolled his eyes.

Cameron narrowed his brown eyes and continued, "We've only just learned that this is our jurisdiction. We're intercepting so the cops don't get themselves killed. Monica's research points to this guy being at the San Diego Museum of Natural History's gala lecture tonight. Monica, floor's yours."

"Um, yes . . . ." Monica passed out folders. "You'll find additional info here. After speaking with Cam, I believe our mark is faerie. He's a Sidhe—"

"He's a she?" Michaela asked. "A trannie faerie?"

"S-i-d-h-e, not s-h-e," Monica replied. "It's . . . like a race of faerie." She looked to Cameron who nodded in affirmation.

"There ain't anything in the Shadow Guard books on shee-faeries," Michaela frowned. "What exactly are we up against?"

"Cam and I . . . ." Monica cleared her throat, looking at the commanding lance corporal. "We've met a few . . . well, I've met one—"

"What was it like?" Roy turned wide-eyed to his sister.

Monica was relieved when Cameron answered. Perhaps he sensed her discomfort; he always could. "Sidhe have extensive telepathy and telekinesis," he explained. "Direct eye contact allows them to breach thoughts. From there, they can plant suggestions, false memories. They can get into heads insomuch that victims are little more than marionettes. Depending on how strong they are, they can, literally, kill with a thought."

"Wait a minute!" Roy looked at Monica. "If he can kill with just eye-contact—"

"He'd be at least a thousand years old," Cameron said firmly. "And if he could, he'd have done it in prior cases, which he didn't."

Monica nodded. "So far, he's only made others kill for him. Like having guards open fire on guests—"

Roy coughed, "*Bulletproofvest!*"

Michaela socked him in the arm. "They have any weaknesses?"

Monica nodded again. "They're mortal, but iron hurts them most. It causes . . . ." She looked to Cameron.

"Ferrous poisoning," he explained. "It's like . . . a deadly allergy. It breaks down blood, hinders magic. Hurts like hell—for them. One this powerful can regenerate from regular bullets. Not as fast as a vamp or a lyke, but still damn hard to kill."

"That would have been a good FYI while I was packing," Roy quipped.

"Sorry," Monica apologized, then continued, "So, um, he uses mind power to manipulate, which is why people don't remember what he looks like. He changes their memories, makes them forget his face . . . ."

"You list some artifacts here . . . he's stealing magic?" Michaela asked from behind her file.

Monica shook her head. "He researches certain guests and forces them to wire him money from their bank accounts. The artifacts . . . are just, like prizes to him, it seems."

"Glorified bank robber," Roy scoffed.

"Unseelie—dark faerie for the unschooled—bank robber," Cameron corrected. "That puts him in a category all his own. Sidhe don't need money, don't use it. If he can manipulate guards to kill, he can manipulate a jewelry store owner to give him diamonds."

"Bored little rich D.O. wants to have fun with humans," Michaela sneered.

Roy smirked, "Well, if fun's what he wants . . . ."

Cameron matched Roy's smirk, but Monica thought she saw more concern behind his eyes than he let on.

Victor Caradoc helped himself to champagne from a passing waiter and meandered around the museum Atrium. *Hors d'oeuvres* tables were set up between plexiglass cases exhibiting artifacts from the Peruvian dig William Harrison sponsored. The Sidhe feigned interest, like most of the guests.

Security was his focus.

His previous work had clearly raised the stakes. Six armed guards decked in para-military gear monitored the Atrium's perimeter, and he'd seen two at the entrance. He calculated at least two more floaters in the surrounding galleries.

Caradoc caught the gaze of the closest guard. As they met eyes, he felt the man tense, then relax as he eased into his mind. He walked closer, digging deeper. Soon, he had the name of every guard, information on their personalities, and the rotation plan for the night.

With a smile, he said, "Carl Wilkes, at exactly 9:30, Mr. Harrison wants *everyone* in the Kaplan Theatre for his presentation. If you find any stragglers, use force to get them into the theatre—"

"Force?"

Caradoc frowned as he felt the man's mind question his control, so he forced himself further into his consciousness. "Yes, force."

"Yessir. We are to make sure everyone is in the theatre by 9:30, by use of force if necessary."

"Good job, Wilkes," he smiled, slapping the guard on the shoulder. He headed back to the food tables but didn't get more than three steps before a young woman slid into his path.

"Hi. Madrid Harrison," she introduced herself with a seductive wink.

Arching an ebony eyebrow, he kissed her offered hand. "Victor Caradoc. A pleasure, Miss Harrison." He moved to walk around her, but she side-stepped with him. He looked into her eyes, willing her out of his way.

She tilted her head. "I haven't seen you around before. New to San Diego?"

Caradoc frowned, feeling his powers come up against a feather-pillow sensation. "You must be mistaken; I've seen you at a few parties."

"No. I'm sure I'd remember *you*." She grinned, still refusing to let him pass.

He gritted his teeth behind his smile and mentally cursed. Point-five percent of the human population could not be mind-controlled by Sidhe. Half a percent! And the daughter of his mark had to be in that percentage.

"Hm . . . I do tend to blend in. Maybe it's my new suit?" He held out his coat and spun for her. "My tailor said it would make me stand out? I'm rather flattered that you noticed . . . Madrid—may I call you Madrid?"

The young woman giggled. "Of course. The suit does look fabulous, *Victor*."

"Why, thank you," he reached to kiss her hand again. If she could remember his face and name together, he couldn't let her out of his sight. He needed to keep her with him until this was done, and he could kill her.

"If I can smell your panic, so can he," Cameron cautioned, picking at a fruit plate.

"I'm *not* panicked." Monica retorted, eyes shifting over her champagne glass rim, resting on the security guards planted around the Atrium. "They have armed guards. Did they completely miss that Caradoc used armed guards to kill hostages in the last two heists?"

"They're rich people stuck in a world of, 'It can never happen to me,'" Cameron replied, popping a grape into his mouth. "They don't actually expect Caradoc to strike."

"Lovely," the woman muttered, glancing at a tight-knit group near a pottery display. "So, now what?"

"Mingle, see if he's here." Cameron followed her eyes, as she kept glancing from the guards to the flock of socialites. "Maybe work yourself in with the artifacts people—"

"Monica Fletcher!"

Both looked over. A man in a tuxedo as old as his face strode toward them, waving. He embraced Monica with two kisses. "What a surprise to see you!"

"Doctor Millovic!" Monica beamed, returning the embrace. "You, too! This is my boyfriend, Cameron Fairweather." Cameron held out his hand, attempting to look more curious than puzzled. "Cameron, this is Doctor Millovic. He's heading this whole Peruvian dig the Harrison's are sponsoring. He invited me out to Iceland a while back, to translate runes."

"Invited? I all but begged after Doctor Carter raved about her work in Antarctica!" Millovic pumped Cameron's hand then wrapped an arm around Monica's shoulders. "It's so good to see you here! Maybe you wouldn't mind looking at some of the Incan hieroglyphs—not to impose, of course . . . ."

"Don't mention it! I'd love to!" Monica replied.

"You would? Wonderful! You simply must meet Bill." Arm still around her, he led Monica to the circle surrounding Mr. Harrison. Cameron followed. "Oh, Bill! Let me introduce you to the brilliant, talented, and quite beautiful Ms. Monica Fletcher!" The middle-aged Harrison gave Monica an approving once-over.

"Oh, Doctor . . . ." Monica blushed. "Really, I'm not—"

"Monica, you do yourself a disservice," Cameron piped in. "You're brilliant and beautiful." He turned to Mr. Harrison and sized the man up, knowing his compliment would leave Monica speechless for at least a full minute.

"And you are?" he asked.

"Cameron Fairweather, Miss Fletcher's guest." He held out his hand. "Monica raves about your work."

"Monica said she'd look at some of the glyphs with us," added the archaeologist.

Mr. Harrison smiled at Monica. "Well . . . I'd love to talk more with Miss Fletcher." He nodded, winking at Cameron. "You don't mind if we borrow her?"

"I couldn't keep her away if I wanted," Cameron replied.

"Excellent. Should we start with the pyramid piece, Cristof?"

"Just what I was thinking, Bill . . . ."

"Could I, uh . . . powder my nose, first? Maybe grab a bite more?" Monica smiled shyly.

"I'll go with you," Cam volunteered, then winked back at Millovic and Harrison. "I promise I'll let her back to you." Once they were out of earshot, he asked, "You alright to do this, Monni?"

"I'm fine, really. This is my element, research and all."

"Not that—" He laid a hand gently on her shoulder, fingers stroking her bare skin. "I mean . . . well, after D'Anarys . . . . Are you really sure you want to handle another Sidhe?"

"I-I can do this. Trust me."

Cameron studied her face, nose twitching as he picked up the scent of her pheromones. Withdrawing his hand quickly, he tucked it into his tux pocket. "I trust you," he told her, then slid his hand back into hers, stepping in closer to conceal what he gave her from any onlookers.

Monica issued Cameron a questioning look before unwrapping the black leather. Her brow frowned even deeper when she saw the iron dagger and a flask filled with an orange-flecked liquid. "What's in the flask?"

He smiled. "Rusty water—"

"Rust? Oxidized iron suspended in water? Brilliant! But—what about you?"

"I have my sword, like always," he flicked his wrist with a whispered hiss so Monica could see the slight glow of the space pocket. "The blade is just as potent as iron, if not more so since he's Unseelie. Don't worry about me, but you—you remember, if anyone is too beautiful to believe—"

"Don't look 'em in the eye. Trust me, I *know.*" Monica fidgeted as he watched her with concern. Placing his gifts in her beaded purse, she said, "Thanks, Cam," then gently patted his lapel before turning into the bathroom.

"Oh, that's Paris," Madrid giggled over champagne.

"I see." Caradoc glared at the black chihuahua growling from its owner's purse.

"Little dogs are so perfect." Madrid's voice elevated, as if disclosing some major insight.

"Mmmm." He took some pleasure in sending fruitless suicidal suggestions into her pathetic human brain matter. Caradoc checked his watched again.

"Oh, look, there's Daddy! Let's introduce you!"

Madrid grabbed his hand and pranced three-inch stilettos across the Atrium, perfect ebony coils bouncing around her head like crazed medusa snakes.

Were it not for his reflexes, he would have crashed into her as she stopped short.

"Who is *that* he's with?" she growled between clenched teeth, an amazing impersonation of her dog.

"Who?"

"That skanky blonde he's talking to. I wonder if Mom's noticed!" She stalked over as Caradoc surveyed the blonde under Mr. Harrison's arm. She appeared clueless and naïve, but far from what the Sidhe would call "skanky."

"Daddy!" Madrid threw her arms around her father, shaking the pursed Paris and evoking angry yips. She shushed the dog and exclaimed, "I wanted to introduce you to—"

"Victor Caradoc," he said, making sure to meet Bill Harrison's, as well as Cristof Millovic's gazes. He glanced at the blonde, who gasped and looked back to the piece of pottery. Caradoc's eyes narrowed. "And you are?"

The blonde bit her lip and seemed to struggle for words.

"This is Monica Fletcher," Millovic said. "She's an old friend of mine, a linguist, though keen on anthropology, archeology, the works!"

"Hi," she said, glancing up, eyes only making it to his lips, then returning to the pottery. "Dr. Millovic, have you noticed the iconological similarity to reign of Horus Djer?"

"You really love your work, don't you, Monica?" Caradoc asked, reaching to touch her.

The woman recoiled. "I do, actually," she said shortly. He smelled fear on her. "I hate to be rude, gentlemen, Miss," she nodded at Madrid, who was still shooting ocular daggers, "but that last glass of wine is getting to me. Excuse me?"

"Of course, Monica," Dr. Millovic smiled, "don't be too long, dear. That's a fascinating point you've brought up!"

"Thank you, Doctor." With a quick nod, the woman all but ran away. Caradoc moved to follow, but Madrid gripped his hand.

He glowered at her perfectly manicured fingers; her voice grated in his ears, "Who's she, Daddy?"

"She's a friend of Cristof's," he frowned. "She's helping with translation."

"Where do you know her from, Dr. Millovic?" Victor asked sweetly, meeting the man's eyes and searching for the information, himself.

"Oh, she helped me in Iceland a few years back. She's the best I know; written several major articles on ancient religious, and supposedly magickal rituals . . . ."

"Magickal rituals?" Victor prodded, scanning the man's memories rather than paying attention to what he spewed on about. When Millovic paused, he pressed, "Did Monica Fletcher come here with anyone?"

"Oh, yes . . . she had a date, I believe." The man struggled to remember the face; he'd been busy staring at the lovely Monica. "Faireweather . . . I think. Cameron Faireweather."

"Faireweather?" Victor broke his stare, pursing his lips.

"You know him?" Harrison asked, looking somewhat relieved. "I hadn't heard of him before, but he's Ms. Fletcher's guest . . . ."

"The name sounds familiar," Caradoc said, his most honest confession of the night. "But I can't place it."

"Curly blonde fellow?" Harrison shrugged. "A few inches under six feet, about your height."

"Well, I'll have to seek him out," Caradoc smirked, "and perhaps inform him that it's a crime to have left his date's side for so long."

Madrid grinned and loosened her grip.

"Oh, Monica's a woman of her own mind," Millovic poohed. "She doesn't need someone who'll hang on her all night."

"I suppose," Caradoc shrugged and looked into Harrison's eyes. "Now, don't you need to get ready for your show?"

Harrison looked at his watch. "My, you're right. Cristof?"

The faerie followed the men a few steps, catching the eye of the last guard he'd been trying to see that night. He only had a moment to silently transmit orders with Madrid on his arm. Verbal commands were much stronger, but he hadn't had that luxury with anyone but Wilkes. Nevertheless, he'd tied their minds enough with brief eye-contact.

Everything was under control.

Cautiously, quietly, Cameron snuck through the empty gallery. At the fire exit, he paused. Relying on his keen sense of hearing, he waited, listened.

Nothing.

Activating the locator on his watch, he whispered, "Got me?"

"Yep," Roy said in Cameron's earpiece. "North fire exit. Disarming now."

"Guards are already making sure everyone gets into the theatre."

Michaela spoke, "Geez, he doesn't waste time."

"Okay," Roy said. "Try the door."

"Copy." Cameron pressed the crash bar. Parting the door slightly, he removed from his pocket a carbon pin the length and diameter of a pencil. Sliding it between the door and the jam, he released the bar, leaving a sliver of an opening. "Done. You should be able to get in easily now, on my command. Copy?"

"Copy," Roy replied. "Awaiting your orders, sir. Fletcher out."

Cameron headed back towards the Atrium. He sidled up to Monica as she exited the ladies' room.

"I met him," she whispered, linking her arm through his. "Black hair, pony tail. Drop-dead gorgeous. Wandering around with Madrid Harrison."

Before they could continue, two guards confronted them.

"The presentation is beginning; please join the other guests inside the theatre." The sound of weapons cocking came from the upper floor where a second pair of guards aimed down at them.

Monica gasped; Cameron pulled her closer, turning toward the theatre entrance. "Right away."

Seat rows spilled toward an expansive movie screen before Caradoc. Alone in the back of the theatre, his shoulders relaxed in the absence of the pooch-purse princess. He'd requested she wait for him in the front row; at this point in the plan, he didn't need her by his side. Joining the applause, the Unseelie watched Harrison and Millovic walk over golden oak stage toward a podium.

"Ladies and Gentlemen, thank you all for coming . . . ." Harrison began.

As Caradoc surveyed the room, security ushered in two more people: Monica Fletcher and her companion. An ill-wind sensation feathered over Victor Caradoc's skin when he saw the blond young man.

Faireweather. Faireweather . . . .

He eyed the guards behind them, pointing at Monica. He mind-spoke, relaying: *"Move her over there! If they protest, shoot her!"*

The guard yanked Monica from Cameron's side, bracing a pistol at her temple. Cameron growled, "Hey—"

Lights dimmed. Flute notes penetrated the darkness. The film danced shadows across their faces as Caradoc looked at Faireweather. "Why are you here?"

The young man, faerie, though not Sidhe, Carodoc sensed, wouldn't meet his eyes. With a smirk, Caradoc walked over to Monica and grabbed her chin. "What do I need to do to get you to talk, Monica Fletcher . . . ."

"I won't," she whispered, clenching her eyes closed.

"Caradoc . . . ." came Faireweather's warning voice behind him.

Caradoc sneered, glancing down at Harrison. "I don't have time for this. Any interference, kill her," he ordered, "then him." The guard nodded.

The dark faerie strode down the side aisle, eyeing the two gentlemen behind the podium. Harrison stopped mid-sentence. A flick of the Sidhe's hand threw Harrison and Millovic against the screen. They hung several feet off the ground, the film distorted over their bodies. Caradoc held them there while he continued to the stage. As he approached the podium, the men thudded to the floor. The crowd stirred. Women gasped; men half-stood, unsure what to do.

"I'm Victor Caradoc." His cold stare sent trepidation into each person who caught his gaze. "I'm taking you all hostage, so I suggest you sit back down, or I'll have you killed." Those standing quickly complied.

Caradoc rounded the podium, removed a BlackBerry and cable from his pocket and hooked into the jack. "For those of you who keep up with current events, you know that I take my work *quite* seriously. If anyone tries to play hero, they will fail." He raised an eyebrow at Faireweather, who stood motionless. "Now, that I have everyone's attention . . . ." He glared over the crowd and called out seven names, Harrison and Millovic included. "You will find prepaid cell phones in your pockets or purses. Retrieve them." He waited, watching them gape at the common device. "Call your banks and complete the transfer transactions currently pending on your accounts. Do this *now*."

"Like hell!" shouted a man from the crowd. Some hostages gasped, eyes flashing back to Caradoc.

"Hell, hmn?" Caradoc met the protesting man's eye. The dissenter grabbed his head, falling to the ground with a howl.

A woman in a middle row stood in terror, screamed, and ran for the exit.

Caradoc smiled and pointed at the woman. The closest guard shot her dead.

Harrison lurched forward. "Penelope!" Simultaneously, Madrid stood from her chair, jumped on stage, and attacked Caradoc.

"That's my mom!" she screamed, punching his chest as tears streaked her face. Caradoc grabbed her and threw her to the ground.

"Anyone else?" he asked calmly.

When Madrid rushed the stage, Monica kicked the guard's leg behind her, raking her heel down his shin. She followed her attack with an elbow jab to his chest. Cameron moved in tandem with her and took down his captor. He turned toward Monica's captor and knocked him cold with a blow to the back of his head.

Cameron touched his ear-mic. "Fletcher, Tyler—good time to crash the party."

Monica heard her brother in her ear. "Trying to, sir. Some guards stuck around upstairs. Be there ASAP! "

"I'm going down," Cameron informed Monica, handing her one of the guard's guns. "Watch these guys."

Paris escaped Madrid's purse and nipped at Caradoc's feet. The dark faerie kicked at the chihuahua; the dog dodged and continued yapping. "Shoot the damned dog!" Caradoc ordered.

The guards fidgeted, confused. They moved weapons between the dog and the crowd. When Cameron Faireweather hit the bottom of the stadium, he reached for the other iron dagger sheathed beneath his coat and threw it. Caradoc's eyes widened as the weapon penetrated his side. Cameron leapt on stage and jump-kicked Victor, knocking him to the ground.

Blackened blue blood pooled beneath the Sidhe, painting streaks across the floor as he squirmed. Gritting his teeth, he retched out the blade.

"Faireweather . . . I know of you," he snarled as he moved to his knees. "Seelie hunters of the Unseelie. I had hoped your line died out. You find satisfaction in killing your own kind?"

Cameron answered with a soft murmur; a silvery sword appeared in his left hand. He lunged. The dark faerie evaded him, throwing the sobbing Madrid into Cameron. He caught the girl with his right arm, shifting her behind him, and still striking. The whisper of the blade sliced the Unseelie's dress shirt, drawing another line of blackened blood from his stomach. Face contorting in agony, Caradoc back-pedaled. He grabbed a sidearm from the nearest guard, who crumpled to the ground, clutching his head. The second guard tried to draw, but hit the ground howling before her gun even left its holster.

"Stay behind me!" Cameron instructed the mascara-streaked debutant, as he squared off in front of Caradoc's gun.

The dark faerie fired three bullets into Faireweather's torso. Cameron fell backward, the force of each shot bruising his chest through the Kevlar.

Madrid dove over him, grabbing for the dog. "Paris!"

Caradoc pistol-whipped the girl, and she sprawled onto the floor. He re-aimed the gun at Cameron, but Paris crawled up his pant-leg, needle teeth and nails shredding his skin. Cam stood back up. He could see the ferrous poisoning and his sword's magic darkening the Sidhe's facial veins; even the tiny dog's attack would be torture. "Surrender," he offered.

Even as he fell to his knees, clutching his gun arm against the blackened-blood-soaked suit, Caradoc managed a *You've-got-to-be-kidding* expression before his gaze shifted past Cameron.

Cameron glanced behind. One guard drew on him, the other on the crowd.

"Hey!" From the second rear entrance, one of the remaining guards saw Monica. He turned his weapon on her. "Drop it!"

"Um . . . ." she whimpered; her own gun trembled.

"Monni!" her brother spoke behind her. At the other entrance, she saw the two guards fall. Michaela emerged and holstered her dart gun.

Relief flooded through Monica. She looked at her brother. "Roy! Cameron's down there! He was shot!"

Roy turned immediately toward the stage. "Good thing HE wore a vest."

Michaela jabbed him. "Get these people out!"

"Yes ma'am." Roy hustled down the aisle.

Monica moved from her post as Michaela took over. She scrunched her petite frame behind a back-row seat and scanned the theatre. Her heart stopped when she noticed Roy standing three rows down, face slack. Monica looked at Caradoc . . . staring at her brother. Roy turned his weapon on the crowd.

"No!" Monica screamed, stood, and fired wildly at Caradoc. The bullets hit nothing but screen and wall, but her target flinched, breaking eye contact with Roy.

Caradoc glared and turned his gun on Roy who, still distorted, didn't duck, didn't dodge, didn't see what was coming. From where she hid, all Monica saw was red. Red blocking her eyes, red streaking down Roy's face where his ear should be. Warm stickiness and the taste of iron sickened her.

"ROY!"

She heard Michaela shout, "EVERYBODY OUT!"

Monica wanted to get to her brother, needed to. But the crowd surged toward the rear exits, a stampede of panic. She fought against them, but they pushed her back. She couldn't see Roy. Was he getting trampled? Monica looked to the stage. Could Cameron do something? Some sort of faerie magic?

Onstage, Caradoc ducked out the emergency exit behind the screen. It looked like the damn dog still gripped his arm. Cameron followed closely. She thought she saw the blade slice through the back of Caradoc's tux coat. Madrid sat on the black-blood-slicked stage floor, looking quite dazed.

When the crowd thinned, Monica saw Michaela bent over Roy. She was giving orders to two other paramedics. He was still alive; he had to be—no use ordering paramedics to do stuff if he were dead, right? SDPD poured in the rear exits. "Lady, this way!" one ordered her.

She shook her head. Down by the stage, she noticed the ragged Madrid Harrison skulk out the same door as Cam and Caradoc. Monica glanced once more at Michaela and Roy; Mike would take care of him, she trusted. She ran after Madrid to find Cameron.

Monica followed piercing yips and a blackened blood-trail up a set of stairs and through an office corridor, exiting onto the floor just above the Atrium; below them was the din of people and shouting officers. Caradoc and Cameron faced off.

Cameron had dismissed his sword in favor of his SIG-Sauer sidearm; Caradoc clearly suffered from his wounds, barely holding his gun. Madrid leaned on a case of Egyptian cartouches, blood smearing the plexiglass as she inched toward the men.

"No, nonono!" Monica hissed. "Stay here . . . it'll be all right. I promise."

"Paris . . . ." the girl muttered.

The woman was surprised at the dog's tenacity as it now gripped the Sidhe's dark-veined arm below a shredded coat and shirt. Monica pressed her lips together and tried to put her arms around Madrid.

"Killed my mom . . . ."

"I know, honey—" Monica began, but was cut off as she watched the dark faerie punch his whole arm, and the dog, through a plexiglass case of burial collars. The dog fell in a lump, and the Sidhe grabbed a handful of the priceless adornments.

"Noooo!" the girl howled.

Monica saw Cameron manage two shots before Madrid intercepted his line of fire to reach her dog.

"Hold her here!" Cameron ordered and pursued. A blue-black blood spatter on the far wall let Monica know he had hit Caradoc at least once.

Madrid scooped her broken pup into her arms. More gunshots sounded and Monica feared the worst. She had a job to do, though, so she held the other young lady and comforted her.

"Ffffhhhhk!" Cameron cursed. He flung off his jacket and tore off his shirt to make a tourniquet for his leg. He eyed the Sidhe's discarded gun; Caradoc had hardly been able to hold it, much less aim, with the degree of iron and magic inhibiting his blood. The bastard still had some power left—enough to throw the lance corporal *through* a three-tiered mineral display. His own red, non-Sidhe, blood pooled on the exhibit and ran down the wooden side.

He mourned the poor dog as he grimaced to tighten his shirt and stem his blood flow. It had been his fault the creature died; he'd told the animal to attack in its own tongue. Mere animal spirits had their gifts, too. He hoped the chihuahua's sacrifice at least saved others.

Makeshift tourniquet secured, he lowered himself off the display and activated his mic as he limped toward the door. "Shot in the leg, but okay. Status everyone! How's Roy?"

Monica froze upon hearing Cam's voice. She didn't dare let herself relax at his safety; she needed to know about her brother.

"Roy's fucking pissed and ready kick some dark faerie arse!" came her brother's voice over the mic.

"Oh, thank God!" Monica tearfully collapsed beside the sobbing Madrid.

"His ear was shot off is all. Getting patched now," Michaela stated. "W—"

"Hey! Where are you going?" Monica shouted, her team's radio conversation lost as Madrid kicked off her shoes and shakily jogged toward the door they had entered. Monica ran after her and grabbed the girl's shoulder.

Blank eyes stared back at Monica. "Roof . . . someone's coming . . . he said . . . I heard . . . ."

"Look, Cam's following him and knows what he's doing. Stay put!"

"No!" A crazed fire alit in Madrid's eyes. She shoved Monica aside.

Monica stumbled, surprised at the girl's strength, but kicked off her own shoes and rushed to catch her again.

"Monica?!" Cameron's voice demanded over her earphone. "Where the hells are you?"

"Another set of stairs, heading up."

"What? Why? I told you to stay with Madrid."

"I *am* staying with Madrid."

"No, Monni, no! It's too dangerous. Stay in the stairwell. That is an order."

"Too late . . . I'm already here."

She silently slipped through the door in time to grab Madrid's arm again. "Madrid . . . please! Cam will be here any minute," she whispered.

A few paces away, Caradoc leaned over, supporting his hands on his knees. "Where the fuck are you—" he choked into a phone, then turned to look at the women. Monica barely averted her eyes. The pause was enough for Madrid to yank away from Monica and rush him.

He batted her down with a backhand and then turned to step upon her throat.

"STOP!" Monica cried. She grasped Cameron's flask from her purse and threw it. It shattered and splashed upon him. His exposed skin blistered immediately as he cried out venomously. Though trembling, she drew Cameron's iron dagger, and attacked.

He caught her wrists and twisted her around, pinning her to him with her own arms.

"Let her go!"

Cameron! Monica thought.

"Oh for fuck's sake!" He held Monica like a shield. Though she felt him shake behind her, breath coming out in gasps, he was still stronger.

Cameron pressed his lips together and squeezed his trigger.

Searing hot pain went through the top of Monica's shoulder. She fell forward, swooning from her injury. Caradoc staggered backward, clutching his chest.

Madrid got to her knees, glazed eyes on Cameron. One step brought Caradoc close enough to seize her hair. He looked at the other faerie with a crazed smile. "You don't win today, Faireweather. Not today."

Dragging Madrid by her hair, Caradoc launched them both off the roof.

"No!" Monica screamed, grabbing only air. She and Cameron looked down. Only Madrid Harrison's twisted body lay below.

"Did we miss the fun?" called Roy, exiting onto the roof in front of Michaela. Monica nearly knocked her brother over in embrace, then yelped at his returned hug.

"You're hurt! I told you you shoulda worn the damned vest!"

"Fat lotta help it did you," she retorted through tears, reaching up to kiss his cheek again. "I thought you were dead!"

"Not quite," he replied and went over to Cameron. "What happened? Where is he?" Roy asked, voice subdued as he looked over the edge. "God . . . ."

Cameron said bitterly, "They both went over."

"Faeries really have wings?" Roy inquired.

"He was calling someone to come get him," Monica said. "But I didn't see . . . ."

"Dimensional shift . . . back into the Underhill," Cameron explained in a harsh whisper. "Some Emanthe can make them; most Sidhe keep Emanthe servants."

"So, you're telling me he got away?" Roy said, eyes narrowing.

"As should we," Cameron stated. "The SDPD will be asking questions; SG clean-up is in charge of settling mundane affairs."

The helicopter roared overhead. After it touched down, they helped each other inside and Michaela pulled open the large med-kit.

"Total casualties?" Cameron asked, summoning his own medical kit. He sat across from Monica, inspecting her shoulder wound. "Clean graze. Nothing a few stitches won't help."

"Just the two females, sir," Michaela replied. Cameron pointedly ignored her double take of the medical kit seemingly appearing out of nowhere.

Monica frowned, "Madrid and her mother."

"Shouldn't have been anyone," Cameron said softly.

"Y'know, if this were a bloody vamp, a werewolf, a cult of elder demons, we'd be all over this shit," Roy seethed. "One faerie . . . one goddamned faerie."

"It wasn't a total loss," Michaela said, re-inspecting Roy's ear wound. "None of the rich white folks lost their money; that'll lessen the din. And I got blood samples." Her eyes hardened. "We'll be prepared next time."

"We'll kill the bastard," Monica said softly, looking at Cameron who gave a small nod.

"No, we'll bring him in. Study him—like all Dark Ones," Michaela declared firmly. "We'll find that bastard's weaknesses . . . and make him and all his kind pay . . . ."

Monica watched Cameron's jaw tighten. She touched his face. Leaning in, she whispered in his ear, "We'll kill him first."

The animal-spirit's face relaxed some, and he started bandaging Monica's shoulder.

"Sir," Michaela said. "Your leg?"

"See to the Fletchers, Tyler. That's an order." He and Monica shared another look. The Shadow Guard didn't need any more blood samples that night.

The Reality Division

Christopher Sirmons Haviland

"MR. BRIDGE? MR. BRIDGE? CAN YOU SEE ME?"
I know it's my name, but I don't know where I am or how I got here. I sees a blur, and my eyelids are sticky. There's a man talkin' to me, and a bright light.

"Yeah," I says, but my tongue feels like a dead fish, and kinda tastes like one, too. And *oh man,* am I thirsty. My jaw muscles feel like they're made-a sand and my lips feel like when you drink Tequila wrong. The man gets closer each time I blink. He's a doctor.

Oh God, what did I do last night?

"Well," he says, lowering a light. "You're a lucky man. Welcome back to the world. I'm Dr. Ackerman. You've been in a coma, Mr. Bridge."

So I sits there and listens to this story about how I contracted Lyme Disease, that I had an allergic reaction to some drug I can't pronounce, that I slipped into a comatose state for two years, and that a living clause in my will kept me alive with help from my personal inheritance. At first I thought he was full of it, but I started to recollect. I was out pickin' apples with that nerdy girl from Accounting. I knew I shouldn't-a dated her.

That inheritance was supposed to be for when I retired, so I could lay up on some beach for the rest-a my life. A little bastard tick took it all away from me.

But two years? Come on. Last thing I remembered I was havin' a beer out back the house, watchin' the game on my portable. I had the day off 'cause that tick bite was sore and I had got back from the doctor after some shots. Seems like just minutes ago I heard the neighbor yellin' at me about somethin'. Now I'm here.

"Where'm I?" I moan as my eyes focus on a couple other doctors in the room.

"New York," he says. I wanted a little more detail but I think he didn't want to overwhelm me with information.

A couple bright lights really bother me.

"Can yooze turn them lights down?" I mumble at him like the Godfadda. My tongue don't hardly remember how to move no more.

"You're optically hypersensitive. Your eyes have been closed for years, Mr. Bridge. They'll adjust."

"How can it be years?" I says. "I was just in the back yard . . . ."

"Comas are like that," he explains. "Even when you sleep, you can perceive the passage of time, but during a coma there is no time perception at all. It's as if it never happened. It's normal, but very confusing."

My eyes get clearer after I blink the gook out, but the lights are still annoying. I come to think they ain't light bulbs, though. I don't know what they are, but they're big and wiry and don't stay put. I begin to stare at them as doctors and nurses probe me, turn me this way and that, play with my arms and legs, change my hospital gown, sponge me down, move me from bed to bed, and say all sorts of things to one another I don't understand. Whenever they ask me a question, they have to snap a finger to get my attention, 'cause those lights spook me.

Am I thirsty? Yes. But they won't let me have a beer.

Hungry? Yes. But they won't let me have a steak.

Pain? Stiff. But I can't take a hot tub.

"Let's turn you on your side, Mr. Bridge." "Try to lift your head, Mr. Bridge." "Look this way, Mr. Bridge." "This will pinch a little, Mr. Bridge."

"Call me Bobby, for Christ's sake," I says.

These light shapes follow me as Doc Ackerman pushes me in a wheelchair into his office.

"We can't locate next of kin," Doc says. "Is there someone I can call?"

"I'm single," I says, watchin' the light shapes float along with me. I can see more clearly now and they look kinda like big glow-in-the-dark wasps. They got long danglin' legs and flaps like wings that wiggle and curl. They remind me a lot of those tiny things in the deep ocean. "My parents are dead," I add.

"Do you have any friends I can call? Co-workers?"

My mind is numb. There's Frank and George at the factory. Leeches, both. I'd rather they not know I was awake. They'd start borrowin' money as soon as I found out how much is left.

What about the girly-geek? Brenda, her name was. Nah, she's the one who got me into this mess. What about Karen? But we just broke up a month ago . . . I mean two *years* and a month ago. She went messin' around with that Puerto-Rican guy, I'm still sure of it. Probably they got kids now.

"I'll think about it," I said, starin' at the glowin' wasps.

Doc Ackerman follows the direction I'm lookin'.

"Do you see something that bothers you?" he asks.

With some effort, I point at the nearest wasp. "These bright spindly things. They been floatin' 'round since I woke up."

More torture as Ackerman checks my eyes again with his pen light. His breath smells like an old Arby's burger but I try to hold still 'cause I want some answers.

"Do they move when you turn your head, or can you look way from them?"

"I can look away from them. They seem to move by themselves, like ghosts."

"Well, before we talk theories, I'll send you to an ophthalmologist tomorrow."

Then I hears this whisper sound, a voice like air leakin' out of a tire, and I knows it's one of those things.

"I think he sees us," it says.

And the other one says, "That's not possible."

"He's been watching us."

"Doc," I says nervously, "maybe get an ear specialist, too. I can hear 'em talkin' now."

Doc Ackerman gazes at me over his half-lens glasses. "What are they saying?" he asks suspiciously.

One of the creatures clenches its legs in disgust. "He must be stuck between," it whispers.

"This one claims I'm stuck," I says, pointin' at it. Tingles run down my back. I'm startin' to think I'm outta my mind.

Ackerman looks where I'm pointin' and still doesn't see nothin'. He scribbles somethin' in his notepad.

"What do you . . . do *they* mean by *stuck*?" Ackerman asks.

I shrug.

"What should we do?" a creature asks.

"Summon the President," orders the other.

"They're going to call the President," I sputter.

"The President of the United States?" the Doc asks, his bushy eyebrows in a furrow.

"Doc, how should I know? Is this an after-effect of—" The giant glowing wasps' legs turn green and a spray of tiny green lights appear and swirl around them. "Whoa! Now there's more lights!"

Ackerman's gettin' very concerned.

Then the little lights form into a funnel, like a tornado, and a thin green man sorta drops into the air like he'd been flushed down a toilet. He lands on the floor athlete style and slowly straightens. I wheel my chair away from Ackerman's desk to the back of the room.

"What is it?" the Doc asks me twice.

"It's a new one," I says, pointin' again. I dare not describe him. "Doc, what's happenin' to me?"

Ackerman picks up the phone and calls a couple other doctors into the room. And some orderlies, who stand back and watch me like security guards while the doctors kneel beside me and look me over.

The green faerie-guy squints at me and stalks around, studying me from behind the doctors. "For your sake, you better not see me, Bobby Bridge," he says with a sinister voice. "For your sake, you better not hear me."

"How do you know my name?" I ask him, my spit flying into one of the doctor's face.

"We know what we know," he says with menace, his mouth a slit with no lips.

"Are you talking to . . . them?" Ackerman asks.

"Yes, there's this guy that looks like Gumby, and I think he's their President. Am I gone insane, Doc?"

"If you think you could be insane, that means you're not."

"I am Elveesh," says Gumby. "President of the Consciousness Investigation Arm in the Imagine Nation."

"I ain't so sure about that theory, Doc," I says.

"You aren't supposed to see and hear us," Elveesh explains.

"That's kinda what *I* been thinkin'," I says back with sarcasm.

Another man steps into the room with long grey hair tied into a pony tail. He seems completely different from the rest of these folks.

"Come in, Ted," Ackerman says. "This is our patient, Bobby Bridge. Mr. Bridge, this is Dr. Panter, your psychiatrist. We were going to schedule you anyway, but—"

"I'm seein' and hearin' things," I says to Panter, shakin' his hand. Normally, I'd never want to see a shrink, but right now I'm desperate for someone to make this stop.

"Mr. Bridge, what are you seeing?" Panter asks.

"Well . . . ."

But Elveesh interrupts me. "My time is not at your disposal, Bobby Bridge. We must finish our negotiations with the Guild."

"Believe me, if I could dispose of you, I would!"

He tilts his head down and peers at me under his heavy brow with narrow, judgmental eyes. "You will have to dispose of *yourself.*"

"What's that supposed to mean?" I ask anxiously.

"Bobby," says the shrink, "stop talking to these people for a moment. I'd like you to close your eyes and tell me if they're still talking to *you.*"

I does so, and the thing says, "You are caught where we are, between the realities. This is not allowed. You must stop your brain."

My eyes pop back open. "Is that some kind-a threat?" I demand.

Panter says, "Nobody's going to hurt you, Bobby."

"Sorry . . . I'm havin' two conversations here."

With hardly a nose and only a line for a mouth, Elveesh looked like an unfinished marionette. But turned out the puppet was me. 'Cause next thing I know, I snatched Panter's ballpoint pen and tried to stab myself with it! Panter catches me just in time, and I'm grateful the old guy's still got good reflexes.

"Bobby, no, don't do this!" Panter shouts, as everyone grabs my arm and snatches the pen away.

"I ain't!" I shout back. "I don't know how, but it's the little green man that made me do it!"

"We're going to give you something to help you relax," says Panter as the orderlies hold me down in the wheelchair. "Larry, let's try some Thorazine."

Ackerman picks up his phone and relays the order.

"What's Thorazine?" I ask Panter as he checks my eyes. *Can everyone stop with my eyes?*

I glance at Elveesh. He makes a gesture with his arm and suddenly I launch my face at Panter's pen light. I would-a poked my eyes out if Panter hadn't jerked away so quick.

"He made me do it again! He's makin' my muscles lurch somehow. He wants me to kill myself so I don't see them anymore!"

Elveesh looks very displeased. His glowing insectoid buddies whisper between each other. I hear one say, "This will be harder than we thought."

Their twitchin' claws are still green.

"Easy now, big guy," says an orderly who's got my head in an arm lock from behind.

"Bobby, look at me. Look at *me*." I force myself to look at Panter. "Whatever you think you're seeing and hearing beside the humans in this room *is not real*. They can't make you do anything."

Elveesh makes a karate-like thrust with his hands from across the room, and I feel this powerful surge of strength through my torso, forcing me to throw my chair sideways. Somehow it's enough to knock all the orderlies down with me.

"Hurry up!" I hear Panter yellin' as the orderlies pin me to the floor. Panter sticks my arm with a big needle while he's talkin' about all sorts-a drugs, and then I black out.

Again I wake up. Different this time. The room's kinda big and quiet. The walls are white and blank. I'm lyin' in an inclined bed with my arms and legs strapped down. I'm alone.

Not alone. Elveesh is here. He's standin' in the shadows of the far corner, wearing a grey robe. His head is down, his arms draped. Very still, like a manikin. I stare at him and try to get up, but my arms and legs are held down by heavy Velcro straps.

"Elveesh," I calls to him. The thin green man jerks and looks up at me with blood red eyes. It gives me a chill, like I just called the devil. He stalks toward me like he thinks he's some kind-a Ninja. "Why can't you leave me alone?" I says.

Elveesh gestures and I feel my biceps jerk, but not so badly this time. And it's held by straps, anyway. His powers don't seem as strong as they were.

I try a new strategy. "Who is the Guild? I want to talk to them."

Elveesh jumps back in surprise. "No, Bobby Bridge, don't call *them!*"

Ahah, I thinks to myself. *I got to him. I need leverage and I found some.*

But my satisfaction is short-lived.

Somethin' rises from the foot of my bed. It's red and bloody, like a baby that'd been turned inside-out. It has no face, at least not in human terms. Just a red and tan mass as a head, with irregular bones stickin' out of it.

I scream even before I fully realize how scary the dang thing is. I no longer think I'm havin' hallucinations; I think this is real. But that frightens me even more.

It floats up several feet, with misplaced stubs for extremities, jerkin' and twistin'. And another appears, also a blood beast, a big one with somethin' like a heart thumping underneath it. And there's more. They all look like mutated human body parts glued, and twisted together and somehow alive. Stomachs, kidneys, bones, and brains, a dozen or more rise up from under my bed.

Even more botherin' is that nobody answers my screams. I twist my head from side to side, 'cause I can't move. I'm a pretty big guy, and I trained with free weights every day in my garage, but I still feel so weak. The doctors called it atrophy, but whatever it is, it ain't helpin'. Still, they all noticed I am stronger than I should be. I remember them takin' note of it.

When Elveesh tries to control me, it makes me stronger.

I stop screamin' 'cause it scratches my throat and make my eyes water, and I got to keep my eyes on these *new* faeries, or trolls, or whatever they are.

I see tubes attached to my arm and wires to my chest, connected to pumps and machines. The machines are beeping frantically 'cause I'm losin' it, but nobody answers that either.

And then I remember . . . I been awake before. Many times, since that incident in Ackerman's office. Awake and delirious, like I was skippin' through an inside-out nightmare, where sleep is my only peace. Each time I was awake, Elveesh had been there, and tried to make me hurt myself somehow. But each time got harder for him, like he's losin' his control over me. Maybe it's the drugs.

I realize what happened. I been committed. I'm in an asylum. *Holy crap!*

"A spy," grunts the voice of one of the bloody things, though I can't see no mouth.

I have to catch my breath before I can answer the thing.

"What are you guys supposed to be? Goblins?"

"He has nothing to do with us!" Elveesh shouts at the dude with the big thumpin' heart underneath, who seems to be the gang leader.

But the thing ignores Elveesh like he ain't even there.

"Who do you speak for?" it asks me. It sounds like its talkin' and garglin' at the same time.

"I speak for *me*. Bobby Bridge. Who am I speaking *to?*"

"Mind your tongue!" says one of the leader's minions. "This is Domo Thum, President of the Reality Division, Guild of the Wall. You will ask no questions, only answer them."

Now I'm startin' to get irritated. Ever since I woke up, I been attacked, controlled, and misunderstood. Enough is enough. I used to deal with wiseguy types back on the street where I grew up, and these guys may look different, but their game has the same rules.

"Don't get snarky with me, you little monster turd!" I shout at the heavy, or whatever he is. "I'll ask what I want and you'll get no answers unless *I* get some."

"Leave us!" Elveesh points at Domo Thum. "This is not your affair!"

"You were in the wall," says Domo Thum to me. "You have the smell. How did you get out?"

"I don't know what the hell you're talkin' about. I was in a coma, and since I came to, Elveesh here's been trying to make me kill myself."

"What??" Domo Thum shakes with anger and blood drips onto my white sheets like tears of frustration.

Elveesh's insectoid buddies reappear in a swirl of lights, their claws still glowing green. He ain't got no eyes, but it seems to me that Domo Thum ignores Elveesh and addresses *them*.

"You are stealing from the wall!"

"He fell out!" Elveesh shouts back. "He's stuck with us, and the Imagine Nation cannot allow it."

The wall must be a reference to my coma, I thinks to myself. I ask, "What do you mean by *imagination?*"

"He belongs back in the wall," says one of Domo Thum's sidekicks. "Imagine Nation tried to cancel him before we found out. That is grounds for a strike."

"Strike?" I says. "What are you, some kinda labor union? What kind of beings are you? Faeries? *Talk to me, goddammit!*"

Domo Thum turns, I suppose to face me. "Humans call us many things. Those who have seen us."

"Back to the wall with you," says a smaller one to my left, with a couple testicle-sized sacks pumpin' on both sides.

It comes toward me and I throw my head back and forth and spit like mad. "Get away from me! *Aaahhhh!* Don't touch me!"

The door to my room flies open and Doc Panter slides in, his big pony tail swingin'. "Shh, Bobby, what's going on, Boss?"

Of course he don't see what I do, so I pay no attention to him.

"Stop in your place!" Elveesh roars at Domo Thum. The whole mob of Reality Division body parts backs away from me, just as Dr. Panter pulls out a syringe and prepares to inject me. I stop screamin'.

"Wait, Doc," I say with a hoarse voice. He hesitates.

"You are in violation," accuses Domo Thum, addressing the giant glowing wasps. Is Elveesh in charge of them or not? I ain't makin' sense of the peckin' order.

Domo Thum, the guy with the heart, is a union leader for his side, I'm guessin'. Doc Panter is still poised with the needle.

"I'm sorry, Doc," I say to him. "I ain't tryin' to disturb the place. But these things, man, they freak me out."

"You're still seeing them?" Panter says with a frown. "After the cocktail we've given you, you shouldn't be still having hallucinations."

"His conscious soul belongs to the wall. We require an increase of one hundred seventy percent. That is our final offer."

Elveesh chops his hand sideways through the air. "No increase!"

"Then we strike!"

"It's illegal for you to stop the machine."

"Alright, *wait!*" I shout at them. "I want both of you to tell me what you are, and what you do! Then I'll tell you what *I* am, and what *I'm* going to do! I have *rights*, dang it, and you will learn them!"

Domo Thum and Elveesh come to the foot of my bed. Now I feel I'm part of this negotiation, but I don't know what they are negotiating and what I have to do with it.

And Doc Panter has resumed filling his syringe. "No, Doc, I'm not yellin' at you, please. Don't stick that stuff in me. Just hold on for a minute so I can talk to these things, okay? But don't leave, just stand there and listen, okay? I need that."

Panter seems very curious now and nods. "Okay, I'm here for you, Boss."

"Thanks, Doc. Domo Thum, that's your name, right? I'm waitin' for an answer."

At this point, I wonder just how much these creatures know about me. Do they know I was used to union politics? Do they know I once knocked my Boss on his ass for sexually harassing a fellow employee? Do they know I had a really nasty temper?

Of course, I could be arguing with a figment of my deranged mind, and I'm now just like one of those crazy people shoutin' at things that aren't there. But what else is there to do? Maybe all those crazy people were "stuck" like I am now?

"The wall is a machine," answers Domo Thum. "It separates realities. And Imagine Nation is the company that owns your reality."

"Imagine . . . Nation. Right." I'm thinkin' that sounds really goofy, but I take it as seriously as I can. What do I got to lose? I look to Elveesh. "First let's get facts straight. Nobody *owns* me."

"We own your reality," Elveesh says. "It's not for you to decide, but for those who manage you. Without us, you have no soul."

"I don't believe in a soul."

"How is that our problem?"

"Domo Thum, if you strike, what happens?"

"The machine stops," says Domo Thum. And with the gesture of a small absurd digit, an amazing wall appears in my room. It makes no physical contact with the real walls, just passes through them like one of those big holograms down at the museum. But it *looks* solid. And it's not made of brick or stone or steel. It's made of bones and organs, like Domo Thum and his minions: body parts all connected in a massive network that turns, twists, throbs, jiggles, puffs and waves as one big wall. Bodily fluids flow through veins woven throughout, like circuit wiring. It gurgles and snaps, belches and pops, and makes all other crude organic noises. I think Domo Thum's gang are maybe components of their own machine. Like the gears we cast down at the plant.

I swallow down the urge to puke and ask, "If the machine stops, what happens?"

Domo Thum's bony companion says, "Realities will blend. Yours and your neighbors'."

"What does that mean?" I ask, starin' at the absurd and grotesque operation fillin' my room.

"You're about to find out," says Domo Thum, and the wall leans toward us. I'm afraid the thing is gonna fall on me, but it stops close enough for Domo Thum to touch it.

"You'll be penalized," Elveesh warns him.

"So will you."

A penile-like tube extends from Domo Thum and plunges into the machine-wall. The tube connects to the maw of veins and it all stops. The organs stop rotatin', the fluids stop circulatin', the membranes stop breathin'. Then they disassemble. Creatures like Domo Thum climb out all over the place and dance around, croakin' and gruntin' and scratchin' themselves. Just when I think I'm gonna barf on Doc Panter, they all fade out of sight. Off to their locals' bar, I guess, if they have stuff like that.

"The Guild has infringed upon the Third Sanction of the Union Contract," Elveesh begins.

While a long list of violations follow, Doc Panter finally asks, "So Bobby, tell me what's going on, then."

I tell him everything I just saw and heard with as much detail as I can. He seems fascinated, though I know he doesn't believe any of it.

"So what's supposed to happen now that this reality machine is stopped?" Panter asks.

"I don't know," I says, "so far nothin' seems any—"

Suddenly there's a weird scratching sound up in the ceiling somewheres, like a rat slidin' across a corrugated box with its claws out.

I'm about to announce it to him when the Doc says, "What the heck was that?" He's lookin' at the ceiling.

"You heard it?"

"I'll have to call an exterminator on—"

Then there's a scream down the hall, and we hear a tray of instruments fallin' on the floor. Panter walks swiftly to the door.

"Wait, Doc, don't leave me here. Untie me at least!"

But he rushes out of the room, leavin' the door open. I hear shouts down the hall, and more crashin', and frantic screams. And I see shadows of people runnin' back and forth, and things fallin' down, and then . . . . A shadow of somethin' big, like elephant size, passing through some room I can't see. And there's a growlin' sound that gives me a chill. I ain't never heard nothin' like it in my life.

I fight against my Velcro, but it's no use: My muscles feel like boiled noodles.

Was it a big dog? Shadows can look bigger than they really are. But what would an animal be doin' here? Doc Panter heard what I heard, so it must be real, right? Or maybe Doc Panter himself is all in my mind?

I never felt so helpless. I'm thinkin' I may as well die quick, 'cause I don' have no other options.

The two gangs of faeries are havin' a big argument but I can' tell what they're sayin' over all the shoutin' and racket outside my room.

And then I notice . . . .

The tubes hangin' down beside my bed turn to dust! I see other stuff disintegrate too. The computer casings fall into a chalky powder and I can see all the circuits and stuff inside. The baggy part of a blood-pressure instrument rains black soot until there's nothin' left of it. Some gloves on a desk become a pile of sand. I jerk my head back and forth, lookin' at all this, and I quickly figure out the pattern. All the rubber and plastic is meltin' away. Which must include some of my Velcro straps, 'cause now my arms and legs are free!

I jump outta my bed and try to run to the door, but my legs collapse out from under me, 'cause they don't seem to remember how. I manage to get up to my feet and stagger about like a crippled drunk. I'm wearin' a gurney that's flyin' open in the back so I try to tie it shut, but there ain't no straps. They must-a been plastic too, I guess.

Before I get to the door, I see some doctors and nurses and orderlies, and I think a patient, rushin' by. Doc Panter's one of 'em. He sees me and skids to a stop. I'm wonderin' if I can fight him in this condition, but he doesn't seem to care I'm outta bed.

"In here!" he shouts to his friends. And the whole group trips over one another comin' into my room. One of them pushes me aside and I fall back down. They slam the door and drag a desk in front of it.

A couple of 'em are hurt bad. They's bleedin' and limpin'. One old gal, a receptionist I guess, collapses on the yella and white tile floor, wheezin'.

"What's goin' on?" I yell at the whole lot.

"We're being attacked by animals!" one of the big orderlies says, runnin' up to a window in my room that has bars on it.

"That was a *monster!*" the lady on the floor screams.

I wanted a better description until a weird screech out in the hall conjured up somethin' in my head that would do.

I joined the orderly at the window. The night was lit up by fire and explosions off in the distance. I saw a plane crashin', buildings topplin', and weird creatures everywhere. There was a big green blob growin' out of the buildin' next to us, and somethin' like giant broccoli walkin' down the street.

I can't look no more than a few seconds. I seen enough.

"I don't believe this," Doc Panter says as he grabs the phone. But the phone's plastics are gone. The receiver is just a bunch of stripped wires and electrical pieces. He slams the mess down. "What the hell is going on around here?"

"Welcome to my nightmare!" I says to him.

The lights go out. Some battery backup kicks in, filling the room with a dim glow. I smell smoke. Most electric wires have some kind-a plastic to insulate 'em, and if all that's gone, this town's in for some electrical fires.

Panter turns on me like it's my fault.

"Don't look at me, I told you what they did!" I shout. "They stopped the machine!"

"What's he talking about?" one of the other doctors demands of Panter. "Is he one of yours?"

Panter stares at me as the noises outside in the hall have faded. The monster out there has wandered downstairs for more food, I guess. We can all hear screams outside the buildin' now, and far out across the city.

Everyone looks in a near panic except the other patient, an attractive girl who's confused but silent. I'm guessin' she hallucinates, so she's probably used to this. Today, it's the crazy people who will cope.

"This all started right after Mr. Bridge told me faeries stopped some kind of machine that keeps realities separated," Doc Panter explains to them. I can tell he's real scared, 'cause his voice is shakin'.

"Yeah, those guys right there!" I says, pointin' at Elveesh and Domo Thum and their entourage. "Can you see 'em?"

Everyone looks. "I don't see anything, Bobby," Panter says. "What are they doing?"

"They're arguin'. The Reality Division's on strike, like I said."

"Not that I'm buying any of this," one of the orderlies says, "but ask them what that big alligator thing was that ate up half our staff!"

"Hey!" I shout at my faerie buddies. They stop arguin' and turn to me. Elveesh is surprised to see I am no longer confined to my bed. "My people want to know what the animal was, out in the hall just now."

"A neighbor," says Domo Thum. I repeat the answer for my human audience.

But of course, as doctors always do, they want a more scientific answer. "I dunno," I says to them, "take a wild guess what it means. What's the difference? It don't belong here; that's all that matters." I confront Elveesh and Domo Thum. "Now look here. The way I see it, that machine of yours is like a utility, or the department of sanitation. It stops working and society goes all to crap. We got planes fallin' from the sky 'cause our plastic is, I dunno, bein' eaten by some alien microbe or somethin'. We got monsters trashin' the city, explosions, people dyin'. You got to start that machine back up, and now!"

"We're on strike!" Domo Thum says, its mottled skins quiverin' on its enraged lumpy body. "The more human accidents we get, the more souls that join the wall. When we got enough, we'll start it up again."

I repeat the answer for the humans, and everyone's payin' attention to me now. As much as to be expected.

"Why does this machine need more conciousness?" I ask. "It was workin' fine before!"

"They do not *need* more," says Elveesh. "They *want* more."

I'm beginnin' to see that consciousness is not just fuel, it's compensation. So I change my tactics.

"Well what about *us?* What if *we* strike? The humans?"

"You said you do not speak for them," says Domo Thum.

"Well, it looks like I do now, 'cause I'm the only one who can see and hear you and the machine."

"Did they vote for you?" asks Domo Thum.

I tighten my lips for a second. "They will when they learn what I can do, and when they find out what you've done!"

"What would a strike by humans mean?" Domo Thum asks. "You're not workers."

"We'll refuse to give you any more consciousness. That's our strike. All coma patients will be terminated."

"Without enough consciousness it will not work!" Domo Thum and his gathering shout at me in protest. *Ahah, I think I got somethin' here.*

"I bet you could get enough just from our sleep. Right? My guess is when we sleep our consciousness is partly borrowed by that machine, and while there, we can see beyond it. That's where dreams come from, ain't it? But for a coma, you get a lot more, stealin' our memories and dreams. Well from now on, sleep is all you'll get. No comas."

'Course, I'm really playin' poker now, 'cause I have no idea if what I'm sayin' makes sense, but it seems to be workin', cause Domo Thum is thinkin' about it.

I explain to the doctors what's goin' on.

"It's a good bargaining chip," Panter agrees. "But Bobby, you know I—"

I hold up my hand to stop him. I know he's about to profess his disbelief or doubt in what I'm sayin', but to make my bluff work, I need the faeries to think at least the humans in this room are behind me. The way I see it, these faeries are like animals in the deep woods who'll come right up to humans 'cause they don't know what we can *do*. They might fall for the dumbest tricks.

"Follow my lead," I say to them. "I've been dealin' with unions for years. I think I can stop all this."

"We need time to analyze your situation," says Domo Thum.

A classic stallin' maneuver.

"You didn't wait, so we don't wait," I says, and I pick up the naked microphone piece that used to be a phone receiver. "I'm callin' the . . . uh . . . ."

"W.H.O.," says Doc Panter.

"*Who?*" I says.

"Yes, the World Health Organization. W.H.O."

"Yeah, we're calling them right now," I says. "No more comas."

"Stop!" Domo Thum shouts at me, moving forward.

I take a step back from the ugly thing. He's so close I can see a tattoo printed on his thumping heart sack, and it grosses me out.

"We will accept a third more coma."

"A third less," I says.

"Not acceptable! We'll not take a cut!"

"Then we strike!" I pretend to push the little sharp knobs under where the buttons used to be on the phone.

"Stop! A quarter more. Final offer."

"A quarter *less*. Final offer."

"A cut is not negotiable!"

"Then both sides meet half way," Elveesh interrupts. "No cut, no gain. No strikes."

Domo Thum is not happy, but it seems he has no choice. "Agreed."

"Now take us out of this place so we can't see you no more!" I says.

"You are stuck," Elveesh says. "We don't know why you can see us. This is not allowed. You must stop your brain!"

He shakes a fist toward me and I twitch like one of those schitzo people, but I don't hurt myself.

"Now you cut that out!" I shout at him.

Domo Thum doesn't care anymore, because if I'm not goin' back into a coma, my life means nothin' to him. So Elveesh and I face off.

"So, it's a fight, is it?" I says. "I gotta fight for my rights? So be it."

I'm much bigger than he is, but he's sure a cocky little fella, walkin' around me with his head down, movin' like a kung-fu black belt plannin' his attack. I glance at the giant wasps 'cause I don't want them behind me, and while my head is turned,

I see them twitch their green legs like spiders and suddenly Elveesh comes at me. I turn to defend myself just as he thrusts his palms toward me, but he's several feet away. Without touching me at all, I feel my stomach muscles jolt really hard. I stumble into some orderlies, who keep me on my feet.

"Stay in the fight, big guy," says the orderly I met before. "I can't see what you're doing, but I think you can take him."

"He can do it without touchin' me," I says.

But I learned somethin'. When the wasps twitch their legs, Elveesh moves. There's a synchronicity goin' on here. So I take a gamble.

I circle around Elveesh, and he circles me. Just when I get near the biggest of the wasps, I whirl and snatch the thing in mid-air. It's cold and sharp in my clutches, like a sea crab, but I squeeze it and shakes it as hard as I can. The green glow on its legs fades back to white, and same with all his friends. When that happens, Elveesh collapses like a Raggedy Andy doll, and disappears.

"I thought so!" I says. "Your President's some kind of collective puppet, right? Well, time to fight your own fights."

The other wasps make for me.

"Back off or I'll tear him apart!" I shout at them. They shudder with fear and float away from me.

"Now I want you to leave me alone, you got it?"

"Agreed!" they all whisper loudly as my prisoner's barbed legs claw at my arm, cutting open my skin. The doctors and orderlies are watchin' with wide eyes. They can see the blood.

"Tell them we want things set back to the way they were," the orderly near the window says. I can see he's pissed his pants, half distracted by his view outside. I can hear something climbin' up the side of the buildin', and the floor shakes. We may not have long.

"We want that machine back up *now*," I demand of Domo Thum, whose body has turned even more grey in reaction to my attack. He's afraid, too! "You want me to make that call to Who?"

"Fine," he says.

A shadow passes over the window, blockin' the street lamp, and everyone's afraid to look out there.

"Then you'll set everythin' back to the way it was?" I ask. "I mean *exactly* back the way it was, before the machine stopped? No destruction, no monsters? All our plastic back? Can you do that?"

"It will be done," Domo Thum says, and he and his group suddenly make this loud farting noise, like a horn blast, and all the crowds of meaty, bony creatures reappear and assemble themselves back into a vast wall. It happens really fast. The wall-machine once again passes through my room. And Domo Thum himself climbs into it, becoming a gear, pipes and intestines linkin' up to him, ball joints poppin' into sockets with sprays of blood. Fluids start gushing, organs start throbbing, skin twitches and stomachs gasp. Bone-shaped wheels start turnin' against one another.

As that happens, we all stand dumbfounded, watchin' damage to the walls repair itself, fresh wounds heal in seconds, pee on the floor dry up, purple slugs on the far wall disappear, and plastic form back from dust into its original bond. The shadow disappears from the window and the chaos outside turns silent. Even the desk moves back away from the door by itself, and everythin' returns to its place like it never moved.

It's like rewindin' a movie while I'm standin' in it.

While that's all happenin', the machine-wall fades from my sight.

I release my captive, and the giant wasps gather together to console one another. "I'm President of the Humans now," I say to them, "and I command you to leave us alone."

"We will go," they whisper. "But as President of the Humans, you will be called upon for negotiations as required."

"What?" I gasp. "But—"

But the wasps vanish in a storm of fireflies.

"You can't do this!" I shout after them, jumpin' into the air where their lights last floated.

Suddenly, I'm grabbed from behind by the orderly that had pissed himself, but was now dry. I'm totally surprised, and too weak to shake him off.

"How'd he get loose?" Panter demands.

"I don't know," the orderly says. "But he must have freed the others, too."

Another orderly grabs the other patient, the nice-lookin' girl who still just stands there in silence. She don't seem to care one way or the other.

"Hey what's the big idea?" I says. "Doc Panter, what are you doin'?"

"Get him in a straight jacket this time," one of the other doctors says, marchin' out of the room with the receptionist. "Good job finding them, Gladys," he says to her. "That would've been a long report tomorrow, if he had gotten out."

They begin shovin' a straight jacket onto me.

"What are you doin' this for? I just saved the world!"

"I'm sure you did, Bobby," says the orderly. "And we're grateful for that." By his sarcasm, I realize he don't have no memory at all of what happened. They all seem to act like I busted out on my own and they caught me.

Reality's been reversed and everythin' was exactly the way it was before the machine stopped. Just as Domo Thum promised.

Oh no!

"Wait!" I scream. "Doc, the monsters, you saw the monsters!"

"They're all in your own mind, Boss," Panter says, preparing a shot as I'm tied into the jacket.

"No, the faeries just set reality back again, don't you remember? It happened! I saw it, I heard it, it's real!"

"This will help you with that," he says. "Just relax now."
And he stuck me in the neck with it.

Of Plunder and Souls:
The Rescue of Mr. Spaghetti

L. Jagi Lamplighter

PIRATES, YOU SAY?" ASKED THE DETECTIVE WHO STOOD ON CLARA'S front stoop. At least Clara thought he was a detective. He was dressed in a fedora and a trench coat and looked disturbingly like Humphrey Bogart. He could have been the claims adjuster. She had talked to so many people that day, she had lost track.

Clara put her fists on her hips. "Listen here, Buster. Maybe you want me to lie to you—like that punk of an ex of mine did last time they took a car of ours. Tell you some comfortable story about car thieves and let it go at that. But that ain't gonna happen!" She shook her head for emphasis, sending her many cornrows flying and wagged a finger at him. "I'm one woman who respects the truth, and that. Is. Not. Going. To. Change!"

Usually, this was the place where they shot her the "You should be locked away!" look, but this guy just nodded calmly, like he was on the set of Dragnet or something. Cool as a cucumber, he was.

"Pirates towed your car, Ma'am. Is that right?" The detective asked again. He spoke with a Bronx drawl, so that his "that" sounded like "dat." Clara had never heard a Bronx accent in real life before. She kept expecting him to drop it and talk like a proper human being.

"Yes!" she snapped.

"That's all right, Ma'am. I believe you."

"You . . . you do?"

"Sure thing, Ma'am. These pirates have been towing cars all over town."

Clara sighed. It felt good to have someone believe her. Still, it took all the fight out of her.

"Any idea who's behind it?" she asked.

The detective nodded solemnly. "A pack of the worst supernatural scum in Faeriedom."

Just great. It would be that the guy who finally believed her was three crayons short of a box. Clara cocked her head and fixed him with the look that her miserable excuse of an ex used to call the "Hairy Eye."

"Faeries towed my car?"

The detective met her gaze square on, completely unphased by the "Hairy Eye." That itself was amazing.

"Ma'am," he drawled, "you just told me that Pirates stole your car on a Tuesday morning and sailed away—in the middle of Chicago—and I believed you. Common etiquette dictates that you should extend me the same courtesy."

Clara frowned. The guy seemed so calm and reasonable. Not what she expected from a crazy, but then she had been an ER doc, not a psychiatrist. Maybe real crazies were as cool as cucumbers. It would certainly explain the way he dressed and talked, like he had walked out of a 1940s movie.

"Look here, Mr. Spade-wanna-be. Pirates is one thing . . . ." Clara froze, her mouth wide open. A terrible feeling, much like what she imagined being stung by a scorpion might feel like, began spreading through her body. Tears pricked threateningly at her eyes. She let out a low warble of a moan: "Mr. Spaghetti! He's locked in the car!"

"Is that your dog, Ma'am?" the detective asked.

Clara shook her head, nearly whipping him with her cornrows. Next time, she would stand a little closer and wap him good. "No. A doll. My son's favorite doll." It shamed her that her voice broke. "He's going to be inconsolable."

"Children lose dolls all the time, Ma'am. Part of life."

Clara turned on him, showing her teeth like a wolf. "Is that so? Why don't you come in and explain that to my son. He's eight years old, weighs nearly seventy pounds, and has the language capacity of a two year old. You come to my house tonight, and you explain to Sammy what happened to his Mr. Spaghetti!"

The detective lowered the brim of his fedora. "I'll get your car back, Ma'am."

Clara lay on her stomach among the trees at the Lincoln Park Zoo and peered through her binoculars. The ground was damp and cold under her shirt. She hoped this would not take too long. Behind her, she could hear the voices of laughing children as a school group toured the exhibits. This caused a pang of maternal longing, as she suddenly missed her son.

According to her research into recent car thefts—she had called her sister's friend at the police department—the roadside parking area she had under surveillance was a likely spot for the car thieves to hit and just after morning rush hour was a likely time. Twelve cars had disappeared from this parking area alone in the last week. Like hers, they had all been parked off by themselves, with no one behind them. Of course, that did not mean one would disappear today, while she was watching, but she could hope.

And hope she did! It had taken a whole boatload of effort to rearrange her work schedule to get today off. It would be weeks before she could arrange another day off, and, to judge from last night's reaction to the loss of Mr. Spaghetti, her household would not survive another day, much less weeks!

Clara rubbed the bump on her nose from where it had gotten broken during the fit Sammy threw the last time Mr. Spaghetti went missing, the time they had accidentally left the   at the grocery store. She used to have a beautiful nose. People on the street would stop her and tell her how she could be a model. Of course, that was ten years and forty pounds ago. Today, she had more important things to worry about than her looks. Besides, what had her looks ever gotten her except her good-for-nothing ex?

She lowered her head, resting it on her hands. How had her life come to this? Ten years ago, it had been filled with such promise! She had risen from the slums to become a top ER physician. She had saved people! She still had a vase of dried flowers on her mantelpiece, the remnants of the first bouquet given to her by someone who felt they owed her their life.

But she had given all this up for Sammy.

Clara thought about her little boy. At eight, he did not talk, he did weird things with his hands—waving them in his face all the time—and he threw fits that made tornados look tame. And the screaming! Bright lights set him off. Cleaning products, in the air or in his clothes, set him off. Food dyes set him off. And not being allowed to eat the brightly colored candies that the other children ate? That set him off the worst of all.

On second thought, no. The worst was when he could not find Mr. Spaghetti! Man, not being able to find that crazy rag doll provoked tantrums the likes of which not even God had ever seen! Whatever it took, Clara had to find a way to get the doll back!

One smile from Sammy made all the crap worth it.

An inhuman choir rang out somewhere above the tree tops. The voices were cold and eerie and soulless and filled with a harsh glee that had nothing to do with gladness. They chanted:

> *The crew of the Plundered Hearts are we*
> *Fearless and peerless and wicked and free!*
> *Deathless and pitiless robbers are we*
> *Our hearts be as restless and cold as the sea!*
> *We do not bleed blood and we cannot weep tears!*
> *Our hearts are as empty and deep as our years!*

> *Sing yo ho, me bullies, and heave with a will*
> *We sail over ocean and hamlet and hill*
> *Cold iron, man's iron, our plunder-holds fill*
> *For men are our cattle and we wish them ill!"*

"This one will do, Lads!" called out a single deep, gravelly voice.

Clara's blood turned to ice in her veins. A God-fearing woman like her should be at work earning bread for her family! What was she doing hunting car thieves?

Her thoughts turned to Sammy. Her son might not be like other children, but when she saw his steady, shining eyes gazing back at her with such love, such trust, it was like gazing into his soul, like looking into the eyes of an angel.

She had to get that doll back! Clara brought the binoculars up to her eyes and stared, gaping. Even though she had caught a glimpse of these thieves twice before, it had not been anything like seeing them up close.

A huge square-rigger with sails the color of swamp fog sailed down out of the cloudy sky. The mainmast bore the symbol of a bleeding moon and a Jolly Roger flew from the foremast. On the side of the hull, flowery loops spelled out: *The Plundered Hearts*.

Aboard the vessel was a crew of pirates, but not like the pirates in any book or movie! Short, squat men in long jackets and boots with crimson sailors' hats served as powder monkeys. They toiled to and fro carrying rocks to the cannons. Huge, hulking creatures manned the guns; their tri-cornered hats, vests, and breeches were of bark and dead leaves. Tiny, winged pixies, no bigger than Clara's finger, swarmed about the lookout. They were not cute, pretty creatures, like from a story book, but cruel, nasty, little things with ugly, distorted faces. In their hands, they held shiny copper cutlasses.

At the helm stood a leering old man with a long white beard. He was covered in barnacles and seaweed and wore a conch shell for a hat. To his left, a horrifyingly ugly creature with an enormous nose and no mouth at all leaned precariously over the railing, holding what appeared to be a pistol made of peat.

The captain and his officers were of another cut. Clara trained her binoculars upon them in fascination and horror. Tall haughty faeries, they were decked out in a traditional pirates' garb of capes, jackets, blousy shirts, bright sashes, and high boots. Only the capes were tattered, the shirts were stained with rust—or worse, and the wide sleeves of their jackets hung down like the specter's shroud.

Tiny pixies with their penny-bright cutlasses flew out from the ship, leaving trails of glittering light. As the bright little motes drifted down upon several passers-by and a beat cop who stood on the corner watching the parking lot, probably for the same reason Clara was, they all looked suddenly puzzled and wandered away. Even drivers in cars looked bored and drove on when the glittery stuff fell on their vehicles. Clara, with her binoculars, was quite a distance from the ship, and none of the pixie dust landed near her.

Two red caps threw down copper hooks, green with patina, that caught on a tree and a bicycle rack.

"Heave! Heave!" the crew shouted harshly. Three large burly trolls winched the ship down to the ground. The tree swayed wildly. Atop, red caps and pixies reefed the mainsail and the foresail. With a rusty creak, the stern of the ship opened outward, descending until it touched the ground where it formed a ramp.

The harsh crack of a whip made Clara jump. A huge creature, muscle-bound and awkward, stumbled forward; one big red eye peered out from the middle of its head. It was bound in chains. A huge, spiked, bronze collar surrounded its neck and similar rings encircled each wrist and each ankle. The greenish chains were held by many red caps, each anchored by a troll.

That was a Cyclops, from Greek mythology! What was it doing on a ship run by nightmares out of the Brother's Grimm?

The horrible creature with the ghoulish, mouthless face held the whip. It drove the Cyclops down the ramp. Shuffling slowly, the one-eyed brute moved to the red Chevy parked by itself and secured the vehicle with the hooks. Then, it shuffled up the ramp again, grunting under the onslaught of the lashes, and began turning a crank. Slowly, with jerks and stops, the car was winched up onto the deck.

Then, the captain gave the signal. An unseen mechanism hoisted up the stern ramp and the faerie square-rigger floated eerily upward. Atop, the pixies raised the sails, and the ship shot off over the buildings, straight up into the cloudy night sky.

Clara lowered her binoculars and stared after the departing faerie ship, her body trembling. That detective guy had been right. She owed him an apology.

She stared after the ship for a long time, fear warring with determination. Then she stood up and headed across town to the library.

By the time Clara scrunched down on the floor of the rental car and spread the blanket over her head, it was already dark. It was cold down here, and the rug smelled faintly of vomit. She had not thought to check on that when she rented the vehicle. She rested her head against her old gym bag. The bag was stuffed with the goodies she had bought after her trip to the library, things the books at the library had suggested she might need. Of course, the gym bag did not smell that great either, but even old musty sweat was preferable to vomit.

Research, combined with her observations, suggested that the pirates favored cars parked near the park but with an open area behind large enough for them to land the ship. This explained why they kept taking Clara's car. She had a phobia against parallel parking and would gladly walk an extra mile if it meant she could find an easy parking spot.

As she waited under the blanket, trembling, in the dark, she prayed. Her great faith in God had never wavered, not through all the curve-balls life had thrown her.

She just no longer trusted that God would answer her prayers. Still, it did no harm to ask. He was a God of Mercy, maybe he would take pity on her plight. More likely, of course, he was laughing his Divine rear off.

The car lurched and bumped. Clara's stomach tensed. Was it them? Maybe her prayers had been heard after all. She snorted: first prayer answered in eight years, and God picks her request to be kidnapped by faerie pirates.

She grabbed her gym bag tight with one hand and braced herself against the seat with the other. There was a moment of stillness accompanied by a low clanking sound. Then the car began to move.

Clara lay very still, listening for the sound of retreating feet. The ride on the faerie square-rigger took about half an hour. Then the car had been lowered again into its current location. There had been some banging around, some muffled voices, and a loud scraping sound. Then, everything went quiet.

Very slowly, she pushed the blanket aside and sat up. She crawled onto the back seat and peered through the window. Another car sat next to hers, and then another and another and another. She sat up higher and peered farther. No one seemed to be about. Opening the door, she climbed out and shimmied up on to the roof of the rental, shading her eyes to help her see in the pale moonlight.

There were cars as far as she could see. They spread out from her current position in all direction except to the left, where a tall building stood. How would she ever find Mr. Spaghetti?

Jumping down, Clara gave the rental car a fond goodbye pat. With the loss of this car went her very last credit card, the one she had been keeping for emergencies. Sighing, she shrugged and threw the strap of the gym bag over her shoulder.

Creeping quietly forward, she peered into each car, shivering a little despite her inside-out sweatshirt—that was one of the tricks she had picked up during her time in the library. Wearing your clothes inside out was supposed to keep Faeries at bay. From time to time, she stopped and listened, but she could hear nothing except the hum of a freeway in the distance.

Her current efforts were futile, of course. The gibbous moon was not bright enough to let her distinguish the details of individual cars at a distance. There was no way to spot her car from afar, and too many cars to search individually. She would have to find another way.

Large bay doors led into some kind of warehouse. She could not see much in the dark, but even objects she accidentally knocked or kicked echoed eerily. She needed to find a light switch. She flicked her gym bag in annoyance and snorted. All this clever gear, and she had not thought to bring a flashlight.

Either her eyes were playing tricks on her, or tiny specks of golden light were falling through the air. Pixie dust! Clara cringed, fearing the worst as she brushed against some of the stuff, but nothing happened. She did not feel dazed or confused. Hey, maybe this inside-out clothes stuff really worked!

After bashing her head on some hanging thingamajig, Clara found a door. Just behind it was a foundry. The place was dimly lit, but the bright yellow-orangey glow of the something molten illuminated the vast area just enough to make it look like a nightmare from the fourth circle of Hell. It smelled of hot metal and was steamy with warmth, a welcome change from the chill outside.

Clara moved forward cautiously. From her position, she could not see the work force. They must be too small in relation to the gigantic cylindrical vats. However, work force there must be because huge cranes were lowering cars—full size sedans and SUVs—into the molten vats.

Far above the factory floor, a wooden command center hung out over the work area, supported by buttresses. Clara stopped beneath it, puzzled. Who would be kooky enough to bother constructing a room of a burnable substance, instead of from steel and glass, in an environment so filled with fiery sparks?

Faeries, of course. Faeries who cannot touch cold iron—apparently not hot iron either. If the faerie overlords did not care to come onto the factory floor, of what did the work force consist? More enslaved Cyclopes?

Clara squinted at the foundry again, but all she could make out was tiny pixie sentinels hovering in the air above the vats. She crouched down into the shadows and held up the St. John's Wort she had located at the local nursery. Either it worked, or the shadows hid her, for none of the guards glanced her way.

With a loud grinding creak, one of the vats tipped. A stream of hot yellow liquid poured into some kind of long trough, illuminating more of the building. Shadows fled from the corner around her. Clara saw something pale dangling on the wall far to her right.

She crept silently along the wall, the St. John's Wort held above her head, until she came to an alcove about half way down. Hanging suspended by a rope was the detective who had questioned her the previous day, the one who had promised to get her car back. He hung by his hands, dangling above what looked, in the dim light, like a circle of toadstools that grew directly from the cement. His coat had been rent by claws. He had a black eye and an ugly purple and greenish bruise on one cheek. He did not seem to be breathing.

"Dear God!" She pressed her hand against her mouth, hard. "Is he . . . are you dead?"

"Nah, it's okay, Ma'am." The voice came from some place in the air to the left of the body. It sounded as if a pair of cymbals had been granted a voice and were speaking with a Bronx accent. "That's just my body. Normally, I stay in there, but I kinda got out of it, on account as I did not like the way it was getting treated."

"What . . . what are you?" Clara's heart beat loudly. All her neat plans suddenly seemed to be unraveling. The wisdom of risking her life on inside-out sweats and a weed she held over her head suddenly seemed ludicrous. She stared at the claw rents and the bruises and forced herself to swallow.

"Ever read *The Tempest?* By that Speareshaker guy?" His voice issued from the air above the closest point of the toadstool circle. When Clara nodded, he continued. "Remember Ariel? Well, I'm his . . . you'd call it a 'brother.' Only I spend my time in this body here, as Mr. Prospero wanted me to be able to help you humans. He's the one who decided I was to be a detective. Name's Mab, by the way."

"Mab?" Clara looked to and fro, but could see no sign of the speaker, which made sense, if he were some kind of spirit of air. She crossed her arms. "I thought that was the Faerie Queen's name?"

"Nah, her name is Maeve. Spenser got a little confused."

"I see. Can I get you down?" Clara gathered her gumption and took a step forward, eyeing the toadstools dubiously. "I brought some herbicide."

"Herbicide? Clever! A girl after my own heart. But don't use it here. There are other spells, you might get hurt."

"What can I do?"

The voice was silent for a moment. Sighing, he said, "Ma'am, I'm going to ask you a favor. I realize you might not be able to grant it, but I . . . I gotta ask."

"Go ahead," Clara eyed the air suspiciously.

"In order to get anything out of here, you're going to have to face the faeries. Faeries don't got free will—well not in the way that a creature with a soul does. They are constrained to obey certain rules."

"Like leaving a poor soul alone if his clothes are inside out, or not crossing a circle of salt?" Clara asked. What had seemed warm when she first stepped in from outside was now uncomfortably hot. She wiped sweat from her brow.

"Right! They have to stick to these rules under which they operate, whether they like it or not. But they're tricky. Comes from having no hope of Heaven, you know; no reason to behave. If you survive whatever they throw at you, they'll let you pick one thing to take away with you. Pick me."

Clara drew her head back and stared at him like he was bonkers. "Pick you, not my car with Mr. Spaghetti?"

"Pick me, Ma'am, 'cause once I get out of here, I can shut this place down. Shut it down forever. Put . . . let's just say I can put everything back where it goes—I could do it now, if I could get to my danged cell phone, but I can't work it in this form, and you can't cross the magic circle to get it for me."

Mab's voice became more serious. "If you pick something else, Ma'am, you'll get to leave with it, but everyone else's . . . stuff will stay here . . . including me."

"What's the number? I could call them." Clara pulled out her phone.

The voice sounded truly embarrassed. "Blasted speed dial! No one commits numbers to memory any more."

Clara put her hands on her hips and snorted. "You think that's going to be hard, Detective Mab? On one hand, I get a doll or a car. On the other hand, I get both the doll, my car, the rental, and I save you, another human be . . . another living being, anyway. You think I'm going to find this decision hard?" She waggled her head at him. "You have another thing coming."

The detective's voice was low and sad. "Ma'am, you have no idea. If you choose to ask for me, I swear I will do everything in my power to return . . . everything here that is yours. But if you do not, I'll understand. Mortals can only bear so much."

"You're crazy," Clara took a step back, unnerved. "You may have believed me, but you're still kooky as a . . . kooky thing!"

"Just sayin', Ma'am. That's all," replied the detective.

Clara held up her hand as if she were saying the Pledge of Allegiance. "I give you my word I will ask for you. There. How's that! I am a woman of integrity. I. Do. Not. Break. My. Word."

"You shouldn't have done that, Ma'am . . . but I thank you."

She slipped around the wall and was about to head up the stairs to the command room when she saw it. Her car! It sitting in the line of cars waiting to be turned into slag. Clara flew down the stairs that led to the waiting area. She hunkered down and ran between the vehicles like a spy in the movies. Reaching hers, she fumbled with her keys, breathing hard. Then, she had the door open and, with a lunge into the back, Mr. Spaghetti was in her hands.

Clara shut the door and sat down against the tires of a green van. She hugged the stupid, tattered to her chest; its fingerprint-stained spaghetti-like hair flopped against her shoulder. Her body felt weak with relief. "You caused me a whole whopper of trouble, Buddy O!" she whispered to the silly little thing. "I don't know what my son sees in you, but he loves you."

Clara gave the rag doll a last fierce hug and shoved it in her bag. She wiped the sweat from her face again. She toyed with her cell phone as she thought about calling home. Reluctantly, she decided not to. The last thing her sister needed was for the phone to wake Sammy. He had cried himself to sleep, the poor baby.

If it were not for the detective, she would leave now. Forget the car, forget that she had ever seen anything like this. Just get the doll back to Sammy, and life could go back to normal . . . without a car or a credit card. But she felt bad just abandoning the guy. Maybe she should try the herbicide on the toadstools after all. Or maybe, she should just call 911 and bug out of here!

As she stood, she glanced toward the factory floor.

Children?

Where had all the children come from? Clara's feet did not move toward the door. Instead, they crept closer to the factory floor..

It was like walking into a Dickensian nightmare. Children, from tiny three-year-olds to burly teens, worked the factory, moving levers, throwing switches, changing the molds into which the molten metal poured. Dirty children dressed in rags with bruises and open sores. Sweaty children working in all that heat. Dull-eyed children, who went through their routines without any sign of that spark that made a child a child.

Human children. Enslaved by faeries. Here in the modern day, in the country of freedom! In all her years of medical school and ER work, Clara had never chucked her cookies. She had been proud of that. But, her Stomach of Iron failed her now. She turned and vomited behind the wheel of a white BMW. Crouching down, she grabbed her knees and stayed like that until her legs stopped shaking. Then, slowly, she stood up and made herself look again.

Little children, like Sammy. One of the little boys even reminded her of him. Despite the heat, a chill traveled own her spine. No, not reminded her—this boy looked just like Sammy. Except, he looked like what Sammy would look if he were an ordinary child—without that sometimes stupid, sometimes benefic expression the real Sammy wore; like what Sammy looked like when he really concentrated and you could not tell that there was anything amiss with him; like what Sammy would look like with a festering wound on his cheek and forehead.

That boy out there, the one with burn marks on his wrist where molten sparks had caught him—the bastards did not even give him leather gloves—looked exactly like her son. How could that be?

Clara glanced over the rest of the children, the ones she could see. Her heart nearly stopped. There! That little girl was a splitting image of Jillian, the sole little girl in the boy-heavy Autistic program at Sammy's school. And behind the giant crane! The boy who was missing an arm. He looked like the twin brother of Nicholas, from that Special Needs exercise class she used to drag Sammy to.

Slowly, her legs gave way, and she sank to the cold cement floor. She bowed her head. She knew how it could be. She had only just read all those faerie stories.

Clara did nothing to wipe away the hot tears that splashed from her cheeks to the floor. Her life, her wonderful career, the lives she might have saved, the husband she had—yes, she would admit it now, she had loved Stan before it all went wrong and the coward ran out on her—all thrown away so she could raise an faerie impostor who had been left in place of her real son, a changeling.

Now that she knew, life finally made sense. The laughing in the face of discipline, the weird behaviors, the lack of empathy with human beings Sammy displayed. Was that so different from laughing at funerals and the other bizarre things faeries were wont to do? And modern chemicals? Of course, Sammy could not tolerate them! He was a freaking faerie!

Were they all changelings? Clara raised her head. Over a million autistic children in America alone. Had they all been stolen by faeries?

She thought of her friend Jenna, patiently enduring the screaming and fits of three autistic boys. She thought of Martha, who spent her days driving from one doctor to another, determined to find the illusive missing cure. She thought of Mrs. O'Conner whose daughter had bugged out, leaving her to raise her two autistic grandchildren.

All these women, all that labor and love, wasted on changelings—while their own children suffered as slaves.

"Samuel!" She took off at a run, sprinting across the factory floor. "Samuel!"

The little boy turned as she approached him, his eyes growing large. Staring up at her in wonder, he asked in a small voice. "Are you . . . my mama?"

Clara grabbed him and clasped him to her heart. "I am! I am your Mama! And I'm never going to leave you again!"

She knelt and hugged him, her missing son, her long lost beloved child. He smelt like metal fumes and smoke, but under that was a scent that reminded her of her mother. This little boy smelt like Nana! Any doubts Clara might have had evaporated. The two of them hugged and cried and cried and cried.

A scrabbling noise startled Clara, just as a red cap lunged for her. Clara screamed and threw her body between the red cap and her son. Frantically, she stuck her hand into the gym bag, feeling around for something of use.

The red cap let out a yowl. His hands clawed at her but did not touch her.

The inside-out clothes! They had worked! Losing no time, Clara grabbed her son and sprinted toward the cars, and the stairs and the door out beyond.

More red caps appeared. One wielded a cutlass. One swung a copper rope. Another held two wooden belaying pins like daggers. Soon five chased her, then six. As she neared the cars, a seventh red cap stepped straight ahead of her. Clara ground to a stop, hugging her boy tight. What had been the counter to red caps? Fear seemed to have driven all her careful research out of her brain.

Oh, right! Bible verses. Made them stop and loose a tooth or some such rot. Clara blurted out the only Bible passage she could bring to mind.

"'Give us this day our daily bread!'"

The five advancing red caps stopped cold. Moaning, they grabbed their jaws and writhed. A moment later, a tooth popped from each of their mouths. The teeth shot across the room, bouncing off of the floor and ricocheting off of vats. From the additional moans and pings she heard beyond the range of her sight, she assumed that more red caps had been on the way.

During all this, Clara had not been idle. She grabbed the Morton carton and spun in a circle, letting the salt pour out liberally. As soon as she was done, she spun around again, to make sure she had not missed a spot. She had to pour more salt on the two gaps she found, but, finally, she had a closed circle.

The red caps rushed up again and crowded around the circle; short, bearded men in dark sailor's suits wearing red sailor's caps and each missing a tooth. They shuffled around the circumference, as if searching for a weakness.

"Hey, little men?" Clara called. When they gathered around, she shouted, "Boo!" and gave them the Hairy Eye, the real deal, with the full force of her scorn. The red caps scattered like leaves before a leaf blower.

"Now that's how it's supposed to work!" Clara hooted triumphantly. "God only knows what was up with that detective. He didn't even blink!"

Samuel looked up from where Clara had pushed him against her body, his eyes wide. "What happens now, Mama?"

"Don't know, Pumpkin. We wait."

A door opened in the wooden command center, and the captain from the *Plundered Hearts* out and dove from the platform, flying down to land before her. His long coat fluttered about him like wings. He leered at her, his expression distant and cruel. When he landed, Clara saw that he had lost a limb at the knee. In its place was a silver peg leg inscribed with Celtic knotwork.

A tiny pixie sat on his shoulder. The pixie, too, was in pirate garb: tricorn hat, blousy white shirt, black, half-open vest, red sash, blue pantaloons, black boots and a copper cutlass—the whole works.

Clara's heart fell. She was doomed. She felt it. These pirates were far older and more cunning than she. She must have fallen into la-la land—thinking she could outfox faeries! Her hand tightened on her son's body. His heart beat so hard, she could feel it through his back. She raised her head and faced the captain. By God, she was not going to give up without a fight!

"What you think you doin'?" Clara always reverted to the language of her youth when she got angry. "Takin' advantage of these poor, defenseless children?"

The captain grinned. His teeth were all sharp; two were made of silver. "My! Aren't you a feisty one, me Beauty! But yer days of wrecking havoc here are over. Hand over the boy and go, before we find more appealing uses for ye. Arrgh!"

"Appeal this, you POS!" Clara snarled, as she rooted around in the gym bag, her hand trembling. Lord, she had better get out more. She had spent so much time around children, she had forgotten how to swear properly. "You let these children go, or you're going to be sorry you ever drew air!"

"Begging your pardon, me Beauty, but are ye referring to me crew?" The captain gestured toward the factory floor. His long fingernails were crowned with slender caps from which needles protruded. He held them up, leering, "The better to claw out the eyes of disrespectful ship hands, Arrgh!"

"Arrgh!" growled the pixie on his shoulder. "Those scurvy louts!"

"They are CHILDREN!" Clara shouted. "They are supposed to be out playing and running around."

"On the contrary," the faerie pirate captain drawled. "When children are left to their own devices, they are prone to cause havoc. We put a stop to that." He leaned back his head and stroked his non-existent beard with a black-gloved hand. "Me thinks ye should be thankin' us for the service!"

"Arrgh!" repeated the pixie on his shoulder. He leered. "Otherwise, you'd be swabbing up the mess, bitch."

Clara glared at the little bugger. What was he supposed to be, the parrot?

"I ain't even dignifying what you just said with a comment," she grumbled, as she searched her bag.

Clara pulled out a handful of powdered chalk and a pile of red thread. She threw it down with a grunt of disgust. That was no use! She plunged her hand back into the bag again. It had to be here somewhere!

"These wee ones are our weaponsmiths. They make pistols and spears, for use against our enemies, the Unseelie Court. Or are we the Unseelie Court?" The captain cocked his head to address the pixie. "So hard to keep these trivialities straight. The Servelings make weapons now. When they get bigger, we give in to their pathetic mewling and let them wield the things. They're given the honor of cutting down our enemies, Arrgh! Fine bully boys, they make, all hot with anger. We cannot make or hold iron weapons ourselves, of course."

"Arrgh!" declared the pixie. "Melts us like slag." It grinned nastily. "Melts our enemies like slag, too, and they don't got themselves a Serveling army!"

"Servelings! The word you are looking for is Slave!" Clara spat. "You've enslaved children to make weapons?"

The captain of the *Plundered Hearts* chuckled deeply. "Aye, the blackbirdy has spunk, do she not? Look at her bristle like a vixen defending her kit. If we had mothers, lads, we would know how mothers get, wouldn't we?"

There was muttering laughter from the redcap pirates, answered by tinkling giggles from the little floating pixies. Clara glanced around, unnerved. She had not realized that they had an audience.

The captain continued, "Besides, me fierce Beauty, the little powder-monkeys do more than just forge weapons. Some are lucky enough to become cabin boys, or personal servants to other fae. They serve many uses, quite versatile, really."

"Very useful, Arrgh!" the pixie leered, "Especially the saucy little wenches!"

"If they are useful," Clara asked through clenched teeth. "Why do you treat them so badly?"

"Fer the fun of it." The captain leered. The audience hooted and howled.

Finally! Clara's shaking hand—more with wrath than fear now—closed upon her *piece de resistance*. She held it tightly but did not pull it from the gym bag. "Listen here, Faerie Face, I'm leaving and I'm taking my son!" she declared.

"Arrgh! I think not. Pirates never relinquish their loot." The faerie pirate grinned, showing his sharpened silver teeth. "However, Ancient Law, far older than the ways of pirates, require that we must let ye go—with a single object of yer choice—if you can successfully answer a riddle."

"Listen here, you Jack Sparrow wannabe!" Clara drew the sawed-off shotgun from her gym bag and rested it against her shoulder. "I ain't playing any of your pixie games! I am a lady of principle! I. Do. Not. Make. Deals. With. Slavers."

"Ye have no choice, me Saucy Lass, yer in our territory now. Our territory, our rules!" The captain leered. Behind her the red caps and trolls cheered loudly.

"See this shotgun?" Clara trained it on the faerie pirate captain's chest. "It's packed with rock salt and iron filings. Iron hurts you guys, doesn't it? Of course it does, or you wouldn't bother kidnapping helpless babies! Do you know what these filings are gonna do to you when they hit you? Suppurating lung wounds. Ripped aorta. Perforated stomach wall. All that med talk.

"Don't you mess with no MD, Punks!" Clara jabbed the gun at him. "When it comes to knowing how to hurt, we can open up a whole can of whup on your sorry ass!"

"Arrgh! Tradition requires that we . . . ." the faerie pirate captain began. Clara aimed the gun at his head. "Or we can choose an easy riddle and move on," the faerie captain amended. "What is black and white and read all over?"

"A . . . newspaper?"

"Right you are, Missie! Now, ye may ask for one thing, and one thing alone to take away with ye. Anything ye likes out of our booty. Cars. Pieces of eight. Magic rings. Whatsoever ye please."

Clara opened her mouth to tell them that it was sure as Hell going to be her son she took with her. Only she stopped. Behind her, laboring in the factory, were the other children, hundreds of other children, thousands of other children.

"What if I want more than one thing? What if I want to take them all?" She asked. "Do you need me to remind you of what is gonna happen to you and your punk pixie mini-me if I pull this trigger?"

"Now don't do anything hasty, Me Feisty One!" The captain urged. "We of the Old Lineage are bound by yer circle, but them thar human Servelings are not. Children love shooting pistols, ye know, and we have many here. What a tragedy t'would be if ye and yer little boy were gunned down by yer own kind. Poets would write ballads about it." .

The captain leered at Clara. "What be yer decision, me Beauty?"

Clara paused, torn. She looked across the factory floor at all the other little damaged souls. Someone else would have to rescue them. Or maybe she could come back with the police. If they believed her. If they knew enough to use chalk circles and not just get enchanted. On the other hand, what if this Mab person could not actually help her? What if his promise was a trap?

Clara closed her eyes and prayed. Then, she knelt beside her son. "Samuel, honey. I love you more than air itself. But I promised someone who can save all the children that I would ask the faeries to let me take him out with me. It's very important to keep your word, and we want to save all your friends. I'm gong to have to leave you here and come back for you. Is that okay?"

In the best of worlds, Samuel would have smiled at her and said, "That's all right, Mama." But, Clara's life had never been in the best of worlds.

Samuel's bottom lip quiver. He grabbed her leg and held on.

"No! Mama, no! You promised!" he cried, his voice heart piercingly shrill. "You told me you would never leave me again! Mama! They hurt me here, Mama! Don't leave! Don't leave me!"

Clara felt as if she had been pierced to the very center of her soul. If some-one had shoved a hot poker through her spine and into her heart, it could not have hurt as much as this. But when the faerie captain insisted she, herself, tear her son from her leg and leave him, weeping, on the factory floor—that hurt more.

Outside on the chilly street, Clara knelt beneath a street lamp, pounding her fists on the pavement. Beside her stood Detective Mab, back in his body again. He was bruised and beaten but seemed able to stand and walk. "Well blow me to the North Pole, you chose me!" he whistled, pulling out his cell phone.

"What happens now?" she asked fearfully, when he folded his phone again. "Will . . . will the children be all right?"

"We wait for the Cavalry."

"The cavalry?"

"The *Orbis Suleimani*," he growled. "Set up by King Solomon to protect humans from the supernatural. Nowadays, Mr. Prospero's in charge. We've been looking for these pirate jokers for a long time, but we were having trouble locating 'em." A look of disgust came over Mab's features. "Stealing from humans! Enslaving children! Appearing during the day! Those punks had to go down!"

"They can't be responsible for all autistic children. There weren't enough children there," Clara murmured, more to herself.

Mab looked grim. "They aren't the only ring of slavers, Ma'am, but we'll get 'em. We'll get 'em all!"

"Why children?" Her voice sounded unnaturally shrill. "Why not just kidnap adults? Adults would be infinitely more useful for fighting a war."

Mab shrugged. "One of those rules, like why they can't cross salt. They are allowed to take children before their first birthday. After that, all sorts of restrictions kick in. Free will, and all that." He made a sour face. "The same restrictions that require that even though they kidnap these poor little tykes, they've got to go and taunt them by telling them stories about mothers and families and all the good things that they are missing."

So that was how Samuel had known he had a mother.

Ahead, perhaps a dozen dark figures carrying tall staffs approached the factory building. Just before the door, they halted. Soon, they were joined by more figures in wide hoods and long flowing cloaks. When what appeared to Clara to be a small army of them had assembled, they moved, streaming into the building. Clara lowered her head and prayed that, in whatever was about to happen, no one would hurt the children.

As she glanced up again, her gaze fell on the gym bag. Mr. Spaghetti's head stuck out of the open top. Clara grabbed him and hugged him. Then, just as quickly, she flung it away from her.

Mab raised an eyebrow. He walked over and picked up the discarded rag doll, examining it front and back. "Begging your pardon, Ma'am, but isn't that what you came here to find?"

Clara snarled. "My life, my health, my marriage, all the sacrifices I made—that . . . thing is not my son, not even a human being, some kind of . . . " tears threatened to spill over her lashes again, "some kind of soulless monster."

It was the pain, the humiliation, of not having noticed that hurt the most—the pain of having loved him so much. It was worse, even, than having wasted her beauty and her youth on Stan.

Mab took off his hand. "Ma'am, you must be a praying woman."

Clara glared at him suspiciously. "What makes you say that?"

"Cause only the Almighty could arrange a coincidence like this one. Less than a dozen beings on this world could tell you what I'm about to say, and only one who's actually been through it happens to be me.

"Before I go on, let me ask you—truthfully now, just using your own judgment. Do you really believe your son—your other son, I mean, Sammy, I think you call him—has no soul?"

Clara closed eyes and pictured the thing she used to think of as her son, the moaning, bobbing freak who had broken her nose. But what she saw in her mind's eye was not the screaming, thrashing Sammy, but his beneficent smile, that open clear look in his eyes—that look that was like gazing into the eye of an angel.

Suddenly, Clara was certain, from the crown of her head to the bottoms of her sneakers, that Sammy had a soul. She had seen his soul gazing back at her. Sammy might not be the son she had given birth to, but he loved her!

Wordlessly, Clara nodded. Somehow, the detective know what she meant.

"You clearly know something about faeries. Have you ever come upon the story of St. Patrick and the mermaid?" asked Mab.

Clara shook head.

"Well, the short version is that St. Patrick once got a mermaid a soul. It can happen. Mr. Prospero, my boss, he investigated it. Found out that the easiest way to grant a supernatural creature a soul is to put it in a body and let 'em live with humans, interact and communicate with humans, learn decency and love.

"Ma'am," Mab put his hat back on and gave her back Mr. Spaghetti. "Before Mr. Prospero gave me this body, I was as soulless as the rest of my fellow airy spirits. But then I started hanging out with Mr. Prospero's daughter, Miss Miranda—you may remember her from the play—and learning stuff about humans. To make a long story short . . . I've won me a soul! The Gates of Heaven are open for me, now. Just as they are for that changeling you've been raising, the one whose goofy you're strangling."

Clara gaped, clenching the doll. "You mean Sammy did not have a soul when I got him . . . but he has one now?"

Mab nodded. He stuck his hands in his pockets. "Bodies change the way we think. Faeries going into a child's body becomes a child the same way immortal souls conceived by the Almighty sent into a child's body becomes a child. That faerie who impersonated your son had never known love. He'd never known courage, or sacrifice, or any of those things you've been doing for him. Do you think soulessness can hold out against the power of a Mother's Love?"

So, now Clara had two children. She had to change her real son's name. Could not have two boys in the house both called Samuel, and it made sense to change the name of the one who had only just learned he was a Samuel. She called him Stanley; she thought his good-for-nothing father would like that.

Clara kept an eye on the news, tracking the stories about the "foundlings." Children arrived in homes far and wide. It was not an easy time. These battered children went to homes that were already dealing with problems. Some families had two or three such children. Her friend Jenna was suddenly the mother of six.

Some families rejected the new children, who were then shunted off into the foster system. Some rejected their changelings in favor of their flesh and blood. But, for the most part, they did what families always have done since the dawn of time, they made do. They found room. They loved them all.

In America alone, over a million faeries had gained souls.

Rogue Fae

A Clear-Cut Case

Elaine Corvidae

PLEASE, YE MUST HELP ME. I DO NA HAVE ANYWHERE ELSE TO turn," said the young woman on the doorstep.

She was a ragged little thing, thin and dressed in clothing worn from a thousand washings. Soot smudged her face, as it did everything in Gloachamuir, and her tears made bright tracks through the grime. The iron collar of a factory slave encircled her neck, and I suppressed an instinctive shudder at the sight, even though I knew that the metal was no threat to the purely-human woman who wore it.

"I take it you are looking for Miss Barrow?" I asked. "I am her roommate, Elizabeth DaTarn. Please, follow me."

I led the factory slave up the steep stair to the second-floor flat that I shared with Sorcha Barrow. The stair opened onto our small sitting room, which was crowded with a number of oddities that belonged mainly to me. Medical journals spilled from every table and were piled on the floor. A human skull served as a paperweight on the writing desk, and was accompanied by the bronze knife I used as a letter-opener. The skeleton of a dog, strung on copper wire, crouched watchfully on the mantelpiece.

Sorcha stood with her back to us, staring out the window at the night. Tall and whippet-thin, she cut a spare figure in her dressing gown. Despite her youth, her hair was pure white, and drifted about her shoulders like cobwebs.

She turned when I shut the door, and crossed the room (forced as she did so to step around an old medical bag filled with colorful stones that I had collected). Our visitor paled and looked as if she would have liked to have fled. I wondered if she was intimidated by Sorcha's height and severe appearance, or if she had a touch of the Sight and discerned something of our fae blood.

"A-are ye Miss Barrow?" she asked hesitantly. "The private detective?"

Sorcha nodded. "I am. You have come late for a client; most of my business is conducted during the day."

"And sorry for it I am, ma'am, but me shift at the mill just ended an hour ago, and I dinna have the money for a cab."

"Quite all right," Sorcha said abruptly, and dropped into a chair. "Sit down, Miss . . . ?"

"Adaira DaNair."

"Miss DaNair. Do you mind if Dr. DaTarn joins us? I have found her help to be most invaluable on other cases, and being a doctor at the charity hospital, she is used to maintaining discretion."

The praise warmed my heart, and I sat down at Miss DaNair's assent. "Why have you come?" I asked kindly.

Adaira swallowed, her hands twisting nervously in the lap of her skirt. "It's me man, Donal, ye see."

"Dead or missing?" Sorcha inquired, with what I thought a profound lack of either tact or sensitivity.

Tears welled in Adaira's eyes. "Murdered! But how did ye know?"

Sorcha settled back, watching Adaira thoughtfully. "There are few reasons that women come to me with cases concerning men. By your attire, I could guess that you do not have the means to simply investigate a philandering lover. Blackmail also seems unlikely. Therefore, it must be something desperate, which leaves death or the possibility of death the only logical choices."

"Ye're right. He . . . I identified his body this morning, before me shift started. I do na have the money to bury him, and what I'm to do I'm sure I do na know . . . ."

Sorcha held up a hand, cutting off her client's tale of woe. "Please, Miss DaNair, begin at the beginning. When did you see Donal last?"

"Last night." Adaira wiped at her eyes, smearing soot across her young face. "We had a bit of a row, ye see. Donal is—was—a good man, but he had his weaknesses like us all. Had a fondness for the bottle, and he did na like it when I'd scold him for it. Stormed out of the flat he did, saying he was on his way to the pub, and he'd be damned if I'd stop him. And that was the last time I saw him alive."

I perceived that the woman held herself somewhat to blame for the death of her man, no doubt wondering what might have happened if she hadn't complained of his drinking. As for Donal himself, I privately wondered just how good a man he had been. I'd seen some of the effects of heavy drinking far too often at the hospital, in the form of black eyes and broken limbs.

"About what time did Donal leave your presence?" Sorcha asked, steepling her fingers before her and peering at her client with strangely colorless eyes.

"About nine o'clock, I'm thinking. We live down by the railroad, where it crosses over the With, and I'd heard the train go by just before."

"I see. And did Donal have a particular pub he favored?"

"Aye. The Stoat's Head."

Sorcha nodded, and I guessed that she was drawing a map in her head, figuring the streets that Donal was likely to have walked. "Pray, Miss DaNair, continue. When did you first begin to worry about Donal?"

Adaira shook her head and sniffled. "I did na fear for him, 'til the police came to the door, asking me to come down to the morgue. He'd stay out all night at times, and been in trouble with the foreman at the refinery for coming in after the bell had rung. 'Twas about three when the police came. Said they'd found a body on Cast Iron Road, and could I come down to the morgue and take a look?"

"And what condition was the body in?"

I shot Sorcha an angry look for asking the question so baldly. And indeed, Adaira promptly burst into fresh tears, as anyone with feeling might have predicted. Sorcha looked taken aback by the display, so I quickly stood up and went to Adaira, giving her my handkerchief. "There, there," I said, patting her shoulder in a motherly way. In the course of my work at the charity hospital, I beheld grief and pain on a daily basis. Some of my colleagues responded by becoming as indifferent to human feeling as Sorcha, but I had determined instead to learn the quickest and best ways of offering comfort, feeling that it was part of my charge as a physician to heal those in distress.

It took a while, but I eventually managed to calm our guest enough to answer Sorcha's question. "He . . . I suppose he'd been stabbed," Adaira managed to say. "His stomach had been sliced open and . . . they said some of his innards were gone."

Sorcha sat up straight at that, and a new look of interest sharpened her features. Only my quelling glare kept her from demanding what, precisely, had been removed, a question I doubted the distraught woman could respond to with any certainty.

"Please," Adaira whispered, clutching at my hand. "The police . . . they do na care about the likes of us. I dinna have enough funds to bribe them to find Donal's killer. I'll do whatever it takes to pay ye—I'm a fair enough housekeeper, if ye need one to clean for ye, or someone to mend yer clothes, or anything ye think just, for as long as ye like. I beg ye—yer me last hope, and the last hope for Donal to get justice."

Sorcha seemed lost in thought for a moment, but at last she nodded. "Very well, Miss DaNair. I will take your case. Payment will be arranged later, upon completion of the work."

Adaira leapt to her feet and seized Sorcha's hand, weeping over it and offering incoherent thanks. Sorcha again seemed at a loss, and I wondered, not for the first time, if her fae blood was strong enough that human emotions were somewhat alien to her. Eventually, Adaira allowed me to escort her back down the stair and out the door.

When I returned to the sitting room, it was to find Sorcha pulling on her tweed overcoat and heavy boots. "I take it that you mean to waste no time?" I asked.

"I do not. Furthermore, I need your help in this case, so ready yourself as quickly as you can. It's a cold, damp night outside, and your seelie blood is far thinner than mine."

Sorcha and I were both faelings—part human, part fae. My great-grandmother had loved a faery knight—one of the seelie, who had dominion over fire and air, and whose power waxed with the long days of summer. One of Sorcha's ancestors—how distant, she had never said, even as she never spoke of her mortal family—had been the antithesis of mine, an unseelie fae who had gifted her with the legacy of winter magic, of power over water, earth, and shadow. Although these differences might have doomed a friendship between us, instead we had used them to forge a partnership in which each of our strengths could be best utilized to cover the weaknesses of the other.

"I take it you wish to view the body?" I called as I hurriedly changed into a heavier skirt and shirtwaist.

"Indeed."

"It will still be at the city morgue, as Miss DaNair lacked the funds to pay for a burial," I said, emerging back into the sitting room and picking up my coat from where it lay discarded over the back of a chair. "They'll hold it for a few days; then, if no one else comes to claim it, put him in potter's field."

As Sorcha had predicted, it was indeed a miserable autumn evening. Gloachamuir was normally shrouded by a haze of smoke from the smelters that blazed day and night, and at times it grew so bad that the streetlamps burned at high noon in an attempt to dispel the gloom. Tonight, the coal smoke was augmented by a nasty, clinging fog that covered everything with damp, soot-laden dew.

The city morgue lay near the outskirts of the city, surrounded by gloomy tenements and a rundown police station. The few people on the streets had thin faces and hungry eyes, and as a precaution we both cast glamours over ourselves, so that we appeared to be large, hulking men. When we drew near the morgue, however, Sorcha insisted on glamouring us both into invisibility, so that no guards would see us. The feel of her magic on my skin was uncomfortable, as though I lay at the bottom of the river, in the water and the cold mud.

The stone building had once been part of some ancient fortification, and the thick walls held a chill even at midsummer. The main entrance was barred with an iron portcullis, but I led the way around the side to a more modest door, which had but a single watchman. I conjured up the illusion of a light, which bobbed through the air like a lantern in the hand of some unseen person.

"Who's there?" the guard called, squinting at the light. When no answer came, he moved toward it cautiously, allowing us to slip in through the door behind him.

Despite the late hour, I knew that there was a good chance people would be moving about within. Death, after all, does not keep banker's hours. Fortunately, we saw no one as we made our way down to the holding area in the basement. I had been there many times before, in the course of my work for the charity hospital, and so it didn't take long to locate the correct room. Bodies lay in silent rows on tables of steel, which would bind our magic if we came into contact with them.

"Stand back and keep a watch on the door," I told Sorcha as I hunted for the correct corpse by means of crude paper tags affixed to their toes.

"A shame that the workers take the boots," Sorcha said, remaining close to the door as I had asked.

I was surprised that my companion felt some compassion for the dead. "A shame it is, but it's part of their pay, and an ancient tradition, dating from the plague-times."

"Still, I might have discovered more precisely where Donal died if I was able to examine the character of the dirt on his shoes," Sorcha replied callously.

When I discovered the body we had come for, I sat my bag on the table and began my examination. Donal had been a rough sort, his clothing coarse and his face shadowed with the beginnings of a beard, as though he hadn't bothered to shave in some time. His eyes had sunk back into his head in death; they had been open when he died and no one had bothered to close them.

His shirt was stiff with dried blood, and I smelled the distinctive scent of bile, suggesting that the gall bladder had been disturbed. Moving carefully, I peeled the shirt back, noting the long slash in the cloth as I did.

The exposed wound was even more brutal than I had expected. Something had sliced horizontally through the lower portion of the man's chest, just beneath the sternum. The lowest ribs had been cut apart and wrenched away, exposing the internal organs.

"What was the weapon?" Sorcha called.

I frowned, examining the shredded tissue. "It appears that a pair of instruments were used. The edges near the center of the body suggest that two sharp objects were thrust into the flesh, then pulled to either side to make the wound. An unusual method of killing someone."

"Indeed. Were knives used?"

"I'm not certain, but I don't think so. The cuts have a ragged nature to them. Perhaps if the knives were dull, they might make such wounds."

"Curious. Pray, continue."

I opened my bag and pulled out a pair of bronze forceps. Normally these would be made of steel, and although I was human enough to tolerate the touch of iron, it nevertheless would bind my faeling abilities. My solution had been to have most of my equipment specially-forged in bronze, explaining to everyone who asked that I had a rare allergy to steel. Using the forceps to manipulate the tissue, I pulled open the wound and examined the abdominal cavity beneath. It didn't take long to determine what the killer had removed.

"His liver is missing," I said, standing back and tugging his shirt back into place.

Sorcha frowned. "His liver?"

"Yes." I went to the sink and cleaned my hands. "His liver. All the other organs are more or less in place."

Sorcha frowned deeply, obviously thinking hard. I started to ask her what she suspected, until I realized that the sound of voices floated down the hall outside. Sorcha heard them as well; moving silent as a ghost, she hurried across the room and stood by me, covering us both with her glamour.

A moment later, the door opened, and I saw two of the morgue workers come in, a body between them. A police officer accompanied them, attending to the formality of noting that the body had indeed been delivered to the room. "We're still trying to round up someone to identify him," the policeman said to the workers. "So yer stuck with this one for a few days."

One of the workers spat. "Third in a week. I dinna like it. Gives me the creeps."

The policeman snorted. "If ye get the creeps, yer in the wrong business. 'Sides, what are ye complaining about? If someone's killing scum down on Cast Iron Road, 'tis more boots for ye, and less drunks for me."

They put the body on one of unoccupied tables; when the policeman turned to the door, one of the workers made a rude gesture at his back. Both seemed uncharacteristically grim as they followed the officer out and back the way they had come.

The moment they were gone, I hastened to the newest corpse and confirmed what I suspected. Like Donal, he had been torn apart for his liver.

"So," Sorcha murmured, coming to stand by me, "it seems that our Donal wasn't the first victim, nor the last."

"Indeed." A shiver ran up my back. A crime of passion I could understand, but the idea that someone was coldly mutilating men on Cast Iron Road and removing their organs was something else altogether.

Sorcha put her hand on my shoulder. "Brace up, Beth. This is indeed an ugly business, but I fear it will get uglier still before the end."

I glanced at her. We were still under her glamour, so through my right eye I saw nothing. But through my left, I saw that her thin mouth was set in a grim line, and her colorless eyes were troubled. It came to me that she knew, or at least suspected, something about the case that she was not yet willing to share.

"Are we to try and apprehend the fiend?" I asked, not without trepidation.

"I fear that we must." Sorcha's slim hand tightened on my shoulder, then fell to her side. "But not tonight. Our killer has already sated himself."

"Sated?"

"Indeed." She smiled, but it was utterly without humor. "Why else do you imagine he would take the livers, if not to eat them?"

Sundown of the next day found us at the head of Cast Iron Road. Sorcha and I had both glamoured ourselves to appear like young male factory slaves, hoping such a disguise would keep anyone from troubling us while we hunted our quarry. As the sun slipped below the horizon, I could see her colorless eyes beneath the glamour gleam like a cat's, a single flash of greenish light to herald the moment night took over from day.

As for myself, I would have preferred to come when the sun was high, and my seelie magic stronger. Our quarry preferred the shadows to do his vile work in, however, so there was no question of that. Fear makes me grumpy, and I thought that most criminals were very inconsiderate, to insist on operating under the cover of darkness.

From the swath of light and music spilling from a dozen open doors, many of the establishments on Cast Iron Road were only beginning their business day. The area mainly catered to the cheap pleasures of factory slaves and other unskilled laborers, and so was a haven of saloons, penny theaters, and brothels.

"I fear that we may have a long night ahead of us," Sorcha said, sounding invigorated by the prospect. "We must be careful to keep our ears open as well as our eyes, as I doubt our killer will be kind enough to commit murder in the middle of the street where we might easily lay hands upon him."

"How are we to find him then?"

Sorcha hesitated, then gave me a false smile. "Although he hasn't been caught in the act, he's hardly been circumspect, either. The bodies were found relatively quickly, which suggests that we have a chance of catching him easily enough if we keep on our toes."

There was another reason, I felt certain of it, but I had learned early in our friendship that Sorcha did not respond well to questioning. So I resolved to be alert and to let nothing odd go uninvestigated.

We began our patrol, from one end of the garbage-choked street to the other and back. A few hansoms clattered past, but for the most part people here traveled on foot. A pack of young children were fighting over some prize in an ash heap; they screamed invectives at one another that would have shamed a sailor. Prostitutes, seeing only the glamour of a pair of young men, called out invitations that made me glad they couldn't see my blush. Sorcha, however, answered them so saucily that I was taken aback, despite the fact that I knew she prided herself on fitting the role anytime she took on a disguise.

Together, we walked up and down the long street thrice, changing our glamour each time so as not to draw attention to ourselves. The head of the street was brightly-lit and bustled with activity. As one moved farther from the light, the nature of the activity changed. It was here that the street women brought their customers, and I found myself glad that my seelie eyes couldn't see well in the dark. Sorcha seemed undisturbed by whatever she beheld, but I had yet to discover anything that could ruffle her exterior. The far end of the road, down by one of the refineries, was dark as an abyss and seemed to be abandoned even by the prostitutes.

It was on our fourth patrol that it happened. As we drew near the deserted end of the street, I felt a cold wind touch me, bearing on it the scent of slime. A moment later, I realized that there was no wind after all.

Someone was using magic. Unseelie magic, to be precise.

Sorcha had frozen in an attitude of listening. The phantom wind touched me again, flowing from the shadows near the refinery, and a moment later Sorcha broke into a run. Cursing silently, I raced after her.

At the sound of our footsteps, something turned in the shadows. I pulled the memory of summer sun from a slumbering tree, the reflection of gaslight from a pane of glass, and formed them into a ball of light that flared sharply, dispelling the shadows.

Our quarry cried out, flinging up an arm to shield its eyes. At its feet lay what I already knew I would see—a man's body. A tremendous amount of blood had gushed from the great veins of the liver, and the smell of rust coming from it was almost overwhelming.

The killer was surprisingly small, all thin limbs clothed in a ragged shift. It dropped its arms, and I saw that it was in fact female. Her face and tangled, filthy hair were soaked in blood, some of it fresh, some of it dried to a crust, and when her lips drew back in a snarl I saw carnivore's teeth.

With a sudden shriek, she flung herself at me, no doubt trying to extinguish the light that pained her. To my horror, I saw that her forefingers were horribly deformed—twice the length of a normal finger, and ridged with stiff blades of bone that wouldn't allow them to bend. I dodged wildly, felt one of those blades slice through my coat and into the flesh beneath.

"No!" shouted Sorcha, her eyes blazing in her bone-white face. Frost shattered the stones beneath the killer's feet, causing her to stumble and allowing me a moment to get beyond her reach.

Letting out an unearthly scream, the creature spun and sprang at Sorcha instead, her dagger-fingers stabbing at my friend's eyes. Sorcha caught her by the wrists; frost instantly coated the creature's flesh, but she only snarled. For an instant they were poised, both of them exerting all their strength, the blades slipping closer and closer to Sorcha's narrowed eyes.

I tore the last of the heat from the corpse on the street, discovered the memory of a forest fire in the wooden joist of the building beside us. Wind buffeted my hair, ripping it loose from its bronze pins, and the scent of scorching rose with my power. Gritting my teeth, I hurled myself on the creature, locking my hands about her throat and pouring every bit of magic I could summon into her.

The thing screamed, but this time it was a piteous cry of pain. Sorcha thrust her back, and she fell limply to the ground. A thin column of smoke leaked from her open mouth, riding her final breath.

"Are you all right?" I asked.

Sorcha nodded, and tiredly wiped her wind-whipped hair from her face before kneeling on the filthy cobbles beside our fallen enemy. "She didn't even know how to protect herself," she said quietly.

"She certainly seemed to do well enough to me!"

Sorcha shook her head. "No. She was just acting on instinct. She didn't know how to fight off a magical assault, just how to bear the pain and push through it. I don't think she really had a chance at all."

I looked down at the body, at the slack face. Despite its inhuman teeth, the features themselves were startlingly ordinary . . . and young. Dropping my gaze to her ragged shift, I realized that she had barely even begun to develop breasts. "Dear God. She was a child."

"Yes." Sorcha rose to her feet. "Come, Beth. Let's dispose of her body, so that at least she can be spared becoming a curiosity in death."

The next evening, I returned from my shift at the charity hospital to find my friend sitting in her dressing gown and staring out the window, her face a study in melancholy. It was unusual for Sorcha to show emotion, and I wondered at it now.

"Our last case has put me in a mood," she said, when I hesitantly questioned her. She smiled a little, but it was a sad look that didn't fool me at all.

"It was a terrible business," I agreed, sitting down beside her. "I've thought of little else all day, save when I had a patient to distract me. She was a terrifying creature."

To my distress, Sorcha's look of sorrow only intensified. "Did you find her so? I thought her pitiable."

"Truly?"

"Of course." Sorcha linked her hands together and stared down at them. "She was a faeling, like us. You knew about your heritage, Beth, but I am guessing that she did not, if only because of her utter lack of training. Imagine what it would be like to find yourself at the age to become a woman—and instead, to find yourself becoming a monster, without any cause or explanation known to you. Your fingers grow distorted, sharpening into daggers. Your teeth change their shape. Perhaps you have already learned how to cast glamour, but perhaps others notice before then, and shun you. Perhaps you have to flee the only family you have ever known."

Her fingers tightened, and the edge of pain broke through in her voice, like the back of some great beast breaching the surface of a tranquil ocean. I shifted closer, not certain how to offer comfort, but she ignored my movement and continued on. "But that is not the worst of it. A terrible hunger begins to grow in you, one that you cannot understand and cannot fight. It burns in you, night and day, until you can think of nothing else. Until you know that you cannot survive without assuaging it.

"You are a child of the lower classes; you know how easy it would be for a woman or a girl to lure a man away from his friends. You've learned to use glamour now, and so you appear to be normal, or maybe even beautiful. And when you finally work up the courage to do it, you find a man, get him to come with you . . . and finally, you are able to feed, to quench the terrible hunger that has been devouring you from the inside." She closed her eyes, as though envisioning the scene, and I saw them moving rapidly beneath the thin lids. "Perhaps you are horrified by what you have done. Perhaps you're too desperate to care. It doesn't matter how you feel, because you are doomed to do it again and again, because it is your nature. You have no choice."

I thought that the bitterness of her words came not solely from sympathy for the young creature's sad fate. I had often wondered what had motivated Sorcha to take up the mantle of consulting detective, or why she felt such a keen need to see that justice ultimately won out, and I sensed that there might be some clue here.

"It was terribly unjust," I agreed at last, heavily. I imagined what would have happened if I had discovered myself a monster, not through some fault of my own, but through an accident of birth which caused my faeling nature to manifest in such a way. "I'm sorry we killed her. Perhaps . . . ."

Sorcha gently put one of her hands on mine. "No. She would have killed you, and that I could not allow. Her nature was what it was, and there was nothing to be done about it. But I grieve." She sighed. "I grieve, because she so easily could have been me."

I looked up at my friend, uncertain whether she wished me to intrude into her past. I think that she sensed what I was about to ask, because she suddenly smiled and stood up. "Enough of this. I'm hungry, and we've nothing worth eating in the flat. Shall we go out to dine?"

"Of course." I stood up as well, and went to fetch my hat. "But not to any establishment which serves liver, if you please."

Bad Clown

D.C. Wilson

ECTOR LOVED THE CLASSICS. SOME OF HIS COLLEAGUES WOULD groan whenever he threw a cream pie in the face of a mark or tumbled around the sawdust-strewn floor, giggling as the children laughed at his pratfalls. He didn't care, so long as he had the children's attention. Classic gags could be miraculously new for them. His taste in dress reflected his love of the old days: black and white checkered vest and black three-belled jester's cap with white hose. The cap fitted over his eyes, doubling as a mask with an obscenely long nose. For a splash of color, he wore red gloves and slippers and a red cape with a gold lining that hung over his shoulders, smoothing over his outline in just the perfect manner. A little white face completed the costume. The only props he carried were his cane and a multitude of colored handkerchiefs tucked inside his vest.

"What is black and white and red all over?" Hector asked the other clowns in the Oberon-Titania Circus who would groan, fully aware he would exclaim the answer before anyone would try to respond. "Me!"

As a small regional circus, Oberon-Titania did not have many individual acts, which suited Hector fine. His double-jointed frame and wiry physique enabled him to not only serve as one of the clowns, but also aerialist, contortionist, escape artist, and, on occasion, human cannonball. Hector also mastered knife throwing, but he rarely showed that skill off in the rings. He preferred to reserve that for his avocation.

The sun was just dipping below the Appalachian Mountains as Hector the Harlequin tucked several sharpened implements into his shoulder bag. He removed his cape, exposing a small hump in the center of his back. With great care, he folded the cape and placed it in the bag as well. Then, Hector took a deep breath and unfolded his wings. Taking a quick glance around the park to make sure none of his fellow carnies were watching, he leapt into the air and flew north.

Leif opened his bottle of beer as he watched the sun go down and felt a twinge of nostalgia. The rolling mountains of Pennsylvania always reminded him of home, so he made sure the circus passed through here every year. He took a swig of the dark ale, so unlike the colored rice water that the big American breweries passed off. Since it was brewed locally, stocking up on the ale was another perk of visiting Pennsylvania. Tetsu had tried to show him how to order a case through the microbrewery's website, but Leif didn't trust all the technology in this new world.

A raven settled on the roof of Leif's trailer. "The Harlequin's about," the bird squawked.

Leif took another swig. "You know the rules, Tetsu. If you want to talk to me, you have to have lips."

The raven let out a noise of protest, "No time, little person!"

Leif finished his ale with a final gulp and pitched the bottle at Tetsu. The raven just barely hopped out of the way and fluttered to the ground. "Shift, now," Leif said. "And I warned you about calling me a 'little person', tengu!"

With a sigh, the raven twitched as he grew, shaking off feathers and sprouting fingers. His face transformed from that of a bird to what appeared to be a handsome young Japanese man, though his long beak of a nose made him look like he was preparing for a high school production of Cyrano de Bergerac. Tetsu straightened himself and smoothed his black silk shirt and pants, tracing the gold embroidery along the collar and lapels with his fingers. "Sorry, Leif," he said. "I was just trying to keep up with the modern parlance."

Leif slipped off of his tiny deck chair and folded it up as he let out a snort of disgust. "I hate that bloody politically correct term. I'm a dwarf. It's what I've been for eight hundred years. It's what I'll always be."

"Eight hundred and six," Tetsu corrected.

"Who's counting?" Leif reached up to open the door to his trailer. "Let's go inside."

Leif kept only a few personal items in his trailer. It served not only as his sleeping quarters while on the road, but the business office for the Oberon-Titania Circus. A small desk and filing cabinet fill most of the front section. A PC sat on the desk. though Leif rarely used it. A few of the circus's framed promotional posters hung on the walls, including one that proclaimed, "Leif Erikson, the World's Smallest Ringmaster!" Leif sighed at its yellowing edges. The date on it was 1936.

Leif settled behind his desk and waited for Tetsu to take a seat. "Now then, what is so important about the Harlequin?" he said, starting to open another beer.

Tetsu cleared his throat. "He's unseelie."

The bottle slipped from Leif's fingers and struck the edge of the desk, spilling foam on his white shirt and red jacket. "What? Are you're sure?"

"Positive." The tengu produced a handkerchief from his sleeve and started to dab at Leif's jacket. The dwarf brushed him away with his arm.

"How long has he been pledged to the Winter Court?"

Testsu shrugged. "I'm not sure. Possibly decades, maybe even a century."

Lief pressed his palm against his forehead. For centuries now, the two fae courts, seelie and unseelie; Summer and Winter, had been in a formal détente. While both courts still sent spies into each other's midst, a precarious truce had been maintained since the Thirty Years War.

"Damn it," Leif said, "Why can't the bloody nobles let me keep the circus out of politics? They know I'm Summer, but I treat them fair."

"The Harlequin is a different matter," Tetsu said. "You know his past."

"The Winter Queen's henchman . . . of course, I know!" Leif snapped. "He promised to give up his ways in exchange for a job."

Leif took another swig of beer. This time, it tasted more bitter than his last. Damnit. Hector had promised. All fae had in their blood a mercurial nature, something Leif took great pains to keep under control. It bothered him when he failed.

"And you trusted him."

"Since 1867, he's behaved himself, and indeed, become one of our top performers. What reason did I have to doubt him? Yet *now* you come to me saying he's been working for the unseelie all this time?"

Tetsu shrugged, his long nose bobbing up and down. "You asked me to look for signs of trouble."

"I did indeed. I just didn't think it would take you a hundred and thirty years to decide he was trouble. So, is he here to spy on us? I can't think of anything the circus has done to warrant the attention of either court."

"But we do travel around a lot. It's the perfect cover for someone who is looking for something important," Tetsu said.

"Do you know what he's up to?" Leif asked.

"He's tracking several online auctions, looking for artifacts from the old days."

Leif glanced at his computer. "You can do that?"

"Oh, sure," Tetsu said. "It's easy once your figure out his user ID. The Harlequin's is Joker69. Not very imaginative." The tengu reached over to power up the PC. "Here, I can show you how it's done."

"No!" Leif pushed his chair back from his desk as if there were a viper on it. "I mean, you can show me later."

"Really, Leif, you have got to get over your fear of technology."

"It's fine."

"Yorak the troll is better with computers than you. He's even got a MySpace page."

"I said, later! First, let's focus on where the Harlequin has gone."

Tetsu leaned back and waved his hand dismissively. "Very well," he said. "He's gone north to a place called Steelton. It's a little town just outside of the city of Harrisburg, about fifteen miles from here." Tetsu pulled out a map of Southern Pennsylvania and pointed at a place right along the Susquehanna River.

Lief glanced at his beer bottle. The label read, "Brewed in Harrisburg, PA." Later, he thought. "What is he after?"

"Ah, that's where things get sticky. I think he's tracked down the Cauldron of Plenty."

Leif stood up. *Damn,* he thought. *Damn it to bloody hell.* "Go get Katie and tell her that I want her and her brood in my truck in ten minutes." Tetsu rose, nodded and started to leave. "And get Yorak, too. We may need some muscle on this."

As Tetsu gathered the troops, Leif started to unhitch his trailer from his truck. He couldn't afford to have anything slow them down. He cursed himself as he worked. Why hadn't seen this? How could the Harlequin have betrayed them? Despite the clown's past, Leif had considered him a friend, a good one at that.

"Bad things happening?"

Leif nearly jumped at the sound. He glared at the scaly creature perched on the roof of his trailer. The chupacabra's green eyes glowed softly in the moonlight as he slid onto the ground and he let out a soft purring sound as he flexed his wiry limbs. The boney extrusions running the length of the chupa's arms, legs, and back quivered and he chattered with excitement.

"Not now, Rafe," Leif said.

"Rafe come along? Rafe help. Rafe good helper."

Lief winced. In the old days, the circus employed Rafe as a geek in the original definition of the term. The little goatsucker would eat anything, dead or alive. But such acts had lost their appeal in recent decades and Leif had to put him on other jobs. Rafe didn't mind. He just wanted to help. He *always* wanted to help.

"Please let Rafe help?"

"All right, fine," Leif said, "Only because I don't have time to argue. We're going on the road, so that means you wear your glamour."

"Yes, yes!" Rafe capered around with joy before dropping to his knees and shifting into the form of a chihuahua. As dog, he continued to hop up and down, yelping and trying to lick Leif's face.

Disgusted, Leif unhitched the trailer. He had just finished adjusting the pedal extensions when Tetsu came back with Katie and Yorak, their children in tow. Fortunately, the family had the sense to wear their glamours already. Katie wore her wetsuit, her long red hair dripping water on the ground. Yorak the strong man, though, was still in his performance costume: A bearskin cape complete with the head attached that he wore as a hood. He also carried his cudgel, which was longer than Leif was tall. Fortunately, their three girls took after their mother, wearing matching wetsuits.

"Take that ridiculous fur coat off, Yorak," Leif said. "We're going out among mundanes."

The strong man sniffed with an indignant air. "It is my totem of power. I must wear it in battle."

Katie rolled her eyes as the triplets nudged each other and giggled. "Don' look at me, Leif. I cannae talk sense into 'im. I gave up sixty years ago."

"All right," Leif said as climbed into the front seat. "Everyone, just get in the truck." Yorak climbed into the bed of the pickup. Fortunately, the rest fit inside the king cab. Leif never understood what a selkie like Kate saw in that troll. *It takes all kinds*, he thought.

"Rafe! Get off my lap! I need to drive!"

They arrived at the house in Steelton too late. The Harlequin had already fled, leaving behind a nightmarish scene that looked like a set from a schlocky slasher film. Furniture had been overturned and ripped apart. All the drawers in the house were pulled out and dumped on the floor. A closet door was ripped from the hinges. In the living room, they found a woman tied to a chair. Her arms and torso were cut in several places. Her throat was slashed to the point where she was nearly decapitated and her head hung to the side, her mouth frozen in a scream of terror. Two buckets full of blood were placed on either side of the chair. All over the walls, the Harlequin had written the words "Ha Ha Ha" in red.

As he looked around for clues, Leif could hear Katie outside as she argued with her three girls, forbidding them to set foot inside the house. Rafe sniffed the floor, stopping only to lap up some milk that spilled on the kitchen floor where the Harlequin had overturned the refrigerator. Yorak put his fist through the wall into the adjoining room. Tetsu sat down in front of a computer to search for information there.

The dwarf shook his head. "He's definitely gone back to his old ways."

Katie burst into the living room, slamming the door closed. "Ye're lucky I saw this mess before me girls did, or I'd be using yer beard to clean the diving tank, dwarf!"

Leif looked down at the floor at her furious gaze. "I'm sorry, Katie. I didn't think he would do," he spread his hands around the room, "this. He was our friend. We all thought he had changed."

"People don' change," she said. "Especially the fae."

Tetsu slammed his fist on the table.

"What's wrong?" Leif asked.

The tengu cursed. "The buyer of the cauldron was Michael Caffrey." He held up a stack of letters and pointed at the corpse in the middle of the living room. "This is the home of Michael and Sharon Caffrey. Assuming that this unfortunate woman is Sharon, then where is her husband?"

"More importantly," Yorak said, "where is the Cauldron of Plenty?"

Rafe let out a loud yelp and jumped a full three feet in the air. "Someone else is still here!" The tiny dog/chupacabra headed up the stairs, sniffing each step along the way.

"Rafe, wait!" Leif said, running after him. "Be careful! We don't know what could be up there."

The dwarf and the other fae followed Rafe into a small bedroom with pink carpeting and a matching bedspread. Several dolls and stuffed toys were arranged on the bed with the care of a child who still held to heart the fantasy that each toy had its own personality. Rafe continued to jump with increasing excitement in front of the bed. "She's here! She's here! Rafe find her! Rafe good helper!"

Leif crouched down and lifted the comforter and met a pair of eyes cowering back him. "It's okay, honey. You can come out now."

"The b-bad clown will get me."

"No, no," he said, "it's okay. The, uh, bad clown is gone."

The little girl shook her head.

"What's yer name, sweetheart?" Katie said as she knelt next to Leif. The girl reluctantly crawled out from under the bed. Leif guessed she couldn't be more than eight.

"Amy."

"Me name is Katie. This is me friend, Leif. Did ye see the bad clown?"

Amy nodded. "He took my daddy."

"Do you know where he took him?"

She sniffed. "He'll kill me!"

"No, sweetie, ye're safe now. But we can help yer da if ye tell us where the bad clown took him."

"He wanted Daddy to give him something," Amy wiped her nose. "Daddy said he hid it at the old factory."

The old factory turned out to be a sprawling steel works complex covering dozens of acres along the river. Much of the factory was abandoned, full of broken windows and rusting piles of old I-beams and scrap iron. Thousands of crows flocked together, perched on the rooftops. They cawed in a chorus of anger. Something must have awoken them.

"A murder," Yorak let the words escape his mouth.

The selkie wrapped both her arms around her husband's massive forearm. "We'll prevent this one, luv."

"Hmm?" Yorak said.

Tetsu coughed. "He means the crows. A group of crows is called a murder."

"Why is that?" Leif asked.

The tengu shrugged. "It just is. I don't understand all of the intricacies of the languages of the mundanes."

The corners of Leif's mouth turned up into a grim smirk. "Can you talk to the crows at least? Get them to create a distraction?"

Tetsu's long nose bobbed up and down as he nodded.

"Do it."

The tengu shifted into the form of a crow and took to the air. The bird/fae flow on toward the abandoned factory, his squawks mingling with the thousands of others.

"Momma, I don't feel so good," one of Kate's daughters said. Faith, Leif guessed. Or perhaps it was Hope. Or Charity. The triplets were hard enough to tell apart in daylight. In the dusk, they might as well be one.

Kate shivered. "I don't like this place. Too much iron here," she said. "I can taste it in the air."

"Send the girls back to the truck and have them watch over Amy," Leif said. "Then, go down to the river and scout the area out." Leif had hoped to use all four selkies for recon work, but the Harlequin's escalation of violence had killed that plan. Leif forced the bile back down his throat at the memory of the bloody scene at the house. They had to slip Amy out the back with a blanket over her head to spare her the sight of her mother's mutilated corpse. Not even the Unseelie Court would sanction such depravity. "Try to cover any possible escape routes. I'll take Yorak and Rafe as the frontal assault once Tetsu is in position."

The troll knelt down to wrap his three girls in a single embrace. "Mind your mother," he said. Kate gave her husband a kiss on his bald head.

"Ye know I'd go in with ye if I could," she said.

Yorak said nothing, but took his wife in a deep embrace before they sent the girls to safety. Then Yorak pulled the hood of his bearskin over his head as Kate jogged toward the river. Rafe capered around the troll and the dwarf, yipping with excitement until Leif shushed him.

"You think the Harlequin could really find the Cauldron?" Yorak whispered.

Leif shrugged. "I hoped not. Imagine if the Unseelie Court had the power to heal their armies at a touch and provide them with unlimited nourishment. It could break the truce between Winter and Summer."

They reached the gate to the factory. A rusted padlock hung broken from a chain. With as much stealth as he could, Leif pushed the gate open. "We can stop him. The mundane who hid the Cauldron here did us a huge favor." Leif gathered up the chain and slung it over his shoulder. He had to wrap it around his small torso twice to keep it from dragging on the ground. "How clever the mundane was, to lure the sidhe to an ironworks. It must be eating away at Hector from the inside." Leif grinned.

"We've got him now!" Rafe said. Leif shot him a stern glance to let him know that he should hush up. But the little chupacabra had been right. The various Folk each had their strengths and weaknesses. Trolls such as Yorak had to wear powerful sunscreen during the day or be turned to stone. But neither trolls nor chupacabras feared cold iron.

And neither, thought Leif as he caressed the chain, *do dwarves. We forged Mjolnir, the hammer of Thor and Gugnir, the spear of Odin. We were shaping iron and steel while the mundanes were still struggling to make a bronze sword that didn't bend at the first strike. We know iron. We came from iron, just as mundanes came from dust. We are iron.*

Finding the Harlequin proved to be easier than they had hoped. They had to just follow the macabre laughter. They found him on one of the foundry floors, prancing around Michael Caffrey. He had strapped the helpless mundane to a board holding him prone on the floor. Leif motioned for the trio to slip behind a stack of old crates where they could hide until Tetsu brought his distraction into play.

The sidhe clown had shed his cap, allowing his wings to unfurl. Leif had seen the Harlequin's wings before. Then, however, they looked like motley gossamer wings. Now, they had changed into twisted, black, bat-like wings. Blood splattered all around his black and white jester's costume.

What is black and white and red all over? Leif thought, remembering the Harlequin's favorite joke. *Me!*

Leif gazed toward the ceiling. Hundreds of crows had flown through the broken windows and gathered among the rafters. "We are ready for your move, Tetsu," Leif whispered.

The Harlequin had brought a bucket full of water and a plastic tarp. Setting both down next to Michael, he sat on his prisoner's chest. "I love knives," the clown said as he drew a stiletto from his tunic belt. "For centuries, I had trouble finding some that I could handle safely."

He coughed, spitting blood onto Michael's face. Wiping his mouth with his sleeve, the Harlequin held the knife above his head.

The iron here is making him sick already, Leif thought. If they moved now, they could easily disarm him and save the mundane. *Where was Tetsu?*

"See how the blade glistens in the moonlight?" The Harlequin twisted the blade in the air, dazzled by the reflection off of its polished surface. "I do so love this modern world. Teflon-coated steel. Titanium blades. So many wonderful things that make my hobby fun."

Now, Tetsu!

Leaning forward, the Harlequin held the knife so that the tip of the blade hovered just above Michael's eye. "Do you know what they call the fluid inside the eyes? Vitreous humor." He licked at some of the blood on Michael's face. "Isn't that a wonderful sounding name? Vitreous humor." The Harlequin drew the final "r" out into a soft purr.

"Don't," Michael pleaded. "My eyes."

The Harlequin tucked the stiletto back into his belt. "Oh, we'll save the knife fun for later. First, though, let's do the water sports."

Jumping to his feet, the Harlequin picked up the plastic tarp and unfolded it with a flourish. He laid the tarp over Michael's face before another coughing fit caused him to double over. The Harlequin picked up the bucket and held it over Michael's head.

Then, he stopped and turned his gaze toward the crates. "Oh, Leif. You might as well come out. I know you're skulking in the shadows there."

Leif felt his heart freeze. Taking a deep breath, he led his companions out of their hiding place. Yorak hefted his cudgel in both hands and stood ready to charge as soon as Leif gave the word. Rafe let out a menacing, if somewhat high-pitched, growl.

"You know we cannot let you torture this mundane."

"Leif, you really should keep up with current events. Waterboarding isn't torture anymore. Think of it as a dry, land-based swimming lesson."

"Let him go," Yorak said.

What are you waiting for, Tetsu?

"The Cauldron is too dangerous for either court to have," Leif said. "It'll break the pact. Do you really want to trigger a war between Seelie and Unseelie?"

The Harlequin doubled over laughing. "You think I care about the old loyalties? Seelie and Unseelie? We're in the era of global warming. Summer and Winter no longer hold any meaning. I'm after the Cauldron for myself and myself alone."

"But, Tetsu said you were serving Winter."

"Yes, I'm sure Tetsu said that." The Harlequin burst into laughter again, which quickly devolved into a coughing fit. The bucket slipped from his fingers and fell to the floor, spilling water in every direction.

"Get him," Leif said. But, before troll, chupacabra, or dwarf could take a step toward the coughing clown, the air around them exploded into a flurry of beaks, claws, and feathers. Blinded by the attacking birds, the trio retreated back toward the crates. Rafe erupted into an hysterical barking fit as Yorak swung his cudgel in a futile attempt to strike one of the birds. He succeeded only in reducing a wooden crate into splinters.

Leif dropped to his belly. Yorak's glamour began to slip as splotches of greenish-grey skin appeared all over his body.

"Boss," said Rafe. "What's happening?"

"Tetsu betrayed us!" Leif gritted his teeth. "Why, Hector? Why are you doing this? We've lived in peace for so long."

"Yes, and it's been a very dull millennium. You'd be surprised how many of the Folk have gotten restless. We want something different. I'll offer them a novelty: A new court with me at its head. Yes, the fool will become the king!"

"Great," Leif said. "He's gone completely bonzo."

Rafe, still in his chihuahua form, barked excitedly and then charged, ducking under the murder of crows flying around them. "No, Rafe!" But the little chupacabra ignored Leif's warning and didn't stop running until he reached the Harlequin and sank his teeth into the sidhe clown's ankle.

Snarling with fury, the Harlequin spread his wings and flew. He kicked his legs in the air in an attempt to shake Rafe off. But the chupacabra had dug deep into his flesh and kept his grip even as the pair rose into the air.

Sighing, Leif crawled on his stomach toward Michael Caffrey. When he reached the mundane, he began undoing the ropes that lashed him to the board. "Don't worry, friend," he said, "we'll get you out of here. Can you tell me where the Cauldron is? We can't let that madman get it."

"I-I," Michael stuttered for a moment. "I don't have it."

"What you mean? You bought it at auction, didn't you?"

"Yes, but I didn't want to pay extra for overnight shipping. It hasn't arrived yet."

"Then why did you tell the Harlequin that it was here?"

"After he killed my wife, he threatened my daughter. I told him that just to get him away from her. Oh God! Amy!"

Leif had worked the last of the ropes free. "You're daughter's safe. We found her at your home. We'll take you to her once this is over."

Suddenly, Yorak howled in fury as he grasped a crate with both hands and held it over his head. Ignoring the dozens of crows pecking at his exposed flesh, he threw it into the air, where it collided with a single bird before shattering against the wall. As the pile of broken wood fell to the floor, Tetsu shifted back to his human form.

The murder of crows dispersed, fleeing back to their roosts in the rafters.

The troll rushed Tetsu and grabbed the tengu by his pointed nose. Leif could hear the cartilage snap in Yorak's fingers as Tetsu cried out in pain.

"You think I'm a fool," Yorak said. "But I know animals. And I know the difference between an American Crow and the Daurian Jackdaw that you turn yourself into!"

Leif drew himself up to his feet. As the Harlequin still struggled with Rafe in the air, Leif spied a catwalk. He climbed the nearby ladder and then continued along the railing until he could reach the steel support beams in the ceiling. He made his way across the ceiling until positioned directly above the Harlequin. Wedging his feet into the truss, he carefully unwound the chain from his body. Then, taking the chain in both hands, he let himself drop. His tiny body collided with the Harlequin's. As they plummeted to the floor below, he wrapped the chain around the clown's neck.

They hit the concrete hard. Leif had twisted his body to avoid a neck injury, but he felt his collarbone snap on impact. He heard one of the Harlequin's wing bones break.

Still, Hector managed to get to his feet first. Despite the pain and the iron sickness, he was able to disentangle himself from Rafe and make a run for the rear entrance.

As he tried to reach the river, he found Kate barring his path.

"Hector," she said, her voice more icy than the Hebrides in winter, "ye frightened me girls tonight." Her fist landed dead center in the Harlequin's throat, collapsing his windpipe.

Yorak arrived just in time to wrap the chains around the Harlequin's waist. "Hello, dear."

"Hello, luv."

"How was your swim?"

She shook her head. "Not much of one. River's too bloody shallow."

"Don't forget to chain up Tetsu," Leif said. He leaned heavily on Rafe for support, his left arm dangling uselessly. "I think Yorak will have to drive us home."

"Tetsu?" Kate asked.

"Yeah, apparently he and Hector were working together."

Yorak hoisted the Harlequin and Tetsu, one over each shoulder, and hauled them back toward the truck.

Leif walked up to Tetsu and said only one word: "Why?"

The tengu coughed. Blood sprayed out of his twisted nose as he wheezed. "Figured I could grab the cauldron while you and the Harlequin were fighting." He burst into coughing fit. "I knew his plan to start up a new court. Thought it might work better for me than with that lunatic."

Leif shook his head and turned away from his former friend. "Damn fool. That's what happens when you spend too much time reading those blogs by the mundanes. Everything thinks they're a politician now."

"What are we going to do with them?" Yorak asked.

"They go before Queen Titania for judgment." He nodded toward Michael. "After we take him take to his daughter."

"And the Cauldron?"

Leif shook his head. He probed his mouth his tongue. At least one tooth was chipped from the fall. "It's not here. Never was." He gave Michael a serious look. "I'm sure Mr. Caffrey here will sell it to us for a fair price."

Michael nodded. "You can have it. I never want to touch it after this."

"Then," Leif said, "we drop it in the ocean. Let it feed the bloody fish forever."

Whiskey Sour

Skyla Dawn Cameron

I THINK I PICKED UP HIS SCENT EVEN BEFORE HE ENTERED the bar.

As I ran a damp cloth over the counter in front of me, it was as if something tickled my nose. I breathed in sharply, my rational brain telling me my instincts were wrong. My instincts and brain are usually at war like that.

In this instance, I ignored my instincts.

I'd never caught his scent fresh like that before, and I guess that's why my brain didn't trust my nose. Weeks after the morning he left, when I had just begun to realize something was wrong with me and hundreds of different scents had assaulted my nose, his was among them. Old, watered down, lingering in the corners of my apartment where I hadn't cleaned. And it was that uncertainty, that lack of trust in my abilities and my instincts that came back to me as I cleaned my area of the bar, sensing someone I knew shouldn't be there.

Maybe it was just wishful thinking on my part, rather than full-blown doubt. If he showed up at my place of work again, I'd have to kill him, and then I'd probably be made to leave work for a few days without pay. And I do like to get paid.

I dropped the cloth in the sink under the counter and went about refilling the peanuts, immersing myself in the noise and smells around me, ignoring the niggling in the back of my brain . . . .

In my peripheral vision, I saw a patron slide onto a barstool near me.

"Whiskey sour," came a voice I wished I didn't recognize.

My grey eyes slid toward him. A cocky grin met my

gaze—one that I immediately wanted to smack away. Given the strength not directly apparent in my skinny arms, I probably could have done it too, and knocked him clear across the bar before he knew what hit him. Bit of glamour to disguise it, make up something about him trying to assault me, and no one would be the wiser.

Instead, I reached under the bar for a heavy glass. I set it on the counter with a noticeable *thud*. My movements methodical, I filled it with ice, lime juice, and finished with a shot of whiskey. I held onto the drink, however, and stared at him expectantly.

"Cash up front."

His eyes, which were a dark brown with amber ringing the inner iris, lit up with amusement. "Think I'll take off without paying?"

"Just looking for an excuse to throw you out."

He pulled a ten from his jacket pocket, set it on the bar, and slid it my way. "There you go," he said, meeting my gaze in a challenge.

Within me, I had the same fight to establish dominance as he did, but luckily I had a strong enough will to not give in to those urges. I passed him the damn drink, took his money, and promptly put him out of my mind. Easier said than done, but I was willing to work at it.

"Juliette," he said.

"Oh, so you remember my name?"

"Can we talk?"

"We are talking."

"I mean in private."

I gestured around the bar. "Quiet night. This is about as private as you're getting, so say your piece, then get out, Toby."

Thankfully, a new customer took a seat a few stools away from him. I went to take her order and clear my head for a minute or two.

"That guy bothering you, Jules?" whispered Luc as he approached me. Luc worked the other end of the bar. He had an annoying sense of what he'd call chivalry, but which I found chauvinistic. At least Toby had that going for him; he didn't treat me like an infant just because I lacked a dick.

"Just an old acquaintance," I said, with what I hoped was a believable smile. "Owes me money is all." Luc must have accepted the explanation, because he returned to his spot to refill the glasses of a couple of regulars.

I decided to look for something else to do rather than leave myself open for conversation with Toby. My hair required some fixing, of course. And I had a new pair of long silver earrings that grazed my shoulders, so I decided to play with those for awhile. All very important work, I might add.

"I really need to talk to you," Toby said as I began obsessively wiping the bar down again. Though genuine seriousness touched his tone, I didn't believe it for a second. It did seem, however, that he wouldn't be leaving until he'd told me whatever it was he'd come there to say. Just in case it was an apology, I decided to hear him out.

"I'm taking a break in a half hour, depending on how busy we are," I said, and then gestured to an empty booth at the back of the room. "Wait over there, but remember we kick people out for not spending money."

I watched him go, his saunter annoying me almost as much as his grin had. He followed my instructions without complaint, though he stopped to charm the new young waitress, Marie, and order something more to drink.

As far as one-night stands go, Toby was definitely the one I regretted the most. Some chicks wake up pregnant, or with herpes, or with a really nasty hangover.

I woke up infected with lycanthropy, which particularly sucks when you're a faerie.

Over a year ago, I had been a "normal" twenty-something woman who just happened to have faerie blood. My fae family came from Ireland to Quebec ages ago during the Great Irish Famine, as faeries need to eat as well. Thus the O'Briens became the Aubrys, and they did what they could to fit in without losing all their culture. That becomes an even more difficult balancing act when you're fae, but we managed.

None of that ever really affected me, however, being so far down the line. I was raised to know my past, even if I didn't care about the history or struggles that my ancestors faced. It's kinda important for a girl to understand why certain things repelled *her* when they didn't bother normal children, and why when the wind picked up and magic beckoned to be used, it probably shouldn't be. Thus I was taught in secret, and forbidden to use much magic outside of the home, save for emergencies. All in the name of seeming "normal."

At least I had passed for normal enough until Toby walked into the bar one night.

Plenty of guys hit on me when they come in. No surprise, considering I'm a bit of a hottie. Big grey eyes, silky brown hair, decent bod—male attention frequently found itself directed my way, so it was nothing new when he strolled over and made eyes at me over his whiskey sour. He had the look of a pretty boy who was just a little rough around the edges; hair short, naturally a dark brown but dyed bright red, multiple piercings, a tattoo of a wolf paw print on his inner forearm, and all in contrast to fine bone structure and a narrow, toned body. Anyone else coming in there looking like that and I might have said they were trying too hard, but he pulled it off. Even then, I wouldn't have given him a second look if it weren't for those eyes. There was something predatory in his gaze—something thrilling, something exciting. Something that made me linger near him for a bit of conversation after refilling his drink.

I was the one to lock up the bar that night, and Toby stayed behind to "chat." Obviously, I'm not supposed to go home with patrons. That was even in my workbook from bartending class. So instead I brought him back to my apartment above the bar. He was gone the morning after, which hardly surprised me. I didn't really mind, either . . . until about two weeks later when the moon was full and I started sprouting fur.

Suffice to say it was *not* an attractive look for me and it put a real strain on my social life, so I hadn't quite forgiven him yet when he came calling again after all that time.

I waited longer than the half hour I'd promised him. The bar wasn't all that busy, but I pretended to have a great many things to do. Forty-five minutes after I'd first spoken with Toby, I untied my apron and hung it next to the bar, snuck a shot of tequila for myself, and went to where he waited.

He must have sensed my approach, but didn't look up as I walked over and slid into the seat across from his.

"French fry?" he asked, pushing his plate of half-eaten *poutine* my way.

I shook my head and downed the shot of tequila, instantly wishing I'd brought more than one. "Start talking."

"Juliette, I need your help."

"I need your balls in a jar on my mantle. Fair trade?"

"Want me to roll over and beg?"

"How about 'play dead?'"

"Look, is there anything I can do to get you to hear me out?"

"I'm still leaning towards castration."

"Okay, sweetheart, the truth is that I didn't know at the time that I had infected you."

The pet name grated my nerves, but I didn't bother saying anything; it would probably just encourage him. "Didn't bother to find out, either."

"And I apologize. It wasn't until I heard through the grapevine about an abnormally large wolf prowling the streets of Montreal that I put two and two together. But hey, except for turning to a bad-ass, uncontrollable monster once a month, it's not that bad the rest of the time. You've got mad strength now. That's gotta be cool."

"I also have to shave my legs twice as often—you're not going to win this conversation." It was clear the guy just *didn't* get it. He'd irrevocably changed my life, basically violated me, and yet he thought it was okay to stroll in like nothing happened. Hell, he'd probably never think it was a big deal. I had a feeling that he had a bit of a disconnect in his brain between the world of charming, irresistible Toby, and reality where the rest of us lived. Men are typical, no matter what their species. Must be something on the Y chromosome. "Hurry up and explain your presence so I can get on with my night."

"Okay, I didn't really tell you what I did for a living before."

"Besides sleep with women and pass on lycanthropy?"

"Well, yes, besides that," he muttered. "I . . . retrieve things for people. Sometimes items, sometimes other people."

"Theft and kidnapping?" *Big surprise—the guy's a criminal.*

"Not quite. I usually retrieve items that have already been stolen and return them to their rightful owners, and apprehend people who have committed crimes. For a price, of course. Usually I work slightly more . . . odd cases that your average human wouldn't."

"Ah, supernatural bounty hunter."

"More or less. That's what I was doing in Montreal last year and why I'm back here again."

"And you need my help why, exactly?"

"I was hired to get something in town—something from a more unusual thief. Generally, a werewolf is pretty good at dealing with just about anyone, but this case is a little different. The thief is fae."

"Oh, hello, Toby's point—nice to see you finally joined the conversation."

"So anyway," he continued. "I figured having a faerie on board for this job would be in my best interest."

"I'll bet." I didn't need to ask why he knew I was a faerie without my telling him—now a werewolf myself, I knew fae gave off a certain scent. Otherwise, we look completely human. We age a little slower, live a little longer depending on the concentration of fae blood, but that's it. No wings. No pointy ears unless you're a pure bred, which I'm not. But Toby knew what I was the very second he stepped foot in the bar the first time. Pity I hadn't had the benefit of recognizing a werewolf at that time. "I'm not interested, however, so you'll have to flip through your little black book for someone else to help."

"It's going to be really simple, and it pays well."

"Still don't care." I slid out of the booth seat and started to stand. "I have to get back to work now."

"Look, it's in and out—under an hour, tops. I just need someone to take care of the magic around the place. Did I mention it pays well? You will of course get an excellent cut."

A little magic, I could take care of. And under an hour didn't seem bad . . .

in terms of having to deal with him, that is. I *have* done just about anything for good money in the past, so a little thievery certainly wasn't below me.

I sat back down. "Fifty percent."

"*Hell,* no! I was turned onto this job by someone taking a finder's fee, so I'm only getting eighty to start with. I'll give you forty of what I make."

"Fifty of what you make. I have a lot of furniture to replace that I tore up when I first changed."

"Listen, sweetheart—"

"Fifty-*five* if you call me sweetheart again."

"Fine."

"So who's this fae thief?" I asked, leaning back in the booth comfortably.

"Chantal Riel."

Luckily, I wasn't drinking anything at the time he said that; if I had, I'm sure it would have come out my nose.

"You've got to be kidding me."

"Is there a problem?"

"Only that everyone knows she's absolutely nuts. Like, seriously batshit crazy. Rumor has it she was Seelie Gentry once upon a time. You *really* don't want her to catch you."

"Uh, yeah, that's why I asked you to help. That . . . and I don't know where she lives."

"You at least know what you're going to steal, right?"

"Yeah, it's this little goddess idol . . . can't remember its name. I've seen photos the original owner took, though, so I know what I'm looking for."

"Well, at least you'll be contributing *something* to this little venture."

After finalizing our plans, I stood next to the bar and watched Toby leave. Satisfied he was out of sight, I looked to Luc.

"I'm going to duck out early. Hold the fort down while I'm gone?"

"Where are you off to?"

Hmm, stealing shit from a fellow faerie to help my werewolf ex-lover didn't seem like the kind of answer he was looking for.

"Some bastard still owes me money," I said instead.

"Be careful, Jules." Luc nodded in the direction Toby had taken. "I don't like that guy."

"That makes two of us," I said under my breath. I grabbed my jacket from the employee room, slipped it on, and went out the back door. Glancing around and sniffing the air, I ensured I was alone, and then pulled out my cell phone. I had to call around to a few friends to get the particular phone number I desired, but once it was in my possession, I put in the call.

"Hey," I said as a woman picked up the phone. "You don't know me, but my name is Juliette Aubrey. I think you and I need to have a little chat . . . ."

I met Toby a block from the faerie's home an hour after my shift would have officially ended. He hadn't specified how to dress, but I'd donned all black nonetheless, tied back my straight brown hair, and slipped on gloves. Toby was similarly dressed and stood with a cigarette between his lips, leaning against a tree. He dropped the cig on the ground when he saw me and stamped out the butt.

"So you're not friends with this fae?" he asked as he walked toward the house. The night was dark, the street empty, but I kept alert for any signs of people around us, and specifically any angry faerie thieves we planned to rob.

"Not friends with too many fae," I said. "So, all business right away—this must be an important job."

"I thought I'd work into telling you how great it is to see you again, Jules."

"Right."

"I mean it—I really did like you. *Do* like you. Still."

"I'm here, I've agreed to help you, so you don't need to butter me up."

"This isn't about buttering you up . . . ." He paused on the sidewalk in front of Chantal Riel's home and drew me into the circle of his arms. Gazing at me with those striking eyes, I could almost think him sincere. "Unless, of course, you're into something involving butter . . . ."

"How about we stick to the job for now?" I snapped, twisting in his arms until I had broken free. He really made my skin crawl—you'd think a damn wolf would have more respect for personal space and boundaries.

We crept through the front yard toward the grey stone house, hiding in the shadows cast by the large oak tree in the center of the lawn.

"Can you sense any magic in the house?" he asked. "Something you'll need to dispel?"

"If Chantal has half a brain, she has some kind of alert system in place—I'll work on it."

Toby moved a few steps ahead of me, waiting in the gardens for his chance to break in.

"How long will it take you?"

"Oh . . . ." I raised my hands, drawing magic from the earth and weaving it around my fingertips. Generations of fae blood lent me strength as I focused the spell. "Not long, I imagine."

Without warning, I released the magic, directing the spell at my target: Toby. The force knocked him to the ground and though his werewolf reflexes would normally have given him an edge, another figure released the glamour hiding her form among the trees upwind of him and appeared at my side to strengthen the magic. Heavy roots leapt from the ground and wrapped around Toby, pinning him down. Both his faerie mark, Chantal Riel, and I stood over him.

"Jules," he began, pleading at me with his eyes.

I gave him a swift kick to the head in answer, knocking him unconscious.

Toby came to about twenty minutes later. Chantal and I had dragged him into her house and we restrained him to a dining room chair. Not one to chat, she all but ignored me while she waited for him to regain consciousness. She did circles around his chair, ready to pounce. I stood off to the side, leaning against the wall and looking around at the faerie's home. *Someone* hadn't quite entered the "new" world yet. A lot of oak, antique furniture and the ugliest floral wallpaper I'd ever seen. The drapes were heavy and tattered, as if they'd been hanging there since before Chantal's birth. Vines crawled out of a pot of ivy on the floor and crept up around the doorframe near me. It was like a page from "Decorating Old, Crazy-Ass Faerie Houses Magazine" if such a publication existed. The few glimpses I had into other areas while dragging Toby inside revealed a lot of junk. Even if I'd had a description of Toby's quarry, I didn't know if I could have found it in that mess.

I meant it when I told Toby that I didn't know her; I don't exactly make time with people *that* much older than me, including my mother. But I knew of friends who had made her acquaintance in the past, so she wasn't hard to track down. On the phone, she had sounded quite pleased at being informed of a werewolf's plans to break into her home, and our own schemes had developed swiftly from there.

As Toby lifted his eyelids open, his head rolled to the side. Those striking dark eyes that had once attracted me were unfocused as they went my way, and then to Chantal. Toby frowned in confusion.

"What the . . . ?"

Chantal swung her open hand toward his head. A foot short of physical contact, waves of magic emanated from her fingertips and struck his cheek. Scratches marred his face as his head snapped to the side.

"Holy shit, what the hell?" he shouted. His gaze went to me again. "Juliette—"

Chantal smacked him again. I admit I got a kick out of the exchange.

"You dare break into my home?" she hissed.

"It was my job," he replied. "Besides, you stole it in the first place, right? Now, I'm sure we can work something out . . . ." He flashed a smile, the blood on his face doing nothing to lessen his charisma. I grinned at the thought that he believed he could charm the older, deadlier faerie; Chantal Riel would kick his ass before he got too far.

"Who hired you?"

"I can't—"

She hit him again. Toby fought his bonds, straining to break free— to twist at least one arm loose, but it was of no use. He swore under his breath.

"Caine Hartman," he said, and it didn't surprise me how quick he sang a different tune when it came to saving his own ass. "I guess he planned to buy the idol from the guy *you* took it from."

"That viper," Chantal muttered.

"Who is it?" I spoke up at last.

She turned to me and stalked away from Toby. "A human with a fondness for artifacts of supernatural origin, which is an interest I share with him."

"So you *do* have it around here . . . somewhere?" My gaze trailed around the place.

"Yes," she said. "But I keep such things locked up safely." Her gaze flickered toward the hallway, in the direction of the sitting room. "Caine would have it on display, just as another decoration. He has no idea what anything does, just seems to enjoy knowing he has something that our kind—and those like us—*should* have but don't."

"Typical stupid human with more money than he knows what to do with?" I guessed.

Chantal nodded. "I thank you for coming to me with this. You are a good girl, Juliette." She spun to face Toby once again, long ashen hair settling around her shoulders. "We should send this one's head," she gestured to Toby, "back to Caine as a warning not the mess with our kind again." She glanced over her shoulder and gave me a toothy grin filled with malice and glee. Pale blue eyes sparked and spoke of violent possibilities.

"And how does one normally contact Hartman?" I asked. "I mean, I doubt we can just drop a head off at his doorstep."

"He's based in New York—the O'Connell family has a home there as well," Chantal said, referring to a well-known clan of immigrant faeries, rumored to be of royal descent. If I were familiar with the name—and I didn't give a shit about most faerie goings-on—then they *had* to be easy to find. A few inquiries among them would yield information about contacting Caine Hartman. "I have some tools that may be of use in taking apart the werewolf." Chantal raised an arm and waved her long fingers in the direction of a cabinet on the right wall. "Have a look and see what you'd like to use."

"Jules," Toby pleaded again. "C'mon . . . how about sixty percent?"

"How about one hundred?" I said.

Chantal turned to look at me in confusion. With a flick of my hand, I released the binds on Toby's feet and he used the chance to kick her shin hard. She slipped to the ground, but recovered. A cold wind struck me and pushed my body into a china cabinet. Glass broke and wood splintered beneath me.

Toby kicked Chantal again, distracting her and giving me a moment to get on my feet again. I snatched her up by the neck and pinned her to the wall. Her eyes widened and she opened her mouth to scream, but there was nothing she could do to stop me. As her interrogation of Toby claimed her attention earlier, I'd used the opportunity to slip brass knuckles on one gloved hand. They weren't exactly brass, however—I'd found one made of iron, which would not only hurt her, but block her magic as well.

Holding a strong, dangerous fae at my mercy like that . . . the sense of power was intoxicating. I'd never felt something like that in my life.

And I liked it.

"How can you . . . betray one of your own?" she whispered. For someone rumored to be so crazy, she apparently thought highly of loyalty. I guess she *was* out of touch with reality after all—or at the very least, my generation.

I shrugged. "I'm *not* one of you, Chantal. Not anymore."

I squeezed her throat until she gasped for breath. Once she fell limp, I let her crumple to the ground.

"Um, thanks," Toby said as I released the rest of his bindings. "But you know killing her wasn't part of the deal."

"I just knocked her out," I replied. "But she'll wake up soon. Get what we came here for."

"I may be awhile. This place is a mess."

Christ, he was dim. "Weren't you paying attention?" I jerked my thumb over my shoulder. "It's locked up somewhere in the sitting room. Hurry the hell up."

I kept an eye on Chantal while Toby obtained the idol. I heard him rummaging around in the other room and the sound of wood breaking. He returned with something tucked in a black velvet bag.

"You had me worried there for awhile," he said with a grin. "I really thought you intended to let the bitch decapitate me."

"I had a few plans in mind," I said. "Hadn't committed to one in particular yet." And that was the truth of the matter, actually. I find it's best to leave oneself a number of opportunities in case things go to hell.

"I see. Now, about percentages . . . ."

"Aw, Toby," I smiled sweetly. "I meant it when I said one hundred percent."

His grin faded and eyes grew huge as I sent a powerful uppercut to his jaw. It turns out "brass" knuckles are good for dealing with werewolves, too.

The second time Toby regained consciousness that night after I had knocked him out, it was in the empty bar. This time he wasn't tied to anything, but left propped up in a booth seat. The streetlights shone through the front windows, casting odd shadows around the room. Chairs and barstools were all on top of the tables, and I hadn't bothered turning on any of the lights in the bar.

His eyes blinked open and adjusted to the darkness.

"Juliette?"

I stepped from the shadows. "I think I'd be more comfortable with Mademoiselle Aubry, actually."

"Look, I get that you're kind of bent out of shape about what I did to you, but—"

"Shut up, Toby." I stalked forward, taking one predatory step at a time, embracing the feeling of power coursing through me. My true nature had been unleashed now: greater than faeries, greater than wolf . . . something new entirely. I'd been a faerwolf for a year, yet this was the first time I really understood what that meant.

Supremacy. I had the best of both worlds. This werewolf thing wasn't entirely a curse, the need to own extra shaving supplies notwithstanding. And I had more than faerie magic now—more than some glamour and elemental spells. I had everything.

I focused my gaze on his. "Tonight, when you walked into this bar, the werewolf instincts you passed on to me made me go kinda crazy. I hadn't really felt like this before, but I realized something . . . . And now we need to have a little chat." I held up the black bag with the idol in it for him to see. His gaze flickered from my eyes to his quarry and a look of worry touched his face.

"You're going to kill me?" he guessed, but I shook my head.

"No. Not today. You have made me a somewhat wealthier woman, so you can leave alive this time. I'm contacting Hartman and I'm collecting the bounty on this. Both you and your friend collecting the finder's fee can suck it. And you're going to leave Montreal."

"Well, duh—"

"This city is *my* territory. If anyone employed in ventures similar to yours requires something from Montreal, I get a cut. If anyone needs to travel through here, they come to me first. I trust you'll spread the word for me."

"Babe . . . ."

"*You* are the exception to this arrangement, however. If you *ever* step foot in my territory again, your balls ending up in a jar on my mantle will be the least of your worries. Any questions?"

He opened his mouth to speak, then closed his lips again as he debated what to say. I expected the usual attempt to negotiate, to charm me, to save his own skin.

At last he let out a snarl. "You double-crossing bitch."

"*Tsk tsk,*" I said with a shake of my head. "That wasn't a question."

Outside the bar, I tossed his ass into a waiting cab that I had called earlier. Contacting Caine Hartman was simple enough and he didn't question the change of hands. I'm guessing that in his business, it wasn't exactly an uncommon situation.

Chantal was pissed but didn't retaliate . . . or at least hasn't *yet*. I still think she might, but I could be wrong. A few vague threats reached me through the grapevine. I'd pay, I'd regret it, blah blah blah . . . it all sounded idle to me. There's something about the older generation of faeries, though. No matter how long they've lived here—even if they're born here—they're strangers to this land. Their people matter to them, friend or foe. Maybe, in the end, she passed off my actions as youthful indiscretions. Maybe she's waiting until she has me where she wants me and then she'll attack. I'm not sure. I think she figured out I'm not your average faerie, however, and I doubt she planned to invite me to her next Equinox party anyway.

After explicitly telling people to watch what they do when they're in my territory, I didn't expect to suddenly become a millionaire with offers to have me help them on all kinds of work, therefore it seemed a good idea to keep my job at the bar. So I keep alert. I pay attention. You piss off enough people—or at least the wrong kind—and you never know what they're going to do to you if they get the chance. That's what Toby learned with me.

Ah, Toby. I still expect to see him walk through that door any day now, despite what I told him. He doesn't seem the type who'd take it like a bitch when I told him to piss off for good. Now every time someone sits down at the bar and I hear those two little words, "Whiskey sour," I glance up, body tensed and ready to move. It hasn't happened yet, but it will. So why didn't I just kill him, as he wondered? I kind of like knowing he's out there, living with a bit of shame. I like that he has to walk through the supernatural underworld and explain to his colleagues that some faerie chick he banged in Montreal outsmarted him. I almost get a kick out of the idea that he might try to cross me again—that he just might be so stupid.

But at the very least, he probably has enough sense to always use protection now. I know I do—I'd rather not wake up a vampire, too.

Zwischenzug:
A Pennidreadful Tale

Lorne Dixon

DOWN IN THE CATACOMBS, PENNI AND VASSILI PLAYED CHESS AS the luxury sedans rolled up the long driveway into Echo Meadow Cemetery. Between moves, they discussed the pest that had been digging up the south lawn, the oldest stretch of graveyard on the property. Penni knew that more than dirt was being disrupted.

"Sounds like company," Penni sang in a bright, relieved voice, leaning against her only remaining bishop and rubbing her wings against its smooth plastic body. She always insisted on playing the queen herself. "Guess it's an early night?"

Vassili clicked his tongue off the top of his mouth as the sound of car engines drifted down into the ossuary. It was a rare night—he was winning. Even if Penni was cheating by consulting the old sea-captains interred in the walls, he was only a half dozen moves away from cornering her king behind a line of pawns and the edge of the board.

"Leave everything exactly as it is," Vassili said as he stood and headed for the uneven carved rock stairs. "I mean it, don't move anything."

She smirked and kicked over his rook. "Earthquake."

She flew after him, up through the ossuary gates and into the camouflage of night. She followed Vassili through the east lawn on the cemetery, past the stone mausoleum, to the reception awning in front of the funeral home. He stood silently on the curb and folded his hands.

Both front doors on the first sedan opened. The driver and front passenger flung themselves out and met at the rear passenger's side door.

They wore bloodstained suits with loose ties dangling from their necks. They murmured to each other—strings of nervous, hushed words—and opened the door. As they pulled the body out from the back seat, Penni heard a tiny gasp escape Vassili's lips.

Pawn to queen's knight four, Vassili thought as the body was carried from the car. He motioned for them to pass into the funeral home through a pair of automatic double doors. One mumbled a few words toward him as they passed, an apology or a condolence. It sounded like a word caught under the weight of a snore.

The driver's door opened on the second sedan and Niccolò stepped out. He dabbed at a single dot of blood on his lapel with a silk handkerchief. He spoke before he even raised his eyes from his jacket. "Uncle Antonio, I know it's late, but I didn't know where else to go."

Vassili turned and watched his brother's body disappear behind the white doors. They shut silently. "What happened, Nicci?"

"Don't call me that," Niccolò said as he stepped up, his adult face much harder than the boy Vassili remembered. "No one has called me that for a long time."

Vassili nodded. "Okay. What happened, *Niccolò?*"

His nephew lit a cigarette. "It wasn't what you'd think. This wasn't the Siffredi family or the Carracci brothers. We were coming back from the Island. We were hungry—and you can't find a decent greasy spoon on that side of the Verrazano, you know that, so we got off the bridge, took an exit, and found this buffet joint. Lo Mien and shit, y'know? Dad gets up to fill his plate. That's when this huge piece of shit comes up behind him and puts a fork in his eye—a fuckin' *fork.* Place is going wild and this lunatic is stabbing him and we rush up there and grab the guy. He just throws us off, so Benny D—he's the taller one—he pulls out his bip gun, just a little .22, and puts one in this guy's back. You know what he does? Fucker doesn't even flinch—he just throws Dad onto the desert trays and starts to eat right off the buffet table—with the same fork."

Vassili's eyes followed the glowing cigarette tip of the as it shook in Niccolò's fingers.

Niccolò nodded. "We jumped him and beat him down pretty nasty. Dragged him to the car. Got him in the trunk."

"Dead?" Vassili asked.

A smile crept across his nephew's mouth, left to right like a zipper sliding open. It wasn't a gleeful grin; it was a twisted smirk full of rage and ugliness. "Naw, I've got another idea for this cocksucker."

Vassili leaned over his dead brother and ran two fingertips over his face. His face felt cool and slick, a smooth plaster mask with a pool of red built up over his sunken right eye.

Niccolò stood in the doorway, shoulder propping open one of the white doors, his third cigarette dangling from his lips just below his threadbare mustache. "You'll fix him up good, right, Uncle Antonio?"

Straightening up, Vassili turned his head toward the young man and studied his face. There was grief, but a distant cousin of the kind Vassili knew. Niccolò's tight face and wild eyes seemed as much relieved as distressed, as if he had long wished his father dead but didn't really know how to cope with the feeling.

Queen's knight to queen's bishop three.

"You know I will. He'll look fine."

Niccolò flicked the cigarette outside and tilted his head, gesturing for Vassili to follow him as he stepped out of the funeral home. Cool air teased the back of his neck; it was no longer a brisk Autumnal evening but rather a cold night full of invisible bee stings hidden in freezing gusts of wind. He felt Penni's presence, her eyes watching him, but could not see her tiny, naked body hiding in the shadows.

The orange glow on the discarded cigarette's tip lost its intensity and disappeared in a wisp of twirling smoke. Niccolò stepped over the rising gas tail as he fumbled a key ring out of the pocket of his pleated slacks. He rounded the second sedan, stopped at its trunk, and waved a hand vaguely toward his men, "This is Benny and Marco. They're okay. Dad hired them to drive."

Dad hired them to drive: it meant something like, *Dad hired them as getaway drivers, or triggermen, or shakedown thugs,* something like that. Benny was tall and thin— probably could have gotten a gig as a rodeo clown; probably should have given the size of his feet. Marco had a few short prison terms etched on his face, probably low-level assaults and the like.

Niccolò slid the key into the lock and popped open the trunk, revealing an enormous, contorted body. The giant wore a stained, threadbare tee-shirt and a pair of straining sweat pants.

Benny and Marco reached inside and struggled to pull him out like fishermen fighting to drag a monster game fish on deck, straining as they counted to three and grappled with rolling waves of fat. Finally, the giant tumbled out of the trunk onto the pavement. As he hit, a metallic missile jingled as it shot out of his body and skittered across the asphalt to Vassili's shoe. He reached down and scooped it up. The bullet must have mushroomed when it hit the behemoth's body, cutting through layers of gelatinous fat and deforming, its head ballooning and body shortening. Vassili pocketed the bullet.

Queen's bishop to king's knight five.

"Stand that fat retard up," Niccolò demanded.

Penni didn't need to hide: all attention was glued to the big man they held captive. This was way better than the sappy Christmas movies Vassili wanted to watch tonight. Perched on the first sedan's side mirror, Penni watched Benny and Marco hoist him up. They groaned as they lifted and were panting by the time they pushed him roughly against the trunk's standing hatch. He was not just the largest man Penni had ever seen but also the tallest, a full foot and a half taller than Vassili.

There was something else about the big man, something new, something she had never encountered before. She could feel the cancer throbbing inside Vassili, the first touch of Addison's Disease tickling Marco's adrenal glands, embryonic Choroid plexus cysts growing on the surface of Benny's brain, and the madness swirling in every atom of Niccolò's body, but in the big man she could sense no death. Despite his gargantuan size, he was entirely healthy. There wasn't a single black dot of death inside him. Nothing was completely free of death. Penni wasn't sure exactly what he was, but she knew that *human* was a poor choice of words. Better to think of him as a monster—a perfect monster.

She saw that they had shot him, but she couldn't feel a dark spot where they had wounded him. Her smile widened. They might as well have hit him with a stone from a slingshot.

Marco reached into the monster's pocket and tore out his wallet. He picked through the contents. "Just a lot of punch cards from cheap restaurants—wait, here. A Pennsy license. Expired in '02. Name's Matthias Joseph Lotts."

Niccolò stepped forward and snatched the wallet out of Marco's hand, "I want you to tell me who you work for."

The Matthias-monster opened one swollen eye.

Biting his bottom lip, Niccolò reached into his coat and slid out a handgun. He struck out, ramming the handle against the Matthias-monster's cheek. Its head swung back but Benny and Marco held him in place as best they could. A trickle of blood wormed its way down his bulbous face.

"You'll answer me—" Niccolò screamed and pulled back his arm, striking a pose that threatened a second blow.

The Matthias-monster didn't flinch. Instead, he reached up slowly and caught the blood drip before it could drop from his chin. Then he brought his finger to his mouth and sucked.

Benny and Marco looked to Niccolò for instructions.

Niccolò's pistol hand shook.

Calm, the Matthias-monster spoke in the friendly voice of a singing hobo, as smooth as white Mississippi gravy. "I was hungry. He took the last of the Xiaolong-bao dumplings."

The men stood motionless. Penni covered her mouth to suppress a giggle.

"They're my favorite," he added.

Niccolò glanced at Vassili. Vassili ran a hand through his thin, silver hair and extended a questioning hand—*I don't know, what you think.*

"Dumplings?" Niccolò asked, rage building in his quivering voice. "You killed my father with a fork because you didn't want to wait ten minutes for a fresh tray of fuckin' dumplings? Am I supposed to believe that?"

Niccolò jammed the gun against the Matthias-monster's nose, pressing it flat to his face. "I think you better tell me the truth, now motherfuc—"

"I do feel a *little* guilty," the Matthias-monster said, his voice distorted by his bent nose. "The dumplings really weren't very good."

Fresh anger spread across Niccolò's face a second before he pulled the gun back and swung it at full force. The Matthias-monster's nose disappeared behind an eruption of blood. Niccolò struck out three more times. The massive man slipped out of Benny and Marco's grip and fell to his knees. Niccolò kicked him in the chest.

The Matthias-monster didn't fight them. Benny and Marco pummeled him with their fists, each blow landing with a wet slap. Niccolò sidestepped them and opened the back door of the sedan. He returned, swinging an arms-length crowbar.

Penni felt a shiver run through the Mathias-monster, starting at the place where the crowbar struck his brow and reaching out to his extremities like a wild crack in a pane of glass. It was the first whisper of death's song.

Vassili watched the big man fall, first to his knees, then onto all fours, and finally flat to the ground. Niccolò continued to bludgeon him with the crowbar. When Matthias' eyes lost focus, Benny and Marco flipped him over. His chest was still moving, but only in shallow, low tide waves. Benny pulled his piece, a showy nine millimeter Luger with a smooth black finish. "I should end this?"

"No—" Niccolò shouted. He gestured for Benny to put the gun away and turned to Vassili. "On the way up, I saw a grave on the hill covered with a tarp."

Vassili nodded. "Mister Calhoun's plot."

"Is the hole already dug?"

Shaking his head, Vassili stepped closer to Niccolò and put a hand on his shoulder. "You can't do that, Nicci. This place is different. I can't bury—"

Niccolò shrugged Vassili's hand away and stared into his uncle's eyes with the scalding intensity of an eclipse's brightest refracted light. "I'm not asking."

Vassili took a step back. "And I'm not allowing it. Go dump it down in the barrens or sink it into the Delaware. But you can't—"

Niccolò sighed. "Jesus, Uncle Antonio. I was hoping it wouldn't be like this. I always looked up to you. You weren't like Dad. You were always good to me. But now I can see. You don't want to help me with this . . . this piece of shit, here. Maybe you don't want to help because you think you're entitled to step up now that Dad's gone. Well, you ain't gonna step up. It's my turn."

"I don't want it—" Vassili said.

Niccolò turned away and kicked Matthias in the head.

Butterfly wings fluttered in Vassili's stomach. "Hey, Nicc . . . Nicc . . . I don't want it. I don't—"

Niccolò nodded at Benny.

Benny drew his Luger and fired twice.

The butterflies scattered. Two suns exploded into supernovas in Vassili's chest. He fell onto his back as his body convulsed. He felt a lung collapse. Blustering heat filled his chest as he gasped; each breath was a volcanic exchange, each mouthful of fresh air only fuel for the fire within. He tried to scream but trying to scream made him *need* to scream, his pain becoming a hall of funhouse mirrors, each torment feeding off the last and giving sustenance to the next.

King's knight to Queen three, captures pawn, check.

Penni trembled. She had been wrong, horribly wrong—this was not better than *The Bells of St. Mary's* or *Miracle on 34ᵗʰ Street* or even the most wretched of the bunch, the numbingly horrendous *March of the Wooden Soldiers*. This was worse. Worse than an entire year full of Christmas movies. She leapt into the air, wings outspread, and flitted in the air. Every instinct in her tiny body demanded that she fly to Vassili's side.

And then what, bitch? she asked herself.

He groaned and clutched his chest. His hands were streaked with blood. He needed help. Soon. She felt death grow out of his wounds like spider-webs, microbe thin but expanding, growing in girth and length, moving through his body at strange angles, infecting him, killing him. She could hear the cancer cells in his blood cheer on their reinforcements like a city crowd welcoming marching soldiers.

She needed to help him, to stop the darkness from spreading, to save him. But the horrible men would make that difficult, probably impossible.

Penni needed help. She flew away from the reception awning, away from the bad men and Vassili, over the cemetery hills and meadows. She heard the voices of the dead men and women under the soil, each chattered away in their graves, telling stories, crying, asking for forgiveness. Normally, their voices enraptured her. She had spent countless nights just listening, sometimes talking back, reassuring them, kidding with them, laughing at the divine punch line at the end of life. But tonight, she didn't want to hear them or to think that Vassili's voice might soon be buried in their chorus. The voices sunk away to a low murmur.

As she approached the south lawn, the voices disappeared entirely. She had noticed the silence months earlier on one of her nocturnal flights. There was nothing left to the dead interred here, no voices, no memories, no love or hate or—

She knew what it meant. She knew what she had to find. And she knew that it would be dangerous, maybe even more dangerous than the men who had hurt Vassili. But really, what choice did she have?

Niccolò dragged his uncle by the loop of his collar into the funeral home and dropped him onto the floor. Vassili tried not to move. Even the slightest twitch would only infuriate the hornet's nest buzzing in his chest. His face went slack and cold. He felt tired. Staring up, he saw his brother's hand draped over the side of the stainless steel autopsy bed.

Sliding only his eyes, he caught sight of Niccolò leaning against a countertop. Niccolò had inherited his grandfather's impatient eyes and his nervous mannerisms, the way he would make a fist around one of his thumbs and squeeze, the way he would see-saw a cigarette in his mouth. For a moment Niccolò was gone, replaced by the image of Vassili's father standing in their childhood kitchen, two boys cowering at his feet. His father's voice—a memory, a ghost . . . nipped at his ears—*I swear you boys'll end up faggots, queers, fairies . . . .*

Fairies. Faeries. Despite the pain that he knew would follow, Vassili smiled.

"What're you smiling at?" Niccolò asked.

Through the open doorway, Vassili watched Benny and Marco heave Matthias' body back into the trunk. Marco ducked into the funeral home breathing hard, "Should just take a few minutes. Benny found a storage shed with cheap coffins. Just have to find one big enough for that ox."

Niccolò blew out a twirl of smoke. "Take your time. It's gonna be a long night either way. Just make sure that fucker's still breathing when you bury him. I don't care if you gotta give him mouth-to-mouth. I want him to die slowwwwww—"

Marco nodded and darted out the door.

Niccolò bent down over Vassili. "And what do you think I should do with you? Can't bury you here. Someone will come looking for you and they'll start looking here. But you know, Uncle Antonio, I did notice that you have a crematorium in back there. I've never used one before, but it really can't be too difficult, can it? I mean, I've burnt enough toast in my life."

The smile on Vassili's face sank. He could accept death if it meant eternity with Penni, but cremation would steal that from him. "You don't have to—"

Niccolò shushed him. He twirled the cigarette for a moment and then slid the burning tip into the bullet wound just under Vassili's right nipple. He shrieked.

"I don't have to do nothing."

Rook to queen's bishop one, captures rook. Check.

Penni flew through a corridor of tombstones over quiet graves. The wind blew stronger on the downward slope of the hillside, making flight awkward and turns treacherous. She scanned the ground as she entered the oldest part of Echo Meadows, the tract of land where a colonial church once stood, now just a single wall of stone and mortar. Holes peppered the landscape, many small enough for field mice to scurry through, but a few wide enough to be groundhogs tunnels, but Penni knew that no animal had dug them.

She found him inside the ruins of the church, sitting cross-legged on the corpse of an eastern cottontail rabbit. He was dining. Not on the rabbit's flesh—on its essence. He was twice as large as Penni and infinitely older, though his age brought only muscle and strength. His body was covered in fine vein lines and thorny growths. A line of spikes rounded his head like a fallen halo.

"You're the ugliest faerie I've ever seen," she announced as she landed on a smooth fieldstone. "And I've seen some real freak shows."

He eyed her with amusement. He spoke softly to her in a language that only the fae could hear, the true language of the old faeries, where every sentence was a poem. It didn't translate into English very well. "What are you doing here, little bug? Come to see the monster? Or maybe you have an eye for bad boys?"

"I've known you were out here for quite a while. The dead used to sing out in these fields, but the graves have been going silent. I knew it had to be one of you," she brushed her long black hair, moving it to cover her breasts. "An ossuary faerie who doesn't talk to the dead; you eat them. *Mangeurs de l'essence* as the French say."

He shook his spiked head, "Human languages are so crude; I'm surprised to hear a fae speak one, but then again, I really shouldn't be surprised, coming from a damned housefly."

"I don't live in his house," she said.

"Oh, you certainly do," he snickered. "Since I see you aren't leaving, you can call me Zwischenzug—its one of my names you should like, since it has a human origin. German, I believe, though I honestly can't be sure. All humans look the same to me. I believe the Germans had stylish marching boots?"

"I've come to ask for your help," she told him.

He laughed. "I don't *do* help. It wastes time."

"Then don't do it for me. Do it for you."

His stiletto ears perked up.

Penni stood up. "I'm sure you're hungry for fresher corpses, more recent memories, less clouds getting in the way of the details. The dead you've had out here in this cemetery are centuries old, too long in the ground to really remember anything clearly."

"I was working my way north, didn't want to miss out on anything," he said. The spikes on his body seemed quivered. "How fresh you talking?"

Penni smiled. "How does *still wet* strike you?"

"I don't have to do nothing."

Breathing hard, chest heaving, Vassili rolled onto his side and spat a mouthful of blood onto the tile floor. He gulped as he spoke, drinking in the air. "You'll. Have. To. Die. Like. Everyone. Else . . . You'll. Have. To. Do. That."

"You threatening me, Uncle?" Niccolò asked. "From down there on the floor, already a couple pints low? You really think you can take me?"

" . . . No."

Niccolò stretched out his arms, a cynical Jesus asking *Eli, Eli, lama sabachthani? God, my God, why hast thou forsaken me?* "If not you, then who? I don't see anyone around here except a whole lot of dead people. And dead people can't help you."

Vassili asked, "Do. You. Believe. In. Faeries. Nicci?"

Penni and Zwischenzug watched from behind a crooked marble spire as Benny and Marco finished covering the grave. They packed the loose soil down with pats from their spades.

Benny said, "Ain't really level."

"Yeah, well, fuck it," Marco swung his spade behind his shoulder like a baseball bat. "I never wanted to be no gravedigger, anyway."

Benny rubbed his hands together for warmth. "Sure getting the practice in, though. I don't know, you think things'll be better with the kid running the show?"

Marco made a sour face, "You?"

"Hell, no."

They started to walk back to the funeral home. As soon as the sound of their footfalls could no longer be heard, Penni flew over to the grave. Zwischenzug followed at a more leisurely pace.

"Benjamin Robert Calhoun?" Zwischenzug read the name on the tombstone as if it were a riddle to be decoded. He quickly ran one callous hand over the stone, his sharp talons leaving tiny scratches down its face.

Penni's lips curled into a disapproving little pout as she landed on the fresh soil. "He's not down there; he's still in the cooler back at the funeral home. Messed up bad—smoking in bed, died in an apartment fire."

She pointed to the dirt. "Dig."

Dropping to the ground, he tore through the soil, both arms working so quickly they became a blur. He tunneled down, leaving a hole in his wake twice the size of his body.

She heard him strike wood and flew head-first down the hole, landing in a handstand on an exposed portion of pine. Zwischenzug pulled back one claw and brought it down forcefully. His talons punctured the coffin like a spike and pulled back. The wood cracked and splintered. Penni glanced up to the surface to make sure the noise hadn't brought Benny and Marco back to the gravesite. She saw only a few stars in the black sky.

"You stay here," she said and squeezed through the narrow opening. It was as dark inside the coffin as it was in the ossuary during a cloudy new moon midnight. She could hear the Matthias-monster breathing.

"You wakey?" she asked as she walked up his chest.

He quivered slightly, probably in surprise, and brought both his hands up, swatting himself. Penni let one of his fingers brush her wings before she flew out of his reach. "Careful, buddy, this is only our first date. Hands at your sides if you want me to help you."

"Who are you?" he asked.

Penni softly set herself down on one of his massive shoulders. "You're buried alive in a burn victim's grave. You've been shot and beaten with a crowbar. And all you can think is to ask me who I am?"

He asked, "Bring any food?"

"You're hungry?" she asked.

He whistled, "Starving."

"Well, there's nothing to snack on down here. Won't be until the wood deteriorates and the wormies wiggle in looking for some calcium. But you'll be in no position to eat by then." Penni distinctly heard his stomach growl. It could have passed for whale song. "But what if I could get you out of here? Plenty to eat up topside, you know. Frozen pizza and candy corn, that sort of thing. If I get this box uncovered and open, would you do something for me?"

In the dark she heard him whisper, "Bean burritos?"

"With fiesta sauce," she told him.

They had a deal.

Though his vision was beginning to dim, Vassili could still make out Benny and Marco strolling through the double doors. Marco carried one of the spades from the work shed; Benny was empty-handed. Beyond them, in a blur, Vassili thought he saw a second spade leaning against his nephew's sedan.

"It's done," Benny said to Niccolò.

Niccolò licked his top lip. "Did he scream?"

"Nah," Benny told him. "Didn't make a peep."

"Too bad," Niccolò reached into his pocket and retrieved Matthias's wallet. He split the bills, and handed them to his men. "But it'll be a long night. He'll be screaming before the air runs out, before the arteries in his lungs burst."

Marco pocketed his cash and dropped the spade onto an empty gurney. He glanced at Vassili. "Yeah, speaking of long nights, what do we do with him?"

"Can't leave him here," Benny offered.

"Wetlands?" Marco suggested.

Niccolò tossed the wallet away. "We'll figure it out on the road." He turned to Vassili as the men moved in and pulled him off the floor. "Uncle Antonio, you remember that summer when you taught me to drive? In that old Studebaker with the one brown door? Well, we've got one more ride to take, me and you."

Benny and Marco dragged him across to the door. As they passed over the threshold, Niccolò stopped short and pointed to a hill on the east lawn. "Now, what the fuck is that? You better tell me it's not what I think it is."

Vassili raised his head and squinted. At the top of the hill, the shape of an enormous man shambled toward the funeral home.

Niccolò turned and faced his men, "What did you do, bury him a couple inches down? Was he able to snorkel under the dirt?"

"No, I swear, he was six feet—"

Niccolò waved Benny off. "You know, really don't give a shit, all I want is for you two to get over there and kill that motherfucker. You think you can handle that? Is he too small a target for you?"

Marco let go of Vassili, popped out his .22, and stepped past the sedan. When he noticed that Benny wasn't following, he stopped and turned. "You coming?"

Benny struggled to hold Vassili upright. "I dunno, man, he looked like he was nearly dead when we buried him. What if, y'know, maybe he died and shit and now he's come back for re—"

"You tweakin'?" Marco asked him.

"Drop that," Niccolò screamed. It took a moment for Vassili to realize that *that* meant him. "And get your ass out there and take care of this—"

Benny hesitated for a second.

"—You. Go. Out. There. You. Die—" Vassili whispered.

With a frustrated grunt, Benny threw Vassili to the ground, scrambled over to Marco, and started up the hill. Hitting the asphalt, Vassili heard Benny warn Marco, "Better *not* be no zombie shit going on."

Turning his head to watch them head off to intercept Matthias, Vassili thought, *King's bishop to king's rook three, captures pawn.*

Marco led the way, marching up the incline. He kept his eyes on Matthias as the big man headed down the hill, their paths precisely locked, two locomotives heading for film reel history. Benny, winded and afraid, trailed behind, pushing off tombstones and keeping his gun aimed. There was no way he could have hit Matthias at that range, but he felt safer with the gun in his hand.

Not turning, Marco asked, "What's with you and zombies?"

"I just don't like zombies," Benny panted.

Marco snickered. "Ain't no such thing as zombies. Only thing you should be scared of is our new boss back there. He likes the meth and he's got a temper."

"You think?" Benny didn't bother keeping the snark in check. Then another thought crossed his mind. "He'd make a really scary zombie."

Matthias' face came into focus, smeared with red like a roughed up whore, mouth sagging open, tongue moving across his lips.

Marco slowed down as they approached the giant. Both men trained their guns on his head. "How did you get out of the hole, Biggie?"

Matthias stood in the moonlight and did not move.

"Just shoot him," Benny pleaded.

Marco turned slightly and threw Benny his best Southern Baptist-fire-and-brimstone snake-handler's glare. "Don't worry, little bro, I got th—"

Something small and dark and thorny buzzed out from behind Matthias, something not much larger than a cicada but moving like a tiny surface-to-air missile. Marco didn't see it coming. It hit his face at full speed and tore straight through his head, emerging from the other temple in a blast of fine blood, diced brain, and sandy granules of skull. Marco stood for moment, his feet firm on the soil, before collapsing like a freefalling building in a controlled demolition.

Benny tried to aim his gun at the blur of motion heading for him, but only for a shadow of a second before he spun in place and sprinted. He zigzagged through the graveyard, trying to evade the missile.

He didn't get far before he felt it tear through his right shoulder blade. He shrieked and dropped to his knees. Looking down, he watched as a hole appeared in his shirt just below his right nipple and a tiny creature emerged. Its tiny, spiked body was covered in his blood. And some of Marco's. It dragged a severed, spitting pulmonary vein in one hand.

It turned its head upward and stared at Benny for a moment, a twisted little face filled with sadistic glee. Then it brought the vein to its lips and blew into its mouth. Benny watched an air bubble travel into his body, a snake digesting a mouse, and felt the first tremors hit his body.

Turning back to Benny, the wicked little face smiled up at him and said, "Drink that pain, you filthy primate; it'll make you sweeter."

Niccolò watched his men fall and Matthias walk slowly down the hill toward the funeral home. He pulled his gun, though at the snail's pace the big man moved, he wouldn't need it any time soon. When he glanced at his uncle, Vassili could see terror in the young man's eyes. "What just happened? Who else is out here?"

Vassili didn't answer. Something caught his eye instead, a tiny figure swimming just behind Niccolò's head, bat-like black wings fluttering, long, pale legs paddling through the air.

Niccolò brought his free hand up to his face and tapped his fingers against his forehead. Then he yelped like a dog, an angry, frustrated sound, and lashed out, punching the window of the sedan and kicking at its door. He turned, waved his gun at Vassili, and screamed, "Who the fuck is out there? Who did that to Marco and Benny—"

Penni winked as she flew past and darted into the funeral home. To Niccolò, it was probably nothing more than a fast black moth or a tiny bat passing by.

Niccolò scrambled over, his feet kicking at the asphalt, and wrenched Vassili up by his collar. His wild eyes pulsed with rage and fright. "Okay, right, whatever. We're going. Now."

He dragged Vassili over to the sedan, opened the rear door, and heaved his uncle inside. Vassili slid one foot into the door as Niccolò tried to slam it closed. He grunted as the heavy door hit. Bones broke, but the door remained open.

King's rook to Queen six, captures knight.

Penni flew into the funeral home, up onto the examination table, and landed on the cool steel a few inches from Vincent Vassili's face. Using her hands like crowbars, she took hold of his lips and peeled them back. Then she reached farther inside and attempted the same with his locked teeth. No luck.

The messy way, then, she thought and back-stepped to the lip of the table. *I must really love him.*

Penni ran and dove into his destroyed eye, penetrating the channel Matthias had opened with the fork, and crawled inside.

"Get . . . ." Niccolò shouted, "your . . . motherfuckin' . . . foot . . . ."

He swung the door open and then reversed the motion. Vassili screamed again as he felt his foot twist at an unnatural angle and the joint in his ankle pop.

" . . . inside . . . the . . . *motherfuckin'* . . . car!"

Again. The third hit tore his flesh open at the heel and twisted the foot completely around. Still screaming, Vassili reached down and latched his hands around his leg. Defiantly, he thrust it farther into the door.

"Okay," Niccolò mumbled and stepped back. The car door crept open. He straightened his arm, pointed the handgun at Vassili's head. "I was going to let you do it yourself, take yourself out, honorable, you know? But I see that you—"

"What warlike noise is this?"

Niccolò turned toward the voice, toward the funeral home's double doors, toward the ramshackle figure standing in the doorway, toward his father.

What warlike noise, Vassili smiled. *She loves Hamlet.*

Niccolò's face paled. "Dad- Dad- you're—"

Penni reached into Antonio Vassili's coat with his hand and withdrew a small black Glock. "I think you should step away from the car, Nicci."

Niccolò glanced back at Vassili, then at his father. His eyes were glassy and unsure, as if he were on the verge of tears or madness- or both. He was frozen in place. "I- Jesus Christ- Dad- I—"

Penni squeezed Vincent Vassili's finger and the gun fired, tearing a hole through Niccolò's jacket, shirt, skin, muscle, breastbone, and heart. At the same moment, a small blur of flashing wings and sharp thorns collided with the back of his skull and burrowed inside.

Niccolò remained on his feet. His eyes closed for a moment and then reopened. A crinkled, devilish smile grew on the dead man's face as his free hand balled into a fist.

Vassili backed up, dragging his foot onto the bench seat. The smile that Penni's *Hamlet* recitation had brought faded as his nephew turned to fully face him.

"This cemetery's mine," Zwischenzug said from within Niccolò's lips. "Every body in every grave, mine. Those two heaps of flesh up on the field, mine. That stinking pile of meat in the doorway? In a minute, you? All mine. I may even eat your little winged girlfriend. 'Cause she's mine too, now."

Niccolò's gun fired. Vassili felt the slug hit his chest. This one was no lingering pain; this was sharp and forceful—and final. He knew that he couldn't survive it. He didn't scream. He didn't cry. He just slowly lowered his head to the upholstery and whispered, "Penni—"

Tears exploded from both Vincent Vassili's eyes and Penni's own. She pulled the trigger on the Glock and unloaded the clip into Niccolò's back. He stammered and fell against the sedan.

Zwischenzug raised Niccolò's handgun and fired off his remaining three rounds. Each slammed home into Antonio Vassili's body. Both bodies slid to the asphalt, both spilling blood, both too damaged to function.

Vincent Vassili's mouth yawned open and Penni crawled out, still covered in gore. She watched as Zwischenzug cut an exit tunnel out between Niccolò's eyes. They stared at each other for a moment, then both leapt and flew toward the other at top velocity. They collided in mid-air, two buzzing figures tearing at the other's flesh. Penni wrapped one hand around Zwischenzug's throat and squeezed. He slashed at her with his thorny arms, slicing into her flesh, one hand twisting in her hair and tearing out a handful from the scalp. She raked at his eyes with her nails.

He was stronger, a born warrior, and it didn't take long for his advantage to become absolute. They fell to the blacktop. He straddled her and brought his arms down, slicing her breasts, her throat. She screamed and sobbed. Zwischenzug began to laugh, a million insults in as many languages mixed with his loud chortle. He reached down with both hands and took hold of her right wing. He snorted into the cold air, spit on her face, and then tore it off.

Penni roared in agony. She watched helplessly as he raised her severed wing over his head and bathed in her pink blood. He backed off her, an expression of pure triumph, of the most hideously birthed orgasm imaginable, spreading over his vicious little face. In the ancient language of the fae, he said, "Housefly, always looking out, wondering what real freedom is like, always too frightened to find out. It was only a matter of time before someone swatted—"

"King me," Penni said.

The spade flatted him; spread his body thin across the driveway.

Penni stared up, shock still swimming through her body, the image unclear, unfocused. Slowly, Matthias came into focus as he scraped the remainder of Zwischenzug's mangled body off the spade with one boot.

"Thank you, big guy," She said, panting.

He nodded. "Bean burritos?"

"Inside, in the fridge," she said as she pulled herself off the ground. She wobbled, her balance hopelessly impaired without her right wing. Matthias carefully stepped over her and disappeared into the funeral home. Penni stumbled over to the sedan, pulled herself up Niccolò's body, and climbed inside the car. Vassili was breathing, but only the weakest, shallowest breaths. She could feel the death inside him, growing stronger, taking over each cell, driving out the last of his life.

She ran up his body, falling twice, up to his face. She pressed herself against his cheek. They cried together, neither for themselves.

"Sorry," Vassili told her, "but. This. Is. Check. Mate."

She straightened up and wiped the bubbling tears from her eyes. She ran a hand over his cooling skin, and sobbing, said, "You're a bet- better- better player than that, Vassie- You still- it's still your turn- and you- you still have one piece- on the board."

He didn't smile—couldn't. But she saw a glint in his eye, a thankful glint, a loving glint.

"—you still- you still have your queen."

Pennidreadful ran, out of the sedan, down the dead nephew, and up the hillside. Her body ached but she didn't slow. Vassili had very little life left in him, very little light left to fight the encroaching darkness. So she ran as fast as she could, ignoring the slap of grass blades, until she reached a tall marble monument.

It read, Gene Murkowski, M.D.

She listened, deep in the ground, and heard the doctor down there—a thousand memories recalled, a thousand surgeries remembered. Into the soil, she said, "Listen, I want to make you a deal—"

Pixie Dust

Steven Earl Yoder

DARKNESS PERMEATED THE ROOM, BROKEN ONLY BY THE GLEAM of grinning white teeth in a narrow beam of moonlight that seemed determined to sneak its way through the black cloth covering the window. Aysa wondered again if things were *really* bad enough to seek outside help. After all, the cuts in her wings would heal . . . eventually. She was used to taking care of herself, having spent much of her life traveling alone. But she had never been alone against a whole gang of Fae before. She had also never backed down from a fight, and wasn't about to start now.

The flare of a match drew her from her thoughts, and Aysa's eyes adjusted slowly to the dim, flickering light as the old black man lit six white candles on the table before her.

What she saw added to the disoriented feeling Aysa had felt since walking through the door. The room was cluttered, both with things she recognized and still others she had no idea what purpose they could serve. A workbench made of a dark wood ran the length of the wall on Aysa's left in the cramped room. Scattered about it were various things often associated with Voodoo; candles, a half full bottle of rum, cigars, and countless jars of unidentifiable powders. Hanging along the wall over the table were portraits of various Loas, the gods so important to practitioners of this art. Some were crudely hand drawn, while others were almost a quality worthy of any prestigious art museum.

What really drew Aysa's attention was the back wall. End to end and top to bottom were cases of preserved insects. In the dim light many of them seemed to come alive, the flickering of the flames giving the illusion that their wings moved.

Aysa was brought from her entrancement by

another flare of light and a stinging scent. The dark man had leaned forward and used one candle to light a huge cigar. The rising smoke made patterns around his head, adding to the otherworldly feel of the room.

His name was Bosun, and he came highly recommended as the best hougan in Baton Rouge, maybe even in the entire state of Louisiana. To Aysa, he looked the part, too. Short and black as pitch; Bosun had yellow eyes and teeth that could blind, if the reflection in the moonlight were any indication of what they would be like in daylight. Bosun's hair was long, and worn in tight cornrows close to the skull. His clothing was colorful, loose-fitting and comfortable-looking, with designs drawn or sewn all over the shirt. Aysa assumed they were wards against evil spirits. Most striking, though, were the lines in his face. Some were age lines; others looked to have been carved there in some ritualistic fashion. All of them were very deep, giving Bosun a tired, but wizened appearance. He looked almost as though he carried all the knowledge of the world, and not being able to share it made each day a lifetime.

"So, *bebé*," Bosun said, leaning back and blowing a huge puff of smoke into the air, "you come here to me because you want protection." Aysa started. So far she hadn't spoken, but this man knew why she was here. She was impressed, but not convinced. A lot of people came to a hougan for protection. It could have just been an odds-on guess.

"Well . . . yes," Aysa slowly replied, measuring how to proceed. "But this is a special case." Aysa thought she sounded stupid. Still, she had to keep going now that she had started. "I know you probably hear that a lot, but my case is *definitely* different from your normal clients."

"I isn't blind, girl. You of de Fae," he said, pursing his lips in a disgusted way that made the lines in his face even deeper. "Any damn fool see dat!"

Aysa was shocked that the man could so readily see her for what she was. Clearly he did have power, because with few exceptions only other members of the Fae had such instant recognition. A surge of joy and hope passed through her, which she tried to suppress before continuing.

"Yes, I certainly am. Unfortunately, I don't have many friends amongst my kind, at least not here in Louisiana." Aysa bit her lip, because this was hard to talk about. "I've tried making friends here, but it just never worked. The other Fae here don't act normally. They have a real mean streak." Thinking, Aysa tried to describe her treatment. "When I wouldn't join their gang, they started picking on me, just like I was a *human*. They're the worst kind of rogues, and they're about ten to my one." She paused, and decided to tell all. "Lately it's gone beyond just taunting." Stifling back a sob, Aysa cried out, "Just look!"

From behind her, Aysa's wings appeared. Normally iridescent and beautiful, hers had been mutilated. Long cuts had been made in them, and their normal shimmering was sporadic. Instead of being things of wonder, Aysa's wings were now dull and crumpled and ugly.

Bosun sat silently for a while. If the sudden appearance of wings on this young girl had surprised him, he was hiding it so deeply that Aysa couldn't tell. Maybe he'd seen much more surprising things in his line of work.

Finally, Bosun stood up. "I see you have good reason for wanting this." He started searching through the bottles on his workbench. "You clearly not happy in your current state here. Maybe I know something to fix dat." Reaching to the far right end of the workbench, he seemed to find what he was looking for. "Maybe I know just de thing for a girl like you," he said, with laughter in his eyes.

Bosun crossed back from the workbench, a jar of glistening sand in his hand. Aysa watched as he reseated himself across from her and opened the jar. He counted out three large pinches of the shiny substance into a cloth bag. This he bound with a string. Then he looked up at her with a smile. "Close your eyes."

Aysa did as she was told, and she heard him get up from the table and move around behind her. As he passed, something about him struck her as familiar, but his chanting distracted her. Aysa felt dusty powder sprinkle down on her head. From the rustle of his clothes, she assumed he was shaking the contents of the bag onto her with sharp snaps of his arm.

"Okay, you all set," Bosun said, crossing back to his side of the table and re-seating himself. Aysa waited as the old man relit his cigar and leaned back. "Now, *bebé*, nothing happen yet. But you wait and see." Bosun smiled, and released a long breath of noxious smoke into the air. It curled around his head, as though reluctant to leave his presence, but started dissipating when he spoke again. "When dem other Fae harass you again, THEN something happen, and dat's sure. What, exactly, depend all on you."

Bosun didn't seem interested in volunteering any more details, and Aysa wasn't interested in asking. She was just glad to have some form of defense against the gang of Fae that wouldn't leave her alone, whatever it might be.

"Thank you, Bosun," Aysa said, "Tell me, what do I owe you? I can pay gold, or grant some other boon, if you like."

Bosun smiled that secret smile again, took another long puff of his cigar, and said, "Dis one cost you nothing. We wait and see what happen." Bosun dropped the butt of his cigar on the floor, stepped on it, and said, "Besides, when Fae gets what deserved, payment is made."

"Bosun, I realize that customs here are a bit different than I am used to . . . ." Aysa started, but the man's quick frown made her stumble. Still, she felt she owed a great debt because certainly the next step these rogues would take could well mean her death, or worse. Determinedly, Aysa continued. "Really, I can't leave a debt of this magnitude unpaid!"

"I say dis one cost you nothing, and dat is dat." Bosun's demeanor told Aysa that nothing more would be said or heard on the matter, so she reluctantly gave up trying.

Aysa stood, hid her wings again and said, "Bosun, if there's ever anything I can do for you . . . ever anything you need . . . ."

"Maybe we talk of dat later," Bosun said with a dismissive air. "Right now you go, get some rest, see what come tomorrow." With that he closed his eyes in meditation, and Aysa left.

"Well, that certainly was a bit unusual," Aysa thought as she started the long walk across the parish. "But I've met more eccentric folk in my time. Maybe the eccentricity is a statement of the power he's said to have." She cursed under her breath at having to *walk* when she should be able to enjoy the freedom of the air.

As Aysa made her way home, a breeze stirred the bottom of the lightweight dress she wore, lifting her mood with the hem. She found herself thinking of her travels, and the trinkets she had collected along the way. Aysa remembered the first time she saw a miniature car, and how she had found it as fascinating as the real ones the mortals drove. She had started collecting them because they were easy to transport, and now had nearly one-hundred of them. Aysa resolved to play with them for the first time in months when she got home.

The next morning Aysa woke refreshed, actually looking forward to the day rather than dreading what it might bring. She didn't really feel any different, and there wasn't the slightest residue of the powder Bosun had used. His spell, at a minimum, left her feeling as confident as the first time she had met the harassing gang of Fae, and there was something to be said for that.

Aysa decided to go for a walk—specifically to the trees in the park where the gang could often be found. She was actually feeling a bit cocky and wanted to confront Mikål, the leader of the group, before any spell Bosun may have cast wore off.

She wound her way down the path and began to lose herself amongst the trees. It wasn't long before she heard the catcalls start from behind her, and rising above the rest was the annoying whining voice she used to dread.

"Well met, Aysa. Normally we have to come looking for you. What brings you to us this fine day?" came Mikål's mocking voice. "Have you reconsidered your attitude, perhaps? You know, it's just not natural for a faerie such as yourself to have no interest in joining with a troupe. What would they say in your beloved homeland?"

Aysa wheeled around, uncomfortable with anyone behind her, especially Mikål. "They would say that I have some level of standards, rather than reveling with any pig or pooka." She had wanted to say this for a long time, but fear had kept her silent before this. Aysa had learned early on that standing up to Mikål and his boys only ever made things worse, so she had all but given up trying.

This time it felt really good to speak her mind . . . even if he was right about the way she was acting. Normally, Fae would gravitate to one another, but something about the Fae in America, and Mikål and his gang in specific, set her completely against doing the sociable thing.

If he were surprised that she had stood up to him this time, Mikål didn't show it. He turned to his gang and with a mocking tone of shock said, "The cat has claws again!" Turning back to Aysa, his face darkened. "Now Aysa, you know well enough not to disrespect your betters." While Mikål goaded Aysa, his gang circled her, entrapping her like they always did. "You know what happened the last time, and it can only get worse from there. Besides, what's wrong with running with pooka?" As he said this, Mikål's wings and donkey ears appeared, as if to accentuate his point. "In your homeland, all may be mostly peace and well between the different kith, but here a war rages, and choosing no side makes you an enemy, and a target."

Aysa tensed up, wishing she could fly away to safety. Her mutilated wings trembled as if ready, and the memory of when they were damaged drove her to infuriation. Even though violence was against her nature, there was no way she would let them brutalize her again.

Aysa conjured her dagger and leapt at Mikål, wanting to destroy his wings as he had done to her. Her inexperienced attack was miscalculated, and she drew a horrible gash in one of his overgrown ears instead. Mikål's howl of pain and rage gave Aysa the greatest satisfaction she had felt in months; she actually began to tingle with it. The pride of this Pook was damaged, and that was no small feat.

Mikål felt at his wounded ear, and instead of rage, a smile of satisfaction crossed his face. "That, my sweet, will cost you more dearly than you can imagine."

Aysa stepped back out of Mikål's reach. She couldn't fathom what he meant, but knew it couldn't possibly be anything but bad. She silently prayed for what-ever it was that Bosun had planned to start having some kind of effect. Anything would do, because she was starting to feel scared and quite out of her league.

The tingling sensation Aysa felt surged throughout her body. The feeling had started, slowly building, from the moment she attacked Mikål, and now seemed to be peaking. Suddenly she was panting, short of breath. Her grip loosened and she dropped her dagger. Everything around her closed in, and Aysa felt as though the very air itself smothered her. The pressure continued until it was like every cell in her body folded in on itself. The park grew huge before her, and Aysa briefly closed her eyes. When she opened them nothing was the same.

Bosun's spell must have backfired and helped them instead of me, Aysa thought as she looked around her. Her thin-bladed dagger lay on the ground in front of her, and the sight of it brought a moan of despair. She could see that she was no bigger than the handle, maybe six inches at most.

The gang seemed to have lost sight of her momentarily, and Aysa used this to her advantage. She had to get away, had to get back to Bosun so he could fix this. As best she could, she stuck to cover and moved away from the group.

"Where is she?" Aysa heard Mikål yell. "Find her! There will be hell itself to pay if we lose her." Even at six inches tall, they would be able to sense her presence and track her. She had to put even more distance between them. In desperation, she tried to fly.

To her surprise, Aysa discovered that she could, just a little. Her wings seemed to be repairing themselves. They were still bent and damaged, but the cuts were closed. *Maybe, that's what Bosun intended,* she thought, *and the rest was just a mistake.* Carefully, Aysa made her way across town and to Bosun's shack. Her wings were healed enough to fly, but only erratically, so the trip was long and nerve-wracking.

Aysa knew there was no way he could hear it if she knocked with her tiny fists, so she kicked the door. Even this brought no response. She had to find some way to get his attention. She moved from the doorway and explored the sides of the building. On the side with the window, she found vines growing from ground to roof. Perfect! Maybe if she could get up there, she could make enough noise for Bosun to hear.

Aysa struggled, but finally managed to pull herself up the vines to the sill. Frantically, she banged on the glass. "Bosun, HELP! Something has gone terribly wrong!" There was no answer, not even the slightest sound to indicate he was here.

Running along the ledge, Aysa noticed something she hadn't seen during her climb. At the far left edge, the bottom pane of the window had a crack in it. The smaller piece looked like it might be loose. She set about dislodging it. If she could just get inside, she could wait safely for Bosun to return.

Pushing, sliding, and working away at the ancient grout around the pane, Aysa finally managed to get the glass to fall inward. It bounced intact, but shattered when it hit the hardwood table. She carefully climbed inside, safe at last.

Before her eyes could adjust to the dark, she found out how wrong she was about that, and so much more. A hand from the darkness grabbed her; loose enough to not cause her harm, but tight enough that there was no hope of escape.

"Gotcha!" Bosun exclaimed, and Aysa believed she had never seen such a menacing grin on any being. "I knew you would end up like dis," he said. "I know dese things, an' you Sidhé kith never disappoint me."

Aysa's mind struggled with the betrayal. The spell hadn't gone wrong at all. She had been set up, and Bosun had apparently been laying in wait for the payoff. She could hear the hatred in his voice, though she didn't know why.

"What . . . I don't understand," Aysa stammered. "What are you doing? I came to you for help!"

"All magic got its price." A smile crossed Bosun's face, the smile of someone who had a nasty secret they were going to reveal, and the confidant wouldn't be happy about it. "You jus' paid."

"Paid?" That one word was all Aysa could manage. Nothing was making sense to her, and fear was making it that much harder to understand anything.

"Yes, *bebé*, paid." Bosun smiled, white teeth flashing like they did the first time she met him. "Paid the moment you act the way you do. Paid with the old punishment for acting out of place."

Aysa stared. She knew a little about the old punishments, and a new fear began to gnaw at her, born of sudden realization. Bosun didn't seem to notice, but continued with what seemed to be a practiced speech.

"Dat powder I use on you was pixie dust. Very rare . . . very powerful." Bosun checked his grip and carried Aysa towards the rear of the room. "Only one source of it," he continued, "and only one use for it."

"You see, *bebé*, pixie are not true Fae, they are made. No one know anymore where the first come from, or how dese things discovered," Bosun looked to the ceiling, as if trying to remember the proper order for a bedtime story. "But pixie dust been effective for a very long time. Sprinkle it on a Fae who might be acting out of turn. If they not, it wear off in a day and nothing happen. And if they are, then they shrink into a pixie." Bosun grinned again. "You should not have attacked. You know better, no matter how compelled you felt."

When Bosun reached the rear wall, he held Aysa fast against one of the boards. "Now de *source* of pixie dust, dat an interestin' matter." He smiled that chilling smile, and the lines in his face deepened, like cavernous pits to hell. "pixie dust come from pixies! Drop off dey bodies, as dey slowly die, done right. The *best* dust drop off dey wings."

Now Aysa knew why the insects on the boards seemed almost alive, and why some of them had seemed iridescent. She didn't want to look to her left and right, but she was unable to stop herself.

All around her were the decaying bodies of pixies. The ones who seemed to be in the best shape were clearly in terrible pain, pinned to the boards with no hope of escape. The ones in the worst shape just kind of hung from their posts. Still, the occasional movements made Aysa realize that even the most decayed were *still alive*. Each time they moved, iridescent dust fell from their bodies, and they became even more decrepit.

Aysa struggled again in the iron grip of the old man, but it didn't do any good. As long as she was this size, she had no hope of escape. Bosun smiled another of those wide and toothy smiles. He knew what she was thinking, and reveled in the control he had over her. He reached into a small box that sat on the dust collection shelf just barely within Aysa's sight.

At that moment, the door to the little building was thrown back, startling her, but like everything, having no visible effect on Bosun. Aysa twisted to look. To her horror, she caught a glimpse of Mikål.

"Bosun! It happened, she attacked just like they all do when you taint the dust, but this one managed to slip away when she shrank."

"No worries, Mikål," Bosun said, without looking away from Aysa. "I got her right here. Now dey be one less enemy in the kith war."

Bosun spoke again, and his tone was almost fatherly. "Oh, baby doll, I give you one las' life lesson." The black man paused, and Aysa shivered as she saw the wings unfold from behind him, and his ears growing to match Mikål's. "Good to know how to pick your friends, but better to know how to pick your enemies!

There was no escaping the grip of a pooka once he held you fast. Aysa screamed the scream of the mad as an insect pin neared her chest.

Shadow Fae

Bottle-Caps and Cigarette Butts

Bernie Mojzes

IT ROLLED LIKE TUMBLEWEED DOWN THE STREET IN THE WAKE OF the SEPTA bus. Rolled like an empty beer can, fluttered like crumpled newspaper and yellowed ginkgo leaves and pigeon feathers, then slipped through a storm grate, where it watched me suspiciously with eyes like cigarette butts and bottle-caps. Watched me watching it, then blinked twice and dropped out of sight.

Can't say I begrudge its circumspection. The city requires a bit of wariness from us all, don't it? Whether we be human or critter or something else entirely, we all show a bit of the same behavior. We all keep an eye out for shadowy doorways. We all take particular notice of those who're giving us a bit more attention than we want. In the end, we're all potential predator, and we're all potential prey. And why should the Fae be any different? At least, that's the way I figure it.

I jaywalked at a break in traffic and peered down the storm drain. Didn't see anything, of course. I might've been looking right at it, but if so, it blended in so well with the trash that had collected at the bottom as to be invisible. I fumbled in my laptop case and found a package of Starburst candies and half a Mounds bar. I opened one of the Starbursts and popped it in my mouth, then dropped one through the grate. Never hurts to leave an offering. Once upon a time these folks were Door Things and Kitchen Things and Stable Things. The spirits of trees and streams and rivers and rocks. I think. But there's no room in this world for Door Things and Kitchen Things. Not anymore.

And the trees are all caged and replaced before they can push up the sidewalks. The streams are all paved over. People don't even have time to notice the Place anymore, much less the Spirit of the Place.

As I walked away I felt eyes watching me—an itch in the center of my back, hair raised at the base of my neck. I turned to look at the storm grate but I saw no hint of the Street Thing I'd seen. Still, the disconcerting feeling remained. I threw another Starburst at the grate (and missed), attracting the attention of a handful of jeering children as they passed me on the street. A flash of movement caught my eye as I turned to walk away. When I looked back, the candy was gone.

I smiled as I continued walking, ignoring my lingering apprehension.

That evening I had dinner with Amy and Taylor, who were visiting Philly for a week, and my friend Stephen, at a small restaurant on Fifth and South. A bit pricier than my post-student budget could comfortably accommodate, but how often do I get to see Amy and Taylor, since she got accepted at the University of Washington and he followed her and became a programmer for the very same Evil Empire he'd spent years mocking?

We were well into our second bottle of wine by the time the appetizers arrived and I was well into a fantasy in which the evident tension between Amy and Taylor turned into a full-fledged fight, and she turned to me and said, *I should never have left you.*

And she turned to me and said, "Why do you keep looking over your shoulder?"

I hadn't realized that I had been. But I had. I kept stealing glances out the window to the street, but there was never anything there. You know. Except for people. And cars.

"I don't know," I said. "I keep feeling like I'm being watched. It's been going on all day."

Taylor grinned. "You become a spy since we've been gone?"

"No."

"Witness in a mafia trial?" Stephen offered.

I rolled my eyes.

"Nikki's stalking you." Amy looked over her wine glass at me. Taylor and Stephen laughed, but Amy didn't. She knew better.

"Gods, no. She's, I dunno, off stalking someone else. I think she moved out of town."

"Good." Amy's lips curled into a crooked smile. "So who's watching you?"

I felt my face flush. "It's nothing. It's silly." I shook my head. "You'll think I'm crazy."

"So what's new?" Taylor flinched as Amy backhanded him.

"All right," I said. I rubbed my temples. "It's like this. I see faeries."

Stephen cocked his head. "Hello? You're just now figuring this out?" His grin would've shamed Puck.

"Drink your wine."

"I hear and obey." He waved the near-empty bottle at the waiter.

I ignored Taylor's mocking look and focused on Amy's skepticism. "Told you you'd think I was crazy."

She gave me a wry grin. "I like your brand of crazy. And I think we most definitely need more wine for this conversation."

There should have been sound. The throaty flutter of giant wings, the grinding of stone on stone. Something.

We'd been somewhat fairly quite thoroughly tipsy when we'd left the restaurant, drunk and pissy, the tension between the fiancé and the ex-boyfriend moving from playful jabs to blatant hostility quickly as Amy played us off against each other. I pretend to think that I understood why she was doing this. Stephen, neutral as Switzerland, but a lover of drama in all its forms, had settled in to enjoy the show, only pitching in to throw some fuel on the fire when things started to die down. He didn't much care about the outcome—it was the battle he loved.

Out on the sidewalk, Stephen gave Amy and Taylor cursory hugs. "Hate to bitch and run," he said, "but I have a date tonight." He smiled and kissed me on the cheek. "If you get lonely, text me. We'll make it a threesome."

"Hot faerie action," Taylor muttered.

"You bet your sweet virgin ass, honey!" Stephen smirked, and then, with his habitual flourish, he was off, leaving us to our anger.

"I'll walk you to your hotel," I said.

"That's not necessary," Taylor said, and Amy scowled.

I shrugged. "It's on the way to my apartment. But if you want I'll walk on the other side of the street."

"Works for me."

"Don't be an ass." Amy linked her arm in mine, and her other in Taylor's.

That's how we negotiated the sidewalk, winding like snakes around signposts and pedestrians, partially parting like retarded nematodes for parking meters and fire hydrants. Taylor kicked an empty Coke bottle in front of him, swapped it for a crushed beer can when we came across one, and traded that in for a broken piece of masonry after Amy almost sprawled on her face tripping over it. We were all a few sheets to the wind, but it was pretty clear by the time we'd traveled a few blocks that Amy was using us for support as often as not.

"Wait," I said, pulling us to a halt. I recognized this spot. This was the storm grate the Street Thing had disappeared into. "Gotta do something." I untangled myself and fumbled in my bag. Yep, still had some Starbursts. I dropped a couple through the grate. I think I may have seen something move.

"What the fuck are you doing?" Taylor was shaking his head.

"An offering. It's good to make friends. It's like that old Gang of Four song. 'Make friends quick, buy them a beer!'"

Amy laughed. "I love Gang of Four!"

"You don't even know who Gang of Four is." Taylor tugged at her arm. "Let's go."

Amy tried to shrug him off. "'*The girls they love to see me shoot, the girls they love to see me shoot.*'" She was off-key and adorable, and I'd have fallen in love with her right then and there if I hadn't already done that years ago.

Taylor dropped her arm, and she swayed. "So there's something down there."

"Maybe," I said.

"There's a faerie down there."

"Maybe. Or maybe there's just rats." I grinned. "As above, so below."

"'*I love a man in a uniform. Shoot! Shoot!*'" Amy sang.

"I suppose next you'll be telling us that the gargoyles are alive, too," he said, pointing up.

"Don't be stupid," I began, and then stopped. The building next to us was host to dozens of gargoyles, winged and fanged, with clawed hands and feet whose talons gripped the stone with ease. They adorned the ledges under each row of windows. They were completely motionless. "They're just stone," I said. But I saw. Those eyes. Oh, yes, I saw.

Maybe if I hadn't been drunk, I'd have been fast enough to stop him. Of course, if I hadn't been drunk, I wouldn't have been telling anyone about faeries, and Taylor and I would still be pretending that we were friends.

He reached down and picked up his piece of brick. "Then nobody will mind this," he said, and heaved it at the closest gargoyle. It turned in the air as it flew, shattering as it hit the gargoyle's face. There was a moment when I dared hope we were safe. Fragments of brick showered us, getting in our hair and eyes, but the gargoyle appeared undamaged. Then stone lips curled into an angry grimace, and the air filled with dark grey shadow.

They dropped soundlessly, the air heavy with granite and cement. It was almost impossible to breathe, the air was so dense. I saw them move. I believed they could, and when they did, I knew what I was seeing. Maybe that's why I was able to duck and squirm and rip myself out of their grasp. Maybe that's why when Amy and Taylor were taken, screaming, I was left torn and bleeding, lying on the ground under the bumper of a parked car.

Or maybe that was just part of the game.

A few feet away, bottle-caps and cigarette butts stared at me out of the darkness.

"I'm sorry," I said.

They blinked and were gone.

I called cell phones, called the hotel, took a cold, sobering shower while mainlining a giant cup of coffee. Not enough Band-Aids to deal with the gouges on my arm and shoulder, so I tore up an old t-shirt and did the best I could.

Then I made more phone calls.

Still no answer from Amy and Taylor. Stephen texted me back, suggesting that I hurry if I want in on the fun. He, at least, was safe. But there was nothing I could do for Amy. Or Taylor.

God. I could still feel her arm linked with mine, her body pressing against mine as she swayed, as we dodged other people on the streets. She and Taylor weren't getting along.

I like your brand of crazy, she'd said.

She still loved me. How could I abandon that? How could I let that go?

Half an hour later I was standing in front of the gargoyle building, holding a lead pipe, staring at an unadorned edifice. Where the gargoyles had perched, only claw-prints remained, sunken into the stone. I think I screamed at the gargoyles, at the wall, at the heavens. At myself. And then darkness dropped from the sky.

I held the lead pipe like a baseball bat and waited. The gargoyle landed silently in front of me, out of range unless I leapt for him. It. It was smaller than I was, but I looked at two-inch fangs, ancient and rain-stained, looked at claws that dug holes in cement, and decided to maintain my distance.

It stretched its leatherstone wings, settled them against its back, and spoke. The sound tore through my marrow, a saw drawn across slate. "You seek something," it said. "Something precious to you."

"Yes." I didn't have to look to know the pipe was trembling in my hands. Formidable I was not. But I didn't wet myself. It's the small victories, right?

"Then you must ask." It grinned, revealing more teeth than I could have imagined, and malice more pure than I'd ever dreamed. So much for small victories. I don't think I noticed until later, though. "But choose your words wisely. Every question must have its answer, as every king must have his queen. A poor choice yields unpleasant consequences."

"Yes, sir," I said. I bit my lip. "Would you please bring Amy back to me?"

It smiled, almost kindly. "Of course." Bat wings stretched and the air thickened, pressing against my chest and throat and driving me to my knees. "We'll bring what's left when we come for you."

There should have been a sound as the immense wings beat against the soupy air, but there wasn't, and then the creature was gone. I could breathe again, and I retched and sobbed until I was empty.

Morning brought the sun punching through the inadequate shades of my easterly facing bedroom windows, burning in throbbing pulses past my sheltering arms and through my eyelids. I'd run home after the confrontation with the gargoyle, stripped and showered. This time instead of coffee, I brought a half-full bottle of tequila into the shower with me. I'm pretty sure that I'd made a significant dent on it before it slipped through my fingers and shattered in the tub. I cut myself less than I should have, and then started in on a bottle of cheap vodka that someone had been so kind as to leave at my house, leaving a trail of blood and water from the tub to the freezer. That one at least was safe. It came in a plastic bottle. I don't know how much of that I drank either. The uncapped bottle had spilled and soaked into the bed at some point in the night.

I buried my head under the pillow and wished for stellar cataclysm, but no such luck. Instead, there was a tap at my window. A minute later, again, something hit my window.

I'm on the third floor. People don't tap on my window. But still, there it was. A few times every minute, now. Insistent. I ignored it for as long as I could, and then I dragged myself out of bed and pulled the shade.

Three Starburst wrappers were stuck to the glass.

I rubbed salt and sleep and tequila and vodka out of my eyes and looked again. Still there. And outside, yes, the Street Thing, huddled inconspicuously between a trashcan and a signpost, watched me. It motioned somehow, and I waved to it.

I was out the door before I realized just how desperately I needed a cup of coffee. I stood there, blinded in the morning sun, while a small bundle of trash bounced against my leg.

"Coffee," I said. Inhuman eyes looked at me with confusion. "I need coffee to think."

The Street Thing rolled down the sidewalk, then clambered up the side of a trash can. It reappeared a minute later holding a coffee cup. It was a little stained and crumpled, about a third full, and not entirely cold. Not the time to refuse a gift. I tried not to think about what else might have been in the trash can, pulled the lid off and downed the contents, trying to minimize the amount of contact my lips had with the cup. It helped.

A couple waiting at the bus stop were staring at me. In retrospect, I wonder what it was they had seen happen. At the time, I didn't really care. The coffee was cold and nasty and full of what I needed. That's all that mattered.

The Street Thing started rolling off down the street and I followed. It took me down 22nd Street to Panama, down to 23rd and into Fitler Square, Center City's nigh-forgotten park. There it scurried toward the bushes near the statue of the ram. A handful of other Street Things waited there. They looked at me with a mixture of apprehension and curiosity.

"Hullo," I said. Then, feeling stupid but not knowing what else to do, I gave a small bow. There was a soft noise, like plastic grocery bags blowing in the wind. "Can you help me get Amy back from the gargoyles?" The noise repeated, and then the Street Things pressed into and under the bushes. The last of them, possibly the one I'd followed, motioned me to follow. I hoped no one saw me.

Safe under the cover of the bushes they spoke to me in their soft voices, voices that echoed the flutter of pigeon wings, the hiss of tires on wet roads, the click of high heels on concrete. And when they were finished talking, I knew exactly what I needed to do.

My quest took me to a place of stone and air. The Benjamin Franklin Bridge rose on massive granite anchorages. I entered through the riverside door at the base of the structure, popping the lock with the aid of a pry bar. I avoided people; sneaked down less traveled corridors, climbed many, many steps. Beyond the abandoned trolley station, I found my way to the base of the roadway and looked out at the exposed girders and cables. I took a deep breath. The street was easily a hundred feet below me. Somewhere ahead of me were dozens of gargoyles, and Amy. I slipped the pry bar under my belt—it would be useless against even one of these creatures, I knew, but how could it hurt?—and stepped out over empty space.

I've never been afraid of heights.

That didn't help.

I clung to the cable and tried to pretend that I was on a balance beam, that there was a sandbox just a few feet down. I tried to ignore the wind that tore at my clothes and made my eyes water, and told myself that it wasn't making the bridge sway. I tried not to flinch every time a truck drove overhead. After only a hundred feet or so, my hands began to ache and cramp from gripping the cable so tightly. Ahead, winged shapes adorned the underbelly of the bridge, so I forced myself to relax, shook out each hand in turn, and went on.

They watched, stone-grey eyes glittering.

I spotted Taylor first. He was dangling upside down over the river, left ankle held in immobile stone. He twisted in the wind and fought uselessly to get hold of something solid. Amy lay draped over a steel girder, motionless.

My breath caught, air viscous in my throat, as one of the gargoyles took flight and landed in front of me. Its talons gripped the beam as if they'd always been there.

"Impatient for your turn?" it asked.

"I've come to get Amy," I said, weak-kneed.

Taylor twisted to look at me. There was murder in his eyes. I looked away.

"You have had your chance," it hissed. "It is too late to save her."

"She's not already . . . ." I couldn't finish.

Its laugh nearly ripped me off the bridge. "Dead? Not yet, no. We haven't finished playing yet."

She was still breathing, I could see now.

"You said I had to ask a question, a good question."

"You have had your question."

"I have another. And how often do you get to play this game nowadays? When was the last time? This year? This decade? This century? People don't even notice you up there anymore, much less understand what you are. And if they did, what would they do? Bring out the rocket launchers, that's what."

Other gargoyles hissed and gibbered, and the bridge trembled under the weight of their speech.

"Yes," said the gargoyle. "You may ask again, for her life. But when you fail, we will keep you here, and you will watch us feed."

And so I began to speak, minding my words carefully. I told them the tale the Street Things had given me, wove the sentences into tapestry. No simple riddle, this. An epic of misdirection and false leads, clues buried under lies, truth tangled into frayed knots. I don't know how long I spoke. I wove elements of movies and novels, history and folklore into the tale, garnished it with bits of my own life.

And when my question, the Street Things' riddle made mine, rang into silence, I looked at the gargoyles expectantly. They were still as stone. Occasionally one would hiss something in their incomprehensible language and others would answer. And after an hour had passed, the gargoyle facing me stretched to its full height.

"It was a good question," it said.

I nodded, barely daring to believe. "So I can take Amy and go?"

"You would drop her. I will bring her."

"What about me?" Taylor was still dangling by one leg.

"What about him?" I asked.

"You didn't play for him."

I looked at Taylor, then back at the gargoyle. "I thought it was assumed."

Its laugh ripped through the air. "You may ask another question. If it is as good as the last one, he may go free. If not . . . then we keep the girl."

I couldn't look at Taylor. "Sorry, dude," I said.

He yelled at me as I turned to make my way back to land, cursed and screamed. "You'd do anything to get me out of the way!"

I spun abruptly, almost knocking myself off the bridge. "This whole thing is your fault," I said coldly. "You had to put me down in front of her, you had to go and throw a damned rock at a gargoyle and almost get us all killed. I'm sorry, it sucks, but it's not like you don't deserve it. And you never deserved her."

Amy was lying on my floor, still unconscious, when I got home. I washed the blood and grime from her face, checked her for any serious injury, and put her to bed. And as I watched her breathing softly under the covers, God help me, all I could think was that he was finally out of the way.

It's taken a bit of effort, what with the crutches. But I've finally made it back to Fitler Square.

I told the cops nothing, not when they found me, and not at the hospital. I just said I couldn't remember. Amnesia. I'd been bashed around enough that maybe they even believed it. But bruises would heal, cuts could be stitched, bones would mend, more or less. I'm not so sure about the rest.

She didn't come to see me at the hospital, didn't leave a note. I guess she's back in Seattle now. But she hasn't answered emails and I haven't dared call.

It's starting to get dark, and soon I won't be able to see what I'm writing.

I don't blame her. And I don't blame him for beating the snot out of me with a baseball bat. I never tried to save him. I never intended to try. Instead, I'd be there for Amy, there to comfort her in her time of need.

Who knew gargoyles had a sense of humor? The rules of the game said they couldn't come after me. Nothing said they couldn't let Taylor go, after I'd signed his death warrant.

Soon, I'll put this notebook away and unpack my backpack. I'll hobble to the row of bushes near the statue of the ram and get down on knees that'll never work quite right again, and I'll set out food and drink. And maybe the rats and pigeons will get it, or stray cats and dogs. Or maybe some homeless guy will stumble across it.

Or maybe the Street Things will feast tonight.

Days like these, it's good to know that somewhere, you have a friend.

Do You Believe?

C.J. Henderson

"Do you believe in faeries? Say quick that you believe. If you believe, clap your hands."

J.M. Barrie

C'MON, FELLAS," THE NEWSMAN SHOUTED PITIFULLY, "GIMME A break!"

It was the horrible sincerity the figure before him could muster, with his pitifully outstretched arms and quickly moistening eyes, that made the balding man grin so. Turning to his friends, he shuddered in mock horror, then asked;

"Well, what'daya think? Can we tolerate his presence?"

"I don't know," added another at the table, a tall, thin gentleman with intense blue eyes. "I do hate it so when his lower lip starts quivering."

"Did I mention," offered the newsman with practiced timing, "that the next round is, of course, on the network?"

"Now I could be seein' my way to forgivin' the lad his indiscretions," offered an aromatic type of extremely disreputable note. "Considerin' his warm proposal of a proper makin' of penance, as it were."

"Oh, good," chuckled the balding man, "now I'm in the dubious position of not only supportin' the local pariah, but also havin' it known that I agreed with Darby on somethin'."

Most who were gathered there that night got the joke. The newsman was Marv Richards, head anchor and main producer of *Challenge of the Unknown,* the only network news show dedicated to covering the strange and the supernatural. He was also one of the only media personalities ever to be allowed within the walls of the Narkane. On every world, there was one spot where all dimensions met. In some it appeared to be a marketplace; in some a temple; some a school. Often it was a library. Whatever the shade of a particular reality, however, that same set of square footage was always a place where people gathered, reverently, to engage in social discourse.

In the reality where they called the third planet from the yellow sun in their Sol system "the Earth," that spot was the Narkane, Manhattan's most exclusive nite spot, and a focusing point for all manner of things. It was known across the widest band of the dimensional spanway as quite possibly the most interesting club experience in the "Hip" universe. Within its walls, any two creatures, entities, or semi-mobilized philosophies could bump up against each other.

The Narkane was, of course, a natural haven for scoundrels determined to transport illicit goods across inter-dimensional boundaries. Which meant on any night there you might be rubbing elbows with smugglers bent on moving anything from Romulan ale to the square eggs of the Andes. In a nutshell, it was the ultimate Spe'keasy—a place where anyone and anything could take to the dance floor. Which was more than proved by the crew at table 15, who were finally waving Richards over.

The oldest was Professor Zackery Goward. Doctor of philosophy and theology, he had spent the better part of his life in the search for the strange and the bizarre. Paul Morcey, the balding man next to him, was not nearly as cultured as "the Doc," but, as a detective working out of the London Agency, he had come across enough of the strange and the bizarre to last most men several lifetimes. And completing the trio was one of the least reputable beings for miles around wherever he went. A storyteller known simply as Darby, he was the last word in "odious," the kind of person who made those rare strains of sentient toilet scum feel good about themselves.

As Richards turned the threesome into a quartet, he indicated to one of the bartenders that the table should be hit once all around by pointing to the claw hammer hanging above it. Sliding into one of the table's two vacant seats, his ears leaped into the conversation as Darby growled;

"Oh, auk now—it t'weren't so bad."

"Not so bad," sputtered Goward. "You had sex with a blind nun by telling her you were Jesus."

"Well and sure, now hasn't every young scamp played a merry prank or two in his time?"

"Yeah," drawled Morcey, grimacing as anyone would who had to admit to knowing Darby, "but you made a tape of the evenin' and sent it in to 'America's Most Embarrassing Videos.'"

"That was you?" All heads turned toward Richards. His eyes filling with admiration, he said, "They won Sweeps hands-down with that. Forced ad revenues up for their network three points. Nice work, dude."

"Sweet bride of the night," groaned Morcey. "Now we got two of 'em." The detective's mouth hung open a moment, as he listened to a chuckling Richards say;

"I'm telling you, oh, when you told her 'This is my body, take therefore of it and eat,' oh, oh my God . . . "

The anchorman broke down into hysterics at that point, first at the memory of Darby's carnal comedy, then at the pun of his own calling on the Almighty during that story. Pounding the table with his fist, waving his other hand, he choked out a few words—

"And then, then . . . oh, and then, when . . . when you blessed her with your 'holy water' . . . ahhahhahhahaha . . . "

And then fell into a tittering fit that left the professor and Morcey looking at each other askance, and Darby simply sitting back, enjoying his pipe. Richards was saved from death-by-fluster, however, in a timely fashion by the arrival of a medium-sized carnivore of some sort or another management had somehow stuffed into a tuxedo, which had brought the new round of drinks, including a Scotch for Richards, his usual, and a complementary bowl of house mix—a random mangerful of goodies in which one could find anything from Rasinettes and Crunchy Frog to golden apple chips or bits of the True Cross.

"So," said Goward, tossing a noncommittal fragment of conversation into the air, "it seems the theme tonight is something of an Art Deco by way of Kate Hepburn/Flash Gordon."

The others agreed. It was one of the more fascinating, yet subtle things about the club, the fact that the decor and design changed on an almost nightly basis. For instance, if Monday the band was blowing big band cool, Tuesday was just as likely to be a combination of jitterbugging and hip hop as it was to be superheroic polkas. The management had long before decided that the easiest way to keep any one faction from dominating the clientele policies was to maintain an ever-changing atmosphere. Thus, if Wednesday the universe's best Klezmer band was on stage, then Thursday might be Jazz James Bond Night, Geeks-Rule Eve, Barbie Nite, or who knew what.

"All right, fine—the decor is swell," responded Richards, never one to let an interesting conversational opener interfere with his primary objective of self-promotion, "but who's got something good for me?"

"Hey, Marv," answered Morcey, setting down his bourbon, "give it a rest, will you?"

"Com'on, you guys," the anchor pleaded. "It's a cold, cruel world out there. I've got my third season justification pitch coming up. I need something new. Something with a little pizzazz. Some kind of shambling creepie, or slinky hell babe—"

"Well, responded Morcey, grinning, "Truth told, I could go for a slinky hell babe myself."

"Yes, quite," said Goward. His fourth Rob Roy firmly in hand, he added, "what a provocative idea. Make that two, would you?"

"Go on, yuk it up," groaned Richards. "I'm still desperate here. Doesn't a finder's fee interest anyone anymore?"

"By the by," said Darby dryly, "I might have a tale you could spin them." Goward and Morcey turned with interest. Foul and repugnant and just downright cootie-a-fied as Darby was, there was no doubting that when it came to storytelling, he was the king of kings. Richards also flashed his interest at the lumpy Irishman, but his was powered by a need far more intense than the desire to be entertained. Turning the full intensity of his personality upon the storyteller, Richards signaled for a waiter while saying;

"Do tell? What kind of story?"

"Well now," answered Darby. "Have you ever heard tell of . . . the cockroach faeries?"

"Hey, that sounds grea—" the anchorman cut his cheer short as his hearing caught up with his enthusiasm. "What?"

"You heard me . . . the cockroach faeries. Do you know of them?"

"I've heard of faeries," said Morcey. "And bein' a New Yorker, it's obvious I know about roaches. But what do the two of them have to do with each other?"

"Let me pose a question," said Darby. Draining his glass as the waiter approached, he indicated he would like three more of the same, then said, "You're all men of substance. All of you over a hundred and fifty pounds, at least. Now, you tell me—is there a man among you who, in his time, that hasn't stepped on a roach, tryin' your best to eradicate the wee beastie's mortal existence?" All three of the others affirmed that they had.

"Of course you have. Now, tell me, how many times have you done so, to then lift your foot and watch the blessed thing run off with nary a harm done to it?" Again, all three affirmed that such was the case.

"I thought so," answered Darby. "That's because there are roaches in this world, and there are faeries—true is true. But the thing most have nary a clue over is the secret of the cockroach faeries."

As Darby downed a full-throated swig of his Baggins Brew Dark Ale, Harry Hausen, a skeleton in a tuxedo complete with top hat and spats, ambled out onto the Narkane stage to introduce the members of the band. Realizing this meant it was time to order a last rounds of drinks for the moment, the club's clientele went into an uproar, calling for everything from Pan-Galactic Gargle Fizzes to Cherry Rolling Rocks. Once the commotion died down, and the Narkane's All Cephalopod Dancers had taken to the stage to mambo to the haunting strains of Kip Bisseldorf and his Elegant Lads, Darby returned to his story.

"Now, as I was sayin' . . . the cockroach faeries . . . . Well, first you have to understand, I'm not tryin' to tell you that all cockroaches are faeries, or that all faeries are cockroaches. No. You see, a long time back, there was a group of faeries, the

Kel'derna, that, well, I hate to cast aspersions, but they were, shall we say, not appreciated amongst their own kind."

"Why's that?"

"They had what some judged to be, bad habits. They weren't as interested in helpin' kindly cobblers or paintin' rainbows as they were stealin' the milk from cows and runnin' away with human babies and the such."

"Faeries from the wrong side of town, like?"

"Oh, aye, Mr. Richards, that they were. And they caused the rest of the faerie community no end of trubble—that they did. Well now, it wasn't long before they weren't welcomed in any neighborhood, district, or region by any type of pixie, sprite, or other winged imp. Their brand was as unwelcome as an undertaker at a wedding. Why, they made the traveling Jews of the fourteenth century look like the Prodigal Son, they did."

Darby drained one of the various mugs before him, then hoisted another with a wonderfully smooth motion, as he continued.

"Now, it was around about the time of the Greeks—I mean, when they were the big kahunas, philosophically speaking—that things came to a boil for the Kel'derna. Gettin' a bit full of themselves, don't cha'know, they managed to upset just about every branch of the magical world. I mean, if you think the faeries were mad at them, oh and now, I'm tellin' you true as dew in the mornin', there wasn't a harpy, hydra, or demi-god that wouldn't swat one as soon as give 'em a glance at their sun dial. They were in it, sure'nd true."

"So that's when they turned into cockroaches?"

"Don't interrupt him," cautioned Morcey. "That'll just cost you more drinks."

And, indeed, the balding man was correct. Darby had the anchor signal another waiter who was given the order to simply start bringing random drinks of any type in any quantity to the table. Morcey smiled, saying;

"This ought to be good. I want to see you drink a mint julep right after a Coconut Pepper Zombie."

The storyteller's only response was to instruct the waiter to combine the drinks just mentioned in one pitcher, add a can of Foster's Lager, a raw egg, and two chicken bouillon cubes and to then bring it to the table with a stalk of celery he could use as a stirrer. As Goward turned a touch green, Darby continued telling the history of the cockroach faeries. And fascinating it turned out to be.

Over roughly the next forty-five minutes, while consuming an Eclipse, a Dubonnet Fizz, a Thunder, two Ninitchkas, a Bulldog, a Bronx Terrace, three Fallen Angels, two Pink Whiskers, and a small tub of Pousse Café, along, of course, with his initial special order, Darby told those assembled the remaining history of the Kel'derna.

Gathering all their remaining clansprites in the forests of Gaul, the outcast pixies debated as to how best protect themselves from a hostile world. The decision was made that the simplest way for them to survive was to disappear. The

Kel'derna would be no more. It was decided they would retreat back into the most inaccessible reaches of Gaul, and create a society for themselves alone. Impossible thoughts such as "hard work" and "moral responsibility" were bandied about, but the clan had brought such down upon themselves, and there was no getting around it.

Now at the time, the common cockroach was not the fearsome and hated creature it is today. A simple, sturdy survivor from prehistoric times, the Kel'derna began to breed them along specific lines. One thing, Darby emphasized, was the importance that they become both delicious and indestructible. If the creatures were to be the cows as well as the horses of the race, they would have to become tasty as well as sturdy.

The Kel'derna bred the race of cockroaches in secrecy for centuries, for both size and speed for when they would be used as steeds, as well as for their further applications after life. The clan increasingly enjoyed the taste of the cockroach, of that there was no denying, but they also found myriad other uses for them, as well. Their wings, especially, became not only shields, but the basic building blocks of Kel'dernian industry.

Homes were made from them, as well as boats, umbrellas, cutting edged tools, serving bowls, et cetera. The roach became marvelously useful to the Kel'dernian community, but their greatest use was yet to be discovered.

"Indeed," said Darby, his voice low and eyes glistening, "that moment dinna come until the Kel'derna had been breeding roaches for nearly a thousand years. By then, Gaul had been overrun with people, and as the Kel'dernian population was finally startin' to show a bit of an explosion, itself, it was decided that some of the younger, more adventurous of the clan might set out on their own. And, dinna they have the marvelous luck then that the Pope, in his infinite greed and deviltry, called at that time for the first of the Crusades."

Richards' hands flew through page after page of notes as the storyteller related how the movement of people out of the cold and damp north into the southlands and back again, over and over for the next few hundred years became the catalyst for the spread of roaches across the face of the world. Morcey and Goward looked at each other a trifle askance, but did not interrupt, wanting to see just where Darby was going with his tale.

And where he wanted to go proved interesting to both of them. As he told it, wanting to see the rest of the world, or at least some of its drier segments, the Kel'dernians decided to venture out from the protection of the dark wood. It was then, as they began to move about in the world at large once more, that they noticed the greater aversion humans had to their friends, the cockroaches, than they did other insects.

The reason, it was assumed, was the roaches' habit of invading the homes of man on a far more permanent basis than the occasional fly or bee that might wander in. Even ants always went home after they found what they wanted. But, the human reaction to roaches was so much greater than these that it was soon decided the Kel'derna would become as closely associated with their livestock as possible. Soon cloaks were added to the utilitarian function to which their cattle were put. The clan also soon began experimenting with a form of rudimentary genetics, breeding themselves to darker and darker shades.

Over the hundreds of years of the Crusades, the clan became more and more adept at mimicking their mounts. They learned to run across floors like them, run in wild circles to avoid destruction, and to vibrate at just the right frequency while standing still in a sudden burst of light so as to appear to be insects. Truth to tell, the secret the Kel'derna learned was the more they pushed their way into the homes of the aristocracy, the less people bothered to look at them.

"It's a sad commentary on folk, but it's true," Darby sighed, stirring a half keg of General Harrison's Egg Nog with his celery stalk, "We live in an age now where Kel'dernian magic has the world completely under its spell. You know as well as I do, some folks, as soon as they see a roach, why, they grow completely irrational, slammin' and bangin' away at the poor dears with anything at hand, while others go completely in the other direction and will turn the lights back out and just tip toe away."

"But, I don't get it," said Richards. His face showing his puzzlement clearly, he said, "When there aren't any faeries around, why do people get so upset over just simple roaches?"

"It's the magic—the magic that the Kel'dernians used to breed their roaches, it's in all of them now. The clan is in every city in the world; they still find it easier to live off what they can steal from human society. Even after spending near an entire millennia on their own, as soon as they came out into the world again . . . well, sigh—I guess it's just in their blood, the little devils. But as I was sayin', the magic they used to breed their roaches has infected the entire species. Now, people can't be around them without reactin' far different than they do with any other bug."

Darby sat back, taking a long swig of no one knew what. Morcey hooded his eyes and gave Goward a what-do-you-think look. The professor smiled, not quite knowing how to answer. Not noticing the non-verbal conversation on the other side of the table, Richards jerked his head back involuntarily once he realized the storyteller had finished his tale, and barked;

"That's it? That's the big story? I shelled out . . . " he did a quick bit of mental calculating, then shrieked, "nine hundred and eighty-five dollars just for *that?*"

"Did you be wanting' more?" As the anchorman's glare blasted its way across the table, Darby moved a bit in his seat, reaching inside his coat, saying;

"Auck, you TV people and your visuals. Well, mayhap this might be of some assistance."

Darby withdrew his hand from the moldering tatters of his overcoat, bits of thread and other debris clinging to it. Then, putting his loosely-closed fist down in the center of the table, he opened his fingers to reveal a large number of roaches.

Everyone else's immediate reaction was to grab his drink and move back a bit. Then, the previous conversation sinking in, they all leaned forward again to find they were not looking at roaches at all—or, at least, not merely roaches.

Several of the figures Darby had set to rest next to the table's candle and the wicker basket of half-eaten house mix were indeed roaches, but two were not. Richards leaned in even closer, at first not believing his eyes, then not believing his good fortune. Morcey and Goward leaned in as well, joining him in his former disbelief if not his latter joyfulness, for there on the table were two miniature human beings, faeries if either had ever seen one, but of a type they had never previously beheld.

Tall and thin, one male and one female, the pair were as brown as mahogany and as spiteful as an old testament deity. They wore helmets adorned with long antennae, vests, and cloaks made of cockroach wings, and leggings and boots fashioned from some other part of roachian anatomy no one wished to question. Two of the roaches that had been set down along with them stood calmly aside their masters, obviously outfitted with saddles and reins. Rubbing his eyes, Richards stammered;

"But, but . . . I can see everything so clearly. When they're in my kitchen, I only see . . . I mean—"

"Ah, an' that's easy to explain," answered Darby casually. "When you snap on a light and you see one of these fellows, your mind thinks 'roach,' and so that's what you see. But, now that you know what you're looking at, well, you see what you know. You know?"

The anchorman nodded absently, his eyes studying the two figures on the table with a growing fascination. He asked a score more questions, but everything Darby told him about the Kel'derna only made him more and more desperate to take the two pixies away with him that night. Finally, they made a deal for a figure that choked the working stiffs at the table. After the storyteller and Richards shook hands, however, Darby added;

"Of course, this is all moot if the Kel'derna won't go with you."

"Go with me?" questioned the anchor. "I thought they were, I don't know, pets, or something."

As tiny hands went for their swords, Darby leaned forward quickly, shaking his hands and speaking in a bastardized elven dialect that hurt the ears. After making Richards' apologizes for him, then calling for another round of too-many-drinks, this time including a set of thimbles so the Kel'dernians could help themselves, the storyteller asked;

"So, what say you two? You've been with me a while, and there's all the fun in that, but this fellow, now . . . he wants to put you on the tellie. What do you say . . . would you like to be exploited for ratings?"

"Did I mention," offered the newsman with practiced timing, "that practically anything you might want is, of course, on the network?"

The offer brought a chorus of high-pitched giggles that seemed to delight Richards and Darby equally. Indeed, negotiations went so swimmingly after that point that it was but a matter of seven minutes before the anchor was on his way to the front door with his new stars, and Darby was signaling furiously for a waiter.

"That was a remarkable bit of history, Mr. Darby," offered Goward as a waiter approached. The storyteller asked for a heavy-duty first aid kit then responded to the professor.

"What, oh, heh heh, sorry, but you might not want to be repeatin' any of that for one of your classes."

Morcey groaned, pulling a hand down over his face as he said, "Owwwww, suckered again."

"Now, now," said Darby as he removed a great wad of blood-soaked linen from beneath his coat, "it was just a harmless bit of fun either of you might have pulled. I mean, well and sure, now hasn't every young scamp played a merry prank or two in his time?"

"You mean to say, sir, that there are no cockroach faeries?"

"There are," said Darby with assurance. "Two, to be exact. Fred and Maxine, and you just met them, may the devil take their hindquarters, the ungrateful little bas—"

Morcey started to laugh as the waiter returned with the first aid kit. In moments, Darby was washing out his left arm pit with hydrogen peroxide while the waiter prepared to sew shut the ragged holes in his arm still dripping blood and loose bits of flesh. While the storyteller groaned at the first threading puncture, he explained;

"I might have promised the two of them a place to stay after a Halloween party a couple of years back. They went as cockroaches. I lost some sort of bet. I can't be too certain of the details, all I know is after drinkin' perhaps a wee bit too much, I woke up with those two livin' in me armpit, and no way in hell of gettin' them out except comin' up with a better deal for them."

"So," said Goward, his knuckles turning white as he unconsciously gripped the stem of his Rob Roy far too tightly, "you're telling us that for several . . . years, *years* . . . you've had a small horde of cockroaches and faeries . . . livin' in your armpit?"

Darby nodded sadly, pleading that anyone can get himself into a spot of trouble now and again. The waiter bit off the last piece of thread knotting closed the last of the wounds in the storyteller's arm. Gathering up his kit, he removed it, along with twenty-some of the empty glasses, mugs, and thimbles, the emptied house mix basket, and the remaining roaches. As he left, Goward sighed;

"I'm sorry to hear the tale was a fiction. It did explain a great deal about cockroaches. I've always sworn the damnable things were magic on some level or another."

"Oh," responded Darby absently as he tested his arm, "but they are. Dinna you know? It was one of the outer gods or the other, created them just to cause trouble, it did."

"Do tell . . . "

Darby looked up, discovering Morcey and Goward looking at him with interest. Finding his arm reasonably repaired, the storyteller told them;

"Oh, indeed. What a tale I could tell you, if it t'weren't for my terrible thirst . . . "

The two men looked at each other for a moment, shrugged, and then signaled for a waiter while Darby said;

"It was the Daemon Sultan, itself, the primal chaos men say sits in its court at the center of the universe . . . "

And, while his story went on, drinks were served, vampires mingled with insurance salesmen, faeries stole mints from the bowls at the bar, and cephalopods danced, as they did every night at the Narkane.

Final Stand

Brian Koscienski & Chris Pisano

HIS FIST CONNECTED WITH MY JAW. I DIDN'T EVEN SEE IT COMING. I felt nothing and everything; the punch happened so fast I didn't feel it, but I knew where all four of his knuckles hit, from just under my nose to the bottom of my jaw. I tried to roll with the punch, pursed my lips for extra protection, but he knocked two of my teeth out anyway.

I hit the ground hard, shoulder first. I spat out my teeth with a glob of blood; swallowing them would be the only way to make this situation worse. Throbbing ruptures of electricity pulsed from the newly emptied sockets through my skull to my right eye. It watered uncontrollably. I knew this was going to hurt, but dear God!

Cheering. I heard the crowd chant his name. Well, two thirds of the crowd, anyway. Luckily, his hubris distracted him from me, forcing him to laugh and wave at his fans. I'd take any time I could to catch my breath. Prepare myself for the next punch. Think of my son and daughter.

My boy was only three, my girl just one year old, when they came. Those winged devils, death-bringers of hatred. The Fae. The Faeries. The war lasted four years, consumed all of Earth, and left humanity completely enslaved.

I remembered that day with the same vividness of a knee-shaking vomit. My daughter's first birthday. I held her in my arms, soaking in every moment, every giggle, every smell. The personification of love. Then they attacked.

I learned that day other dimensions were real, because that was where the Fae came from. They tore a hole between our reality and theirs, flooding our world with wings and weapons and pet monsters.

They also brought with them their lust for conquest. And none liked to do so more than Akilay, their greatest warrior, the one who just punched me in the face.

Taking enough time to collect my thoughts, I stood. If only I had a better plan! The surrounding crowd displayed mixed reactions. Many laughed and whooped, most cheered and chanted Akilay's name. Not the humans, though. I heard their silence. Twenty thousand still tongues. Their closed lips cried out with hopelessness, ground down into submission, feeling like nothing more than crushed sand on a scorched beach. They had seen this before and knew very well what the outcome would be.

I held my fists in front of my face, classic boxing style, but little good that did. With buzzing wings, Akilay flew to me like a missile. His left fist connected with my gut, forcing all the air out of my lungs. Doing a midair pirouette, he backhanded my head with the force of a runaway train. My neck hurt from just trying to keep my skull attached to my body. I writhed on the ground, my body spasming from trying to remember how to breathe while doing anything to get away from my attacker. Blurry vision and the taste of blood consumed my world. The same way the Fae consumed Earth.

Confident and by surprise, they appeared from nowhere, attacked all parts of the globe, and disappeared. They did this every day for the first year, weakening all militaries the world over each time. The good news was world peace resulted. The bad news was the limited time to celebrate it. The greatest scientific and military minds collaborated in trying to find the doorways to their world, predict where they would appear next, or create one of our own. Again, that was all for naught. When the Fae opened the doorways one final time, we had nothing left. And they were just getting started.

Dragons blotted out the skies like sticky ash from angry volcanoes. No airplane or helicopter stood a chance; they simply cracked and discarded them like broken toys. The heaviest tanks from every corner of the Earth were ground under the thunderous heels of trolls. The sick beasts laughed with each twist of metal. Monsters with snapping jaws and slicing claws roamed the lands, invading every country no matter how sparse the population, stopping for nothing other than their masters' commands. And their masters commanded them to stop very infrequently. We had speed and dexterity, but they had numbers. Endless numbers.

We resembled them without wings, making us one rung lower on the evolutionary ladder, and they enjoyed celebrating that fact, mocking us for not being quite perfect, and sodomizing our souls for their pleasures. Men sturdy enough to stand fought for their amusement while those who couldn't joined the children and elderly enduring back-breaking labor, while women . . . women had it worse, reduced to meat, playthings at best.

The Fae stayed in our world to push our faces in the dirt with their heels not only because our suffering amused them, but because they had been here before.

And they wanted revenge. The stories, the books and tales, movies and whatever form of media spun a yarn about faeries were true. All true. The Fae invaded us before, thousands of years prior. Yet somehow we repelled them, shoved them back into the dimension from which they came and sealed it shut! But they returned like a revenant disease. All those faerie stories were supposed to be cautionary tales, hidden within them the answers, the magic to thwart our enemy.

When I stepped into the arena for this battle, I was adorned in cheap armor, and given a flimsy shield and bent sword. Akilay's golden armor glistened in the sunlight, making him look like the god he mimicked, like he wanted us humans to believe him to be. He had no use for a shield, but his sword, long and thin like him, blazed with blue licks of fire. At first, the humans were silent, most averting their eyes so they wouldn't have to bear witness. But then I did something to make them look. I dropped my weapons and stripped.

After seeing enough of these events, I knew they would be useless. And if I were going to be a martyr, I had to make sure I did it the right way. So, there I stood, naked and unarmed. The arena fell silent, dead silent. Fae and human alike, no one could comprehend what they saw. Then I raised my fists, showing him I was still willing to fight. The Fae crowd erupted with laughter.

Akilay laughed as well, even displayed great theatrics as he wiped a tear from his eye. Still smiling, he raised his sword above his head and beat his wings. He charged forth, and I didn't move, didn't budge. The closer he came, the higher he raised his sword and adjusted his muscles to cleave me in half. But I stopped him with one word.

"Weak."

The sword sliced downward, but stopped short of my skull. Drops of liquid fire splashed my forehead and cheeks. The searing ate holes in my skin; the smell of burning flesh was worse than the pain.

That split second of time was worth it; I knew it would be. Confident eyes turned confused. The din of the crowd quieted once again. I had him, and I told him why with one word. There would be no parades for him, no adulation from even his own kind, had he split an unarmed man in two. He sneered through clenched teeth as he dropped his feet to the ground. I didn't blink. Then, his smile returned, telling me that he would enjoy tearing me apart with his bare hands. He dropped his sword and undid his armor. Then his fist connected with my jaw so fast that I didn't even see it coming.

There Akilay floated, his wings abuzz, hands clasped together over his head in celebration. My vision cleared enough to see that. I could breathe again, and I thanked every god I could think of. The Fae crowd cheered and chanted while the human crowd . . . the human crowd finally stirred, sensing this battle would be different than any other. There was only one thing I could do.

I stood.

Gasps echoed through the stadium. The Fae could not believe my audacity, my blatant disrespect. The humans gasped because my actions only egged him on, ensuring more pain for myself.

And the pain came.

Anger turned Akilay's azure eyes murky, storming with diabolical emotions. He became a buzzing missile, punches and kicks smashing into all parts of my body. I used both arms to guard my head and crouched to protect the rest of my body, to little avail. His fists were like rockets ripping through wooden palisades. Frustration must have consumed him; he pulled my left hand from my face then, with a blinding chop, snapped my elbow the wrong way. My tearing skin and shredding muscles did nothing to muffle the sounds of my bones cracking. With an equally fast kick, he did the same to my left knee. I fell again, not prone, but near enough. The left side of my body became shattered glass wrapped in wet cardboard. My right side bore my weight as fire charred my guts with every move.

Akilay spat on me, and then turned his back to face the crowds. The gasps disappeared, replaced once again by cheers from his kind.

I leaned forward and placed my forehead on the dirt wet with my blood, so I could dry heave unnoticed. My stomach cramped from the pain until I could barely inhale. Each exhale brought ruddy strings of mucus and spittle. I couldn't help but smile, though. I had lasted longer than any human in the arena.

The Fae were smart creatures. When they came, they learned about our world, read our history books, understood us. And used it against us. Used our very own arenas against us.

They started with our Presidents, Prime Ministers, and kings, ripping our hearts out by having our leaders slaughtered in fair competition. Then they stole our souls by taking our athletes, our strongest and fastest, and reducing them to corpses. Keeping us weak, mentally and physically, they set regularly televised gladiatorial games where the only people left to compete were regular people like myself. I joined the circuit after the Fae claimed my wife. There were benefits, though. I lived in a small community where no harm befell my remaining family. My children were why I willingly challenged Akilay. Why I was on the ground with a broken arm and leg.

I finally got my breathing under control. Well, as best I could. I disallowed myself to look at my left side, knowing very well if I saw the impossible angles of my limbs I might go into shock. Tears streamed down my face as I recalled the twinkle in my son's eyes and the brilliance of my daughter's smile. My muscles wanted to reject my commands, but I forced them to obey me anyway.

I stood.

One third of the crowd cheered. My third. My people. I bent my right leg a bit to adjust my balance. My functioning hand curled into a fist and took its position, guarding my face. One third of the crowd rose to their feet.

Akilay lost patience, but not control. I could only withstand three quick blows before I dropped back to the ground. Again, I crouched, balancing on my right hand and knee. I still refused to even acknowledge the left half of my body. The humans no longer cheered, but I heard random clapping and the occasional voice encouraging me, begging for hope.

Hope was all we had left. Rumors and rumblings made their way all though the gladiatorial community. Our numbers were always replenished whenever they dwindled; those lost to the games replaced like inventory. Word came in every day of rebellions, underground movements hoarding scientists, procuring and maintaining whatever supplies they could find to research and discover the secret to sending these demons back to the Hell that spawned them. The rumors slowed. Once every two days we would receive news. Then once a week. Soon, the newest members of our fold brought no news from the outside. They brought no hope with them. I knew what I had to do. I knew my purpose was to be right here, right now. If I could stand up to our oppressors, others could as well. The rebellions would continue. The magic necessary to send the Fae back would be learned.

Although my body begged for me to be any other place than right here, right now. Still on my hand and knee, I panted and wheezed like a cornered cur. Then I saw my opportunity, my chance to turn the world around, to bring hope. So furious at his pugnacious opponent, Akilay paced around me. He *walked* around me!

Taking advantage of his one mistake, I lurched forward, pulling my hand from the ground to my shoulder. I drove the full weight of my falling body into my elbow, into his foot. I did no physical harm. But the blow to his ego would scar him for the remainder of his years. The sound of the human crowd exploded into one unifying cheer that would haunt his nightmares. Disgusted, he immediately took flight, then swooped in to kick me square in the gut with such force I spun through the air before landing on my left side. He was on me before I even stopped rolling, pummeling my face, grounding it into the dirt. He stopped when the humans stopped cheering.

I could no longer see out of my right eye. I had no idea if it was swollen shut, or if it was simply no longer inside my skull. Lightning crackled through my face. I coughed and saw a dozen teeth fall to the ground in a steady stream of blood. My breathing turned into painful choking, gargling until I coughed out blood to clear my esophagus. My fingers sank into the ensanguined mud. I pushed. I pushed past it. Because I could *not* stop until I knew I had won.

I stood.

The arena trembled with voices shouting and hollering. Humanity cheered me on. Although I knew it was purely delusional, I heard the *world* chant my name. Akilay attacked again. But this time as his blows rained upon me, I heard the crowd—the humans in the crowd—getting louder. I was *winning*.

The crowd cheered for me, but their voices faded from my mind. All I heard was just one person saying one word, the most powerful word I had ever heard in my life.

"Daddy."

For my son, did this. I wanted him free of this stadium, this arena of death. And for my daughter, I fought. As soon as she was old enough, those winged bastards would take her and . . . they'd use her for . . . NO! Damn it, no! I couldn't . . . I couldn't let them . . . I had to . . . I had to . . . *move!* Fight through this! Get up!

I stood.

I did it. I won. Akilay lost control. He picked up his sword and flew toward me. I heard the pure outrage in my people's voices. The walls of Jericho would crumble to give way to hope, I made sure of that. Smiling, I clenched my fist and held it pugilist style in front of my face as I made my last stand . . . .

Within the Guardian Bell

Danielle Ackley-McPhail

SUZANNE WAS WORRIED. VERY WORRIED. LANCE HAD NEVER FELT so much anxiety from a fae as what flowed through her now. Even though the pillion pad behind him was empty, Lance could feel her clinging to his right arm. Sparing a fleeting glance from the road, he looked down to where the black muscle shirt left his arm bare. The tattoo image of his lady had shifted as only magic could allow. A link to her soul, tied to his empathic gift, the tat reflected whatever Suzanne was feeling. Right now the skin art hid itself between his arm and the curve of his chest, all four limbs wrapped around his biceps as if it were a lifeline. It was the closest he'd ever seen Suzanne get to being clingy.

She might have been seamlessly healed after their encounter with the *Dubh Fae*, but her spirit bore the scars absent from her body. She worried about him, because the Faerie Court had decided he, a Halfling, was too much threat to let be. They'd hurt her to get to him, and she still wasn't over it.

Neither was he.

It left him raw and sent him raging if he thought on it too long. This was the first time he'd left her side since he and the Club rode to her rescue a week ago. It couldn't be helped . . . club business that couldn't be put off, but she wasn't handling the separation well.

Again: neither was he.

That was the reason his fool ass was out here, without gear, in weather even a SQUID would have more sense than to ride in. His teeth ground against one another as he revved his '47 Knucklehead.

His business done, he now raced back to Delilah's, where Suzanne waited for him, reasonably safe and surrounded by the other members of the club. He had to keep telling himself that. Though mindspeaking was not one of his gifts, Lance thought real hard at her. *I'm coming, babe. I'm coming.*

The power of his engine thrummed through him, making him one with leather and chrome and steel. If he listened real close, he almost dare believe he could hear a mad tinkling as Suzanne's latest gift, a tiny pewter guardian bell she'd attached to his swing arm, was buffeted in the wake of his speed. Whether it was truly audible or not, he could certainly sense its magic, subtly flavored by Suzanne's special touch.

Behind him, the hiss of four wheels on wet pavement blended with the muted rumble of some cager's engine, a reminder he had to keep his mind on the slab. He wasn't riding Front Door right now, with the club strung out behind him, and any biker going solo had to watch his own back.

As if to reinforce his thoughts, a Q-Tip in an equally ancient Buick passed too close on his left, sending him swerving toward a rainbow-covered puddle.

"Ah, crap!" Lance swore as his tires hit the slick and lost their grip on the road. The Knucklehead dipped sideways, surely setting the bell to ring wildly. His stomach clenched hard until he brought the bike vertical once more.

"Get some glasses or give up the license, Grandma!" he yelled after the oblivious old woman.

He fought the skid and won, but it was close. When he got back, he'd be sure to tell Suzanne how well her gift had protected him. Mostly potholes lurked in puddles these days. Helmet or no, hit one of those in this weather and he'd earn himself another set of broken wings. *That settles it,* he thought, *time to get off the road a while.* A quick glance down at his gas gauge confirmed it was time for a fluid exchange, anyway. Lance moved into the Bike Lane, triggering a string of horn blasts from the cagers to either side as he passed them by.

As the biker rode away down the center of the road, the puddle bubbled and seethed. Up from its shallow depth popped an odd, tiny creature, clutching at its ears. "Smear doesn't like the faerie-man. Not at all. Or his bloody little shrill bell. Smear wants to grind his face, crush the bell." Crouched upon the road, he slammed his thick, meaty fists against the asphalt. Microfissures formed: the conception of a pothole.

He was joined by another, and then another, crawling up through the fissures, expanding them, until the puddle was gone. Standing in its place was a troupe of inch-high gremlins, identical in every way: Skin as grey as asphalt, with an oily, rainbow shimmer. Hair long and thick and spiny, like a porcupine mated with a box of nails. A thick white line ran down the center of their faces, like war paint, and along their arms were thick, black squiggles. Like tats or tribal markings, only with the dull gleam of tar snakes. Each finger was like a spike, reminiscent of those found at toll booths and security gates, only jointed. The miniscule troupe rumbled and grumbled as they watched the bike speed away.

"Smear doesn't like him, wants to snap his bones, crumble a fender," one of them muttered. "Smear doesn't like him, wants to bash his head, crack the tranny," added another. Each of them offered up a world of pain they planned to inflict upon the biker and his cycle; each of them punctuated their threat by pounding upon the blacktop, splitting it further.

Why do you wait? a lethal voice hissed in each of their heads. It was beautiful and horrible all at once, leaving them as cold as icebound pavement. *He escapes you!*

"Why? Why? Smear doesn't wait! We go! King-fae says we can; says we must. Smear listens," they vowed in one voice. "But King should know, biker's been belled."

Go, now! I will take care of the bell, the King's voice answered.

Cackling with as sound of shattering windshield, one gremlin grabbed the next, each of them melding until there was but one the size of a particularly ugly cabbage patch doll. It crouched upon the roadway as a Mustang went zooming by. With supernatural precision Smear reached out, his spiky digits piercing vulcanized rubber as if it were water. Swinging up, he perched on the rim of the wheel, his fingers still in place. It wouldn't do to have the ride spin out . . . until after Smear reached his target, anyway.

As they sped away, the only sign the gremlins had been there was a scattering of nail-like spines and the crumbling edges of a pothole just waiting for the next car to come along.

The rain had settled down to a pissy mist by the time Lance pulled into the truck stop and right up to the pumps. Kicking down the stand, he shed his helmet, setting it on the saddle as he got off the bike. In minutes, he'd topped off both his gas tank and the reserve and headed inside. With the rain letting up, he didn't want to stop long, just enough to fill up and drain.

"What'll you have?" asked the hot, young mattress cover masquerading as a waitress. Lance kept his expression neutral as she gave him the once-over, making it clear she was offering a bit of distraction along with what was on the menu. She was good. He could practically feel her gaze running from his segmented ponytail clear down to his ass. Too bad he could also feel the ribbon of hatred spiraling through her. One of the benefits of being an empath . . . .

He'd never even seen her before, so what was her hang-up? He might have suspected she was a part of the *Dubh Fae's* crowd, gunning for the Halfling, only he couldn't sense anything fae about her. Anyway, not that it mattered.

"Just a cup of joe to go," he answered. "And the way to the john?" She acted disappointed on the surface, but not very surprised, as she pointed down the hall.

By the time he came back, the coffee was waiting, and the waitress was nowhere in sight. Lance threw down a couple of singles and headed out without the cup. He didn't know what her issue was, but he wasn't about to trust anything she poured out of his sight. At the very least, she was likely to have spat in it.

Nearing his ride, he discovered where she went. He stalked up behind her, more silent than could be imagined given his leathers and biker boots, and cleared his throat.

"Oh!" She spun around. Her hand slid into her apron pocket while her eyes shifted to the side as if looking for where to run. Instead she laughed, slipped on that fake invitation smile, and let her eyes roam over him once more. "I just had to come out for a closer look. Nice ride."

"My old lady likes to think so," Lance let a bit of steel creep into his voice. "Now, how about stepping away from it."

Again that flash of hatred deep in her eyes.

Before she could say a word, a couple of drivers came strolling out of the truck stop. "Hey, Jolene, Mac's lookin' for ya," one of them called out. With a huff, Jolene hurried away, her eyes slicing across Lance in a much different manner than moments before.

"Whack job," he murmured as he inspected his scoot. Everything seemed in order. He couldn't find anything that she might have disturbed in the short time she had alone with the bike. Even the bell was still in place. Dismissing the episode from his thoughts as just one more example of everyday craziness, Lance pulled out his cell phone and hit the speed dial for Suzanne's brother, Gavin.

"Hey, bro," he said as his best friend and lieutenant answered. "Just checking in. I'm about half an hour out . . . . No, everything's fine, just some road-trouble this trip, it seems. Tell Suzanne I'll be there soon."

He flipped the phone closed and slipped it in his pocket. Adjusting his helmet the best he could, he swung onto the bike and gunned it out of there loud enough he couldn't hear the bell.

Faerie-man was coming!

Not far past the truck stop, Smear released his grip on the wheel where he'd hitched, letting the spikes shred the treads as they pulled away from the rubber. As he flipped himself to the ground, there was a *pop*, and the tire blew, followed by the crunch of crumpled metal. Not as glorious as Smear would like; just a bit of bent steel and a bumped head, no blood or flame or final breath. Several Smears broke away from the whole and, despite all reason and their one-inch size, they shoved the 'Stang out of sight of the road before scampering back to meld once more.

"Faerie-man, crunch your head, hose your ride," the gremlin chanted. "Dance in your blood and wear your stupid bell as a hat."

Continuing to mutter, Smear stalked to the center of the road, called every bit of Smear from every crack and crevice, every slick spot and crumpled zone. As they rallied forth like blowflies to roadkill, the gremlin beefed up, absorbing all that came until he was the size of a pitbull, and then a rottweiler. He stood there in fine fae challenge, idly whirling a bit of chain swept up from the side of the road.

The roar of the cycle drew near and Smear crouched at the ready, blending with the asphalt like a chameleon on a log. Only a chameleon never had such teeth.

Lance throttled down. His head went up, and his muscles went taut. If he used Jolene's hatred as a baseline, what he sensed now was off the charts. He strained his senses trying to pinpoint it, but things were a bit weird now that he was more fae than human, rather than the other way around. He had Gavin to thank for that. He still didn't know if he should thank him, or redesign his anatomy. Ever since his friend had sabotaged his shields while they were fighting the *Dubh Fae*, things hadn't been quite right. Of course, Lance would have never survived the encounter otherwise, but from time to time he lost that fine empathic control he used to have, and that just pissed him off.

Anyway, if he believed what he felt right now, he was surrounded by an entire roadbed of people who hated him . . . only they were all invisible.

Yeah, not totally impossible . . . he should know . . . but frankly the only people that hated him that bad were all fae, and he could always sense them. Right now, all he sensed was the road and the hate.

Taking it slow, he kept going. Just in case his empathy wasn't screwy, he took a deep breath and started drawing magic to him slow and easy. It was a new sensation for him. He had to fight the thrill of it filling him up, the feel of his shoulder fins expanding, the crackle of the magic trailing from those fins as they rose through the slits in his muscle shirt and formed his wings. Man, he could *almost* sympathize with the 1%ers that indulged in meth. If it felt anything like this, it was no wonder the addiction was damn hard to shake.

Ready to blast whatever came at him, Lance rounded the bend. Still he could see no source of the hatred. The road was smooth and bare. Writing it off as his body still adjusting to recent changes, he started to open up the throttle. This close to home he had no interest in taking it slow.

Out of nowhere, the wind rose, sounding like ground glass and a cackle mixed in a blender. The Knucklehead hit a bump camouflaged by the roadway. Again the front wheel threatened to skid. Lance growled and fought it back, only to hit another on the other side.

All around him the wind both whispered and howled.

Goin' down, faerie-man, crunch your head, shred your wings.
Goin' down, faerie-man, spill your gut, blow your gasket.
Goin' down, faerie-man, skin nothin' but rash, bike nothin' but trash.
Goin' down . . . goin' down . . . goin' down . . . .

"What the hell?!" Lance swore. There was nothing around but him, the wind, and the road . . . . So what was the deal with the voices in his head? Mindhearing wasn't one of his gifts any more than mindspeaking was. His lip twisted in a snarl and his brow dipped low, as he opened up the throttle all the way, ready to power through the creeped out stretch of road.

What was that Irish blessing . . . .

Oh . . . yeah . . . *May the road rise up to meet your feet* . . . . Someone needed to tell them that wasn't necessarily a good thing.

Before his eyes, the road rucked up in front of him. Malice met his gaze from bright red eyes glowing like lit brake lights. A chain whirled idly in the creature's hands. Any moment Lance expected the links to fling out, tangling in his rims. Maybe that was why he wasn't quite ready when it dropped to the asphalt, and what could only be a road gremlin incarnate launched itself straight for him.

Yeah, there was that hatred loud and clear now. It still streamed from all around, but that made sense; Lance was surrounded by nothing but road . . . and gremlin.

"Bring it on, skidmark," Lance sneered. He had faith in the bell, knew it's magic firsthand; its specific purpose was to ward off gremlins and trap those already in residence on any bike. And as it was a gift from Suzanne, who loved him, its power was double-potent.

Besides, new to it or not, his own magic evened things a bit.

Goin' down, faerie-man . . . .

" . . . Yeah, right!"

Even as he watched, his cycle collided with the creature. His windshield snapped and the gremlin shattered into countless pieces. Each one grimaced with hatred, tried to stare him down with light-bright eyes. Only they didn't fall away.

They cackled and again he heard the grind of shattered glass on the wind. It was then he realized he couldn't sense the bell. The swiftest of glances confirmed it was still there, but the clapper was silent. Then he remembered Jolene, crouched by his bike, and he cursed with enough venom to put a goblin to shame.

Goin' down, faerie-man . . . crack your balls like a walnut, crumple your pipes real good . . . chew up your bloody bell into itty bitty bits.

One of the buggers chomped on his ear; another slammed a fist full of spikes through his engine block. The others followed suit, in one manner or another attacking him or the Knucklehead. Lance snarled and fought to keep the bike stable while smacking the creatures away. But there were too many of them. He could feel the bike start to fail; smell fluids he ought not to have been able to smell . . . both his own and the bike's.

Tearing one of the creatures from his neck, Lance roared and slammed the bike into a skid, laying her down on the road, scraping dozens of the gremlins off as he surfed the asphalt. Both his wings and the cycle sent up sparks. There were little puffs of acrid smoke where the gremlin bits got caught by either. There was some satisfaction in that, but there were too many of them left for it to count. He leapt to his feet, leaving behind a good bit of both leather and skin, but snatched up his bell and pocketed it.

Goin' down, faerie-man, goin' down right now, put you out like a candle.

"Come on and try it, slick," Lance growled. "You look like you could use a tune up."

The gremlins hissed at him as they gang-banged back into one mass. He could see its bulbous nose twitch and its finger spikes flex. It stalked forward now, roughly the size of a bull mastiff, only much uglier.

Lance's wings crackled behind him as he lashed out a side kick at his adversary. The kick sent the creature flying, slammed it right into the downed bike. He winced at the added damage; the gremlin, on the other hand, exploded back into a thousand smaller selves. They scrambled to meld together as Lance stalked forward and brought the heavy tread of his biker boot down on a choice few of them, leaving nothing but smears on the pavement. But there were still too many and he already faced a once-more unified foe.

Bloody bells! Bloody biker! Smear smash 'em and crash 'em and leave 'em in bits!

The gremlin fairly frothed as it spat and cursed. It also gave itself away. Lance knew what to do. He dropped the creature again with another kick, but this time, the gremlin anticipated the strike and mostly kept itself together. While it was distracted reabsorbing the few bits that popped loose, Lance drew out the bell.

With a vicious grin, he held it up high, dangling a silent threat. But was it an empty one? Lance could see the clapper was gone, hastily ripped out by the bitch at the truck stop.

Still . . . nothing that couldn't be overcome . . . for him, anyway. Drawing a bit of magic to his fingertip, he drew it down the slope of the bell. There was a subtle hum that turned Lance's grin wolfish. In his thoughts, he pictured a clapper of pure, hard light. The more he focused the more solid it became, and for a fraction of a second, the creature missed a step.

No! Turn you to pizza, tear you to shreds, crush the fucking bell like a bug!

The gremlin's raging took on a frantic edge as it launched itself at his hand, spikes extended as if to slice the bell to bits. With a laugh that any member of the club would have known to back away from, Lance sent the bell ringing right in the gremlin's face.

Once in flight, the gremlin had no hope of avoiding the hollow. Caught fast by the clapper, every bit of the creature disappeared within the depths of the tiny bell. It rang even more, frantically swinging as the gremlin fought his new prison.

Nothing escaped the bell but sound.

Lance smiled and gave it a little shake of his own . . . not even minding that it rang with a new tone, like screeching metal against metal. It was a delight to his ears, actually. With a sadistic grin he reattached it to the swing arm and righted his battered bike. Propping it up, he pulled out his cell phone, hitting speed dial as he flipped it open.

"Yeah, Delilah . . . . I need you to send out the Wrench."

The Seelie Seven

Lee C. Hillman

"ALL RIGHT, YOU MISERABLE CHANGELING-SPAWN CHUCKLEHEADS," the Sergeant-Major barked, "you all know why you're here. You're each facing eternal fire—condemned to pay the Teind because of crimes you've committed against the Court.

"You've got one chance to save your worthless hides: Serve with distinction on this mission, and Her Majesty might just see fit to pardon you."

Robin leaned over to Spike, standing next to her. She muttered through tight lips, "Didn't you rent this movie a couple years ago?"

"Something you wanna share, Marshmallow?" The Sergeant-Major hovered in front of her face. He was typical military pixie scum: almost blue skin and translucent dragonfly wings, and fatigues crisp with starch.

"No," she drawled.

The Sergeant-Major pointed a blue-tinged finger menacingly. He held the pose a moment, wings buzzing, then his hand retreated to pull the gingerroot he habitually chewed out of his mouth. He waved the root for emphasis as he talked. "You of all Seelie should pay attention, you depraved, over-privileged, white-wing crook. And you a direct descendent of one of the Royal family's best servants." He shifted his gaze to Spike. "And you! What are you, her lap-dog?"

Under normal circumstances, Spike would have turned invisible and high-cottontailed it. But expert guards staffed the compound and each prisoner wore a collar that kept him from using magic. Spike wasn't used to close scrutiny, Robin knew, and his six-foot-two frame shuddered.

Although the Sergeant-Major was a jumped-up garden faerie and about ten times smaller than Spike, Spike paled. His ears laid back.

"Wassamatta?" the sergeant taunted. "Not used to Fae being able to look you in the eye? Are you a pooka or a pussy?

Eh?"

Spike bared his teeth. Robin understood: he didn't retreat from observation because he feared it; he avoided notice because a pooka backed into a corner found it difficult to suppress his feral side. It was part of his attraction, as far as she was concerned.

Sure enough, Spike in his agitation brought up paws to swipe at the Sergeant-Major. But the faerie beat his wings hard to fly out of reach easily.

"Nice try, but you telegraph like mad," the Sergeant-Major told him. The pride in the faerie's voice surprised Robin. He addressed them all again.

"I'm Sergeant-Major Milkweed. I've been given the task of transforming you sorry bunch of faerie-dust specks into a crack unit. There will be no screwing around, no attempts to escape. Any one of you tries to go back to your thieving, darn-near Unseelie ways will scupper the chances for all of you—you'll all go straight down to the pit. Got that?"

The motley group to Robin's left all grumbled half-heartedly.

"What?" Milkweed demanded. For a little pixie, he could sure make noise.

"Yes, Sergeant-Major!" Spike shouted along with the others.

Milkweed flitted back into Robin's face. "That goes for you too, Sidhe-devil."

"Jealous?" Robin's lip curled.

Milkweed snorted. "All right, Bonnie, Clyde," he continued, bringing in Spike, "and the rest of you. Across the compound, there's a well. In the well, there's—"

"An egg, and in the egg is the heart of a giant," one of the Fae on the end drawled, sounding bored. "Sergeant-Major, do you think the Unseelie are still so unimaginative? After all these years?"

Milkweed chewed on his gingerroot. Robin could have sworn a faint smile crossed his face as he flew down the line and dropped to the speaker's eye level.

"Well, well, Doc Halloween: the Summerlands' most infamous dwarf."

"We prefer Svartalfheimrs or Dvergar."

"Like I give a plague rat's ass," Milkweed told him. "You have an objection to the exercise, Doc?"

The dwarf—Dvergr—sniffed haughtily. "Aside from the fact that it's trite, over-done, cliché, and useless, being completely inapplicable to our situation and, I strongly suspect, our mission, none whatsoever, Sergeant-Major."

"That's where you're wrong, Halloween," Milkweed returned. "I'll decide what's related to your mission and what ain't." He backed wind to give himself a better view of the seven of them. "It so happens that the Unseelie don't seem to have learned many new tricks when it counts, even if they've changed their . . . their MO's in the last two or three centuries. We have between this new moon and the next one to train for our objective. That objective is to infiltrate an Unseelie waystation and retrieve an item that was stolen from the Queen recently."

"And the item holds her heart?" the Sidhe on Spike's left spoke for the first time. She wasn't as tall as Robin or Spike, and her coloring was closer to a ripe peach than the white of Robin's skin. "Sweet. I've always wanted to be Queen."

"Keep dreamin', PeasePorridge," the Sergeant-Major quipped. "What it is ain't none of your business—just that it's ours and the Unseelie are gonna use it to gain advantage in the war."

"Permission to ask a question, Sergeant-Major?" a voice down the line asked politely.

Milkweed frowned. "Tachidhemarbhiguin, ain't it?" he asked, rolling his tongue and teeth in an impossible combination of sounds, even for Gaelic.

"That's close, Sergeant-Major," the owner of the horrendously unpronounceable name said. A creature with so long and pretentious a name could only be a Brownie.

"All right—what did your masters call you, then?"

"Two-Bites, Sergeant-Major."

"Ask your question, Two-Bites."

"What is the item—that is, what is its glamour, and where is it now?"

"That's two questions," Milkweed observed, but he was already smiling. The little kiss-ass was good, Robin had to admit. She could smell the pheromones from the other end of the line. "It resides in an Unseelie hideout outside a mortal town called Boston. It's a headquarters where they recharge, soak up human energy and not too surprisingly pick up their new arsenals of strategies to use against us. The destination is a club called 'Luminescence.' And the target item is glamoured for use as their mirror ball."

The news hit with a thud. A mirror ball. The Unseelie couldn't have chosen a more treacherous camouflage—glamours would be useless in the mirror's reflections and, depending on the protections placed on it, so would magical means of removal. Robin just bet there were plenty of protections.

"Now," Milkweed continued over their subvocal groans, "You've been given this opportunity because while you're the lowest scum and the most reviled creatures this side of the Danaan, you're also the most conniving, sneaky, effective bunch of mischief-makers we've known in a generation. So let's get cracking."

Milkweed, it turned out, had a point. Robin and Spike, of course, were the most skilled con artists in any town they cared to visit—most recently Chicago by way of Osaka, San Francisco, and Vancouver. She'd heard of Doc Halloween. He had single-handedly brought a dozen changeling children to the Court . . . only to hype them up on sugary snacks and run the Queen's handmaidens wild satisfying their demands and moods. Two-Bites . . . he was a technical genius, according to Spike. "He can bend human machines to his will," he told her at mess one night. Rumor had it that Two-Bites had spent his master's fortune bribing the border guards to let him bring in a "harmless" computer—that turned out to be a hacker's paradise. Within a month, all the shipping assets the Court had invested in Jötenheim, Hy-Brasil, and Avalon had been diverted into Two-Bites' humble milk fund. He'd been caught trying to import entire dairies' worth of cows.

"What's with those two, then?" she asked Spike, pointing to two diminutive figures sitting by themselves at mess. One had the bright coloring and dragonfly wings of a pixie; the other bore the distinctive grey mottled fur of a gnome.

"The pixie's name is Pussywillow," and Spike added a snort to the end of the name. "Unfortunately, of the two of them, he's the *less* intelligent. His friend there is the mastermind who thought it'd be a good joke to resurrect the Golem to help at the palace."

"Yeesh. He got a name?"

"Sugar, you know's well's I do . . . . Gnomes don't use names. Heard Pussy—" and again, he snorted—"call him Hal."

"They together or what?"

"Dunno. Looks like it."

Then there was PeasePorridge—another Sidhe like Robin, except from the lesser branch of their species, and hardly a credit to her family. Robin had heard that she'd been caught in the palace itself, less than a dozen doors away from the Queen's private chambers, wearing about four pounds of explosive goblin powder. That first night, the little radical had hung back from mess. When Milkweed ordered her to join the others, she'd said archly, "I don't eat with Brownies."

She'd been lucky Spike had only held her down so the others could take their turns. If he'd joined in himself, she probably wouldn't have had teeth left. It took him almost an hour afterward to change his paws back to hands.

Seven of the most reprehensible Fae this century—and they were expected to save the Seelie Court's collective asses. Whoever thought this up was a total whack job.

"Sweet stone of Tara, it really is a Goth club," Robin said when they cased the place a few days into their preparations. "Can't they think of anything more original?"

"You'd rather it were a honkytonk?" Doc Halloween asked.

"Why not? I'm tired of leather."

"Hey," Spike said.

"Not on you, sweetie," Robin amended.

"I hate country music," PeasePorridge offered, unasked. "It symbolizes the inferiority of humans."

"Oh c'mon, industrial metal is just country music with more cutting," Robin said. "They have common roots—"

"Quiet," Milkweed shut Robin down before she could get going. "We've got a lot of details to decide on here."

The club was fairly nondescript outside. Cement steps led to the basement entrance. Blackout curtains covered narrow transoms on either side of a solid metal door. The building stood alone on a short block; around the back, the alley opened up to a door at street level. Presumably steps led down on the inside. Milkweed and Pease had gotten blueprints from the city records. According to them, the chamber inside opened up on high ceilings and a spacious dance floor. In daylight, it appeared to simply be a small, squat building set between storefronts and restaurants. Like vampires, the Unseelie were at their best by night.

"Tell me again, Sarge: Why not do this now, when it's empty?" Robin grumbled.

"Because, it ain't necessarily empty. They rest up in there, remember? By day there're no humans and no distractions. The wards around the place are too strong for cat-burglary and anyway, if we cause a disruption to the club, it'll hurt them more than if we just steal the item back quiet-like. But if you go in and they don't have anything else to worry about—the seven of you against who knows how many Unseelie? There'd be nothing left of you to send to the Fiend."

"All right, let's not get nasty," Robin said mildly. "No need to bring up the pit."

"The pit is what's waiting for you if this mission don't succeed, so I suggest you put your considerable mind to how we're going to blend in as humans when glamour will be next to useless."

"Easy," Robin said with a feral grin to rival Spike's. "We don't."

The plan was simple: infiltrate, create a diversion, snatch and grab, and hightail it back to the Summerlands. Its execution? That was more complicated.

"Let's review it again," Milkweed insisted during dinner the night before the raid. For three weeks, they'd been drilling in hand-to-hand and working as a unit, mostly, while Milkweed decided who'd be doing what in the plan. They'd had their collars removed so they could use magic, but they were still under heavy guard.

"One," he prompted.

"We're at the club; we've just begun," they chanted.

("I did see this movie, I'm sure of it," Robin muttered to Spike.)

"Two."

"Spike and company go on through," they answered.

"Three."

"Doc covers the back with Pease."

"Four."

"Pussywillow(snort) comes to the door."

"Five."

"Unseelie take him for a dive."

"Six."

"Spike gives the door a fix."

"Seven."

"Sarge and Hal climb to Goth child heaven."

"Eight."

"Two-Bites has a date."

"Nine."

"It's *Phantom of the Opera* time."

"Ten."

"Spike and Robin subdue their men."

"Eleven."

"Doc and Pease come in and make seven."

"Twelve."

"Into the sewers we all delve."

"Thirteen."

"Back to homebase without being seen."

Robin twitched the corners of her lapels so they'd stay upright. "You okay in there?" she whispered to Hal.

"*Sí*," the gnome told her. Three weeks and they still hadn't figured out why Hal spoke Spanish, if he spoke at all.

"All right, Spike," Sergeant-Major Milkweed's voice sounded in her ear. Two-Bites had given them all earbuds and mikes to keep in touch. "Nice and casual."

Spike brought up a tiny bit of glamour to assume his usual human guise, keeping the height common in pookas but suppressing his rabbit's ears. The nose ring, earrings, black nail polish, lipstick, and leather clothes—those were all Spike's customary attire. With her arm in his, Robin made no attempt to hide her delicately pointed ears and chin, her glowing skin, or her lithe and tall shape. She tinged her skin a bit to the green side and spiked her purple Mohawk even higher. The two sauntered up to the bouncer.

"We're next," Spike told the humans at the head of the line. The little human girl's eyes widened at the sight of the couple.

"Cool makeup," she stammered.

Her companion didn't seem nearly as impressed, or perhaps he was just more pissed at being cut. "Buddy, you can't—"

"Oh, yes, I can," Spike said dangerously. "You going to stop me?" He stepped into the man's personal space, looming a good six inches over him. Robin felt him stretch himself to make the man crane his neck to meet Spike's eye.

"Nah, go ahead," the guy decided. Robin favored him with a predatory smile as they squared off with the bouncer.

"I know you two?" the bouncer asked through a deep frown.

"Know us?" Robin echoed snootily. "Of course not. We don't associate with servants. Let us in immediately." She nudged her aura to brighten it.

"Yes, Miss, of course." He shifted to let them through. "Enjoy yourselves."

The two crossed the threshold. Inside, Robin's skin prickled. "Feel that?"

"Yeah," came Milkweed's growl over the earpiece. "It's the Unseelie wards—they're gonna damp our magic some. Pussywillow," he added a snort, "you in position?"

"Sure-yo," the pixie said. "Is it time?"

"Not yet. Give us five minutes from my mark. Doc? Pease?"

"We await your signal, Sergeant-Major," Doc Halloween answered.

"Right. Mark. Spike, get all the way in and see if there's a good place to let me and Two-Bites out. Robin, stay with us. Hal?"

"*Sì, yo se,*" Hal said.

Robin rolled her eyes at Spike. Gnomes were all a little touched, but Hal was particularly . . . eccentric. The Spanish affectation alone deserved years of therapy.

They went toward the dance floor so Two-Bites could get to the sound equipment. The noise was nearly deafening—almost impossible to hear through the earbuds because of the relentless driving, pounding technobeats. Robin twitched a little in time to what passed for the music. Spike, of course, was quite happy. *Crazy pooka.*

He held out his hand to her, offering to gyre and gimble as a cover to get them closer to the stage and the DJ. Robin took his hand. They ground together.

"Hey, careful! You've got passengers!" Milkweed protested.

"Sorry, boss—just a little show for the foe," Spike laughed. "Look up, baby," he whisper-shouted into Robin's ear.

She did. The mirror ball was directly overhead, hung at the equivalent of at least three floors above, and it was huge. Moons and stars glittered in the shapes adorning the sphere, every phase and every planet in the heavens seemingly represented in the flashing light that bounced off its surface. Robin stopped moving. The stratosphere was hanging above her. Or maybe she hung above it. Any moment, she would fall upward . . . .

"Hey!" Spike shook her. "Wake up! Mission? Escaping eternal hellfire?"

"Right," Robin said. She blinked and looked into Spike's eyes. They'd turned to a cat's slits in his worry. He stroked her cheek. She covered his hand in hers.

"Problem?" Milkweed demanded.

"No. I'm okay. But there's a spell on the mirrors. Don't look directly at them."

"Good to know. Everyone copy that?"

Affirmatives dribbled through her link. "What kind of spell?" Pease asked.

"Look at it, feel pulled off into the cosmos."

"Huh. Okay, copy."

"Let's get moving," Sarge said. "Spike? Pussywillow(snort)?"

"Has it been five minutes?" he said. "I been countin', but I lost track."

"It's been five minutes. Go."

"Okey-doke," the pixie said pleasantly. Spike positioned himself at the edge of the stage. Robin cuddled up to him, covering the movement of their coats as Two-Bites, Milkweed, and Hal disembarked. Spike then left her to stand guard and moved into the shadows. He disappeared.

A few seconds later, her earpiece picked up the pixie at the door. "Hey, you big ugly momma's faerie! Bet you can't catch me!"

"Buzz off, you gnat," the bouncer's voice sounded faintly.

"I heard Unseelie Fae were cowards, but you're really just big cuddly teddy bears, aren't you?"

"Take that back!"

"I bet you're wearing pink underwear! I bet you play with soap bubbles in the shower! Your mother told you bedtime stories about rainbows and uni—" he broke off suddenly. Robin saw the door gap open wider at the bouncer's departure. Spike was invisible, but he must have moved to the door, because a second later he appeared, looking like the bouncer who'd just left his post to chase Pussywillow.

"Doc?"

"A moment," the dwarf said. They heard some grunting.

"Guards are down. Pussywillow's, too," PeasePorridge said a moment later. "Sarge, he's got a Seeing Stone on him—should we grab it?"

"Negative," Milkweed said, breathing heavily. Robin assumed he was climbing the light towers. Flying would be too conspicuous, even if the lights strobed constantly and half the population of the club was high.

"His weapons are sure to be warded," Milkweed continued. "If you touch—"

It was too late. PeasePorridge must have ignored his warning. A klaxon sounded. The DJ's hands stilled over his tracks. It took the dancers a few seconds to realize that the siren was not part of the music. They too looked around, confused.

"Fire!" Robin shouted into the pause. "Fire! The club's on fire!"

It worked. Humans pushed toward the exits. The DJ dove under his table.

"Oh no, you don't," Two-Bites said over the comm.

"We can move in the panic," Milkweed added. "Two-Bites, give us more diversion. C'mon, pixie-dust, move, move, MOVE!"

"Sí, Commandante," Hal answered.

"Don't climb, ogre-brain, fly! Grab on. No one's looking. There's no time for subtlety!"

A handful of Unseelie responded to the alarm. "Look alive, sweetie," Spike warned Robin. She prepared to intercept.

"Doc, Pease, now would be a great time for backup!" Robin called.

Three more Unseelie came streaming from the other side of the bar. They brandished silver chains and clubs. One, dressed in baggy pants and an overlong tanktop like a gangsta, fingered a slender dirk. They must have been in a back room, because the club didn't have any sublevels according to the blueprints. "Spike, Doc: are the doors secured?" she demanded.

"Yup."

"Affirmative."

Gangsta-Fae snapped his wrist and the knife flew. She ducked, but as she righted herself, she saw two more arrive: a large male and a female with Elvira hair, long nails, a net shirt, black leggings, and stiletto heels.

"They've got another way in or something. I need backup."

"We're coming in," Pease said.

"The front's full of people getting out," Spike said. He sounded amused. *Typical*, Robin thought.

"Well, then get your lazy ass over here and help," she ordered. The female Unseelie charged, nails first. She caught her arm and twisted her aside.

"I'm right next to you, sweetheart," Spike told her. This time she heard him in stereo—through the link in her right ear and for real on her left. The second Unseelie's chain got yanked sharply and he flew across the room.

"Bastard," she muttered affectionately. The Unseelie Sidhe pulled off her shoes. Daggers slid out from the heels. *Stilettos out of stilettos: cute*, Robin thought. She drew her knife. As the Unseelie lunged, Robin swung her blade in an arc and sliced the blade off the right shoe. The woman screeched in rage. Robin brandished the knife at her. She squared off, tried to aim a kick. Robin slashed at her leg. She cut through tendon; the Unseelie dropped, clutching her leg in pain.

"I've located the source of the reinforcements," Doc said. "They've a stairwell to a lower level. Possibly the sewer or an underground Court."

"I thought the blueprints didn't show a subbasement," Milkweed groused.

"Apparently the blueprints are out of date. Shall I disable it?"

"Can we use it for our escape?"

"I doubt it. Even if it opens on the sewers, I recommend we avoid going underground per the plan. There will surely be more Unseelie there."

"Right. Take it out."

"With pleasure," the Dvergr said.

Robin had her hands full with two more Unseelie who faced off at angles, trying to divide her attention. She drew on the confusion in the club and felt it surge through her hands. It tingled uncomfortably—that was the effect of the Unseelie wards—but they hadn't planned on a descendent of the greatest trickster of their race coming on this raid. Mayhem was her crack. It made her feel invincible.

She waved her hand in front of the Unseelie Fae's faces. "These aren't the droids you're looking for!" she muttered. Louder, she told them: "Isn't there something you should do to put out the fire?"

They blinked and rushed to the walls in search of the fire extinguishers. One of them found the fire alarm and pulled it.

The new alarm was about two half-tones and as many seconds out of synch with the ward klaxon. Robin expected her ears to bleed from the dissonance. But her marks, convinced that the club was in flames, now ran out the back.

Meanwhile, the female she'd sliced wasn't as out of the fight as Robin figured. She held her hand up and it glowed blue. The eerie light floated higher, bathing the club. Robin could feel the spell press on her, making her head throb. She threw her knife at the female. It hit hilt-first, but had enough force to knock her out.

Spike had taken on three, still invisible. Correction, Robin realized: not invisible, but appearing as each of his opponents in turn—landing blows against each in the guise of the others. He pulled out a leather sap from his coat and faced off against one of the Unseelie, a female biker-type. She threw a pulse toward him, which knocked him off his feet. He rolled away and came up swinging at a bruiser in a baggy shirt and ball cap on backwards. Spike closed, one hand still clawed and vicious, the other brandishing the heavy sap. The guy stumbled backward from Spike's swing. Robin caught him by the throat as he passed her. She applied pressure. The Unseelie wrapped his hand around and sent a jolt of dark energy into her. Robin cried out in pain, but didn't let go. She countered with a surge of her own power, choking him until he sank to the floor. By then, Spike had subdued the third "gangsta" with a kick to the jewels.

"Great, kid! Don't get cocky," Robin quoted, on a roll now. As the Unseelie woman's spell dissipated, the energy from the confusion went to her head like fine, aged nectar. Her hands burned, but she could fix that later. She blew on them to cool the sting. The second female sent another pulse at Spike, but he winked out of sight. Two seconds later, her head tipped back and she dropped.

A bomb went off—sound, light, and a miniature earthquake exploding all at once. Robin hadn't noticed whether the sprinklers had activated already, but now there really was a fire for the water to combat. The floor caved in on the far side of the club. Looking over, she saw Pease guarding Doc's back while Doc threw a grenade into the cavern. Six Unseelie pixies flew out of the hole. Pease produced a concussion blast, grunting with the pressure of the wards, but nonetheless bringing the pixies down.

"The breach is temporarily neutralized," Doc reported calmly. The floor rocked again. Heat and light from the fissure bathed the corner. She could hear screams from below. "The underground exit would be an extremely ill-advised escape route," Doc continued. "We should seek alternate egress. This won't hold them off long."

"Pussywillow(snort), come in, over," Milkweed said.

"Sarge? Should I come in? Is Hal okay?"

"*Sì, querido*. Major, dju ready to go?" he continued in Gaelic, heavily accented.

If Milkweed were surprised that Hal could speak a language other than Spanish, he didn't betray it or miss a beat. "Everyone give me a go/no-go for *Phantom of the Opera* time. Robin?"

Robin skidded back over to the dance floor. "Go."

"Spike—"

"Go," he said, loping to the bar to intercept two Unseelie there—both of whom wore leather jeans and not much else. Unless body piercings counted as clothing. He hesitated when one pulled out a sword from under the counter.

"PeasePorridge."

"Go."

"Doc."

"Go."

"Pussywillow(snort)."

"Huh?"

"Go/no-go, pixie-dust."

"Oh. Go, I guess."

"Two-Bites."

As an answer, the music changed. The drums switched to the pulse of waves on sand and rock; the scream of electric guitars morphed to ethereal chanting. The few humans still in the club, soaked by the sprinklers, drifted toward the speakers on the stage. The Fae about to jump Spike stood fixed to the spot.

"Remember that this is not real," Two-Bites said into their earpieces. He added a low-level drone and a soft drumbeat to counteract the song. "There are no sirens here—focus on the job."

"Mark!" Milkweed shouted, so loud that Robin looked up at the source. He glamoured into a menacing Goth king: a death's mask on his face and dark, long hair cascading over a drover's coat. Jackboots completed the look. Such an extensive glamour had to hurt like mad, in this place. Hal waved from atop the mirror ball. Robin tossed up a huge pair of wire cutters. Milkweed caught them, then he and Hal began to saw away at the cable just as Pease arrived next to Robin.

The siren song swirled through the club, but didn't transfix all the Unseelie. A few shook it off, including the sword-wielding Unseelie from the bar. Spike danced out of his range. He gripped his knife resolutely. The Unseelie sketched a sigil in the air; Spike's eyes went wide and he froze. His ears laid back.

"Spike, go invisible."

"Can't . . . . Spell . . . " he stammered.

"Hang on!" Robin barreled into Spike. She pushed him to the ground just as the Unseelie swung. The blade whizzed over their heads.

Something small and grey landed on the Unseelie's shoulder. The Sidhe reached up as if to brush whatever it was away. Instead, he cried out in pain when Hal bit into the flesh of his hand.

Spike shuddered all over. "I can move! Thanks, Hal!" He winked at Robin. "Better get back to your post, babe," he told her. He disappeared, but Robin felt him slap her ass affectionately. She hustled back under the mirror ball where Pease swatted away another group of Unseelie pixies.

Milkweed finally cut through the cable. "Heads up!" he yelled. Robin caught the ball, staggering under its weight. The jagged corners of the mirrors stung her hands. She resolutely refused to look. "I've got it," she said to Pease. "Go help Spike. The Unseelie are still a problem."

Pease's mouth twitched. There was an instant where they locked eyes. Pease held up the Seeing Stone and looked directly at the ball.

"Told you I'd rather be queen," she said with an evil smile. She held up her hand and before Robin guessed what was coming, she conjured a bright green gun and pointed it toward Robin.

"A water pistol?" Robin asked incredulously.

"Think again," Pease said, pulling the trigger.

Robin dodged, but the stream of liquid caught her sleeve. It sizzled corrosively, smelling like Troll blood, but not thick enough. Maybe Pease had laced it with Holy Water. Robin ditched the mirror ball to focus on neutralizing the acid.

Meanwhile, Pease used her distraction. She snatched the mirror ball and ran. Spike had sneaked inside sword-range and wrestled the Unseelie to the ground, but occupied with that, he couldn't stop Pease. As she headed for the door, she appeared to be carrying a much smaller object than the ball. Robin figured that was the result of her cutting through its glamour with the Seeing Stone.

"Wrap me in iron and burn my skin," Spike said in Robin's ear. "Did she just . . . ?"

"Yep. Dang, what is this stuff?" None of her attempts to counteract the acid were working. She pulled off her jacket and threw it toward another Unseelie assailant who was immune to the siren song still streaming through the speakers. The acid-soaked sleeve hit him in the face. He screamed.

"Milkweed, you've got a problem."

"*You've* got a problem," the Sergeant-Major shot back angrily. He flew to the floor, glamour removed. He threw the wire cutters at the Unseelie with the sword. It hit him on the head; the iron left a burn mark. "The tithe, remember? One of you screws up, you all go to the pit."

Robin tugged the mike off and threw it onto the floor. "No way," she announced. Grabbing Spike's arm, she turned and ran for the exit. They pulled off their earpieces as soon as they were away from the siren song. Behind them Milkweed shrieked loud enough that they didn't need the link to hear him.

They commandeered a motorcycle on the street. Pussywillow—she hadn't even realized he'd followed them—and sent a jolt of energy into the bike to hotwire it. It roared to life; Spike lifted the kickstand and they fled.

"Hal says he'll catch up with us once he and Two-Bites subdue the Sarge."

"Kinda liked Sarge," Spike said with regret.

"Are you kidding?"

"Nah. He was all right."

"Hey, Pussy(snort)?"

"Yeah?"

"Why're you two deciding to run with us?"

"You're fun. Hal says—"

"Hey, I've been wondering: Why do you call him that?"

"It's short for Jalapeno."

Robin leaned out while Spike rounded a corner. "Never met a Mexican gnome."

"He's from Spanish Harlem. But that's not why I call him Jalapeno."

Spike groaned. "On second thought, don't tell me."

The corners of Robin's mouth twitched in a grin despite herself. "Listen, can you talk to Hal without Sarge hearing?"

"Sure. We're life-bonded. I can talk to him no matter what."

"Well, tell him and Two-Bites, if he wants to come along, to rendezvous at the Charles T station and we'll track down that bitch for that orb."

"We're still taking it?" Spike leaned back to ask.

"I'm not letting some lesser Sidhe steal something so important to the Queen. I'll take it back to Court myself before I let her have it."

"But not really, right?"

"Oh, no. I want that sphere and that Seeing Stone, to boot."

"What are you gonna do with it when you get it?" Pussywillow asked.

"Dunno yet. Something. But for Puck's sake, let's not get caught before then!"

They sped off toward the river to plan their next caper.

Enforcer Fae

REPOstiltzkin

James Daniel Ross

MY EYES QUEST AROUND THE ROOM AND SEE HALF-OPEN SUDOKU books, *The United Nations Space Fleet Engineering Manual*, crosswords, *A Brief History of Everything Else*, and copies of *America's Most Frustrating Riddles* lining the shelves. None of the well-worn pages hold any interest at the moment. I had loaded up my *Spellcraft Horizons* account this afternoon, but all I had done was watch guys line up on the computer screen, flexing virtual muscles and flourishing kilobyte weapons. They'd come, they'd go. I just sat with my bored avatar on the screen.

I am supposed to be a master wizard, weaver of mighty enchantments, brewer of eldritch potions, caster of spells that can crack mountains and boil oceans, scourge of evil and slayer of dragons . . . my heart just isn't in it tonight.

I log out, staring at the *Spellcraft Horizons* logo, groaning a bit as the scantily clad elf princesses flashed on the screen. I grab a stale can of Blur Dog and take a swig, wincing as the caffeinated herbal infusion spreads its hangover all over my tongue. Remembering stern glares from my mother, I get up to pour the dregs out in the bathroom. I pause at my dresser, take Goldie, my lucky polyhedral die, and roll it cleanly off my palm, bouncing it off my second place chess trophy. There are twenty sides, but of course a small, laughing number one is what comes up.

"Figures." I run a finger over the forward phased torpedo array of my model of the UNSF Indefatigable.

"Captain Lockhart, what would you say about a dusty ship?"

My eyes wander to the large, ornate mirror

above the chest of drawers. My cargo jeans are the expensive, looks-too-old-to-be-new type in fashion now, a gift from my parents. The hoodie, likewise is a gift, from Toby. It proudly sports the Assassin's Guild coat of arms from *Spellcraft Horizons*. Unfortunately, the rest of me is still the same as ever.

Flippy, lifeless, mouse-brown hair? Check. Oversized nose? Check. Adams apple like a grapefruit? Check. Acne? Present and accounted for, sir! I salute, giving myself a wry smile without much humor in it.

"Samuel, you are not just a nerd. You are THE nerd, the template from which all other nerds are drawn." But I didn't say: and you are alone on your birthday, and worse, a Friday night, to boot.

I open the door to my room and go downstairs. Pictures of me are everywhere, a legacy of a shutterbug father with an only child. At least he is out of town on business tonight. I have no real desire to have a permanent record of Toby and me at L33T Games. I mean, we still had a blast playing Cybermarine, Purple Heart; Postmodern Warrior, and Light-speeder online against thousands of others, but I still can't get over the fact that it was just he and I.

"You can't . . . all there . . . I won't let you . . . ."

I hear my mother speaking angrily downstairs. I hope beyond hope that she isn't meddling. The last thing I need is her getting all orcish on the guys' moms over the lonely party. It sucks, but having mom riding to my rescue would be worse.

"Don't you give me . . . sixteen years! This is his home . . . ."

She's just always so protective. I enter the kitchen and see the Gunnery Sergeant from Cybermarine cake cut into little squares. Mom had taken one; I had eaten one; Toby had scarfed five. I immediately feel it's my job to catch up to him. I scoop one piece up and bite it in half, letting the soft green icing and rich chocolate chase away the depressing cobwebs from the corner of my head as I toss the can of Blur Dog at the trash. Immediately afterward, I have to pick it up off of the floor and put it carefully into the can.

" . . . You've got another thing coming, mister!"

Whoever she is talking to, she is really going tonight. I finish the cake as I reenter the hallway, cramming the other half between my teeth and chewing. I am trying to pull myself out of my funk, repeating to myself over and over that I'm young. That I have straight A's. That I am already studying REMIX, X=+, and SuperBasic. With a firm grounding in enough computer languages, soon after college I'd have a stellar resume, full fluency in computer code, and . . . .

I glance over my shoulder as I catch a new voice, a strange voice, much quieter and gruffer than Mom's. It sounds like it came out of a massive, round, barrel chest that had somehow been shrunk in the wash. "Look, you signed da contract, right? Now ya wanna tell me dat da contract means nothin'?"

The idea of some strange man in my house arguing with my mom at this time of night sets off all kinds of bells and whistles. I reach back into the kitchen and snatch my Mom's cell from its charging cradle. I dial in 9-1-1 and then hide the little phone in my hand in the front pocket of my hoodie. I try to pump myself up;

standing as tall as I can, I walk into the living room, wanting to be intimidating as possible and back up my mom.

"You can't—"

"I can, and I'm a gunna, lady. Da only reason I'm even talkin' to ya is because you were kind enough to supply some coffee. Can't get good coffee back home."

I enter the front room trying desperately to convince the universe that I am six-foot six with a chest muscled like a bag of basketballs. It's a tough sell. I want to sweep my eyes left and right like a stone-cold killer with pockets full of death, but the sight of my Mom's jewelry piled on the coffee table completely catches me off guard. Then, I see her: Short and dumpy, I can remember how she seemed to magnify like a djinn whenever I screwed up. She would tower over me like a thundercloud, shooting sparks from her eyes and fiery condemnation from never-ending lungs. She's not towering now. She looks shrunken, old, frightened. I spin around, desperately seeing what kind of gargantuan goon could cause, would dare cause, my mother to cower.

"Well, well, well, if it ain't da boy of da hour."

And there he is. The first word that hits me is "short," but closely on its heels is "greasy." Then "portly," "unshaven," and "smells like mutton" crowd into my head like jocks trying to be first into the cafeteria. His slacks are rumpled, his button-down white shirt stained and threadbare, sleeves rolled up. His vest is patchy, and made of some kind of black leather that glittered the way you'd expect dragonhide to behave. Despite the modern nature of the rest of his clothes, his boots were hobnailed, thick, and practical. Just then, the last word saunters into my head fashionably late: Ancient. Not old, not venerable, but Ancient, like a tree that has not only never been cut down, but doesn't even know what an axe smells like. Ancient so old it would forever be spelled with a capital A.

I shake my head. And the feeling passes. He smiles at me from around crooked brown teeth. He lifts one of Mom's kitten-festooned coffee mugs to his mouth and drains it in one go. "Dis will make tings a lot easier. I likes easy."

He parks the mug and hops off the couch, smacking his lips and cracking his fingers. Even at his full height, he barely comes to my hip. His hair is scarce and frizzy, tamed a second later as he took a British pancake hat out of his back pocket and pops it on. I think I see pointed ears tuck themselves into the cap. "Alright, time ta go, Romeo."

And suddenly I feel like I have walked into an episode of *Star Tales* where the main character takes an unexpected trip in time, or another possible dimension, or a holographic simulation or—

My mother's scream rips me back to the here and now. "You can't have him!"

She lunges forward, grabbing only air. The little man slides around the room as if made of wind, and when he comes to rest in his hand is what looks like a TV remote control whittled out of wood. He tosses it in the air with the same air as a cowboy playing with a Peacemaker.

Mom rounds on him, hands clasped in front of her as if in prayer, tears escaping her eyes in quickly widening streams. I stand in shock, numb from the heart out as she pleads with the dwarf, "Please, you can't take him. He's my son! Please!"

But he simply waves the remote in the air, and I catch sight of a glass star glowing on the face above all the other buttons. It's not a friendly light, "Sixteen red diamonds, Babe. Dat was da deal. No red diamonds, no kid."

A sense of dread begins to pound in my stomach, threatening to evict the cake.

"But I thought you were a dream. We were trying to have a baby for so long, I thought you were just a figment of my imagination! I thought you were a stupid dream! You can't—"

The little man rolls up his sleeves in businesslike manner and rattles off the next bit by accentless rote: "In due accordance with the Laws of Magickal Contracts and Binding Oaths, I am taking possession of one human male," he takes out a dirty scrap of paper from his vest, "one Samuel Williams, unless you can forthwith give the name of the duly appointed and bonded faerie agent, that being myself."

He crosses his arms and taps his foot impatiently.

In the hungry silence that follows, my mother affixes me with eyes full of loss and sorrow, bereft of power. I feel tears welling up inside my belly and making a beeline toward my head as she says, "You can't! He's my—"

The little guy points the remote at Mom and hit a button. The star flashes and suddenly, her words go quiet, though her mouth flaps all the same.

"Yea, yea, yea, I heard dat part already." He pops the remote into a little holster—no, it was definitely a sheath—on his hip and he turns to me. "So, you coming along quietly, or am I gunna hafta get rough-like?"

I try to say something intelligent, but all I manage is a gurgle composed of a thousand questions at once.

He purses his whiskery lips. "I thought so."

And then he hits me in the crotch. The pain is excruciating and I fold over like a flower in a stiff wind. Despite his small size, he leans me over his shoulder. The little cell phone, my insurance, bounces from my pocket onto the floor. My head bumps the ground by his heels while my toes drag the ground in front of him, but he manages with ease. I watch my mother flush and snarl silently. Her mouth forms a word that would have gotten me grounded for a week.

His shoulder digs into my belly as he shrugs and draws his remote control, "Not even close, lady."

I see it all, framed by his tiny legs: A spray of sparkles blast from the end of the remote, swirling malevolently around my mom, freezing her in place. Then the world spins as he bounces toward the front door. It takes a bit of juggling, but another blast from the star remote opens his way and he carries me out into the night.

Behind me, my childhood home grows smaller and smaller, my mother paralyzed just beyond the door as if by the eyes of the Medusa. Only the tears on her face move. Then the door swings shut as if by some invisible hand.

My kidnapper whistles a wordless limerick as he bounces me jauntily on his shoulder. I hear the sound of a metal door opening on hinges and then the world twirls as he dumps me into a car trunk. He smiles at me past brown teeth barely above the bottom lip of the trunk. "Did you know you got cake on your face, kid?"

He points his wooden star box and the lid slams shut.

The pain begins to clear as the car starts, but then utter terror creeps in. I am being thrown violently all around the confined space as cold sweat instantly soaks my clothes. It isn't fear of the unknown, or of the little man and his little remote, it is the quickly shrinking space into which I have been thrown. I can't see, I can't breathe, and this trunk does not appear to have the handy little pull cord that lets people locked into trunks let themselves out. I don't know if I panic and then scream, or scream and then panic. In fact, I think it was pretty much simultaneous. It seems to go on forever, the darkness full of crushingly close walls and a distinct lack of air.

I guess he hears me, because the car swerves to a curb, I barely hear his door open over the sound of my screams, and then the lid opens, letting in the sweet open air.

"Whaddayawant, kid?"

"Claus- Claus- Claus-." I gasp, as I fight ineffectually against his too strong hands as he slaps my back, "Claustrophobic."

"No small spaces, huh?" The little guy shoves me back again and then sets his fists on his hips the exact way my mom does when she's had it up to *here*. "Well, it's against union regs, but I can bring you up front if you don't make any trouble."

Up front. Glass. No walls. Air. I nod dumbly.

And then he takes the little wooden remote control out of its sheath and points it at my face. "And, trust me, kid, you do not want ta make trouble."

I carefully consider his words as my eyes pick out details on the remote. Each button is a separate gem, and all of them are labeled like a language out of *A Halfling's Marvelous Journey*. The brand name lovingly carved into the base plate reads *Gandr*, but most striking of all were the patterns in the whorls of wood. They looked like mocking faces. I'm a nerd. I know mocking when I see it. I nod solemnly.

He sneers a little and motions me out of the back of the car, and I discover two surprising facts: Firstly, my kidnapper's vehicle is one of those old fashioned art-deco cars that were used in the 1940's. It is loud, with a burpy engine and rust spots, but still the exact kind used in NightKnight comic books. Secondly, the little man has stolen me without any shoes. The spring pavement is cold and damp, and I feel a shiver roll up my spine as he motions me toward the passenger door.

The dwarf (and let me be clear: by dwarf I mean beards, picks, thanes under the mountain, and battleaxes) hops up onto the seat next to me. Immediately, he grabs a half-smoked pungent cigar from a stack of them in the ashtray and lights it with a touch from his remote. The smell of burning excrement is instantly everywhere.

Then he turns the key, grabs the steering wheel with one hand, and we're off like a shot. He has to stand on the seat to see over the dashboard, and while he is too short to reach the gas and brake, the car apparently does not need them to function. I get thrown from side to side, pressed back into the seat as if by a pair of giant hands. Whoever this guy is, he has no concept of speed limits, traffic lights, turn signals, or inertia. I think of the trunk and weigh no air against not having to see my doom coming. It's a close thing.

As the city screams by, I feel the weight of the last half hour crash into my brain like a blaster shot. Tears peek from beneath my heavy lids. Bright lights seem to laugh at me, and the darkness of the witching hour reaches into me and settles for a good long sulk. I glance at the small man, who is whistling something both perky and perverse and creating smoke rings at the same time.

And suddenly, right then, I fully realize that I am being taken, and I am never going to see my home again.

I feel that seed of helplessness begin to gibber behind my eyes again, given strength by the incessant whistling. I clear my throat. "So, what's going to happen to me?"

He looks annoyed, and obviously considers whether talking constitutes making trouble. He settles on answering, "I dunno; not my department. I just fetch and retrieve."

"Oh." He looks pleased that he was able to shut me up at the low, low price of ten words. But I wasn't done. I need some kind of certainty to grab a hold of. "So, sir, um . . . not to be rude or anything, but . . . uh . . . what are you?"

One eye nails me into my chair as he growls, "Whaddyoumeanbydat?"

And then he takes a sharp turn that slaps my head into the window. I clear my throat twice, rubbing my temple as if to scour away the pain, before I can continue, "I mean, you are obviously not human. The pointed ears alone throw that theory overboard. So, what are you: dwarf, elf, halfling, gnome, faerie, redcap, goblin, knocker, sprite—?"

"You're not a wizard, are you kid?" The tone of his question, not to mention his hand straying toward his remote, ensure that I shake my head vigorously. "Good. Hate wizards. Would be just my luck ta pick one up on a repossession."

Uncomfortable seconds click by, settling on the seat like tacks. I find myself asking, "Where are we going?"

He doesn't even look at me. "Mind your own business, kid."

I roll my eyes and lean my forehead against the window of the DeSoto. More streets flash by before the empty seconds build up too much pressure. "You know, eventually we're going to get where we are going. I'm going to find out then."

He mumbles something surly and huffs. We pass through two more stoplights without even pausing before he digs into his vest and takes out a ragged piece of paper. "Lawrence E. Bannister, 1909 Mulgrove Place. Standard asset retrieval." And then he shoves it away again.

Apparently he has no concept of keeping his eyes on the road, either.

"Retrieval? You're kidnapping someone else?"

He bristles, "Look, kid, don't make me put you back in da trunk."

I feel every inch of my skin go cold. "There's no need to be a jerk."

"Hey, don't get feisty wit me, boy." He takes out his cigar and uses it as a pointer, waving it uncomfortably close to my face. "Just relax, kiddo, it'll be over soon."

I huff and cross my arms. "Well, what's your name, at least?"

The little guy turns slowly toward me and leers like a professional, "What, do I look stupid ta you, kid?"

And then the car comes to a sudden and complete stop.

His door opens and closes as I peel myself off the dashboard. I hear the trunk open, and then close, as I get my bearings, then my door is yanked open and I am bodily dragged from the car by a tiny, hairy fist wrapped around my shirt. The little guy keeps me bent over at his eye level, the huge, muddy brown orbs sinking their teeth deeply into my soul. "Now look, kid: You are goin' ta come wit me. You are goin' ta behave, and when we are done we are comin' back ta dis car." He waves the Gandr box under my nose. The star winks conspiratorially. "Unnerstan'?"

I nod. He lets go, pops the still-lit cigar into his vest pocket, and marches briskly toward the front door.

We had come to one of those neighborhoods where the front lawns could have doubled as a golfing green, both in size and consistency. Every blade is uniform and perky even in the semidarkness. Pure white cobblestones, probably mugged from some historic village, wind around meticulously trained bushes and flower beds. I look up to the pool of radiant light at the center of the gorgeous lawn and am struck by how it seems to continue up, up, up. You could fit an apartment block inside of the place, and the garage seems built specifically for those who look toward collecting cars, rather than driving them. Even so, the driveway is covered in a multitude of vehicles, all of them expensive. Right at the top is a Ferrari so sleek, and so red, it looks like it's going two hundred even standing still. I groan with desire and my kidnapper elbows me to keep me moving.

As we reach the front porch, the distorted sound of music bubbles through the door. The faerie agent spends a wasted moment straightening his rumpled clothes and smoothing down his hair before pounding on the frame. It makes the booming sound of the fist of an ogre on a steroid bender.

The door opens, the music ramps up to full volume, and the woman standing there simply blasts my mind to bits. Her mouth moves and she smiles. My face flushes and all I can feel is my heart in my ribcage bouncing around like a jack-rabbit. Her mouth moves some more and I nod like an idiot. My eyes keep flashing around from her long, sultry legs to her full, pouting lips, silky golden hair, and gigantic yet firm—

—My kidnapper grabs me by the belt buckle and draws me inside.

"Stay close." He growls just above the sound of Master Mix and the Beat Crew singing 'Hootie Tootie Thuggie, Bam Bam Ma'am.' He needn't bother. As long as the golden-haired Aphrodite continues to walk away, I will blindly follow her into a Robatoid ambush. Well, not exactly blindly, it's just I can't take my eyes off of her—

"Mom. Mom!"

My head spins around so fast I get a crick in my neck. The room next to us is filled to bursting with teenagers. It looks a bit like a Simmeon's Diamond store, a SuperUrban Chic, and a Tomorrow's Electronics stalked each of the partygoers and gave them an intense reverse-mugging. Coming through the doorway, and closing the pocket doors behind him, is one of my least favorite people in the world: Ted Bannister.

"Mom, we're out of . . . ." Tall without being lanky, always found in the company of every wonderful new gadget, car, or fashion (and the girls that brings), he sees me and spits out, "I didn't invite you!"

Ted's mom purses her lips. "Dear, don't be rude."

But Ted doesn't listen. He isn't just thinking about being rude, he is promising me that he will wield all his wealth and power to make me miserable at school on Monday. I feel myself shrink. Going to the most prestigious private school in the state means I get the best education my parents can afford, and the choicest bullies for sixty miles in every direction. One of them was Ted.

I am saved by the arrival of the dapper figure of Lawrence Bannister, Ted's dad. He is a tall guy. Broad, too. He walks into the room like a man who could buy and sell it a dozen times before lunch and never lose a single cent on the deal. The full complement of techno gadgets on Mr. Bannister's belt would shame NightKnight; I wonder idly if it ever comes off.

As I understand it, he played football in high school and college, but then became something of a business mogul upon graduation. He is a corporate raider, a title that sounds cool until you realize they basically buy companies and sell them off in pieces to other companies. Then again, exciting or not, it obviously provides him with more than just a living. Even the air in here smells expensive. "So-ho? The birthday boy, huh?"

"Yes, Dad." says Ted, but of course out of reflex I say, "Yes, sir."

Ted doesn't stare daggers at me, he stares an entire armory. His father misses it however, because he's playing kissy-face with his wife and asking, "So, what did you need, dearest?"

She pecks the end of his nose, leaving a red lipstick mark, as she motions in my direction, "This little man is here to see you."

Mr. Bannister looks at me quizzically. "This one of your friends, Teddy?"

"NO!" Ted exclaims, a little more forcefully than needed. Even if it is, checking over both shoulders for unauthorized ears is completely uncalled for.

But then the gnome shoulders his way past everyone's legs to stand in the very center of the conversation. Ted was going to say something rude, but the sight of his father going stark white stops him. I can't blame him. I am beginning to worry if Mr. Bannister is about to have some kind of medical emergency.

The little man simply grins like a rat about to eat everything in the cupboard and then crap over anything that was left. "Hello, Mr. Bannister. I believe you owe me something."

Mr. Bannister is still pale as death, and his hands tremble slightly. His breathing is shallow and he is sweating a bit as he says, "Thank you, Monica. Teddy, take your friend to the party." Next he clearly addresses the little creature, "Sir, if you will come with me to the study."

But those ten words give Ted enough time to develop a real head of steam. "This is NOT my friend. I didn't invite him to—"

Ted's father cuts him off with one of those looks that his boy usually reserves for me. "Not now, Teddy. Go back to your party!"

Ted scowls. His mother slides open the doors and he grabs my arm, yanking me through as Mr. Bannister and the gnome go through the door opposite. I strain to see into the study, but everything looks pretty much normal, if normal for you is a mahogany desk that could fit four normal men, a crystal chandelier, carafes of amber liquid and a roaring fireplace made of white marble. Mr. Bannister lets the dwarf go first then closes the door behind them.

Then music cocoons me in severe levels of bass and Mrs. Bannister shuts me inside with a crowd composed of the most popular people in school. Ted immediately abandons me to the wiles of the party, disappearing amongst knots of people wearing clothes specially treated to look old and ragged, and showing off five-hundred-dollar haircuts that make them look like they are always standing in a wind tunnel. Some had already turned to glance at me, and every one of them gets that same, there-is-suddenly-a-turd-suspended-beneath-my-nose face Ted always has. I wonder if they took classes in it.

I seek refuge over by the refreshments, crowding past preppy students, singers, dancers, the theater club upper crust, and other wealthy dilettantes. As the music takes a pause between songs, I hear them snigger at my back. I am just looking for some punch, but I see the bartender and am thrown completely off. I briefly wonder if someone is still a bartender when there is no alcohol, but he smiles glassily and hands me something red. I follow his hands as he points down the table, and I forget I was thirsty as the feast spills out into infinity. There are cocktail shrimp, each the size of a gerbil. Four cakes, each built in layers on stilts. Thinly sliced meats and minced vegetable pastes sit in artfully arranged toast points, and a Japanese man skillfully works razor-sharp knives in a flurry to keep a steady stream of sushi flooding onto the table.

Past them is a massive ice sculpture. It calls to me, and I find myself fording the streams of popular kids again to stand before it in awe. Then a realization hits me and I have to groan: it is a picture perfect one-eighth size Ferrari, removing all doubt who the car belonged to.

I had wanted a car for my sixteenth birthday. Then again, I would have been satisfied with the gnome's DeSoto. I shrug and sigh, raising the punch to my lips before a sharp, piercing pain takes up residence in my butt crack. I stumble and fall, drink splashing into my own face and spilling down my front. I feel someone yank again. My feet leave the floor and I am dumped in an unceremonious lump.

I had become a connoisseur of bullying during my high school career and I should have seen this coming a mile off. A wedgie like this one is obviously given by a rookie, what with the strong beginning but the necessity of a second yank to fully seat the underwear showing a lack of practice. Still, it has the desired effect since the music comes to a sudden stop and people start to laugh. It hurts. It's embarrassing. It is in no way unusual.

I pick myself up off the floor and come face to face with Ted, who manages to scowl, sneer, and grin all at the same time, "Why, Samuel! Your mommy appears to have forgotten to write your name on your shoes and someone stole them." He raises his voice to a stage whisper and leans in real close. "Thankfully she didn't forget your name on your underwear, so it's right where it belongs."

Everyone starts to laugh. Instinctively, I shove my briefs back down my pants even as I feel my face flush, my pulse race.

Unwilling to let it alone, Ted glances down at the snowy red carpet, stained with the leavings of my drink. "You've ruined my father's oriental rug. If your parents take a mortgage on your house, you may be able to replace it."

I curl my hands into fists and feel the urge to knock his perfect teeth askew. Ted always had money to throw around at anything that got into his way, always had the best of everything. I just wish it would all go away. I want to see what he would do if all the shrimp, all the electronics, the expensive car, all of it simply vanished one day.

And then we hear arguing outside in the hall.

Ted goes first, but I am close on his heels. He slides the doors open to reveal his father and the gnome in the middle of a heated exchange. The taller man wags his finger in the face of the smaller, but the smaller has unsheathed his wooden star remote and spins it like a gunslinger.

Mr. Bannister argues like a lawyer, hands filled with bundles of hair bound with ribbon, some dull yellow, but a few gloriously gold. "You said a lock of hair from my true love for every year of my son's life. I have the payment right here!"

"You're not da first to try ta cheat an agent of da faerie queen, ya know. I knows what da contract says. Dat," he says, waving the remote at the bundles, "is only tree-quarters of da payment."

Mr. Bannister grinds his teeth, his words seething past them with great effort, "There is a bundle here for every single year."

"Very good, mister rich-guy, dere is a bundle for every single year." The gnome took delight in letting the conversation hang as he removed the cigar from his pocket (amazingly still lit) and shoved it into his mouth. "But, ya see, twelve of dem bundles are from da love of your life. The others are from her." And he jerks his thumb at Mrs. Bannister.

Ted's father drops the bundles and lunges forward, grabbing the gnome by the front of his vest and hauling him up to eye level. His voice makes sandpaper look like silk, and a field of magma seem like a skating rink: "Look here, you little freak, my ex-wife left me a long time ago. Monica is here now, and so she fulfills the re-quirement. You will take what you are given and be glad of it. Or I will—"

The gnome, completely unruffled, takes a drag on his cigar and blows it straight into Mr. Bannister's face. The taller man coughs and gags, dropping the bandy-legged creature to the floor, where he bounces up onto his feet and drones around the cigar while spinning the remote. "In due accordance with the Laws of Magickal Contracts and Binding Oaths, I am taking possession of," He takes out a dirty scrap of paper from his vest, "one 'fortune of kings and emperors,' unless you can forthwith give the name of the duly appointed and bonded faerie agent, that being myself."

The only sounds in the entire house are the ticking of a far-off grandfather clock and the crackling of the fire inside the study. Party guests begin to shift from foot to foot, wondering if this was some kind of joke, party trick, or mentally distressed relative. I get a cold feeling in the pit of my stomach as the little gnome smiles wolfishly.

"I didn't think so."

He tosses the spinning remote into the air and catches it with a flourish. He presents it like a fencing foil, pointing it at the room behind Ted's dad before hitting a series of buttons. The star flashes wickedly and a strange sound comes from inside the den, followed by a stranger sound. The first is like a cross between a metal crash, a glass shatter, and a chain mail jingle. The second is like a bonfire sneezing. In fact, it's very much like a bonfire sneezing.

Sparks sizzle out of the fireplace, past the demolished guard, fanning across the room. They settle on everything like anti-snowflakes, carpeting the entire den in low serpents made of smoke. The hallway progresses past silence, becoming a black hole of sound as every single set of lungs paused. Then there is a snap; a hot chip of wood flies out and tips over a glass of amber liquid. It hits the floor and smoke flares into angry red life. Deep inside the cavorting flame, a phone rings. The guests back away from the room in shock as it instantly becomes an inferno, but no one seemed to fully absorb the magnitude of the situation.

Inside the den, an answering machine picks up. A tinny voice fights against the crackling blaze. "BEEP. Mr. Bannister? This is Edward Hep, your insurance agent? I'm sorry to call so late, but this is somewhat urgent. It turns out the check you sent us last month was unsigned. Your bundled coverage has been discontinued until we can get this taken care of-" Then the plastic warps and runs like wax, merging wires and ending the message with an inhuman "—zsxsircksssryck!"

Then the people understand, and they begin to run.

A confused babble tramples the previous silence and I glance left and right for the gnome, but he is nowhere to be found. Someone gets the front door open, and people eject onto the lawn like soda from a shaken can. The whole crowd of them pours onto the furthest end of the yard, and cars roar into life as those with vehicles clear the driveway to get them away from the burning house and out onto the street.

The scene is utter chaos, with smoke belching out of the upper stories as an angry red glow glares at the mob through the windows. I glimpse the gnome smoking lazily and smiling at the quickly growing house fire. I weave through the crowd, past the sushi chef, a future fashion model from my class, the bartender, and the butler. I move within earshot of Mr. Bannister, who speaks into one or another device off his utility belt, "Investigated for insider trading? Are you nuts? . . . . That is absolutely ridiculous! . . . . No, of course not! . . . . SEISURE OF ASSETS?! . . . . Well I hate to disappoint you, but I have incontrovertible proof of my innocence at my . . . home . . . office . . . . Oh, God."

I flip back my punch-soaked bangs and glance over at him, but he's not looking at me, he's staring at his home and his home office, both of which are becoming equal parts carbon and air pollution. An explosion causes the entire crowd to jump back two feet, as a hot-water heater becomes a rocket that bursts through the roof, arcs high in the air, and then smashes down on the hood of the last vehicle in the driveway: the brand new, cherry red Ferrari.

Elder and younger Bannister scream in unison, a sad, lost sound against the night sky. It reaches in and squeezes at me, safe in the crowd of partygoers on the street. Everyone else is watching the obvious display, but I can't stop watching Ted and his dad. Flickering flames cast their faces like masks from a Greek tragedy. Ted, especially, looks like he is at a funeral: Tears of unparalleled woe careen down his face. Monica Bannister steps out of the mess of onlookers. She gently places her arms around her husband and his boy. She seems strongest of all, just happy to have father and son safe. I think about my mother, and suddenly, I can't take joy from pain, even the pain of a royal jerk like Ted.

The cold night air reaches in to tickle the areas of my shirt soaked with punch and I shiver. I make my way to the little man as the fire trucks arrive, but they can't reach the house because of the multitude of cars blocking the street. People race around trying to figure out who should move where to let them past, but it becomes clear that long before hoses meet hydrant, the home will be a total loss.

"Hey, kid, no drippin in da car." The gnome purses his whiskery lips, pulls out his remote and dries me in a flash. "Wa-LA!"

I get into the DeSoto and sit there, a little drained. This time I make a point of searching thoroughly to find the position of the frickin' seat belts. Of course there aren't any.

The gnome climbs into the driver's seat, looks at me, pumps his eyebrow twice, and grins around his cigar like a fox with a belly full of baby chicks. "Well, dat was fun. Who's next?"

The gas pedal slams itself into the floor, and though there is no possible way for the big black car to get through the street packed with cars, it does. We don't even slow down from the normal blur as it dodges like a mountain goat from gap to gap and finally breaks into open street. We go left, and then right, and then I lose track again.

Then something clicks in the back of my head. Old things, half remembered. I murmur " . . . Unless you can give me my name. . . . You're Rumplestiltzkin."

The little guy laughs like a crow atop a dead body. "Dat dere was a pretty good guess, kid. Stiltzky's been out a da game for centuries. He moved and worked elsewhere for a bit, but pretty soon da story got around. Can't get nuttin' done when everybody knows your name."

It hits me like a full pint of milk hurled across a cafeteria: The story is real. Or, rather real-ish. "But it's the same thing, though, right? Magic? Granting wishes, making contracts, and collecting on debts?"

"Yeah, kid. Hell, you is sharp as a tack. Lotsa people make deals. Bannister wanted wealth. He got wealth until he couldn't pay his debt. Udder people wants udder tings: fame, land, peace, power. I sees all types." He smiles proudly at me— well, he smiles because he is pleased about what he does and glad someone other than himself could actually put it into respectable sounding words. "Gotta say, though, Magick has a 'K' at da end."

That seems perfectly reasonable. In fact, some fantasy novels actually spell it that way as a matter of convention. "How did you know I didn't say Magick with a 'K' in it?"

"Word didn't feel right." The gnome guffaws and slaps his leg. "Magick is nothin' but words, ain't it? But still, you's smart. Gives me hope for ya yet."

I smile back at him, but something at the back of my head taps me on the shoulder and goes over the exact phrasing and tone of his last sentence. "Hope for me?"

The-man-who-is-not-Rumplestiltzkin looks a little sheepish and shrugs. "Well, yeah. I gots ta deliver youse, kid."

"But I'm being taken to a magickal realm, right? I mean, dragons and wizards, faeries and trolls? Goblin armies and dwarven kingdoms? Elves?"

The gnome hunches over the steering wheel and pulls his cap down lower, obviously uncomfortable with this turn in the conversation. "Eh, kinda, kid."

"What do you mean, kinda? I mean are there elves or not?"

Not-Rumplestiltzkin shrugs, "Well, yeah, dere're elfs, but dey're kinda mopey. Not da kind of guys you want ta have a beer wit or nuthin'."

I feel the color drain out of my face and the world spins more than is accounted for by the gnome's driving, "But elves are tall, graceful, cunning and beautiful—"

"Look, kid, firstly: it's elfs, with an 'F'. Secondly: elfs are short, hairy, and pretty depressing much of da time. Makes sense. I mean once dey were once fertility spirits. Now DAT'S da job I wants," he barks another laugh, "but now people gots dere 'medicine' and dere 'health care' it's not like dey need da help of little spirits to make a baby . . . unless of course da parents need some kind of miracle. Now youse? You are probably goin' to be given a job by da faerie queen."

I poke my head out of the whirling vortex of my trashed future at those words: "Faerie queen?"

The gnome rolls his eyes. "Don't get your hopes up, kid. You're probably going to be cleaning out cesspits or somethin'. I dunno what it's gunna to be, so don't ask, but my guess is it's not gunna involve a magickal sword or nuttin'."

And completely without warning, I'm slammed into the windshield again. I pry myself off of it, shaking my head to clear the stars from my eyes. Then the gnome grabs me by the belt loop and spins me toward the next house. "Come on, kid, time's a wastin'."

This is a more modest home, much like my parents'. Another party in the offing looks like it takes up the entire back yard, which is four times the size of my own. Lights blaze like a stadium and the music is thumping and screeching like a rave. Instead of going to the front, the gnome leads me around back to where dozens of high-schoolers leap and thrash to synthetic tunes from the huge speakers.

First I see the Olympic-sized pool, but there is also a tennis court, a basketball court, a batting cage, and evidence that football is played somewhere in the margins. Ted had the upper, upper crust of our academy at his party. This place had people from everywhere: troll-sized football players, quick and sprightly soccer players. The swim team flows through the group like water spirits as the basketball team watches over it all like smiling tree people. Here and there, cheerleaders flit from group to group like pixies. I shake my head to clear the disturbing image and find the gnome has left me alone again.

Still stinging from the last time I was left in a crowd of popular people, I keep very close to the gnome as he tromps right through clots of cliques, straight up to the door, and right inside. I follow like his shadow, but once inside the family room, I am nearly blinded by the sheer weight of the memorabilia.

There are pictures, there are medals, there are ribbons of every color and engraved plaques and trophies of gold, accolades covered in balls of various sizes or with little sportsmen on top in the midst of some sportily heroic action. It seems improbable, if not impossible, for one human being to collect all this in any lifetime. I screw my eyes shut and quietly count to three, but when I open them up, nothing has changed. That means I am in the home of Kenny Jackson, and I am going to get my legs broken if he finds me here.

A mahogany-skinned man walks in, and I know in my heart of hearts he's Kenny's dad. It isn't just the family resemblance: broad shoulders, shaved head, sharp eyes, and wide hands; it is a distinctive confidence bred of pure personal and physical power. I find I am holding my breath as the gnome steps forward proudly and extends a hand in greeting.

"Good evening, Mr. Jackson. I trust you remember me." It's not a question.

Mr. Jackson's head bobs once. "Yes, I do, sir. I think you will find everything in order."

"Ah good." And without further pleasantries, Mr. Jackson takes trophies and medals off of the wall and passes them to Not-Rumplestiltzkin. The gnome produces a sack from one tiny pocket and shakes it out until it's the size of a bedspread. One by one the trophies go into the sack as Kenny's dad keeps up a litany of pride.

"Soccer, Basketball, Football, Baseball, Three Hundred, Six Hundred, One Thousand, High Jump, Pole Vault, Long Jump, Triple Jump, Shot Put . . . ."

Kenny has been busy. More than that, Kenny has been GOOD. He won everything he ever tried his hand at, and without breaking a sweat, swept much older competitors before him like a tsunami. Everyone says he is going to be a professional player one day; what nobody can agree on is a professional player of what. He never had to practice much. He just showed up to the matches and blew everybody else out of the water. Lately, however, Kenny has been focusing on the big money sports: Basketball, Baseball, and Football. All of his later trophies and awards were from these three. For my part, I have a chess trophy, and a whole bunch of Math-Olympic ribbons, but none for first place. And I'm guessing they won't have nerd challenges at the court of the faerie queen.

"MVP, MVP, MVP, MVP," Mr. Jackson chuckles, "the WEBN Cornhole Championships . . . are you sure you need them all?"

The gnome just nods and continues to stuff trophies into the sack. The Homeric litany continues, and finally, I cannot stand it any more. I wander out into the tossing waves of Kenny's court and head for the refreshments. This table is laid out much more like I am used to, with cookies and brownies, chips and dip, cans of cola and a massive sheet cake with, 'Happy Sixteenth Birthday, Champion!' across it. I groan a little as I reach for a cola. I almost make it.

Then the familiar twinge takes up from my scrotum all the way to the base of my spine. It hurts so bad it took my breath away. I'm jerked so hard my knees slap against each other. My eyes cross, the world spins, and I am dumped unceremoniously onto the grass. Again, a picture-perfect wedgie, but this one is administered by a professional, and again, someone has the presence of mind to take the music off as I get to my feet amongst the chatter and laughter of the guests.

I find my eyes level with a brand new pair of cleats, size twelve. My gaze travels up, up, up, past calves carved of black marble, past thighs like tree trunks, up to a washboard stomach rippling with muscle, to a broad chest that could shelter me from rain. I crane my head back to look into Kenny Jackson's smiling face. It's not a nice smile. His voice is polished and hits like a fist. "I didn't invite you, Sam."

"I—" my voice squeaks and the nearest guests howl with laughter. I pull at my underwear though my pants so my vocal cords will have proper room.

Someone in the mob jeers, "Look, his name's on them!"

And everyone starts laughing again.

I hold up my hands to try to placate the sparkling God of Sports. "Look, man, I'm not trying to crash your party. I'm just here with a guy to see your dad—"

"Oh, you're not crashing my party all right, but whether you're walking or limping out of here has yet to be seen." And Kenny turns to his adoring audience, waving for them to pour it on.

"Come on, Kenny. I've had a pretty bad night as it is." I hate myself a little more as my ears tattle that my voice is whiny.

Kenny's lips become a thin line and he leans in close, whispering with the finality of a saw felling a tree, "It's about to get worse."

And then he grabs me and turns to his fans, presenting me like some kind of pale, stunted, kid brother. He raises his voice, the powerful tones carrying across his parishioners like a wildfire. "Well, folks, we have a party crasher here!"

The crowd immediately starts to boo and hiss. One or two people throw food at me, being extremely careful to not hit Kenny. A catsup-encrusted hotdog hits my brand-new cargo pants, leaving a cheery red stain. I start to shake with rage, but Kenny's vice-like grip makes any move pure suicide. His other hand waves the crowd off, his tone of chiding clearly faked, "Oh, no, no, no, people! Let's not be barbarians about this. Instead, let's give little Sammy a fighting chance!"

His smile makes his words a lie. Grabbing me by the base of the neck like a kitten, he steers me past jocular knots of people until we sit before a table lavished with gifts. There, in the center, is a beautiful black and white marble chess set. The wrapping paper was spread out in a halo around it, with a little card discarded in the grass, which read:

To: Kenny; From: Grandpa.
Remember that the hardest games do not involve a ball at all.

He maneuvers me around and drops me into the chair, all the while addressing the guests. "Now, folks, I say we play Slink or Swim!" The crowd cheers, as if they know what is coming next. "We'll play one match, and if Sam wins, he gets to slink away. If not . . . ."

Groups of people part to give me a picture-perfect corridor along the length of the yard, all the way to the Olympic-sized pool. Everyone chuckles darkly, a single entity that wants to see me humiliated and, if possible, wet. Kenny sits in a chair opposite and grins over his steepled hands. "You first."

"I'm sitting on the black side of the board. White goes first." Kenny scowls and spins the table with the flick of a perfectly athletic wrist. He doesn't even topple any of the pieces. I sigh, and move a pawn.

Immediately, he moves a pawn, and the crowd cheers for him. I move another pawn, and they boo. He moves a seemingly random piece, and they cheer. Move after move, progressing faster and faster, cheers and boos melt into a slush of meaningless noise. The crowd becomes a faceless thing, and my opponent's towering physique disappears past the edges of the board.

It's just me and him now, and the whim of the masses means nothing. I'm not a grand master, master, or even ranked, really. But it doesn't take a great player to recognize someone who hasn't played more than a handful of times. He moves, I move, he moves. Pieces fall from the table like dust from a chainsaw. At some point I notice that my kidnapper has emerged from the house, looking like a disgruntled elf escaping with stolen back-pay from Santa's workshop.

He doesn't matter, nothing matters as my pieces fly like an army, attacking incessantly as they die, stripping layer after layer of his defenses away.

And then, the moment: I grab my rook and slam it down on the board so hard the pieces rattle. I raise my arms in triumph and cry out, "CHECKMATE!"

But instead of the adulation of the audience, there is silence. I look around, but they're all wearing blank faces. Someone coughs. A few people snicker.

Kenny stands slowly, fake smile plastered on for his fans. "All right, all right, nerd. You won. Slink on home."

And that's when I see the cunningly laid trap. Nobody writes stories about a dog biting a man, that's expected. Nobody would be talking Monday morning about some nerd beating God-Jock Kenneth Jackson in chess. He took a small risk in playing, figuring if he won he would inflate his legend even further. Now that he has lost, he can dismiss me and tell everyone he graciously allowed me to furtively run home like a very small rodent. My arms drop, but my heart is not ready to let go of the moment. I need to be a hero. I need that right now.

"NO!" Kenny stops in his tracks, and everyone glances around to find out who was so foolish as to question the King in his own Court. In less than a second, everyone decides that it had to be me. I am a little shocked myself.

"No," I continue, a little less forcefully, "I beat you, fair and square. I deserve a little respect."

For a moment, Kenny looks out at the crowd, measuring their shock. Then he walks back to me, placing one muscled arm over my shoulders.

"You know, you are right. You won. For that, you deserve a little respect." My head is spinning. I am certain this is it. This is the faerie tale part of the story where everything turns around and starts to go good. I do not watch where we are walking, do not see where we are going. "But you didn't do it fair and square. See, Sammy, the game is called Slink or Swim. And since you decided you are too proud to Slink away like a good little dork . . . ."

And then he tosses me into the pool.

I hit the water, but my body was already convinced it was ice in a clever disguise. I thrash around a second, listening to the muffled squeals of delight and peals of laughter from above. I find the edge of the pool and lever myself onto the lip, expecting at any second to be pushed over again into the depths, or for some degrading cheer to be taken up by the party at large, or perhaps for people to begin throwing food in earnest. None of that happens.

Instead, Mr. Jackson and the gnome, near the edge of the pool, in the midst of a vicious argument, are riveting the attention of the assembled high-schoolers.

"He cheated!"

Mr. Jackson leans down to be face-to-face with the gnome. "It was just chess!"

"It was just chess until da meathead issued a challenge, made a bet on da outcome! Den he trew Sam inna pool. Dat made da stakes real. It makes da game real, ya moron!"

"Kenny's won every sporting event he's ever been in! Chess is not a sport!"

"Yeah, den why do dey give trophies, huh, smart guy?" The gnome drops the bag of awards like so much trash and unsheathes his remote, setting it spinning around his hands like a living thing. "Da moment dere are stakes and winners and losers, it's a GAME, and HE'S NOT ALLOWED TA CHEAT!"

Mr. Jackson's right eyelid twitches, his hands clench and unclench. The gnome takes two careful steps back and declares in a clear voice, "In due accordance with the Laws of Magickal Contracts and Binding Oaths, I am taking possession of," he takes out a dirty scrap of paper from his vest, "one 'athletic prowess of the ages', unless you can forthwith give the name of the duly appointed and bonded faerie agent, that being myself."

Then he takes a long draw on the cigar and blows it out in a cloud right in front of Mr. Jackson. He doesn't speak; he just launches all two hundred plus pounds of muscle at the little guy.

The faerie agent just shrugs and points the remote. "I didn't think so."

And the smoke becomes black, vicious hornets. The cloud stops Mr. Jackson like a wall of iron. He swats and yells as people jump away to avoid the storm of angry insects. The little guy runs right up to Kenny by the side of the pool, dodges an incoming fist, plants the remote between the giant's eyes and pushes a button. There is a blinding flash and then a horrific scream.

I blink away the ghosts of light from behind my eyes and watch Kenny look around, bewildered that he is not being stung, eaten, blasted, or burned. Figuring someone blessed him with unheard of immunity, he smiles and draws back a fist so big it could hold four baseballs comfortably.

The gnome crosses his arms and smirks nastily, "I wouldn't try it, champ."

But try it, he does.

If I were not watching I would not believe it: Somewhere between drawing back his fist and throwing it, Kenny trips over his own feet. He tries to stabilize, but he slips on the stone lip of the pool. The gnome simply breathes on his fingernails and buffs them on his vest as the fist sails so far over his head, it might well have been aimed at a satellite. Then Kenny staggers, slips again, and falls into the pool, arms windmilling.

The gnome winks at me. "Time to go, kid." And off he goes, bouncing like a ball through the riot of confusion and screams.

I start to follow him, but I have this horrible feeling Kenny is about to reach out of the pool like some lagoon creature and drag me down. I dodge away from the edge, and glance back, only to find all six foot of athlete fully underwater, flailing like a madman. My eyes trail to the sill of the pool, where written in black block numbers sat the number ten.

And I watch Kenny panic.

And I look at the number ten.

And I see Kenny thrash.

And I look around at the crowd who are busy avoiding the wasps.

And I watch Kenny flounder.

And I realize I am watching Kenny *drown*.

Without any thought, I am back beneath the crystal cold surface of his private pool. I find the King of All Sports with little problem, but then he claws at me, desperate in his animal drive to get to a badly needed lungful of air. I wrench him to the side, pushing him with all my might until he gets to the ladder, and pulls himself out. I follow, freshly restocked rivulets of water finding their way to my warmest places and making me miserable.

Kenny just stands there, and shivers, mumbling over and over to himself, "I've forgotten how to swim. I've forgotten how to swim. I've—"

He turns to me, takes up a boxing stance and throws a punch. I'm so shocked I don't have time to move. I needn't have bothered: He misses me by a mile. He whimpers and runs. I realize he is flailing at the air, limbs wild, as if he has never run in his entire life. He gets to the basketball court and picks up an orange sphere out of the can. He throws it at the basket, but it actually flies out of his hand and lands behind him. He cries out. Then he runs to the batting cage. He flips switches and grabs a bat just as the first ball comes rocketing at him. He swings. He misses. He wails. Another follows. He swings. He misses. He screams. The third ball comes racing out as he leans in, low, low, low over the plate—

—the ball beans him in the head and lays him out on the ground.

Behind me, the chaos is clearing up, mainly because anyone not being attacked by little hornets forged from cigar smoke has long since left at a run. Mr. Jackson is inside his house, his attention captured by the swarm of angry stingers taking chips out of the glass in his patio doors. But he isn't looking at the wasps, he's looking at the batting cage, at the crumpled form of his son. I've seen the face he's making on the evening news. It's the one that reaches down inside you and twists good and hard, the one that makes you glad you aren't the poor guy wearing it.

Then the gnome, back from the DeSoto, snatches my attention. "Kid! I gots udder appointments. Come ON!" and he waves his remote at me menacingly.

One eye on the disfiguring welts on Mr. Jackson's stricken face, I go along.

I get to the car and the gnome mutters and flashes me with his remote again, instantly drying me off and taking the catsup stain out of my pants in one fell swoop. We pile into the car, then it coughs to life and we're off again.

I shrink in the seat, reveling in my bad mood. I had just been a hero, saving a fellow human being from drowning, but my only reward at the end of the night will be getting delivered to the queen to be executive toe-jam picker or something. We just left behind another set of crushed dreams, but I can't help but think that even while having a faerie repoman call on their doorstep, the popular kids were all luckier than me. They are still home. I'm going to some kind of Dickensian work house inside of a mushroom circle staffed by clinically depressed elfs.

The little guy keeps glancing over at me quizzically, and I guess I'm bringing him down or something, because he seems to go from glee to frustration in just a few minutes. Finally he just throws up his little hands. "OK, kid, what gives?"

I throw up my hands. "I'm tired of being an outcast. I'm tired of being alone."

"You tink youse alone now? Just wait, kid."

And he's right. Soon, I will be surrounded by people and things that aren't even the same race as I am. But still, I am not ready to let it go. "I always wanted to be special. I wanted to be a hero. I'm tired of being ordinary. I'm tired of having my mother write my name on my underwear."

The gnome grumbles a little, tightening his grip on the steering wheel. "Dere ain't nuthin wrong wit your mudda writin' your name on your underwear, kid." And then he mutters, much more to himself than to me, "How else can you keep da goblins offa dem?"

And finally, the rage building all night explodes. "Look, stop trying to cheer me up! I'm not the one with a magickal remote that turns smoke into bees! I'm not the one who gets to ruin jerks' lives! I'm not the one who kidnapped YOU! I'm not the one—"

But this brought on a burst of rage that swallowed my petulant tirade whole. "I'm not da one dat promised sixteen red diamonds in exchange for a baby! I'm not da one dat didn't pay! I'm just here to do a frickin' job, kid!"

And after a second of two of stripping his self-centered perspective out of that last monologue, a question surfaces from the depths of my heart. "My mom did that?"

My voice sounds so soft, so alone, so young. I guess it even touches the gnome, because when he turns an appraising eye on me, it holds some pity inside. "Happens all da time, kid."

"How?"

"Usually by wanting it very, very badly."

In the silence that followed, something hits me. I had spent my entire life wishing for so many things. I wanted to be a superhero. I wanted a magical sword. I wanted to discover warp-drive. I wanted to see elves, dragons, faeries. I had wanted these things, wanted each and every one so badly the desire hurt, but nobody had ever shown up and offered me a deal for any one of them. Then I realize something that brings tears to my eyes.

My mother had wanted me much more than I had ever wanted anything, ever.

I have to get back to her. I have to.

My mind begins racing, turning over stones that haven't seen the light of day since I was in diapers. I run though the legend of Rumplestiltzkin. It's pretty simple: Mom brags about girl; king hears and makes her spin straw into gold; Rumplestiltzkin shows up and offers to do it for a kid; King marries girl; Rumplestiltzkin offers to give up the baby if girl knows his name; And then a woodsman hears Rumplestiltzkin in the woods bragging to nobody about his name and the queen's kid; Woodsman tells the queen; Happy ending. The car comes to a screeching halt in front of another, well-appointed home. Only one thought ricochets inside my head as I open the door and get out, *'Now all I need is a chatty, eavesdropping woodsman.'*

We walk up the well-appointed walkway to the front door, but no drums, guitars, or synthesizers sound through the walls. The driveway is empty, and only the blue-cast shadows in the front room say anyone is awake at all. The gnome pays these clues no mind. He walks up and knocks on the door, causing it to thump hollowly like falling stone lids in a tomb.

Then the door opens, and I fall in love the second time that night.

Within every school, there is a hierarchy, as rigid as a medieval kingdom. At the bottom are people like me, and at the top is Janice Griffin. Her flaming red hair falls in full, gorgeous waves that always smell of strawberries and vanilla. Her full lips lovingly caress every word that comes between them, and her pert nose always seems to be scrunched up in laughter at some private joke. Above all, her sparkling green eyes make the seniors act like toddlers, and those eyes burn me to my bone on her doorstep. She answers the door, and oddly her hand moves to cover her mouth. "Sam? What are you doing here?"

She is always majestic. She is always aloof. She is not cruel, but she never stops the cruelty of others. In that one second, however, she became the greatest humanitarian on the face of the planet. She knows my name, and doesn't say it like a disease.

Before I can faint, the gnome shoulders his way past her into the foyer, casting a surly gaze this way and that, finding nothing to his liking. "Alright, cutie, where're your parents?"

Janice is taken aback, perhaps by his lack of manners, or maybe because of the smell. In either case, she was shocked enough to answer honestly, "My dad's in New York opening a play. My mother is in Milan doing a photo shoot."

My mouth feels numb around the words. "But it's your birthday."

Janice glances at me, looking surprised and a little embarrassed. Then her wayward hand slaps back across her mouth. "Well, yeah, but . . . I didn't feel like going out or having people over."

None of this sits well with Almost-Ruplestiltzkin, who paces back and forth, puffing harder and harder on the cigar. He is only interrupted when Janice works up the courage to say past one perfect palm, "Um, sir? Mom doesn't let anyone smoke in here."

The gnome fixes her with a baleful glare, obviously running though options until none were left available. He takes out the cigar and pops it into his vest pocket. "All right, missy, it's all up ta youse, den. Your parents made a deal wit me some years ago. I was ta be delivered sixteen perfect blood red roses, one for every year of your life, on dis night. Do you have dem for me?"

She is obviously taken aback, and blinks her perfect eyelashes rapidly, as if to wipe this smelly little man out of existence. But when he stubbornly refuses to be disappeared, she motions deeper into the house and says, "Follow me."

She keeps up a running dialogue past her hand as we move though the richly appointed home. She trips once on the edge of the carpet to the living room. "Well, I always thought it was a weird obsession for my mother; she was always on the lookout for this breed called the Black Baccara rose."

I take the moment to glance around, because otherwise I would just stare at the girl and even a nerd like me knows that staring isn't the best way to pick up a date. The house is richly appointed in places, and spartan in others. The only theme linking every object in every room is symmetry, beauty, perfection. It is easily the most coldly beautiful place I have ever seen.

She opens a door into the basement and turns on the light, but nearly walks into the doorframe before finding the first stair with her foot. "Every year she'd find one and bring it down here. I was never, never allowed to touch them." The stairs barely creak as we move into something between a rumpus room and wine cellar. She nearly bonks her head on a low hanging beam just to the side of the staircase. "I just don't get why she'd be collecting these things all my life, or why you'd want them now."

She leads us into the back, where the finished basement became a whole lot less finished. By the washer and dryer, next to the water heater and furnace, sits an industrial-strength freezer. There is a note under a magnet. It reads:

Sorry we had to be out of town, but this is an important opportunity for me.
Didn't want to upset you with the details. Just give him the roses. Love, Mom

Janice looks a little stricken, and to be honest, I can understand. At least my mom was there tonight. I glance at the freezer again, but I think the temperature readout is broken until she opens it up. Arctic air instantly turns humidity into spiraling microscopic crystals of snow. Every breath we exhale tinkles musically as the fog clears and exposes the bare, white interior. And inside, perched on a wine rack, are little glass cylinders filled with roses so dark, they are indeed the color of old blood.

"I guess these are what you're talking about. Take them, they're yours."

I look over the gnome, and feel the need to run for cover. He looks like a cartoon of a prospector in front of a field of gold. His eyes twitch in funny ways, and he makes grasping motions at the freezer. I nudge him and he seems to come to a bit of his senses. He clears his throat and nods as he takes out another small-that-turns-large sack out of his vest and opens it up, "Yep, dose look like da roses ta me. Da only problem is: I'm not allowed ta just take dem. You have ta give dem ta me, freely."

Janice shrugs, "No problem."

And she reaches in to get one.

"No!" I yell, startling the girl and earning a smoldering look from the gnome. The only thing that would be as cold as the outside of the freezer indicated, the only thing that could have kept roses as beautiful as the day they were frozen, is liquid nitrogen. These aren't really roses; they are rose-shaped and colored ice cubes. "Those flowers are cold enough to burn. You need gloves."

She looks at the freezer, then at me, putting two and two together. I find a set of welder's gloves as hand them to Janice. She smiles at me. Suddenly, it's very warm in here.

She ferrys cylinders to the gnome, who grabs them without protection with no obvious ill effects. He examines each one through a jeweler's loop, muttering happily each and every time. Janice grabs the last one and shuts her long sleeve in the freezer door. As she turns around, the sleeve stops her arm from moving, but the flower keeps going. It sails in slow motion as I lunge for it dramatically. I actually manage to brush it with my fingertips, but the searing pain of subzero temperatures keeps me from getting a better hold.

The sad, dead rose shatters in a storm of glass, flower, and vapor.

The gnome cries out wordlessly in rage, and stamps his feet against the ground. He takes out his remote and spins it angrily as he pops his cigar back into his mouth. "Why can't it ever go smoothly? Why do I always get da trouble cases?"

Though the door is shut, the temperature in the room continues to drop as she tries to watch me running numb fingertips underneath lukewarm water at the sink and the gnome stalking toward her at the same time. "I- I- I don't understand. It was just an accident."

"Yeah, but it's an accident dat will cost you, little girl."

I let out a low moan as he fishes around in his vest for a stained bit of parchment. "In due accordance with the Laws of Magickal Contracts and Binding Oaths, I am taking possession of one 'legendary beauty', unless you can forthwith give the name of the duly appointed and bonded faerie agent, that being myself."

Janice backs up a step and finds there is nowhere else to go. "I don't understand."

The stealer of dreams levels the star end of his remote at the girl. "Dat is not my name—" And then someone cries out like a wounded lion, tackles the little man, and rolls around trying to get the remote.

Several seconds later, I realize it is me.

We roll about on the floor, but he is just too strong. He tosses me like a dog with a rag doll and slams me into the base of the fridge. He gains his feet, brushes himself off, and takes delicate aim at Janice with his remote, until he hears "RUN!" from directly above and behind him.

He turns just in time to get a sack full of nitrogen cylinders in the face.

There is an explosion of gas from the sack. A deep fog whirls in every direction for just a few, critical seconds. I hear Janice open the door and bolt, and I lunge to follow her, but somewhere in the fog, I get turned around. My face meets the doorjamb with a crisp snap and I fall to the floor with stars in my eyes. It takes several seconds before the little blue-white comets resolve themselves into one, big, red star. Of course that big, red star is on the end of a remote being waved in front of my face.

The gnome is covered in frost, with little icicles drooping from his heavy brows and little icework bridges linking his whiskers. He may have even looked like a cute garden decoration, if not for the unquenchable blaze that burns in his eyes.

"It's to da trunk wit you, kid. I'm gonna to get dat girl's beauty and den I'm taking you ta da queen." The gnome draws himself up to his full height. "AND I HOPE SHE MAKES YOU MUCK OUT DA DRAGONS FROM DA INSIDE!"

And he kicks me in the crotch so hard I nearly pass out.

I've heard that the difference between a hero and everybody else is razor thin. I never believed it before, but as the gnome bounces over my prone form and up the stairs, I manage to turn onto my stomach and crawl. I hear pots clang against the walls in the kitchen and a puff or two of magick occur with many pushed buttons. I get to the bottom landing and nearly fail to push myself to standing. Every step is a monumental chore, with throbbing pain eating away at my will as I get higher and higher into the house. I nearly overbalance and tumble back down the stairs. My feet are shaking and I can feel my heartbeat deep inside my stomach. I get to the top and nearly give up right there.

But then I hear Janice wail, a frightened, alone, little sound. Equal part tears and despair, her words carom off of the walls like little dying birds made of gold. What she said was: "Sam! Help me, Sam!"

I nearly fall on my face, but somehow it turns into a staggering run.

Pots and pans are everywhere, heavily dented and cast aside. One or two have been turned into confetti, and a large wok is bobbing like a balloon around the kitchen. I push it out of my face and stagger into the entry hall to find Janice curled up in a corner, sobbing and grasping her face as the gnome stalks toward her. He gets closer and closer, mumbling all the while like a bubbling caldron, "Trouble . . . never easy . . . ungrateful . . . never get paid . . . ."

Janice whimpers, "But my mother won't love me if I'm ugly."

And I swear, true or not, I know that she believes every syllable. It is pure tragedy given sound out of the world's most beautiful lips. It's the kind of thing that could even stop a rockslide in its tracks, make it reconsider the misery it is about to unleash on the village below.

The gnome doesn't even pause.

Both legs, and everything in between, scream in protest as I lunge forward and do the only thing I can think to: I sink my hands into his dirty, grungy pants, grab, and pull hard.

The little man is lifted off of his feet and he dangles there, spitting curses with the texture of venom. A blast from the remote hits a vase, and another hits a picture, and a third the floor, before his undergarment rips and unceremoniously sends him tumbling. I glance up to see the flowers wilt and rot; the painting cracks and ages, the wood panel floor becomes gap-toothed, and the polish yellows and cracks.

And as the gnome picks himself off of the ground with the bearing of a giant, I wonder if I am only nearly going to survive.

He is incoherent, spinning the remote so fast, the star becomes an angry pulsing streamer of color in his hands as he punches in combinations that he aborts and reconfigures as he thinks of a more fitting punishment. Janice gets to her feet and shoots up to her room like a gazelle.

I trip and fall over the uneven floor, and manage to substitute my buttocks for feet until I come to the far wall. Still, the gnome marches toward me like time itself, grinning maniacally and giggling out of tune. I look left. I look right. Nothing glows, nothing appears magickal, nothing emerges to provide even the slightest bit of help against this faerie and his wand of gems and wood.

He raises up the remote to point at my nose, trembling with unheard of pique that can only come after centuries of practice. His lips barely move as he whispers to me.

"Any last words, kid?"

I glance down at the scrap of fabric in my hands, the scrap torn from his underpants. And suddenly, I hear his voice echoing in my head, 'How else can you keep the goblins offa dem?'

Written there in bold faced letters is a name. I speak it aloud. "*Lahlicifesboren.*"

The word grows large, filling up the house. It is a wave, a pulse. My hair stands on end and a rush of air dances by like a hot breath. Perfect glass figurines and artistic bric-a-brac shudder slightly to hear it, but the effect on the gnome is immediate. He freezes, tremors becoming a near palsy as he fights against The Laws of Magickal Contracts and Binding Oaths. He towers above me, a titan of fire and hate as the glow from inside his chest seeks to blot out the world.

And then it stops. He shrinks. He sighs.

"All right kid. You can go home."

The words hang there, a glorious prize at the end of my horrible nightmare of a night. But it isn't enough, it isn't. "And Janice. She gets to keep her beauty."

Lahlicifesboren scowls like a redwood hit by lightning. Then he nods. "All right."

And then something else hits me. "And Kenny, and Ted. Give them back the skill and money."

Lahlicifesboren puckers his lips like a man force-fed lemons. "Now, why would you ever ask for dat? Da pretty girl I can understand, but da sportsman and da dilettante? Dey have done nothing tonight but make you miserable. Dey won't thank you. Even if you tell dem, dey will never believe it was you who saved dem."

The thing is: I didn't know, not until he asked. "They are shallow people, with shallow lives. They each only had one thing that defined them and you took it tonight. If you give it back, maybe they will learn to see past themselves to the people around them. Without it, they will live short, miserable lives."

Lahlicifesboren's eyes narrow and cigar smoke comes barreling out of his nose like a cartoon bull. "Why should I give dem back anything?"

I stand, ignoring my protesting legs, and all parts related, so I can face him as an adult, like a man, like a hero. "If you do these things I ask, I will keep your name safe until the day I die. I won't tell a living soul. You can keep working at the job you love."

"And if I refuse?"

I set my jaw. "Have you ever heard of the internet?"

That word hit him like a freight train, and he nodded slowly. "I have your word, kid?"

I nod.

Lahlicifesboren says something unprintable, and manipulates his remote. The wok in the kitchen stops floating and smashes into the floor. Confetti reassembles into cookware. The painting rights itself, the floor becomes perfectly smooth and the flowers rebloom into youthful beauty. I sigh, hoping it's all over.

Lahlicifesboren is already heading for the front door, chewing on his losses with no good humor. I follow him out to the front porch and pat him on the shoulder. "So, how long will it take to drive me home?"

The little man slaps my hand away and gives me a brown-toothed grin. "Dat wasn't part of da deal."

He whoops and runs off, jumping into his black-and-rust DeSoto and driving off into the night. I jump when Janice touches me on the arm. She shrugs a self-conscious apology for having run away and asks the question out of the story books: "Is it over?"

I smile at her. "Yeah. Yeah it is."

She smiles and I can see that her front tooth is chipped at an angle, obvious and obscene against the perfection of her face. She notices me staring and covers it with a hand. I realize the true reason she is home alone instead of out celebrating. I grin and shrug. "It's just a tooth. You're still pretty."

She hugs me fiercely, and for just a few seconds I can only smell strawberries and vanilla, can only feel her endless softness against me. When we part, I feel the question come out all on its own. "Janice, would you like to go out on a date with me?"

For a second she looks stricken, then a flash of panic. Then she slowly lowers her eyes to the ground and says, "I'm sorry, Samuel. I'm thankful for you helping me, but I don't like you in that way."

I chuckle honestly, cleanly, a sound that comes up from my throbbing toes. "That's all right."

And more amazing: It is true. She is her, I am me, and it is all right.

I shrug. "Can you give me a ride home?"

She has the decency to look abashed. "I don't have a driver's license or a car."

I laugh at the stars above, honest stars that laugh with me. "That's OK. Happy birthday."

"Thank you." And she smiles again as I walk off of the porch. She keeps watch as I walk down the path to the street, and then keeps watching as I get my bearings and start down the road. I feel her eyes on me for a very long time after that, as well. I wonder what that means.

I walk home, with no shoes, for two hours. I take four wrong turns, and by the time I get to the front door of my little home, dawn is breaking behind me. I don't even have time to knock on the door before my mother throws it open and tries to crush me with her arms. I hug her back, tears streaming down my face as she thanks God and every saint she can bring to her lips. She brings me into the kitchen and cooks a massive breakfast like Grandma always used to. Hours pass before she fully convinces herself that I am real and not going to disappear in a cloud of faerie dust.

I never speak of it again. Not to Dad, not to anybody. I'm not just carrying *my* secret. I am carrying hers.

I go to bed at noon, surrounded by starship crews and fantasy heroes. Dice are set to clatter next to compendiums of myths and things that never were. I still like them, but I no longer envy them for being fiction. I changed tonight, for I learned three things that will follow me until the end of my days:

The power of a given thing's name.

The love a mother bears for her child.

The heroic nature of the word . . . nearly.

Shadowcutting

Jason Franks & Steven Mangold

I KNOW I'M NOT DEAD BECAUSE THERE ARE NO ANGELS, NO trumpets, no lights.

"Theo."

My ears are still ringing, but my eyes start to clear. I can smell gunsmoke, caustic soda, and cooking chicken.

A silhouette leans over me. "Theo. Theo."

I'm lying sprawled in an almost-dry creek bed. Got some broken ribs, something sharp sticking out of me. I look down to see a twelve inch blade on a broken-off haft sticking out of my guts.

"Theodore." The silhouette resolves into a tattooed, bearded visage that I know and hate: Julian Keneally.

"Fuck off."

"That's not a very gracious way to greet an old friend, Theo," he replies. "Especially one who saved you from a cockatrice."

"Wasn't an ordinary cockatrice."

Keneally smiles. "Somebody thought it would be funny to crossbreed one of its parents with a demon," he says. Yeah, some smart-arse fucking sorcerer like Keneally.

"Fuck you." A few specks of my blood settle on his face, but his smile remains.

"You should thank me; I ruined the organ harvest saving your miserable skin."

The meat of the demontrice is still cooking; it makes farting, squeaking noises. Keneally's favorite spell is one he calls 'Microwave Madness.'

"The bounty's mine, of course," says Keneally. "Since you didn't even scratch the fucker. The state of the art left your glaive behind decades ago, I'm afraid."

I try to speak, but blood fills my mouth. Hard to argue the point with the weapon in question broken off in my stomach.

Keneally waves a hand and his filthy sorcery raises me into the air. "You look like shit, Theo. I'll give you a lift to Doctor Langer." He turns away. "No, don't thank me; we'll stop off on the way so you can sign the bounty check over to me."

I pass out while Doc Langer works on me. It's not just pain; it's the feeling of my guts moving around inside me, the tingling of my flesh rapidly resealing. Or perhaps it's the Doc's singing: bassy and trebly at once; a melody I can't quite predict, lyrics I can't quite understand.

This is faerie magic, I'm pretty sure. Makes me uncomfortable, but I know the Doc's a purebred human. Doesn't have the sheen on him that the frips do.

"There you go, Theo. All done."

"Ugff." Sitting up hurts a lot more than it should. I look down: there are rows of stitches snaking all over my stomach, my arms. "What the fuck?"

Langer is pealing the bloody latex off his fingers. He smiles. "Something wrong?"

"I got fucking *stitches!*" Yelling hurts my stitches. "Goddamnit!" Swearing hurts, too.

"You're not covered for muscular or epidermal repairs. Your internals should be working, though."

Fuck. I can't work if I'm injured. "I can write you a check for the full workup," I say, confidently. Then, just as confidently: "But it won't clear."

Langer chuckles a little.

"I mean, it won't . . . . I don't . . . ."

"Give it up, son. There's truth floss in the stitching."

"I got insurance!"

"Your Monster Hunter's Guild doesn't cover jack shit, Theo." He sighs. "I'm not even going to bother invoicing them for the kidneys or the liver. They won't pay it out."

I glower at him. "We don't all have fancy-pants Sorcerer's Guild insurance."

"That's because you need to be a sorcerer to qualify," says Langer, "and *that* requires you be at least *partially* literate."

Before I can reply he puts his hand on my shoulder. "I'm sorry, Theo, you're just going to have to take it easy for a while."

When I open my wallet to give the receptionist my twenty dollar co-pay I find a business card I've never seen before: DB WEAPONS.

Fucking Keneally. Is he getting a referral fee?

DB WEAPONS is located in an office block on the eastern fringe of downtown. Finding the building is easy; getting up to the fourteenth story is another matter. I ride the elevator up, but it doesn't stop on 14. I ride the second elevator back down from the 16th, but it doesn't stop for me, either. Back on the ground floor, the kid at the reception counter tells me that the 14th floor is inaccessible during the renovations.

"Service personnel are supposed to use the stairs," he says. "I'm sure you've been warned."

I lower my shades and spread my lips. My eyes are red with broken blood vessels, my teeth are stained from the combat supplements I take. The kid looks away. "I've been warned," I tell him.

I walk up fourteen flights of steps, forgetting that Americans consider the ground floor to be level 1. I'm hurting when I turn to go back down a level. Still a long way from fully healed: my back is stiff, my stomach hurts. I've lost three kilograms of lean body mass. I'm not breathing hard, but I can tell that I've lost about a third of my cardio fitness.

Level fourteen is under construction. Partition walls have been knocked down. The carpet has been pulled up due to apparent water damage. Exposed cabling hangs from ragged holes in the plasterwork. There's no furniture.

It stinks with the unstench of faeriekind; odors that do not commingle or associate themselves with anything other than their source object. There's a Gate here, and it's a new one. I'm not a sorcerer, but I've been around long enough that I sense it.

The elf peels away his glamour and steps into my vision in a way that offends me utterly. Back home, Dad and I used to hunt them with dogs and .22s, bounty or no bounty. Now the Guild forbids it: faerie citizens cannot be hunted unless they exhibit 'monstrous tendencies.' PC bullshit, I dunno.

The elf is wearing a white suit and an open-collared black shirt. Gold necklace. Long brown hair covers the points of his ears. He's too soft to be a warrior, too sociable to be a full-blown magus; but beyond that I can't tell what Breed or Species or Nation he's from. Could be anything from a dryad to a townie.

"Ah, Theodore," he says. "I've been expecting you."

"You're DB?"

"I'm called that," he says.

"What's your name?"

"I'll keep that to myself. I hope you don't think me rude."

"You're the weapons dealer, right?"

"Indeed."

"Then show me some fucking weapons. I don't give a shit about your manners."

DB smiles. "I imagine not." He waves a hand—he's wearing a gold Rolex—and three wooden crates appear. DB picks up a glossy catalogue off the nearest one.

"I have many fine implements of death and destruction, never before available outside of the Faerie Realms."

"Yes, but will they actually *work* outside the Realms?"

"New spellcrafting technology allows them to work in any world that has even the slightest ambient magic field."

"I'm on a budget."

"I'm sure I have something within your budget that can add value to your business . . . and I do accept trade-ins." He raises an eyebrow expectantly.

I scowl. "I have a Glaive of St Konin." The Glaive has been in my family for centuries. After the Korean War my father went AWOL to reclaim it from the branch of my family still living in Derry. He killed six cousins and two uncles in single combat before the family let him take it back to Oz.

DB peers into my duffle bag. "Ah, yes." He sniffs. "It's obviously not worth as much as it would be intact."

"The blade is fine. The haft can be replaced."

"Yes, but it's never the same, is it?" The elf opens the catalog. "Never mind, I'll give you a good deal. Let's not haggle until you've seen my merchandise."

"Then put the fucking brochure away and show me the weapons."

DB puts the catalogue down. We approach a crate that's labeled with unreadable script. It takes him three strokes with the crowbar to get it open.

The crate is filled with daggers and dirks made of a black, lusterless metal, lying on a bed of plastic straw.

"Shadowsteel," says DB. "Forged in the Ore-lands, enchanted by true magi. Cutting power proportional to the amount of magic available; indestructible and ever-sharp on any world."

"Perfect for killing baby frips in their prams," I say dismissively.

DB picks up the crowbar and points to another crate. "Something bigger, perhaps?"

I grab the crowbar from him and open it.

The new crate is full of swords, also made of the shadowsteel. They're good, unfussy weapons: straight, double-edged blades, undecorated guards, fat round pommels.

"I also have clubs, flails, sickles . . . ."

"I prefer blades."

DB nods. "More efficient and cost effective. You buy a flanged mace, you're paying for a lot of extra metal that's only going to weigh you down."

I find myself about to give the anecdote about the Chinaman, the Mace and the Unbreakable Door, but I stop myself. He's a salesman, he *wants* to develop a rapport. "What are the specs?"

"The same entry-level features as the knives," says DB. "And of course, all the standard options are available. Magic-proofing, spell thwarting, sensory enhancement."

"My glaive already does that stuff. What else is there?"

He flips through the catalog. "Some, ah, *fruitier* options that I don't think you'd go for. Singing blades, fire plumes, illuminate evil . . . ."

"Pass. What else?"

"I do have some new weapons with Next Gen features. Upskilling. Full Dynamic Variable Geometry. Smart logic, programmable to your technique."

"I don't need some sorcerer's spellgorithm telling me how to swing my sword."

"You'd be surprised by how effective it is." He sees the look on my face and adds: "But that would only annoy a professional like you. Come, I have something that I think you'll *really* like."

We open another box of shadowsteel swords. They're still quite plain, but it's clear that some design has gone into the look and feel of them.

"These are shadowcutting models."

"Shadowcutting?"

"These weapons allow you to strike down your opponent with your shadow."

I reach down for one of the ungleaming blades, then retract my hand. "These won't . . . I don't know . . . suck out my soul, or anything, will they?"

"Of course not."

I'm still suspicious. "This is pretty fancy magic—it has to draw power from somewhere."

"It's pipelined from the factory plant," says DB.

"I've heard of that. The wielder is the conduit?"

"Yes."

"That has to have side effects."

"Of course it does." DB smiles. "It will enhance the wielder's personal attributes. Strength, speed, endurance." He shrugs. "It's quite pleasurable, actually. Try it."

Biting the insides of my mouth, I reach down and pick up the faerie weapon. I heft the blade, point with it, make a small cut. It's well balanced and light, but it has some weight to it. I can tell how sharp it is just from the sound of it. It's a damn nice weapon, and the longer I hold it, the better I feel. My wounds aren't healing, but I feel stronger, quicker, more agile. I want to cut something. "How much?"

"Eight thousand."

I splutter. "Daylight robbery."

"That's two thousand below MSRP."

"Fell off the back of a truck, did they?"

DB shakes his head mournfully. "The Realms have fallen on hard times," he says. "It pains me to be here, haggling for your mortal pennies, but since the Apocalypse, it's the only currency with any worth in our Land."

Of course I've heard that there was some kind of apocalypse in the Faerie Realms, that's why there are more godless bastards around than ever. Not much of an apocalypse, I reckon, if there were this many survivors.

"Not my problem." The longer I hold the sword, the more I want it. I need it. I know that it should be mine. I force myself to put it down. Its absence leaves me with a residual, sticky feeling.

We haggle. I get him down to 7500, but it's difficult. I can't get more than 2000 out of him for the glaive. He won't allow me to finance it, so it goes onto my MasterCard . . . which leaves me just about maxed out. Injured or not, I'm going to have to find some work right away or I'm not going to be able to eat.

"A pleasure doing business with you," says DB, turning away and peeling himself off my retinas again. "Next time you need to upgrade your arsenal, I trust you know where to come."

I slam the door behind me and start down the stairs.

"Those motherfuckers."

I'm on my way to my first job since the demontrice beat the crap out of me. I've been stuck in traffic for a full hour, and I've been cursing DB and Keneally the entire way. I've tried the sword out, and the shadowcutting works great . . . if there's light. In darkness, where there are no shadows, it's useless. I do about 60% of my work in cellars, catacombs and sewers.

Fifty-five hundred bucks is a lot for me, but it's jack shit to Keneally. I know he's out there somewhere, laughing at me.

I pull my van over outside the containment fence and enter on foot. This is the location where the first Gate opened into the city. Used to be an industrial suburb, gang territory—then the influx of faerie refugees turned it into a *real* mess. The elves were bad enough, but then the true nasties started using the Faerie Realms as a thoroughfare. Monsters, demonoids and worse. When the government finally noticed, they reacted predictably. Couldn't have the general public learning that faerie creatures were running loose—not until they'd worked out how to exploit them properly. So they moved out the human residents and fenced the whole area off. Toxic soil from the factories, they said.

If they'd put together a proper, old-fashioned refugee camp we'd have none of this.

Oh, well. Good for my business.

Today I'm hunting leprechauns. They're big in Brazil this year; apparently the latest thing is to use their heads for oracles. I don't think they're particularly reliable, as far as foretelling goes, but the Brazilians are mad for the accents.

I buckle on the Kevlar vest, strap the greaves and vambraces onto my forearms and shins. I hang a big, serrated knife on my belt—I'll need that to saw off the heads. Some small canisters of homemade napalm in the belt pouches. I carry the shadowsteel in my hand.

It's been a while since I've been here, and I'm surprised at how bad it's gotten. Houses are boarded up and barred. Spray paint everywhere, whole blocks are burnt down—goblins, I'm guessing, or some kind of firebreather. Or perhaps just careless cooking.

It *is* a bit of a stretch to classify leprechauns as monsters by the new Guild laws, but if I close one eye and squint I can make a case for it on infrastructure damage. If I get called to tribunal over it I'll just act like a dumb redneck and turn up my Aussie accent. Maybe get a fine, but I expect to more than cover that with today's takings.

I come to an intersection a couple blocks away from my van. I pour out a half circle of napalm across the streets heading north and east.

Kneeling on the cracked asphalt in the middle of the intersection, I produce a barely-circular coin of True Gold from inside a lead box. On one side is a faint image of a crone; on the other are some barely-legible words. It tingles against my skin. Fiddles and flutes play at the edge of my hearing. I read the words aloud: "Tuatha De Dannan."

I don't know what the fuck it means. My family were thrown out of Ireland two centuries ago and shipped off to the furthest of penal colonies; I hate that Celtic shit almost as much as I hate the English.

I put the coin down on the bitumen when it starts throwing off prismatic sparks.

I stand there with my sword in hand, feeling like an idiot, listening to barely-audible goddamn fiddledy-dee music, but eventually my patience is rewarded. Waddling footsteps and a sinister giggling precede the first of them. A pasty-white, inhumanly happy face with a mane of red hair pokes out from behind the house on the northeast corner. He's wearing a green hat with a buckle on it, of course.

"I know this be a trick," says the leprechaun, suspicious.

What a genius. I'm standing over the coin with a big black sword in my hand. "True Gold is True Gold," I say.

The 'chaun comes around from behind the house, both hands behind his back, whistling a jig. He's shorter than a goblin, proportioned more like a toddler than a midget.

"A trick this be, and yet . . . and yet . . . who am I to resist the lure of True Gold?"

Somewhere to my left, another little cocksucker starts giggling. He pokes his head around the base of what used to be a street lamp. "The True Gold is *mine,* says I."

The first leprechaun runs at him, waving his hat around and screaming. "No, tis *mine!*" They all fucking talk like this.

A third one jumps down from a rooftop. "Laddies, laddies, let's not fight! A trap this surely be!"

All three of them are charging towards the coin, raving and giggling. It's as if they don't even see me. I cut two of them down with one stroke, turn my wrist and aim. The point of my blade's shadow rises up off the road and the third one runs right onto it.

All hell breaks loose. Leprechauns start coming out of the trees, out of the houses, out of holes in the ground. Rainbows shimmer as more of them arrive. I'm surrounded. The giggling crescendoes as they mount a charge.

I pop a flare and toss it at the napalm. A curtain of sticky flame roars up behind me and the giggling rises to inchoate screaming as a wave of short, green bastards goes up in fire. Their cooking flesh makes me hungry for pot roast.

The leprechauns come on and I lay about me with the sword. They're angry now, but they still want the coin. They're fearless, I'll give 'em that much. They keep on coming, no matter how high the pile of bodies rises. The sheer weight of them pushes me back toward the flames, dragging the gold coin with my foot.

The sword has amped my endurance. I feel like I can just keep hacking away all day . . . and the more of them I butcher, the better I feel.

One of them locks onto my right leg. I try to shake him off, but his little hands are locked onto my bootlaces. He's trying to chew through my fatigue pants. Another grabs my left leg. A third one gets behind me and starts using his fellows as a ladder. I back up a couple of paces and he catches fire, but now they're all over me and the weight is just too much. I'm bleeding from dozens of bites and gouges. My stitches have opened up. I can't hold my position; I can't swing the sword with five of the bastards hanging onto each arm.

They pull me down. A dozen tiny pairs of hands and feet are prying at me, pummeling me, mashing my face into the pavement. My nose crunches loudly.

A cry of triumph and, suddenly, they're off me. The screaming and giggling abates. I hear lots of little feet retreating. When I roll over I can see one blood-covered leprechaun standing above me, holding the gold coin over his head. He puts it in his front coat pocket and skips away.

"Fairly won, laddie! Fairly won!" They grab him up and carry him away like a champion footballer. They're singing. One of them is playing the fiddle, another is piping away on a flute.

I wipe the blood out of my eyes and push myself to my feet. There are maybe eighty corpses, not a bad harvest. I pull the serrated knife off my belt and get to work.

Doc Langer stops singing about halfway through my procedure. He was happy enough to pull out the stitches after I gave him a fat roll of greenbacks, but once the real work starts, his voice falters. He hums for a minute, then ceases altogether.

When he's done, he wipes his hands on a towel and gives me a serious look. "All of your organs are joined up and functional again. The skin is sealed. Shouldn't be much scarring. I've managed to put most of your nose back on, although I couldn't replace the tissue you left behind."

I sniff, wiggle my nose. No pain. I wave away the mirror, but he frowns at me. "You should have a look," he says.

"Don't give a shit about me nose."

Langer shakes his head. "It's not your nose," he says. "It's your eyes."

I look into the mirror reluctantly. There's still blood in my eyes . . . only now it's black, not red. He grabs one of my hands. "See that?" My fingernails are black. "Open your mouth." My teeth are mottled black, too. "Even your hair looks darker."

I'm not concerned. "Everything seems to be functioning."

"It worries me that I can't fix it," says Langer.

"Yeah, well, you're an HMO doctor. Was there anything else?"

"Well, I was going to top you up on plasma, but you seem to have plenty," He frowns. "I think."

"You *think* I have plenty?"

"No, I think it's *plasma*," he says. "But it *might* be something else."

"Whatever."

I slide off the table and reach for my shirt.

"I'd like to see you back here in three weeks," says Langer.

"When I had no money and my guts were hanging out, you couldn't wait to see the back of me," I say. "Now, you want me to come back—even though I'm fully healed?"

"Theodore, I'm telling you—"

I pull the faded black t-shirt over my head. "Yeah, doc, whatever you reckon."

"Theo . . . ." he says, but I'm already gone.

I shift down and yank the van around, forcing a late model Civic onto the shoulder as I muscle the van through. The wheel gives a crack, breaks in my hands. Time I upgraded this old piece of shit, anyway. There's a hostage situation at the local community college and there's a nice fat bounty if I can get there before too many people die.

It's twilight by the time I arrive. There are black-and-whites everywhere. Ambulances, lights cycling. SWAT cops mill around in flak jackets and polycarbonate visors, toting MP3s, looking grim and useless.

This isn't an ordinary school siege. The miscreants aren't issuing demands, they're not killing many people, they're just holding the place. Waiting for night.

I get out of the van and step over the yellow tape. I'm wearing a cheap pair of wraparound sunglasses. I have the brim of my cap pulled low—don't need anybody asking what's wrong with my eyes. Nothing, so far as I'm concerned. My vision is sharper than ever.

A cop with sergeant stripes approaches me. "You the private contractor?"

"Yeah." He gives me a look of disgust but he doesn't even ask to see some ID. He's dealt with the likes of me before. I turn and walk around to the back of the van. "Tell me the situation."

"No word from inside. Phone lines cut, security feed is down." The sergeant's eyes go wide for a split second when he sees the cache of weapons and the bloodied cooler boxes. Haven't bothered to clean out the van since the leprechaun hunt and I'm actually starting to like the smell.

The sergeant coughs and covers his nose. "They have the hostages in the library block. A man on every entrance, sniper on the top floor. These are pros, not a bunch of shitheads who watched too many action movies."

"How many of them, total?" I'm having trouble fastening on my vest. I've bulked up a bit more than I thought.

"Six. Maybe seven."

I'm pretty sure I know what's going on. The hostage takers are ghouls, enhanced as well as handsomely paid; no doubt promised immortality and lots of necro sex by their vampire masters. Probably ex-military; the vamps are getting smarter about their daylight guardians these days. I squint up at the sun. I can take the ghouls, but vampires are a different proposition. I need to do this before full dark.

I strap on the Glock 17 and the Sig Sauer, check the action on the Mossberg shotgun. Six grenades, a dozen spare clips. The shadowsteel sword is slung across my back.

"You're taking grenades into a *school?*"

I shrug.

I work my way around to the maintenance area on the eastern edge of the building, well away from the library. The hump of the generator there will give me some cover from the sniper, but I still have to cross twenty meters of open ground.

"Fuck it."

I charge the building. I get about halfway across the open ground before the sniper's first shot zings over my head. I zig; the second goes by on my left. The third slams into my vest below my left clavicle. It spins me around and knocks me down, but I roll out of it and zag back towards the window. The Kevlar's kept the bullet out of me, but I'm surprised I'm able to shake off the shock so easily.

I pitch a grenade through a window and run straight into the storm of exploding glass and burning gases, fumbling for a pistol.

I can't get my finger inside the Glock's trigger guard; seems to have swollen up a bit. I discard it and pull the Sig, unlimber the Mossberg with my other hand. Inside, amidst the flapping of loose pages and clearing smoke, is the first of my enemies. He has the greyish skin and marbled eyes of the halfway undead.

Although he's blinded and disoriented, the ghoul opens up with his Uzi, spraying the walls and the ceiling. I stop him with a 3.5" magnum load from the shotgun and head up the stairs without even slowing.

I emerge in a hallway on the first floor. A ghoul comes out of one of the doors and another comes charging around the corner. I fire the Mossberg and then the Sig. The first ghoul's head vaporizes; the second one slams into a wall. He lands back on his feet, hissing like a cockroach despite having four slugs in his chest. I smash his head open with the butt of the shotgun.

I reload as I jog down the hall. Right, then left, through a pair of double doors, and suddenly I'm on the main floor of the library. One ghoul right in front of me, two more up on the mezzanine. I can hear a fourth barking orders at the hostages somewhere in the back of the room. I fire with both weapons and the first ghoul goes down without getting off a round.

I toss the guns; the sword is thirsty. I draw the shadowsteel as I move into the stacks.

A ghoul jumps down from the mezzanine, opening fire as his feet hit the top of a twelve-foot bookcase. I swing the sword up, through the collapsing shelving, the avalanche of paper, the hail of gunfire, and split him in half.

I've taken some fire in my arms, in my chest, even in my face. I don't really care. In fact, I feel pretty goddamn good.

The last of them is in the back, amongst the study carrels, with the hostages. They're kneeling, their backs to him, their hands behind their heads. A few bodies lying amongst them. They're weeping, praying, gibbering. Some of them have fainted. Fucking college nancies with their teased up hair and their rock'n'roll t-shirts, never worked a day in their lives. When I was their age, I'd already put in three years on the slaughterhouse floor.

The ghoul has an AK47 tucked into his shoulder. He keeps the gun on the hostages. "One more step and I'm gonna open up full auto."

He smiles, thinking we're at some sort of impasse. I move forward, pulling off my shades, meeting his marble greys with my black and bloody eyes.

I look up at the lights, step around to the left, and extend my sword arm at an odd angle. He watches me curiously, not feeling threatened by a man with a sword at a distance of fifteen meters. "What are you doing, semaphore?"

"Working out how to kill you."

"I'll kill every one of these bastards if you try anything."

I bring the sword around in a long arc, throwing its shadow across the floor. It rises up, cuts through a bookshelf, then three or four panicking students, before it finally strikes the ghoul, opening him from shoulder to hip. He falls to the ground in two pieces.

I *think* killing humans would have bothered me a few weeks ago, but I'm not positive. Right now, it seems that taking out the ghouls is more important. The shadowsteel certainly doesn't care whose blood it drinks.

Gunfire from the mezzanine. I take it full in the chest, it knocks me off my feet. I'd forgotten the sniper.

The sniper watches me get up, incredulous. He weighs his chances and decides to make a run for it. The students have panicked; they're up and running around, screaming, crazy.

The sniper shoulders open a door into a concrete stairwell and disappears up through it. I rumble up the stairs to the mezzanine after him, my breath steaming out of me, swinging the sword. My clothes are burning off me; my body hair's crisped away. My muscles flow like lava underneath my skin. My dick is loose, slapping against my thighs as I run.

It's only two flights up to the roof; I'm only a few steps away when he finally bursts out onto the roof, crying and yelling. When I smile, my teeth feel surprisingly pointed on my lip.

The sniper stands there screaming at the moon, wailing the blasphemous names of his masters. I can see shapes coming in from the east, following the darkness. I hear laughter on their wings.

I advance on the sniper, the sword loose in my hand. He backs away.

"Come on," I say.

He glances over his shoulder at the flapping wings and something breaks in him. He charges at me, laughing and weeping. I extend the sword and he rushes right onto it, his breastbone slamming against the crossguard. His claws continue to slash at my face until I slap his head off with a casual backhand.

The laughter is closer now, crueler. The laughter of a master amused by the antics of a pet dog.

Movement behind me. When I turn, something rakes my face, tearing through skin and cartilage like paper. My nose is off again. A second blow, aimed at my eyes, scrapes off my corneas. Eyelids and part of my forehead comes off, but my vision is unaffected.

It's full dark.

"You ruined our party, you appalling . . . thing . . . ." The vampire sounds like a Pom. She's wearing jeans and a leather vest; short, dyed-black hair. Biker chick.

"That's okay, you might still get on *America's Funniest Animals*," I say, gesturing at the sniper's corpse.

I swing at her, but she leans out of the way and kicks me, sending me stumbling. She follows up with a kick in the back. I roll, come to a half kneel with the sword angled defensively . . . just in time to see the second vampire alight.

"Y'all killed our little helpers," she says, indignant, "and *then* y'all ruined the food." This one's pure Alabama trailer trash: a skinny girl dressed in a cheap lamé evening dress and a pair of thigh-highs with six inch heels. Fake boobs, slathered on eye makeup—guarantee she used to be a stripper. Vamps have no class anymore.

The stripper looks like the easier target: How mobile can she be in those stilettos? I surge toward her, bringing the blade up in a diagonal cut. She pivots on one heel and swings the other one, roundhouse, into my throat. Very mobile, I guess.

She holds me there, hanging from her heel. When she withdraws her foot, I fall to my knees. My breath whistles and bubbles through the hole in my neck.

The biker vamp grabs me by what's left of my Kevlar jacket, hauls me up and puts her teeth to my neck. I'm about to black out when she freezes and lets me go. I fall down on my arse.

The biker-vamp's choking, her hands on her throat. Shadows spray from her mouth, her nose. She falls, darkness gushing from her eyes.

I tighten my grip on the shadowsteel and rise, as though yanked up by a puppet-string in my back. I grin at the stripper vamp and come *en garde*. My face is mostly gone, my neck has been torn right open, but I feel just dandy.

I try a cut. She slides under my blade and delivers a right cross that splinters the vertebrae in my neck and shatters the left hinge of my jaw. I return my head to its accustomed position. Only the muscle is holding it together.

I can't take this one, not without trickery . . . but there's no moon, there are no shadows to cut with. I curse and circle with her, hoping she'll let her guard down. Maybe she'll slip in my blood, or something . . . there's enough of it splashed blackly around the place.

My blood. It's darker than venal blood, so black it doesn't reflect any light. It lies about in swathes and puddles; it runs out of me like viscous liquid shadow. Oh, yes.

Oh, yes, indeed.

I turn in a direction the vampire doesn't expect, swing a cut that can't connect . . . but the shadowblood I've spilled rises in sympathy with my blade; stretching across the floor, bending up the wall and snaking out to strike her from behind. A black line bisects her face above the cheekbones. The top of her head comes off.

I've killed all the monsters. The mission is a success, far as I'm concerned, but I have a feeling that nobody else will see it that way. The longer I ponder, the less interested I am in whether I'll be paid and the more concerned I am about finding something else to kill.

The shadowsteel blade is so dark and unshiny that I can't tell if there's blood on it. I think it's cleaned itself, like a cat. I'm fascinated with the sword until it vanishes.

I blink, look a second time: my hand's vanished with it.

I fall down.

Without the shadowsteel in my hand, I'm starting to feel my wounds. There's no way I should still be alive . . . and I won't be for much longer.

"Hello, Theodore."

I turn my head a little; it's the only part of me I can move.

"I hope you don't mind me saying it, but you *really* look like shit." Keneally's standing over me with my Glaive of St Konin in his hands. It's been refitted with a new cherrywood haft.

I try to tell him to fuck off, but the words gurgle in my ruined throat.

"I told you the glaive would be useful."

I can't turn my head anymore, but I recognize DB's voice.

"Forgive me for not trusting a faerie salesman."

"It belonged to his family for hundreds of years."

"Yes, and it hated him, just like everyone else who ever knew him."

Keneally slits me open with the glaive. He squats down to peer into my chest cavity. "I had my doubts, I admit, but the shadowsteel reacted to him even better than you said it would." He starts rummaging around in my guts with his bare fingers. "Interesting. You don't see these configurations in a born monster. Look at these kidneys!"

"I bet the eyes are worth a pretty penny."

Keneally crab-walks to my head and pries out an eye with a knife. "Infrared filters, look at that."

I gurgle.

"I'm sorry, Theodore. You were an asshole, but you were a skilled hunter," says DB. "Unfortunately, your business model was tragically dated."

Keneally starts on my other eye. "I'm keeping the glaive."

"Of course. And the shadowsteel comes back to me, as we agreed."

Keneally eyes the sword nervously. "Well, I don't want it."

DB picks it up, removes my severed hand from its grip, and makes it disappear into his Armani jacket. "That's going right back into stock."

I'm feeling pangs, now; terrible pain, though it's not physical. It's as though my soul is being wrung out like a dishrag. I think of my prey: every monster I cut down. Poor bastards. For the first time in my life, I feel for them. They couldn't help their needs, their natures. Who was I to judge them? To shed their blood for money?

Keneally works the remaining eye out of my face, but there's no darkness; everything is bright. Illuminated. Enlightened.

I wish I had turned to some other trade. I wish I were born to some other faith. I wish could be reborn. If I had my time again, I would fling the Gates open wide and invite them all here, in their legions, their tribes, their hordes and their covens. I would hoard gold for the dragons; I'd stoke flames for the hellspawn; I'd give my blood to the vampires, my teeth to the tooth faeries. I'd farm children for the boogey-men, women for the goblins. I'd remake the world as a place of tolerance and charity, of light and love and peace, where none could be persecuted for the way they were born or they way they evolved.

They have no gods, these faeries and monsters and demons; no heavens or hells, as we mortals do. They live their days in suffering and then they pass on, and are gone. Would that I could make this place a heaven for them.

I know that I will be unmourned in death, I know that I deserve it. As I go to my grave, my only regret is that I cannot share my vision of paradise.

Loopholes

Phil Brucato

TAP. TAP. TAP.

Jack's there at the bedside. I can't see him, but I hear him. Feel him, too, a dense presence with barrel-thick arms. The club in his hand falls without striking a blow. He doesn't need to. The sound is enough. Jack Dunning's clever enough to hurt you inside.

TAP. TAP. TAP.

Oak shouldn't fall so lightly. Calloused palms shouldn't sound so thick. There shouldn't be an ogre in a three-piece suit standing at the foot of my bed. And I shouldn't owe him something I just can't pay.

"You 'wake?" Jack says. His voice rumbles through the framework of my bed.

"Keep it down," I hiss. "You'll wake my roommate."

The dark-on-dark shape shrugs. I shouldn't be able to see that, but I can. My eyes must be accustomed now to the light-less room we share. The club keeps falling steadily, soft as rain, hard as thunder.

TAP. TAP. TAP.

Sigh, deep, finally.
"Okay, Jack," I say. "Let's talk . . . ."

It's the American way. Make money, spend money, borrow more money for both. I'd spent the better part of a decade as a hotshot law-shark, acquiring all the toys such status brings. New cars, new house, new clothes, new stuff. My wife Mari and

I lived well. If we seemed extravagant, there was always more coming in.

Until there wasn't.

Boom. Bust. Pretty words. Harsh feelings. Economic onomatopoeia doesn't capture the crushed-chest pain of bills you could have paid a year earlier. My credit was still high, though, so the plastic got a workout. It was only a matter of time, we figured, until the good times rolled back up again.

Something stalled, though. So did my career. Soon, my marriage did the same. The bills, though, kept arriving. The good times, then, seemed over and done with.

But you don't get where I had been without accumulating a few favors along the way. So about three years after the boom had busted, I walked down a flight of stairs I promised myself I'd never descend again.

He was still there, waiting.

The door to his office swung open, silent as a Mob witness on testimony day. Inside, the office was much as I recalled. Floor-to-ceiling bookshelves. Clutter everywhere. Burnt tobacco and paper rot. Endless ticking from countless clocks. Gargoyles perched on precarious shelves. Occasionally, they moved. It'd been that way since I was a kid, when Dad first brought me down to visit . . . .

"Gino," he said in a cigarette voice. His parchment features crinkled with something like joy.

"Hello, Sal," I replied, raising my hand to wave. My fingers, I noted, were trembling.

Salantazi DiVoraccio was from what you might call the Old Country. The *very* old country. Not my ancestral lands of Sicily, but someplace far more ancient than human civilization. His name was a convenience, not even truly Italian. Like most names, though, it conveyed certain hints about his identity.

"It's been too long," he scolded, unfolding from his overstuffed chair. On the table he'd been sitting at, a watch spilled its guts across black velvet. A jeweler's glass overlooked a glittering dissection of bright lights and miniature tools. Sal liked things that ticked. The walls of his shop clustered with cuckoos and other novelty clocks. He couldn't care less about passing hours, but precision fascinated him. If something stopped ticking, Sal would want to know why.

I arced a shoulder to shrug. "Time gets away from me."

Sal chuckled like wax paper. The watchmaker's spotlight cast his dry features into sharp relief. He stilted toward me, trailing smoke like a grasshopper with a nicotine fixation. "Such a busy boy," he said. "So many things to do." He reached out to hug me. I hugged him back, of course. He felt like old twigs wrapped in steel. "It is good to see you, *bambino*."

"Good to see you, too."

His wagged a thin finger at me, smiling. "Ah, ah, ah . . . lying again. Haven't you learned better than that?"

I half-smiled. "Sal, I'm a professional liar."

"Small wonder, then, that you are doing so poorly with it."

"You know?"

"I always could read you, *ragazzo*," he said, motioning to another chair. "Sit."

"Then you know why I'm here," I replied, sitting. The trembling in my hands went bone-deep.

He shrugged, sitting back and turning his chair to face me. "Tell me anyway, yes? Confession is good for the soul . . . ."

I hadn't planned on the law degree. I liked solving problems, though, and Dad always claimed I was great at arguing. "You can debate circles around me," he'd said once. "That doesn't make you right." I didn't need to be right, though. Just paid. As long as I was getting paid, everything seemed fine.

Sure, I made compromises. Who doesn't? Law school teaches that your client is never guilty, even when he *is*. I had plenty of "never guilty" clients, and lots of favors I didn't cash in. One of 'em sat at the bottom of a flight of stairs that sometimes was there and sometimes was not. "Stay away from him," said Dad after I asked about his old "friend" Sal. "Some people, you don't deal with unless you're ready to meet their price. And trust me, son, you never are."

Dad wouldn't discuss the prices he'd paid. I only knew about my own. Late nights bleared with arcane facts. Precedent and argument. Missed meals and brokered deals. Mari spent many 4:00 AMs with my nightmares and compromised positions. Shakespeare said, "First, kill all the lawyers." He didn't have to. Our livers do it first.

It was my friend Stephen, though, who helped me soldier through. Over more beers than I'd like to count, he claimed we lawyers kept the American clockworks greased. "This is why it all works, Gino," he'd say, his lanky frame hunched over the bar stool. "It's us. In a nation of 'laws, not men,' we're the men who work the laws that work the men." He didn't understand that some laws are stronger than men. I didn't understand it, either. I sure as hell get it now.

Our firm seemed to be rolling right along. Then the track ran out, fast. When Stephe hopped off, I saw the end coming. A few months later, the pink slip hit my desk. I thought my client base would take care of me. I thought wrong.

Folks say you're only as good as your last paycheck. Soon, I wasn't feeling too good. Pride made things worse. I couldn't admit how desperate things had become. "Never let 'em see you sweat," and all that. Or bleed, in my case. Lawyers deal in the red stuff, real and otherwise. Sharks smell blood, and I know the scent well. I smelled it all around me, even as I slept. Stepping out of the shower, I stank like a slaughterhouse. The smell drove me insane. It clung to me in each interview and got stronger with each apology. Three years out, I was breathing failure.

That's when Stephen called again.

By that time, Mari and I were history. Most of my cash and credit had gone with her. I was fighting wolves back from the door, and had the bites to prove it. Sure, I scored the occasional client. Getting ahead, though, took money I didn't have. So when Stephen called, I jumped. You need me, Stephe? You got me.

Jack looms across my bed. His breath smells of garlic and alfredo sauce. Faint light through the curtains glints on the tusks jutting from his lower jaw. Jack rumbles in his chest. Is that interest I hear from him, or hunger?

Tap. Tap. Tap.

I choose my next words carefully . . . .

"Thanks, Sal," I'd said to the papery old troll. His eyes held a sympathetic light. His dry hands, however, held something far more valuable: a contract with my name on it. No blood—nothing that melodramatic. Just ink, the blackest kind. The kind that won't come off your hands no matter how much you wash.

"You're good for it, *mio piccolo bambino.*" He offered a single nod and a vaguely barbed smile. On a nearby bookshelf, one gargoyle flapped lazily and settled back onto its perch. I tried to act like that wasn't unusual. Instead, I nodded back. "I am, Sal. You've got my word on that. Literally."

I tried not to notice the scent of blood there, either. Was it something in the room, or was my wounded pride bleeding again? Underneath the paper-rot smell and subtle glide of watch-oil hovered a rich, carnal aroma. Maybe I just knew, then, what my bargain with Sal would cost.

Like Dad said, some folks cost more than you want to pay. Sal was one of 'em. He didn't ask me for anything right then, but I knew that when he smiled and said, "Just you remember me when I come calling," I had better damned remember. There are worse things than broken knees and concrete shoes, and Sal dealt with those "worse things."

My trembling had nestled south of my heart, and my ticker was doing its best to stomp its way out through my ribcage. My wallet, however, held a check for a quarter of a million dollars—the buy-in price for partnership in Stephen's practice, plus a bit extra for me to live on. Who'd have thought that something worth so much could weigh so little?

That thought shook me. I glanced at the clock guts scattered across black velvet on the table. "You realize," I reiterated for the third time that afternoon, "that I *cannot* pay back this kind of money yet. Not now. Not soon. Not for a while."

Sal waved his parchment hand. "Money? It means nothing. Nonsense and trickery. Five thousand years and it still amazes me that you *ragazzi* take it so seriously."

"So why do you have this shop at all?"

He waved his hand at the clockwork corpse. "To see why things tick, *un giovanoto*, even when they are taken apart."

"Is that what happens, Sal, if I can't pay you back?" My voice stuck. "You'll take me apart?"

DiVoraccio shook his head. "I won't have to." He replied, lighting another cigarette. "You will."

"I'm waiting," Jack says. The words remind me of Mari's tone just before a fight. Drop the voice three octaves and you'd have a perfect match . . . but then, I know why it sounds familiar. It's part of Jack's nature to embody your guilt.

They train you, in law school, to keep your voice steady. Some things, though, can't be trained away. Facing down a jury is easy. When you've faced down a seven-foot leg-breaker with Boschian dental work and a tone like your ex-wife, talk to me about training.

Deep sigh. "I know I can't pay you right now," I say as steadily as I can manage. "You know it as well as I do."

"And . . . ?"

"And you know why I can't."

I feel the shadow shrug again. The pressure in my chest grows. Pain swells. The ogre hasn't moved an inch.

Maybe it's the dawn light through my curtains, but I can see him now. He fits in my room with appalling ease. Given his height, Jack should be stooping. Instead, he stands like a butler of the damned. Folks say that Jack was once a man—a warden in an English debtor's prison. Stories of him, though, are as old as debt itself. In Hebrew writings, he's called Yacob the Mountain. Sumerians referred to him as Gud-alim, "The Bull." Germans named him Jakob der Golem, while Chinese debtors regarded him as Fang Yu, enforcer for the God of Justice. I've had plenty of time to study him, see. Jack's been assigned, you might say, to my case. This isn't the first time he's dropped by, and mere bankruptcy won't make him leave.

It had been going so well for a while. Once again, I was nailing my game. Castrovinci & Hall, Attorneys at Law, had a small but busy practice. In a year, we'd broken the two-mil mark. Not bad for a couple of has-been hot shots. The beer tasted sweet then, and though my bed lacked Mari, it didn't lack company.

Sal's first client showed up around then, long after I should have gone home. The doors were locked but he found his way in. There were spiders between his teeth. "Sal sent me," he hissed before I could protest. "I have a special case . . . ."

Some laws are stronger than men. Stronger than other things, too. There are laws carved in the pillars of heaven. And they have loopholes, too. That was Sal's payback from me: he wanted a lawyer to find loopholes for his friends. God help me, I did.

They weren't *demons*. I knew that much. Sal didn't handle Hell's trade. Some things are worse than demons, though. Things with baby-skin belts and razor-blade eyes. I began putting aside funds to pay Sal back. A quarter-mil didn't seem like much of a price for a good night's sleep.

And then? Well . . . .

I noticed it first when my card was declined. I checked my balance and almost died. Sixty grand and change had vanished overnight. The shock took me like a hammer to the chest. Shaking, I hustled out my laptop. Logged in. Checked my savings.

Gone. All of it, gone.

I flew to the office without stopping for lights. Our doors were open. Our furniture, gone too. Five staffers wandered, dazed, appalled. Regina, Mark, Valerie: stunned. He'd even taken their private things. In Stephe's office, one word—"Sorry"—stared back at us from a single index card propped up in the center of the room.

I counted five holes in the wall before my fist started hurting.

He took our money. Took our books. Took our client lists, notes, computers. Worst of all, he took my files, the ones I kept for my "special" clients. He took the library of loopholes I'd started to amass. And my copy of the contract with Sal.

What could I do now?

I never saw the knife coming. I hadn't wanted to. Stephe had always felt above the law. For a while, I had, too.

Soon afterward, I learned better. I was poison in town, untouchable. The black-ball went rolling through, squashing every job in sight. My contacts dried up. My references disowned me. Each compromise I'd made came down on me like a thick oak club.

And that's when Jack showed up, to make me pay my debt.

The thunder in my heart deepens.

"You signed a contract," Jack murmurs. "How are you gonna make good?"

Deep sigh. "I have no idea."

Tap. Tap. Tap.

"That's not good news," Jack rumbles.

"It's been a while since I've had some myself."

"I can make it worse," he says. His eyes narrow, dangerous.

I don't have words for what he does to me then.

But by the time I can think straight again, my throat is raw from screaming.

My roommate Ben never so much as knocked.

"It's just you and me," Jack says when I can think clearly enough to understand his words. "No one else will know."

There's not a mark on my body. They're all on the inside.

I can't speak, just moan.

Jack shakes his head as he fades into gloom. "Don't make me come back again . . . ."

Sal had spread his nicotined hands when I told him about Stephen's theft. "Bad business," he kept saying. "Bad business."

"So what can we do?" I asked. My left eardrum pulsed in time with my heartbeat. My right hand featured a cast for the five bones I'd broken against the wall.

"Do?" repeated Sal. In the background, a gargoyle gnawed on something that could have been a mouse skull.

"About my contract. My work. My debt."

DiVoraccio grimaced, stretching the corners of his wide mouth down. His eyebrows bristled like silver thickets. "Our old arrangement has not changed."

I'd been afraid of that.

He brought his hands together, rubbed them vigorously. "*Un poveraccio*, this changes nothing. You asked for a favor. I granted it. You got what you needed. Now *I* need things. Your partner is no concern of mine, *capisci?*"

"But my books. He took them, too."

DiVoraccio tapped his bald temple with a steel-twig finger. "You're a smart boy, Gino. You go to school, you learn many useful things. These things are not so easily forgotten. Debts still need to be paid."

I felt as though I were drowning in that over-cluttered office. "But . . . I *can't!*" I insisted. "I can't do the things you want without my books . . . ."

He dismissed me with a wave. "So buy more books."

"With *WHAT?*"

DiVoraccio glared. "Make *do!*" he snarled. For a moment, I glimpsed the thing he truly was. A face that made centurions crap their togas 2000 years ago.

I didn't crap my toga. But as I stumbled up the stairs a minute later, I threw up on the landing.

I refused, then, to take on more clients from Sal.

Jack dropped by for our first session a month later. He's come once or twice a week in the two months since. And each time, I feel a bit more dead.

I hate the hours before dawn. The twisted-sheet sickness of a mind against itself. A bed peopled with too many ghosts. Small apartment. Memories. A roommate I hardly even see. Boxes of junk. A knotted gut. A Rolodex of phantoms that never call back . . . .

Pain chases my mind in circles. I can't get away from myself.

Jack will be back soon enough. I have no more to give him than I had before, and no way I can think of to come up with what I need.

A handful of favors and a few scraps of paper are all that remain of my professional life. Bastard even took my diplomas and the contract with Sal. If I had even *that* much, I might be able to figure a way out of this mess.

Contracts have loopholes. Even Sal's. If I could only *see* it again, I could find my way out of it. Figure out what makes it tick . . . .

Problems. I solve problems. Puzzles. Rubick's Cubes. Debates. Rhetoric. Creation itself. Everything has laws. Laws have loopholes. I *find* loopholes. There's got to be one here.

God's a lousy lawyer. His contracts are full of holes. Maybe He didn't want to get stuck with the details. Point is, there's lots of room in reality for interpretation. If you can find the loopholes, you can bend or even break the deal.

Folks like Sal, Jack and their kind . . . they're not bound by many of our laws, but they're utterly bound by their own. Mortals often use that to their advantage. In the case of Rumplestiltskin vs. The Miller's Daughter, for instance, the little guy could no more break his sworn oath than the girl could spin straw into gold. We know how that case went, and I can't say poor Rumpie got a fair shake in it. Arguing by that precedent alone, you can see why Sal's friends wanted to change the deal. They don't like mortals "pulling a Rumpie" on them. My job, then, was to find ways around those laws so that folks with blood-red caps and razor-blade eyes could cheat like humans do.

Yeah, God's a crummy lawyer. He just keeps paralegals busy with the details. Me, I became part of the opposing counsel. The price of my quarter-mil from Sal was to take on clients *pro bono*. Clients like the faceless woman, or the sea-stallion with a thing for kids. They weren't *all* horrors, but I parceled off enough of my soul for that partnership that by the time Stephen made off with the office, I halfway thought I deserved a knife in the back. Funny thing about loopholes: just because you can use 'em doesn't mean you'll feel good about it afterward.

And that's Jack's loophole: guilt. That's why I can't get away from him.

I can't tell you what my contract says, but it's as binding as any physical law. That contract was 26 pages long, with more clauses than a Christmas mall. It's the contract that binds Jack and me together. The legalese would make your head spin, but the gist of it is this:

Jack Dunning is Sal's insurance policy on me. He can't be bribed, bought, distracted, or defeated. I fly to Tahiti, he'll be there when I arrive. Why? Because he's part of me. I signed on that dotted line myself.

Jack is guilt incarnate. Everything you owe, every mess you ever made, that's him. That club in his hands only *looks* like wood. It's actually something far heavier: regret. He doesn't even need to hit you with it. You do that for him. And compared to what I feel like after *that* kind of beating, I'll take the oak club any day.

Like I said, Sal's people don't work by human laws. Jack's immortal, but he's part of me as well. The money ogre lives inside of me, the part of me that feels obligation and guilt. Jack manifests the shitty way I feel about myself. And as long as I'm bound by my contract to Sal, Jack will come around to make sure I fulfill my end of it.

Ironic, really: my inner leg-breaker works off the feelings that made me quit Sal's service. No wonder he hurts me so bad.

When Stephen cleaned out the office, I lost everything that helped me handle Sal's clients. Not that I wanted to, anyway. Guilt is something every lawyer learns to live with. I mean, no matter how ethical you try to be, you'll help some lowlifes to get things they don't deserve.

In my case, the lowlife that had broken my nerve had nine tails, a big mouth and a taste for little girls. When I'd read his profile (courtesy of some really nasty Japanese folk tales), I tried to turn the case down. Sal waved me away like a handful of smoke. "Gino," he wheezed, "you're a good boy but you think too much."

"This isn't a matter of letting some brownie skip K.P.," I protested. "This guy eats . . . ." My mouth didn't finish the sentence. My imagination did.

Sal had turned back to his black velvet playground. That day, he'd been eviscerating a Mickey Mouse watch. Mickey smiled despite his missing arms. I thought of my nine-tailed client's dietary preferences. "I don't think I can do this, Sal. Not even for you."

His parchment hands stopped. His thin shoulders stiffened.

"Let me buy you out," I offered. "I know I owe you, Sal. I never forgot that, and I'm grateful to you. But this . . . this is something I cannot do. *Capisci?*"

A drift of smoke rose from the face turned away from me. I'm not sure it came from his mouth.

TICK. TICK. TICK.

"I understand, *bambino,*" he said at last. His voice sounded drier than usual. "Half a million of your dollars and your debt to me is paid."

"Half?" The word caught on its way out of my gut. "I borrowed a quarter . . . ."

He turned back to me. Seeing his face, I understood why Dad drank so much. God needed better lawyers when He made things like Sal.

It took me almost a full minute to find my voice. "Half a million, then. I'm good for it."

A voice like paper burning. "You'd better be."

From that point on, I swore never to help Sal or his clients again. I'd clear my debt the same way I'd incurred it: with cash.

I'd been six grand short when Stephe took it all. And if he hadn't taken Nine-Tails' file, too, I might have sicced my would-be client on that bastard just for fun.

The cops had searched for Stephe, of course. Nothing. Wherever he'd gone, it wasn't stateside. South America, probably, maybe Eastern Europe. Someplace where the law couldn't touch him.

Man's law, anyway.

I knew other kinds of law.

If only I'd had my books . . . .

It had taken me almost a year, and some really messy favors, to acquire my *other* library. The one my daytime clients never saw. The faerie tales books weren't too bad, and the Bibles looked downright respectable. It was the rare books, the ones bound in moonlight or human skin, that I hid from everybody else.

At times like this, when there's nothing left to do but think, I wonder what Stephe and his crew thought when they dug *those* books out.

I wonder if he's kept them.

If he ever reads them.

If he knows what to do with them.

I doubt it.

But what if he tries to *sell* them?

People would notice. People I know.

Of course.

I was a fool not to have thought of it before.

And just like that, I've got a plan.

It's not great, but you work with what you have.

Stephe didn't leave me much to work with.

And I owe *him*, too, for that . . . .

I was *raised* Catholic, but I'm not a *good* Catholic, if you know what I mean. The things I've seen and done don't fit in anybody's book. Still, I know there's *something* out there, and before I get started I figure it's time to set things square with the Man Upstairs.

Figure I should make this a one-on-one conversation. There's this lawyer-client privilege thing to think about, and I should honor the rules of the game, especially if I want turn 'em to my advantage. So I light up some candles and dust off my Bible and take out a rosary I haven't used in ages, kneel down in near-darkness and make the opening statement no Catholic ever forgets:

"Hail Mary, full of grace, the Lord is with thee . . . ."

Soon, my eyes go dark and my knees go numb. I keep speaking. After a time, I feel like someone hears me.

And I let it go.

All the guilt. All the shame. All the compromises and "never-guilties" that I still feel guilty about. It takes forever, this conversation. By the time I see the room again, it's full morning out and the world feels lighter.

"Thank you," I say. And I rest.

My clock is digital, but ticking haunts me.

Time is my loophole . . . and Stephen's noose.

Her name is Dami, and she lives outside of time. Dami could go walking through Pompeii's gardens, cop a bender with Edgar Allen Poe, and show up at your door a few minutes later with Poe's booze on her skirt and 2000-year-old grass on her heels. Not long ago, I helped Dami bend a few rules so she could step through time and still retain her clothes. When I head toward her favorite oasis, I've got favors of my own to ask.

Benito's opened just before the Civil War. It hasn't closed since then. A 24/7 Manhattan rat-hole, it is timeless as a broken clock. I wave at Francesca behind the bar and snort some forbidden tobacco air. The smoke's so thick, Jack the Ripper would get lost, and I have to wonder whose mojo keeps the Breath Gestapo away. "Perfumes of heaven," I declare, and the bartender laughs. Faint light catches diamonds in her shark-tooth smile.

A few quick words, some flattery, and a half-serious peck on the cheek later and Fran sets me up with a bottle of green faerie at the table near the back. Sure, the stuff's illegal as hell, but so's a barroom full of smoke. Dami always had a taste for absinthe. She claims the stuff was better a century ago, but she'll knock it back like a frat boy on a binge. I can't stand the stuff myself, but I get two glasses from Francesca anyway. Best to appear sociable when Dami arrives.

On the table, I lay out the charm: Six Indian head pennies, a few drops of mercury, and a pinch of burnt oak ash. Dip my finger in the ash and draw a circle on the deep-scarred tabletop. Whistle "Greensleeves" badly, and wait . . . .

She steps up a few minutes later, a tall shadow in the nicotine gloom. Thick silver hair cascades across a black velvet jacket stitched with matching silver filigree. Dami spots the green bottle and glasses, and she smiles.

"Someone," she says with an English twist, "is speaking my language tonight."

"Thought you might like it."

"That I do," she says, sitting. "So is this a social call, then?"

"More or less," I say, breaking the seal on the absinthe bottle.

"You're a very bad liar."

A shrug from me. "If I was that bad, you'd be standing there naked."

"And you'd hate that so."

She spills some of the green stuff in her glass. No sugar, straight up. Dami swirls the liquor around. Inhales with cat-eyed pleasure. Sips a bit of green faerie and grins again. "So what's this job, then?"

"No job," I assure her. "Just a favor . . . ."

Stephe was my mentor and the big brother I never had. Skinny and pepper-haired, he stood a half-head taller than me. I think he was gay, but never asked. His real lover was his work, and he taught me well. Too well for my own good.

He'd convinced me, one beer-soaked night, to sign non-triggering full partnerships with one another. That way, both of us had full access to the firm's resources without consent from the other. He claimed it would allow either one of us to tend the firm if anything went wrong. His dad, after all, had died suddenly without provisions, leaving his estate and business tangled in red tape. Stephe had health problems of his own, and didn't want to make them my problem. "It's all business, partner," he assured me as we signed. "We've got to take care of each other."

He'd taken care of me, all right. Cleaned out our bank account, and forged his way into mine for good measure. Stupidest decision I ever made, that contract . . . but that decision cut both ways . . . *if* I could find the contract to prove it. That's why, I think, he'd stripped my office clean. Stephe wanted to make sure I couldn't pull the same stunt in reverse.

But he didn't know about Dami. Or Sal. Or Jack Dunning.

If I'm right, that's about to change.

May 25th. The day Stephe knocked me from powerhouse to poorhouse. It's easy enough to give Dami directions to our office and tell her where to leave certain files. She can't take things back and forth through time. She can, though, move things around. So I send Dami back to the night of May 23rd, to copy and stash a few items of interest before Stephe cleans the place out. Items like our partnership papers. Sal's contract. And a few select books and files.

Dami can't make major changes in history, but Stephe won't miss what he doesn't know exists. I figure he was looking for the contracts we shared between us, so I ask Dami to photocopy those and put 'em back where they'd been that night. He didn't know about my gig for Sal, though, or the details of my special collection. So over liquorish-and-peppermint bites of absinthe, I give her access passwords and ask her to shift my stuff to a safe location: a box in my closet that I haven't opened since before Stephe cleaned out our office.

Like I said, Dami can't change history. Here's the loophole: if I suddenly "remember" those things I forgot until now, it doesn't count as a change. Stephe still cleans out the office, my life still goes to hell, Jack still shows up to collect his due . . . until I "remember" the box that winds up containing my things. Coincidence. Sure, there are risks: Dami might get caught in our office. She might put things in the wrong box. My past-self might catch her rifling through things in my old apartment. She might not even be able to pick the locks on the office or my old apartment. Hey, no plan is perfect. This way, though, I had a chance to "find" the long lost files, books and contracts. With them, I'd have the tools I'd need to set things right.

One more call to make. To my favorite bookseller, the place in Soho with a back room only certain people know about. On my past-due cell phone, I call in one more favor from the guy with rainbow hair. Give him a list of books taken from my office. See if he can track down any recent sales, and then find out where they came from. If I'm lucky, Stephe won't think I've got that covered. He might stick a tome or two on E-Bay and use an address I can trace. It's a long shot, but that's all I have left. Long shots and loopholes and promises in the dark.

When I get home, Ben's cleaning out our dishwasher. He says nothing as I walk past, but his silence weighs heavily. *Did I miss something?* I wonder, heading toward my room. Another bill I forgot to pay? Rent due? Something I borrowed and didn't return? This is nuts. I can't live like this anymore. No matter what happens with Dami's errand, I need to sort my life out. Fast.

Jack's waiting in the shadows as I open up my door. The kitchen light shines on his three-piece suit. As I softly close my door, he begins to tap his club against his palm.

TAP. TAP.

"Drop the drama, Jack," I whisper. "It's getting old."
"Sal wants to see you."
Oh.
"When?"
"Now."

The clocks have stopped ticking when we enter his shop. Even the gargoyles are still. Sal sits at his workbench, his back turned to me. A cuckoo clock lies scattered on black velvet, its innards glaring in the worklight shine.

Jack shuts the door behind us. Click.

Sal turns around in his chair to face us, his smoke-wreathed smile more awful than a wound. "Gino! What's the good news, *mio piccolo bambino?*"

Try to smile back in that terrible stillness. "I've almost got it, Mr. DiVoraccio."

He uncrumples from his chair, the creases of his suit smoothing into devastating sharpness. "A half-a-million dollars, yes?"

"Maybe that," I allow. "Maybe better."

He picks his cigarette off an overflowing ashtray. "I like the sound of 'better.' The 'maybe,' not so much."

"The devil's in the details, Sal."

He stops smiling.

"It's an expression, Mr. DiVoraccio."

"I know what it is," Sal replies, taking a puff from the cigarette.

Beneath my jacket, my heart pounds like a heavyweight. "I was just saying that I'm working a few things out."

He takes a single step. "When you worked for me, Gino, you worked much faster, yes?"

Nod. "I did, yes."

"So you will be working for me again. Yes?"

Swallow hard. It's tempting. But then I remember little arms and a promise made to God. "I don't think so, Mr. DiVoraccio."

His smile disappears.

"I'm changing my line of work."

He shakes his head. "I asked you for good news. This is not good news. Not to me. Not to my people. Not to you. Especially not to you."

Stillness.

"I may have good news."

A thick puff. "Go on."

Here goes. I breathe deep and assume my best case voice.

"What do you value, Sal? I mean really *value?* It's not money, you've told me that. What is it you really want me for?"

He waves a parchment hand, impatient. "You know this, *un giovanoto.* I have problems, you sort them out for me."

"That's true." I press my case. "I *can* sort out your problems. But I have to do that my way. I must be able to say, 'No'."

He shakes his head. "This was not part of our agreement."

"You're right. It's not. But it can be part of our new agreement."

Behind me, Jack cracks his own neck.

Sal scowls. "Explain to me this new agreement."

And I do.

Jack looks dubious when I finish. Sal seems slightly more impressed. "If," he says, "you can do what you claim, and pay my fee, I will call our old deal done. This, I promise you."

Inside, I feel like the cukoo clock. "Thank you, Mr. DiVoraccio."

He lights a new cigarette with a loud fingersnap. Old-school, but it works. "I promise you this, too, *ragazzo o giovane*: If you make me send Jack for you again, he will take you somewhere *else.* And then, there will be no more deals."

Now I feel like the ash on the end of his cigarette. "I understand."

Sal nods. "You have seven nights to do this thing."

Try to smile as if I'm not shaking inside. "I've done more with less."

I try not to run on my way home. Has Dami taken care of my errand yet? The empty streets seem to stretch into endless hallways of fitful light and passing shapes. My steps *clop-clop-clop* on sidewalks flecked with dog poop and spit. My guts throb softly in time with my heart. I want to check the box in my closet, but know that it's a one-time-only deal. If I open it before Dami's had a chance to put my stuff in there, the laws of the universe might keep her from placing it there afterward. New things in that box would create a paradox. I'm not sure what would happen if she tried that, and I don't want to find out.

These thoughts keep my brain spinning all the way home.

Almost there, I change my mind, turn around, and head back toward the subway. Benito's is open as always, its smoky depths shadowed with the desperate and damned. I fit in well. Francesca's gone to whatever passes for "home" in her world, but the new guy behind the bar has a message for me. Taped to a bottle of Horka Absinthium 1792, there's a note in elegant script:

> G.
>
> *You've forgotten something in your closet. Best go check it again.*
> *Have a drink, darling. And no sugar, either!*
> *P.S.: You owe me, hugely.*
>
> Cheers,
D.

It tastes like burning mouthwash going down, but I step lighter on my way home.

My room feels cleaner as I step inside. Jack's gone to wherever phantom leg-breakers go when they're off-duty. Through thin walls, I hear Ben snoring. How he slept through all my screaming, I can't imagine.

Quiet as I can, I open the closet and move the boxes within.

Hands shaking hard, I check the proper box.

It's all there.

Thank God and all His little loopholes.

Fire up my computer and get to work.

In my e-mail, there's a note from my Soho connection. Yep, Stephe's tried to sell my books. They'd even bought some from him. Yes, there's an address.

Paydirt.

For the first time in months, I can truly breathe.

By the time my eyes blur, it's past noon. I haven't slept, but that's okay. Everything I need is here. Stephe even used his new Belize address as the contact point for the book sale. I'm half-surprised by that. After all, he's a wanted felon. Then it occurs to me that he might secretly *want* to get caught . . . at least by me. That fits what I know of Stephen, and it suits my plans perfectly.

Normally, Stephe's beyond guilt. He could care less about laws or ethics. He's such a hotshot because he holds most people in contempt. Law is his power trip, and working it is his compulsion. Normally, that would make him immune to the likes of Jack Dunning. You have to *feel* guilt in order to be hurt by it. Like everything, though, Stephe's immunity has a loophole. And that's where I'll take the bastard down.

Like I've said, he and I shared lots of beer and conversation. He was kind of closed off about personal stuff, but every so often, the beer would take over and you'd see what made Stephe tick. One night, I remember, he was especially depressed. It was near Christmas but Stephe was spending it alone. No family. No longtime partner, no kids, no relatives. I think I may have been his closest friend. It gutted him that night.

Now normally, Stephe was all piss and vinegar. Nothing ever seemed to bug him. That night, though, he drank lots more than usual and wound up toasting his dead brother, his mom, his dad, and everyone else in the bar. Seems he hadn't spent much time with family back when they were still alive. Once he hit law school, Stephe had better things to do. One year, he didn't even go back home. That was the year his brother hit a patch of ice and slammed into a phone pole two days after New Year's. His mom went a few months later—heart attack, I think—and then his dad, slightly afterward. The following Christmas, there wasn't a home to go back to.

Now, I was never much of a family guy myself. I never had a brother. No sister, either. I was an only child—a weird thing for a Catholic household, but there it is. Talk to my folks once in a while. See 'em on holidays. That's about it. So when I admitted that I've never felt especially close to my family, Stephe leaned in close and gave me hell. Breathing a brewery in my face, he told me never, *never*, to forget my family. "You might wind up like *me*," he slurred, "spending your holidays buried in other people's misery." *No wonder he works so hard*, I thought that night. *It's all the poor guy has left.* That was the only time I'd ever seen him feel guilty about anything. I used it to get nice Christmas bonuses for all our staff. That felt good.

Now I'd use it as Exhibit A in my case against him.

That was gonna feel good, too.

Seven drops of blood, dripped in a circle. Seven drops of blood on an oak leaf placed at the center of my overdue cell phone bill. It's the first time I've employed the charm to call Jack Dunning. Normally, he comes on his own. In the darkness of my room that night, I light three candles, cut my finger, arrange the charm, and wait.

Tap. Tap. Tap.

"I can always tell it's you, Jack."

"You got the money?"

"I needed to check certain provisions in our contract." For the first time since we met, my voice remains steady. This is my turf, now. The realm of law.

The club stops tapping. Jack scowls.

I press my advantage. "Section 1, subsection B, employs the term 'perceived mortal value.' Am I right to assume this means the human value of the money lent by Mr. DiVoraccio?"

"Umm . . . I think so."

"Just as I thought. And Section 9, subsection C, where it refers to 'agents of collection.' I assume that's you?"

His tusks flash in the candlelight. "Yes."

"So in Section 13, subsection E, when it refers to 'tangible and external manifestation of the Lendee's internal sense of moral obligation,' that describes you as an extension of my sense of guilt."

"Yeah."

"And in Section 14, subsection F, the reference to 'all and sundry locations on any or all planes of earthly existence,' means that you can go any place that I have gone. Correct?"

A growl. "Correct."

I'm having fun for a change. "Now, when I read Section 1, subsection E, I take it to mean that any party that benefits from the 'perceived mortal value' of Mr. DiVoraccio's loan is also bound by the provisions of this contract and its strictures, provided that they are also beholden to the legal provisions of partnership with the signee of the contract."

Tap. Tap. Tap.

"Please answer the question, Mr. Dunning."

"I . . . guess so."

"So by my reading of Section 13, subsection E, you should also be able to manifest for collection purposes to anyone who shares a legal obligation to the holder of this contract, provided they have an associated feeling of guilt about that debt."

Jack's brow crinkles like a Park Slope sidewalk. His eyes roll back and forth, as if reading an answer from invisible cue cards. Finally, he speaks. "I think so."

"Yes or no. This is important."

"I need to check with Mr. DiVoraccio."

"Understood. But I need an answer tonight."

Confused by my sudden shift from shrimp to shark, Jack nods. "Okay," he rumbles.

"Here," I say, offering Jack a copy of my partnership contract with Stephe. "This contract verifies my full and legal partnership with a Mr. Stephen Robert

Hall, current benefactor of my loan's 'perceived mortal value.' Please take this to Mr. DiVoraccio."

Jack frowns. "I think you'd better take it yourself. With me."

Damn. Ah, well. I didn't think it would be that easy. Fortunately, I'm ready this time out. My briefcase is already packed and I'm wearing my best courtroom suit. Blowing out the candles, I hope it's enough to win this case.

There's no clock on black velvet this time. The chronographic operating theatre is bare. The gargoyles perch, expectant, as Sal crackles his parchment hands. "So," he breathes with nicotine malice. "You plan to pull a Rumpie on me, *bambino?*"

"Not at all, Mr. DiVoraccio. I have the new agreement here for you to examine."

Sal squints at the papers I hand him. I've seen snakes with kinder eyes. As he reaches for a pair of wire-rimmed glasses, I glance around the clock-lined walls of Sal's cluttered shop.

"Ever wonder," Jack rumbles, "where Mr. DiVoraccio gets all these clocks?"

Shake my head. "Not really."

"Maybe you should."

It takes a moment for me to understand.

My bones turn to cold glass inside.

God *really* needed better lawyers when He made Sal DiVoraccio.

I truly hope this works.

"Oh, shit. It's you."

I'd had my rainbow-haired friend whip up a pretext for sending me to Stephen's office in Belize. Some nonsense about verifying Stephe's book collection for future business. The details aren't important. What *is* important is that two days later, I'd passed gratefully from the humid streets of Orange Walk into an air-conditioned office where I now stood face-to-face with Reginald Robert Hallister, alias Stephen Robert Hall.

Stephe's aged. His face has lines that his new tan can't disguise. His salt-and-pepper hair has gone almost totally grey, and several patches of it are just plain *gone*. Stephe still knows how to dress for success, but his tailored suit can't cover the skinny frame beneath it. He looks ten years older than when I last saw him, but it's been less than ten months since he left. "Jeeze, Stephe," I say. "You look like hell."

He tenses behind his polished oak desk as I close the door. "How did you find me, Gino?"

"That's not important."

"It was the books, wasn't it?"

Nod.

"I knew I should have left those damned things behind." The look in Stephe's eyes lends extra emphasis to *damned*.

Sit down, uninvited, in one of his client chairs. "So why *did* you do it, Stephe?" My voice thickens. "Why did you dick me over—dick *all* of us over—that way?"

He looks down, away, anywhere but at me. "I really can't talk about it, Gino. It's . . . complicated . . . ."

The sun-washed room seems to darken.

"Complicated?" My voice sounds like a stranger's. "*Complicated?* I'll bet it's complicated." My fingers tighten around the armrests with five months' worth of pain. All it once, it hits me: what I went through, what everyone in our office went through, when he disappeared. Our clerks. Our secretaries. What we *all* lost to bring him here.

"So tell me, Stephen," I continue, "how 'complicated' your life is. Tell Regina, whose kid had to drop out of that special school of his because you took Mommy's job away. Tell Valerie, whose old yearbooks wound up in a Dumpster three blocks away after you cleaned her office out. Tell Mark and Merci and the half-dozen people you put out of work because your life was 'complicated.' And while you're at it—" I lean forward in the chair—"tell your partner, your best friend, the guy who's spent the last four months with a goddamned sledgehammer in his chest, just how *complicated* your life had to be before you *cleaned out his fucking bank account* without so much as a 'Goodbye.'"

Lean back. Take a long, deep breath.

"Tell me *that*, Stephen. Because I'm really dying to know."

Stephe looks back to me at last. "You were getting ready to do it to me."

"*What?!?*"

"Tell me you weren't." He stands up tall, his old courtroom self. "Tell me you weren't conducting business behind my back. Tell me you didn't have clients coming to see you after hours—clients you never told me about, never processed through the partnership." He leans across his desk. "Tell me you didn't have books of *sorcery* and God-only-knows what else hidden in your office, Gino. I'd noticed you moving money around in our account, checked up on you, and found out that you were getting ready to screw me over."

He folds his arms across his chest. "So I decided to screw you over first."

Silence. I honestly hadn't expected this.

Stephe goes on. "I had . . . medical problems . . . I wanted to talk about them with you, but . . . when I found out about your off-the-record business and the money shuffling and the weird things you'd been up to in *our offices*, well . . . I knew I couldn't trust you with that information. Or with much else."

For a few seconds, I almost feel sorry for him.

Then I spot his new Rolex. One bought with the money he stole from our firm.

TICK. TICK. TICK.

"Oh, bullshit."

Stephe glares back at me.

"Sorry. I'm not buying it." Rise to my feet. "Maybe you *were* sick . . . ."

"I was. I *am*."

"And you know what? I. Don't. *Care*." The word falls like a dagger on his desk. "Once, Stephe, once I would have given you *anything*. Anything you needed, you would have gotten from me. All you had to do was ask. But you had to be clever. You had to assume you knew what was going on."

"I did . . . ."

"You had no idea, and you didn't even try to find one. Thing is, you've *always* been like this, Stephe, and you always will be. *That's* your sickness, your real sickness. You have to be three steps ahead of everyone else, even if those three steps are wrong."

He glares back. "I wasn't wrong about this . . . ."

"You were *totally* wrong. It had nothing to do with you, nothing to do with us. Yes, I had some extra business, extra clients on the side. I *had* to, to pay off the bill for buying in with you. But I was *loyal*, Stephe. Loyal in ways you can never understand."

I pause, then let the bomb drop:

"I was loyal like a *brother*, Stephe. You were the brother I never had. And I was the brother you threw away."

That hits home.

"And that's where you and I differ, Stephe. I still *care* about people. And you never did."

Slience.

"So what do you want me to say?" Stephe asks, finally. "What do you want to hear?"

"I want to hear you're *sorry*, Stephe. I want to hear my old friend apologize to me."

"Is that it?" He looks hopeful.

"Of course not," I reply. "I also want back the money you stole from me. My books. My things. My client list. My trust. All the things you took from me and our staff and from everyone else who depended on us and looked to us to make things *right* for them. I want that all back."

He looks ten years older now than he did when I walked in. "I can't do that."

"No," I say heavily. "You can't. You can't undo that day and all the days since then. You can't turn back time, Stephen. Neither can I." I grant myself a private smile. "But I *can* demand a half-million dollars from you. Now. Right now."

Stephe sits down. "I can't do that, either."

Minor flash of panic, but I don't let it show. "Where *is* it, Stephen? Where *is* all the money you stole from us?"

Now it's Stephen's turn to smile. "What are you going to do, Gino? Call the police? Tell them that the respectable businessman who's been handling exports here for almost half a year is actually your ex-partner from New York?"

"Something like that."

"Get out of my office, Gino." He waves me off like a gnat. "Get out and go back home to your witches and gremlins and your other faerie tales." He leans back in his chair. "Go to the police if you want—hell, I'll call them myself. I'm covered, Gino. I'm *legitimate*. Sure, you might get an investigation started, but no one's listening here. By the time somebody takes you seriously, I'll be long gone."

I see him now like the stranger he is. Guess I never knew him that well. But at least now, I know myself better.

Get up and take out the papers I've been carrying. Set 'em on his desk. Our contract. "Remember this?"

His eyes widen. Then his sneer returns. "Yes. And?"

"Our agreement. Our partnership. Our signatures. What I have is yours. What you have is mine."

For a second, he looks fragile. Then he sweeps the contract off his desk. "That was another life, Gino. Another man. Not me."

I pick it up again. "Believe that if you want, brother. But a contract is a contract."

He shrugs. "Only if you can enforce it."

I head for the door, then, like a shark tasting blood. "I won't have to, Stephe. You will."

I get the e-mail two days later.

> *Swiss bank.*
> *Credit Suisse*
> *Reginald Robert Hallister*
> *CH10 0023 000A 1098 2234 6*
> *Take what you want.*
> *Just make it stop.*

Thank you, Jack Dunning. He'll make *this* deal stick.

I take out exactly half of Stephe's account. After the half-million buy-off for Sal, that leaves me with just shy of two million for myself. I resolve to pay a hefty chunk of that to Dami. The rest I set aside for other creditors, our former employees, and some seed money for my new business. And that night, I thank God for a very long time.

I leave Sal's office the next day with a new contract and the lingering smell of stale tobacco on my clothes. Under the terms of this agreement, Sal still sends clients to me and Dami. We have right of refusal, though, and there's no money ogre clause to twist my arm. I take on the cases I *want* to take on, and my word—yes or no—is final. All other debts are paid. This time out, I owe Sal nothing but good work and a fair shake. The rest is at my sole discretion.

Yeah, I'm still working with God's little secrets. I get paid well, but not *too* well. Now I work a fair practice. My clients, after all, need someone to keep things ticking smoothly. A mortal who knows loopholes and how to work 'em right. Every so often, the Rumplestiltskins of the world can use an edge when some wiseass thinks she can cheat her way to a golden future.

So yeah, I'm back in business. Ginelli Castrova, that's my trade name—some folks shouldn't know your true one. I provide a necessary service, and I do it well. Hey, *someone's* got to read the fine print on Creation! And after what I've been though, no one's better suited for that than me.

Twilight Crossing

John Passarella

GEORGE THOROGOOD WAS PLAYING ON THE JUKEBOX WHEN I tossed Ollie Janks out on his ass. Wasn't the first time. Wouldn't be the last. Or so I thought, when I said, "Nothing personal, Ollie."

Little did I know everything was about to change.

The grizzled drunk staggered to his feet and made a half-hearted attempt to brush off the seat of his bib overalls. Lacking the coordination to complete that simple task, he decided to flip me off instead. "The fuck, Ray?" he shouted. "My money ain't good enough for the Willowbrook Tavern?"

"Not when you confuse Shirley's ass with the produce aisle."

"Practically keep this dump in business," Ollie said, "much as I spend here."

"We appreciate your support," I said. "But Shirley's not on the menu."

"And what do I get for my hard-earned dollars, eh? Watered down liquor and the bum's rush, that's what!"

"Time to walk it off, Ollie. Or should I call you a cab?"

"Need no fuckin' cab," Ollie said with a dismissive wave of his hand. He plodded toward the shoulder of the road. "Live three damn blocks away."

Shaking my head, I returned to the dark confines of the Willowbrook Tavern. By morning, Ollie wouldn't have the slightest recollection of the events preceding or following his unceremonious ejection from his favorite watering hole.

Something happens often enough, you begin to expect it. That's when you need to worry.

Moments later, the door hinges creaked behind me.

I turned, bracing for round two with Ollie, but the drunk had stayed true to form. Instead, a slender young man with dark hair and a harried expression on his gaunt face brushed by me, tossing a mumbled apology in his wake. My first thought was: *Underage*. My second: *Trouble*.

The clock above the bar displayed midnight.

Then the red second hand began to descend.

Ignoring the social invitation of the bar stools or the shadowed privacy of the side booths, where most of the evening's crowd were huddled, the young man chose the nearest of three unoccupied, wobbly tables, and dropped into one of the four rickety chairs that surrounded it. A hanging brass light fixture seemed to deconstruct his face into pale slivers of flesh and harsh shadows. Otherwise, he looked unremarkably ordinary in a green and tan Rugby shirt, dark jeans and black running shoes. One heel beat an insistent tattoo against the warped floorboards, as if he were keeping time with a frenetic drummer.

About ready to vibrate out of his skin.

Wearing her customary red-and-white-checked blouse, jeans, a beer-stained apron, and calf-high leather boots, Shirley strolled over to the table to take his order. She gave him a one-second appraisal. "There's a law against serving minors."

The young man looked at her, gauging, challenging. "Is that so?"

"That's what they tell me," Shirley said, punctuating the comment with a little chuckle. "So what can I get you?"

"Whatever you've got on tap."

"Gotcha. Back in a jiff, hon."

I shook my head in disbelief. *She's flirting with him! Ben finds out, he'll break that kid in half.*

"Thanks." He tapped both index fingers against the side of the small bowl of pretzels in the center of the table, ran one hand through his hair, then heaved a sigh.

I drifted back to my regular booth, first one on the left, and picked up the well-worn baseball I'd snagged at a Phillies' game over a year ago. Foul ball, unsigned, no sentimental value, but it helped me think. And I needed to understand what was happening.

From my booth, I could observe the entire front half of the tavern, and peek down the short hall to the back room, with its side-by-side pool tables. Only the modest kitchen, with its small grill and deep fryer, was hidden from me. Although, occasionally, through the porthole window in the scuffed kitchen door, I caught a glimpse of the bald head of Oscar, our night cook. With Ollie gone, the place was relatively calm, but I sensed trouble brewing, an inexplicable prickling of the short hairs on the back of my neck. Wasn't sure from which direction the trouble would come. But I knew its target. Had since the moment he bumped into me.

I scanned the crowd, seeking anything or anyone unusual. The tavern was less than a quarter filled, all regulars, fewer than twenty people, huddled in the booths that lined the walls. A few pairs quietly conversed. Some loners scanned the sports pages or worked crosswords, while others watched the muted TV over the bar, tuned to ESPN's continual stream of scores and highlights. Steady night, not too busy. Sometimes the back room could get rowdy. Tonight, there was a companionable game of eight ball in progress. Nothing more. As the Thorogood tune faded, the only sound rising above the whispered conversations was the muffled thwack of billiard balls colliding. An expression came to mind . . . .

The calm before the storm.

Shirley delivered the young man's draft in a stein. He paid attention long enough to hand her a five and tell her to keep the change. Instead of drinking the beer, he traced his fingertips along the surface of the glass, creating parallel trails in the condensation.

I was the Willowbrook Tavern's resident bouncer. At six-one and less than one-hundred-seventy pounds, I hardly looked the part, but I maintained order with the fairly rough trade that frequented the place. I'd needed a job and convinced Quentin Avery, the owner, that I had mastered some inscrutable far eastern martial art whose name I'd made up on the spot and had since forgotten. Self-defense came naturally to me, on some instinctual level I was reluctant to question. In my first two weeks on the job, I proved I could handle the bullies and belligerent drunks, as well as the occasional knife wielders and those making death threats with the borrowed courage of a tire iron or baseball bat. Compared to them, Ollie Janks was a cream puff. Since then . . . .

How long had I been rubbing my arm? Where the young man had bumped into me, my skin felt as if it had been charged with a current. The sensation was spreading, as if he had infected me with his nervous energy. I debated leaving my booth to have a little chat with him, to determine what the hell was happening, when the front door burst open.

Cloaked in shadows, I settled back into the booth and watched as three burly men in black leather garb strode down the length of the tavern, their boot heels striking the floorboards like a succession of hammer blows. Could have been bikers, but I would have heard motorcycles arriving. Two took positions around the nervous young man, one to each side, while the third, presumably the leader, stood in front.

Here comes the storm.

Behind the bar, Shirley tucked a bottled-blonde strand of hair behind her ear. Nervous gesture. She cast an expectant look in my direction. Hank, the greying bartender, stood by the cash register, drying glasses with a frayed cloth. Despite his casual pose, I noticed a slight tremor in his hands. Oscar cast a wide-eyed look through the porthole window, decided it was none of his business and ducked out of view. Most of the bar patrons darted curious but discreet glances at the three men, careful not to draw unwanted attention to themselves. Dan and Elaine, a young couple in thrift shop clothes but with no shortage of common sense, slipped from their far corner booth and practically tiptoed out the back room exit. Resigned to witnessing whatever mayhem ensued, the rest or the crowd seemed to lean a bit further away from the leather-clad trio. The instinct for self-preservation had begun to assert itself.

I leaned forward, my right hand pressing the baseball hard against the tabletop as I studied the new arrivals. All three stood several inches over six feet, had reddish hair and fine facial features, almost delicate in an odd way. *Brothers,* I thought. Though the leader's hair was cropped short, the other two sported locks halfway down their back. Belatedly, I realized they were twins. All three had knives in scabbards looped through their belts. I wondered about concealed weapons.

"Well now," said the leader to the seated young man. "Look what we have here."

"Do I know you?"

Genuinely puzzled, I thought, surprised. *He really doesn't know them.*

"Name's Darius," the leader said. "My brothers, Maleck and Mortenn. And you would be Kevin. Kevin Robb, to be precise. Correct?" The young man nodded nervously, as if confessing a felony to a police officer. "Don't expect you know us, but . . . ." He reached into the chest pocket of his jacket and took out a snapshot. After a quick glance, he nodded and tossed it on the table in front of the young man. "Bet he looks familiar."

As the three brothers leaned forward, into the pale cone of light, to witness Kevin's reaction to the photo—my breath caught in my throat. "What the hell—?"

At first I thought something dark and slimy crawled along their skin and clothes, but then I realized it was some sort of dark *light* or energy rippling around them, a visible aura, something malevolent, if my gut reaction were any judge. I scanned the bar, wondering if anyone else could see the strange phenomenon enveloping these men. Everyone seemed oblivious to it—

—except Kevin Robb. Something had rattled him. Sweat glistened on his brow. His lips trembled as he said, "That—that's a picture of me. Dead. But that's impossible."

"You're half right, Kevin," Darius said. "He is most certainly dead. Did the honors myself. Three days back."

Kevin gulped. "Three—three days?"

"Yep," Darius said. "Problem is, you ain't him."

"Of course not!"

"You've just been pretending to be him," Darius said. "Ain't that right, boys?"

The twins nodded. Mortenn, who stood closest to me, said, "Nine years running."

Jasper Long, a toothless old geezer with a perpetually grizzled jaw and a hollow leg he liked to fill on a nightly basis, demonstrated an alarming knack for bad timing by heaving himself up out of his booth, which was nearest the brewing confrontation, and attempting to sidle past Kevin's table. Maleck's right arm reached out in a blur, palm flat against Jasper's barrel chest. "Stand down, old man," Maleck said. The unspoken threat was clear in his deep voice and steady glare.

With an impatient shrug, Jasper said, "Gotta take a piss, is all."

"Later." With a quick motion, Maleck shoved Jasper back into the booth.

Jasper was no fighter. I heard him grumble, "Young punks got no respect," but that was the end of his protest.

Normally that scuffle would have been my cue to intervene. But something held me back. Something about Kevin and the three leather-clad thugs.

Perhaps hoping to take advantage of Jasper's distraction, Kevin tried to stand, but Mortenn clamped down on both his shoulders and forced him back into the chair. Kevin shook his head. "Listen, there's some kind of mix-up. I have no idea who you are or what this is about."

Darius chuckled unsympathetically. "You being kept in the dark, figuratively, don't matter much. Our job is to put you in the dark, literally."

With practiced ease, Darius reached back under his loose jacket and pulled a dark automatic from where it had been tucked into his waistband.

"Wait!" Kevin leaned back in the rickety chair, hands raised, palms out. "Why?"

Darius extended his arm, the gun's muzzle aimed at the center of Kevin's forehead. "Because the price was irresistible."

The moment Darius reached for his gun, I was out of my booth and rushing toward the brothers. No conscious thought involved. Later, I would realize I hadn't waited to act out of doubt or fear. I had been gathering as much information as possible before unstoppable events began their inevitable motion. Later, I would marvel that my rush down the aisle over warped floorboards made not the slightest sound to betray me. Later, I would recall how time seemed to slow, how the reactions of Shirley, Hank and the other bar patrons seemed to be frozen in amber. Later, many things would resolve themselves. At that moment, my response was pure instinct, that other-self taking over my actions, my own sense of self-preservation choosing, as it always had, fight over flight.

Sensing movement, Mortenn glanced my way. As his long hair whipped around his head, I noticed a slight point to the tip of his exposed ear. He shouted a warning to Darius: *"Fae!"*

Too late.

My arm had already whipped around and was coming forward, the baseball leaving my fingertips at a speed any major league radar gun would have clocked over one hundred miles per hour. Trust me. And my control was uncannily precise. The regulation stitched cowhide ball slammed into the grip of the automatic, knocking Darius's arm off the mark. A 9mm round ripped a furrow into the floorboards. Darius yelped in pain as the gun flew from his hand.

Kevin heaved his chair backward. The rear legs struck an uneven floorboard and split under the force directed against them. The chair collapsed, taking Kevin with it, but he recovered quickly, crab-walking out of the danger zone, momentarily forgotten.

Decorative wagon wheels had been nailed to support beams on either side of the open table area. I grabbed the rim of the nearest one in both hands and swung my legs up and around. My right heel caught Mortenn in the throat. Cartilage crunched. Choking and sputtering, he dropped to his knees, a panicked look in his pale grey eyes as he struggled to breathe, hands pressed to his neck.

Maleck hadn't been idle. During my aerial assault, he went for his knife, slipping it expertly from its scabbard. The blade and hilt were flat, I saw, balanced for throwing. As his brother dropped in agony, he shouted: "Mortenn!"

Rusted nails creaked and the wagon wheel pulled free of the post.

I landed awkwardly, the wooden wheel falling into my lap.

Maleck cocked his arm. A blur of motion and a flash of silver.

Again, reacting instead of thinking, I hoisted the wagon wheel in front of my face, a fatally flawed shield, and with a split-second twist, caught the point of the blade in one of the wheel's spokes. Protruding through the back of the spoke, the tip quivered two inches in front of my right eye.

I sprang to my feet, wrenched the knife free and tossed the wagon wheel aside. The knife seemed to vibrate in my hand. I had the odd notion that it was imbued with some sort of mystical energy.

Maleck's eyes widened in sudden alarm. He darted a warning glance at Darius before returning his attention to me. The dark light of odious energy skittered around his frame. Some hint of recognition prodded the back of my mind, but the words remained too elusive to grasp. "It's him," Maleck said. "Silverthorn."

"Whisper Guard?" Darius said, then shook his head. "Can't be. Silverthorn was executed."

Shirley had crept around from behind the bar and had recovered Darius's gun. Too brave for her own good. Likely to get herself killed.

Raising my arms dramatically, I said, "My name is Ray Thorn!"

Maleck scoffed. "He doesn't know."

"So tell me!"

Abruptly, Shirley stood and stepped forward, arms outstretched, gun clutched in both hands, directing the barrel at Darius. Trembling, she nevertheless stood her ground. "Get out! Now! I'm calling the police."

"Take it easy, madam," Darius said in a soothing tone. His hand fiddled with his belt buckle. Nerves, maybe. I suspected another concealed weapon. But he raised his empty hand and waved it casually toward her. "You're too tired to hold onto that gun."

Something glittered in the light near her face, like a shower of dust.

"Too tired," Shirley repeated softly and yawned. Her eyes rolled back and her knees buckled. As she crumpled to the floor, Darius snatched the dark automatic from her hand, a look of triumph on his face.

Kevin lunged from a crouching position and swung a broken chair leg overhead like an axe handle at Darius, but he was too far away. Maleck stepped between them and took the brunt of the blow across the side of his head and left shoulder. He wrestled the young man to his knees and held him pinned there for the kill shot. Darius leveled the weapon.

I had already flipped the balanced knife, my thumb and fingers now pressed against the tip. Expediency chose my target. With a lightning flick of my wrist, I hurled it at Darius. He shrieked as the blade sank several inches into the meat of his forearm.

At that moment, Kevin pulled free of Maleck and flung himself against the wheezing Mortenn. Concealed from view, Kevin's hand darted toward the fallen twin's belted scabbard. Maleck's pale eyes blazed with fury. He bent over and grabbed Kevin's Rugby jersey in a white-knuckled grip. "Had just about enough of your shit, ch—"

Gasping, he staggered backward, and Kevin rose with him, both hands clutched around Maleck's knife, now buried to the hilt in Mortenn's abdomen. The dark energy sparked and spiked and sputtered around the twin's body. His face became gaunt before my eyes, his body sagging—no, *withering*, moment by moment. In contrast, Kevin seemed to swell with an influx of energy and strength.

Words came unbidden to my tongue: *"Soul blade."* Each one of the brothers carried a soul blade. That explained the energy I had felt vibrating along the hilt of Maleck's weapon.

The gleaming knife in Kevin's hands slipped free as the lifeless husk—all that remained of Maleck—crumpled to the floor. In a moment, the body faded away. Then Mortenn, witnessing his twin's death, made an enraged gurgling sound as he attempted to climb to his feet. Alarmed, Kevin reacted instantly. His right arm lashed out in a brutal backhand, plunging the bloodied knife between two ribs high on Mortenn's chest.

With a last, weary exhalation, Mortenn's wheezing ceased and he slumped back to the floor. A moment later, his lifeless body vanished into oblivion as well.

Not oblivion, I thought. *Otherworld.*

That word had bubbled to the surface of my mind, and I had no idea what it meant.

"What the hell is this?" Kevin said to Darius. "Who are you people?"

"Unbelievable." Darius grunted. He glanced at me and then nervously at Kevin, who still wielded a soul blade. He was outnumbered. And he'd dropped his gun again. "You two really have no clue."

"No," I said and strode toward him, "but you will tell us. Everything!"

"Like hell," Darius said. He raised a booted foot against the edge of Kevin's table and shoved hard. The untouched stein of beer went flying; pretzels scattered from the upended bowl; and the table slammed into Kevin, knocking him off balance. With a howl, Darius pulled Maleck's knife from his forearm. Not in the hands of an attacker at the moment, the soul blade posed no extra threat and had no additional ability to harm him, beyond the wound itself. Darius spun on his heel and hurled the knife toward me, then scooped his gun off the floor and thundered down the hall to the rear exit. "This is not over!" he called. "My brothers will be avenged!"

Despite Darius's haste, his knife throw was uncannily accurate. Reflexively, I twisted my head and torso aside and still felt the breeze of the blade's passing. It thudded into a supporting post behind me. I debated giving chase immediately, but Darius had the gun and his own soul blade, while I was unarmed. Instead, I yanked the knife from the post and caught up to Kevin.

Old Jasper lumbered past me, his gaze fixed on the front door.

I grabbed Kevin's arm. "We need to talk."

Gulping air, he nodded.

With the apparent end to the violence, the rest of the crowd cleared out as if the tavern were ablaze, including Gus and Cal, retirees who had been playing eight-ball in back when the commotion began. A rush of overlapping voices trailed out into the night, "The hell was that?" "—those two just vanished." "Did you see—?" "—a fuckin' hallucination!" "Didn't see a blessed thing." "—the hell outta here!"

Most of the regulars had had more than a few drinks. I wondered what they would remember—or believe—in the harsh light of morning. A brief fight resulting in two deaths, but the bodies had disappeared. Literally vanished into thin air. I imagined a few of the tavern's patrons would begin the new day by entering a twelve-step program.

"Ray? What happened?" a woozy Shirley asked as she pulled herself upright, using a bar stool for support. "Believe this is yours."

My baseball. I took it and thanked her.

"What should I do here, Ray?" Hank said, "Call the cops?"

"Place is empty," I said. "Close early. Quentin will understand."

"What are you gonna do?"

"Hell if I know."

I paid cash for a room at the Riverview Motel. The place was a dump and the nearest river was five miles away. Not that it mattered. We needed a place to regroup and the motel was within walking distance of the tavern. Besides, we also needed to stay near the tavern. Add that to the list of things I knew without knowing *how* I knew.

I stared at the corpse in the photograph.

Throat slit. Eyes vacant. Definitely not a fake. Beyond that, I had my doubts. "There is a resemblance, but . . . ."

"Resemblance, hell!" Kevin said. "That's me!"

"Setting aside the obvious rebuttal," I said. "Have you looked at yourself in the mirror?"

"What?"

"Your hair, it's not dark brown or wavy, it's almost golden and you have these little . . . ringlets." Weird thing was, I remembered his features from the tavern differently. But I was looking right at him now.

Kevin's hand brushed his hair, his fingers combing through the curls. He frowned, walked over to the full-length mirror on the back of the closet door and said, "Jesus! What's happening to me?" His hands pressed against the side of his face. "My ears, they're almost . . . pointed."

"They said you weren't Kevin Robb."

"They were mistaken."

"What if they were right?" I said. "What happened to you three days ago? When Darius said he'd killed the Kevin Robb in the photograph three days ago, you reacted."

"A panic attack."

Curious, I walked over to him and tried to recall the moment when he first burst through the door of the Willowbrook Tavern. No denying it: That Kevin Robb *was* different from this Kevin Robb. He was changing, his physical attributes metamorphosing slower than the conscious level of human perception. Something time-lapse photography would certainly reveal. "Explain."

"Three days ago I had my first panic attack, an overwhelming sensation that my life was in danger. I needed to get out of my apartment. I couldn't go to work. Certainly couldn't stay there for hours. I chalked it up to restlessness, lack of sleep. But every time I tried to fight it, to return to my normal routines, the sensation returned. Been living out of my car for the last two days, moving whenever I *sensed* danger. Until my car broke down, about a mile and a half from the tavern. I started walking. When I saw the tavern, something clicked."

"Clicked?"

Kevin shrugged. "Don't know. Like it was a safe haven."

I chuckled. "First time anyone's called the Willowbrook Tavern a safe haven."

"None of this makes sense."

"What happened nine years ago?"

"Nine years?"

"Something Mortenn said after Darius said you weren't Kevin Robb."

"Right," Kevin said, remembering. "I would have been ten. Not much . . . . Wait! The traveling carnival. Henderson Acres. My parents took me. I got lost."

"Tell me about it."

"All week long, I watched the carnies putting together these fantastic rides, like this fairytale city rising from the field. It seemed magical. I begged my parents to take me. I was so excited. So much to do, so many rides, and games, and the food. Stuffed myself on cotton candy, fries, and hot dogs. I felt sick and got separated in the crowd. Too much noise and confusion. I walked into the woods and got lost. Seemed like hours. Eventually, my parents found me asleep, curled under a bush near the edge of the woods."

"The edge?"

"Yeah," he said. "They wondered why I gave up so close to the carnival grounds, figured I must have been exhausted."

"Is it possible somebody left you there, where you were sure to be found?"

"No," Kevin said, "I was alone. Don't remember anybody else."

"Maybe you weren't supposed to remember."

"What are you saying?"

"There's a gap in your memories," I said. "And, since the moment you bumped into me, I've been *recalling* things I couldn't possibly know. Somehow, we're connected."

"Those men—or whatever they are—they recognized you. And how did you learn to fight like that. It was almost . . . "

"Fae."

"I was going to say 'inhuman.' What about 'Fae'?"

"The word Mortenn used when he first saw me."

"Maleck called you Silverthorn. And Darius, he called you something else . . . "

"Whisper Guard."

"He also said you were dead."

"Makes two of us," I said wryly.

"According to Maleck, you don't know who you are," Kevin said. "And I'm not who I think I am."

"What if they're right?"

"About us?"

"What do you know about the Fae?"

"Fae? You mean Faeries, right? Folklore stuff. Read about it in English lit. *A Midsummer Night's Dream*. Can't recall too much."

"Anything about changelings?"

"What? Alien shape-shifters?"

I shook my head. "Faerie children swapped for human children. The human parents unknowingly raise the Faerie child, while the Faeries raise the human child."

"Are you trying to say I'm a Faerie child? That I'm not Kevin Robb, that the real Kevin was raised by Faeries, and murdered three days ago? That's ridiculous!"

"More ridiculous than bodies disappearing in front of your eyes?"

"But I look just like the other Kevin Robb—"

"Past tense. You're changing. Reverting."

"—and I have his memories—*my*—memories."

"We've seen how memories can be tricked. How much do you really remember before that day at the carnival?"

"A lot, ten years of my . . . ." Kevin pounded the heel of his palm against his forehead in frustration.

"What about your parents? We could call them, ask them about that day."

Kevin shook his head. "They died, fifteen months ago, electrical fire. Smoke inhalation. I was at a party when . . . ." He sat on the edge of the bed, shaking his head. "Why? What's the point? This changeling nonsense."

"Maybe the Faeries thought you would be safe here," I said absently. I was staring at my own reflection in the mirror. The hair I had assumed was prematurely grey was, quite possibly, naturally silver. My ears, so like Mortenn's—and now Kevin's—rising in back, unmistakably pointed. As I examined events in my life, those remembrances began to tatter under my mental scrutiny, a life's scenery constructed from tissue paper, flimsy and unconvincing. Only the past year held the solidity of truth. And my name, Ray Thorn, perhaps only a half-truth. Could my life, my home, my job, all of it, be nothing more than a way station? Silverthorn was real. Ray Thorn was the illusion.

I had been in a holding pattern, marking time. Another word bubbled up to the surface of my consciousness and it held the sad ring of truth. Darius had thought me dead, but the hidden reality was a crueler fate. *Exile* . . . .

Inevitably, the answer came to me. "Henderson Acres."

"What about it?"

"Those woods aren't far from here," I said. "Few blocks behind Willowbrook Tavern."

He nodded. "We should go. Agreed?"

"Not yet."

"When?"

"Twilight."

Though Kevin seemed too restless to sleep, I took the first watch. Made bad coffee with the in-room percolator and supplies. One sip and I swore off the stuff. I angled the ratty armchair toward the front window and widened the gap between the putrid orange curtains enough to reveal most of the parking lot—an island of fractured concrete under the pale wash of streetlights—while maintaining our own privacy. We'd been up most of the night, so the plan was to sleep through the morning and into the afternoon, to bide our time during the day and await twilight. I doubted it would be that simple. Darius had found Kevin once. I had no delusions about his ability to do so again.

I settled into the uncomfortable chair with my legs extended, feet crossed at the ankles. In fifteen hours, we could walk into Henderson Acres. A long time, maybe, but we had no choice. We would wait. And if the situation called for action, instinct would take over. It always had. I glanced at the bed and was not surprised to see Kevin asleep. He'd been on the run for three days. I, on the other hand, had only been drafted into service several hours ago.

Kevin's referring to my disreputable place of employment as a "safe haven" had brought a smile to my face. But I began to wonder if it had been the tavern that had lured him inside or its proximity to me, a trained guardian. *Whisper Guard.* We were connected in all the craziness. Would we find the answers we sought in the woods where a young boy had gotten lost nine years ago?

A weird sensation overcame me. Sitting in the lumpy chair, staring into the illuminated night, my awareness seemed to slip out of the moment. Disconnected
from my flesh, in some sort of trancelike state, I heard an old woman's voice, a frail
whisper on the edge of a dream.

"So soon you begin to remember, Sunray Silverthorn."

I spoke into the heedless dark of the hotel room. "Bits and pieces, Elder. Not
nearly enough."

"Four years too soon," she said. *"But it was necessary to interrupt your pretender life. To
protect the heir."*

"Kevin? Then he is one of the Fae?"

"Miles, last heir to Clan Evergreen."

"And who am I? Who is Sunray Silverthorn?"

*"Also of our clan, disgraced of our clan, a captain of the Whisper Guard, slayer of a Royal
in a duel sprung from a lover's jealous rage—"*

With her words, a rush of images tumbled up through my mind, lost memories
and forgotten faces revealed for a split second before falling away again. And with
the images, glimpses into my past, the familiar sound of names lost to the shell of
a man I had become. "Allemara chose me!"

"—betrayer of protocol—"

"Prince Raganel was the challenger. Honor dictated—"

"—and, ultimately—"

"He refused to yield!"

"—an exile."

Remembering, I sighed. "A five-year sentence."

"By my proclamation," the elder said. The walls of the motel room faded into
translucency, as insubstantial as my *pretender* life. Beyond these hollow walls, I saw
a rich forest glade and, standing in its center, a majestically old woman in a
shimmering golden gown with impossibly long silver hair, tinted emerald green.
Despite her advanced age, her features were delicate and beautiful. Motes of light
sparkled from her green eyes and took flight with an aerial dance akin to the passage of butterflies. *"Knowing the truth of which you speak, it was I, Ellisandra Evergreen,
who waived the execution order and spared your life."*

"This is not a life," I said. "Not the life I was meant to live."

*"You seek pardon? A commutation? Then do what you must. Bring the heir safely home to
us and it may yet come to pass."*

"I will not fail."

She nodded, pleased. *"Now tell me of his would-be assassins."* After I recounted
the fight with Darius and his twin brothers, she frowned. *"As I expected, clanless
rogues, no lasting allegiance other than to coin.*

*"A rival clan, out of the Unseelie Court, seeks to steal our land and holdings without the
consequence of retaliation. For years, we have been unable to expose them."*

"Darius will talk."

"Remember, the heir's safety takes precedence. May fortune favor you, Silverthorn."

Pins and needles in my feet. The walls of the cheap motel room were solid again. Seemingly in the blink of an eye, my *other* awareness had fled. The gap between the curtains revealed it was nearly dawn. Almost two hours had passed. Other than the minor discomfort of my feet, I felt invigorated. Rising, I walked toward the bathroom.

Kevin sat up, yawned, and looked around the drab room. "My turn already?"

"That won't be—"

A sound like an explosion behind me.

I whirled as the door slammed against the wall. Darius rushed in, gun leveled in the hand of his bandaged arm. Kevin rolled off the far side of the mattress. Two rounds blasted into the headboard behind where he'd been sitting. I grabbed the coffee pot and flung the scalding liquid at Darius's face. A third shot, intended for me, slammed into the ceiling as he recoiled from the heat.

A spin-kick dislodged the gun from his hand. It clattered against the wall to my left. Without pause, Darius reached for his soul blade. I charged him, pinning his arm against his body as I drove him backward and slammed him into the television set bolted to the dresser. He grunted, regained his balance, then pushed off, using his superior height and weight to force me back on my heels. "I promise you a slow death, Silverthorn."

A glance over my shoulder caused me to adjust the angle of my retreat.

"If you hadn't interfered—!"

"It's in my nature," I said. *Just a little bit more . . . .*

"Maleck and Mortenn will be avenged!"

I spied Kevin, circling around the foot of the bed, wielding the soul blade he'd snatched from Mortenn. *The heir's safety takes precedence.* I shook my head vigorously to stop Kevin. Darius frowned in apparent confusion. So I chose that moment to stop resisting and fell backward, using his forward momentum against him. I hit the floor and rolled on my back, tucking my legs between us, then pushing out with both feet, hurling him overhead with all my strength.

Upended, his body smashed through the bay window in a tangle of curtains and a shower of glass, and he fell hard against the pavement outside the motel room.

I rolled onto my hands and knees and scrambled for the gun lying against the wall, under the shattered window. Darius roared in anger a split-second before Kevin yelled, "Look out!"

Unable to secure the gun, I rose from a crouch as Darius hurled himself through the broken window. His shadow swept over me, the only light glinting off the soul blade clutched in his right hand, sweeping toward my chest. Peripherally, I saw Maleck's knife on the end table—out of reach.

Kevin yelled. "Catch!"

It all happened in a moment. My left arm shot out, seizing Darius's right wrist, below his injured forearm, to thwart his attack, even as my right hand opened to catch the soul blade Kevin had tossed to me. And again Darius's momentum worked against him. I slipped the point of the blade between us and his own charge drove it into his chest, up to the hilt, as we both fell against the side of the bed.

He grunted, fear ablaze in his eyes as he tried to pull away from me, but I held tight. Groaning, he staggered upright, lurched sideways a few steps, and fell to his knees. He pounded my right arm with his left fist, but I stayed with him, one hand pressing the knife into his flesh, the other keeping his own knife turned away from me. "Who hired you?"

"Go to hell!"

As he struggled, I felt myself becoming stronger, infused with a heady rush of power. I twisted the knife against his ribs for emphasis. "Which clan paid you?"

"Too late," he mumbled weakly.

Too late—? The soul blade! "No!"

I tried to remove the knife, but he clamped his hand over mine, perversely holding it in place for the last few seconds of his life. The hilt was slick with his blood and slipped within my grasp.

He collapsed, spittle on his chin, grinning insanely as he held the knife inside his flesh, literally willing his life away in defeat simply to deny me a vital piece of information.

Before Darius's body faded back to *Otherworld,* I found in his jacket pocket, tied to a leather cord, an irregular chunk of dark crystal, the tip of which glowed when I waved it in Kevin's direction. One mystery solved, if not all of them. But the crystal was a potential clue to the identity of the Unseelie Court clan, so I took it with us as we fled the damaged motel room. We killed time in a diner a couple miles away, drinking coffee, exploring fragments of recovered memories as the day expended itself. Eventually, we made our way back on foot to Henderson Acres, and walked deep into the woods.

Instinctively, we ignored the will-o'-the-wisps, as they would only lead us astray, and we waited for the true path to reveal itself to us. Miles Evergreen had been kept safe, hidden among the humans as Kevin Robb for nine years, in anticipation of this twilight crossing. Fortunately for me, our paths crossed. Redemption was within my grasp.

At last, the path appeared, weaving through the underbrush, gilded in Faerie lights like a bridge into dreams. For me, it was a passage out of uninspired dreams and back into my true life.

With a flourish befitting a prince of a Seelie Court clan, I bowed from the waist and extended my arm toward the path. "After you, Miles Evergreen."

He chuckled. "I'll never get used to this."

"You'd be surprised."

He stepped onto the path to reclaim his birthright.
My road back was simpler, but no less important.

Grim Necessity

Jeffrey Lyman

FEATHERLIGHT AND HER PARTNER, REMY, STRODE DOWN THE corridor of the pixie wing of the maximum security prison, boots clacking on the floor. Remy tapped his billy club against his hip as he walked, a nervous habit. Full-sized bricks, painted white and stacked four high, had been used in the construction of the walls, and there was iron plating behind those bricks. Iron didn't bother Featherlight, but Remy said it felt like an uncomfortable itch.

"I can't believe Clank's getting a visitor," he said.

"Happens to the worst of us," she replied, keeping her eyes open for trouble. "I can't believe the warden's allowing her to see a visitor."

The corridor ended and P-wing opened up around them. They were on the top floor of four stories of cells, wrapped around a central, open core. The core had been strung back and forth with steel wire to keep the pixies from flying.

There were a lot of pixies inside today. The prison was on semi-lockdown because of an outbreak of fighting the day before. The warden was limiting the number of races out in the yards. Right now the brownies and faeries were out, and the pixies, ogres, and most of the dwarfs were inside.

Featherlight and Remy stopped in front of a cell. "Clankerbell. You have a visitor." Remy grunted.

She didn't agree with the warden allowing Clank to have a visitor. All evidence indicated that she hadn't been in the fight, but Featherlight knew Clank had been involved somehow. She always was. Clankerbell stood from her cot, looking bored. Plastic dog tags hung proudly on the wall behind her. They were a trophy, taken from the body of the rottweiler that had bitten off her right wing.

"My reputation must be growing," she said, staring at Featherlight. "They sent the Big Pig to fetch me this time." She fanned her remaining left wing like a butterfly and glanced at Remy. "Who is it?"

She had gotten a new tattoo on her arm, Featherlight noticed. An inverted rainbow, meaning something like an upside-down cross. No matter how hard the warden tried, he couldn't keep the pixies from getting colors for their prison tats. They practically shat colors, so what was the use?

"I have no idea who it is and I didn't ask," Remy said. "He's either a dwarf or a short, hairy man. You ready?" Clank nodded and Remy bellowed back down to the guardhouse, "Open up number seventeen."

The bars of Clankerbell's cell clicked and whirred on their servos and slid to the side.

Featherlight tensed up. "You know the drill. Keep your hands to yourself and I won't crush you."

"Chill, Big Pig. We're cool." Clankerbell smirked and stepped out of her cell.

Featherlight was a protean shapeshifter who could change not only her looks, but her size. She could swell up in the corridor and mash Clankerbell into the wall in a second if there were trouble. She could also close up her wounds if someone knifed her. The warden always sent her into the fights, and the prisoners respected her abilities.

Clank carelessly sauntered down the corridor, whistling the same cheery song all Pixies whistled. Featherlight heard it in her head sometimes after long days. Remy walked behind them both to stay out of the 'crush zone' should Featherlight's abilities be needed.

They passed a smaller cell with a single bell hanging from the ceiling, and it rang off-key in time with Clank. An ugly gremlin peeked out below the rim and Featherlight pointed at him. "Go back to sleep, Smear." The greasy head vanished.

They passed through security, where Clankerbell was searched from top to bottom. Featherlight then led her through a mouse hole and into the secure visiting area. Birdcages hung where pixies could talk to their visitors. More docile inmates were allowed out into the larger Visitor's Room to meet with family members directly. Clankerbell had never been docile.

Featherlight and Remy locked Clankerbell into a birdcage securely.

"Yo, Feather."

Featherlight looked up as an elf guard leaned into the secure room. He was holding a telephone receiver.

"What?" she shouted.

"The Man wants to talk to you."

Featherlight quickly passed through pixie security, and, swelling to near-human size, climbed down to the floor of the guard booth. The elf, who was now shorter than she, handed her the phone.

"What's up, Boss?" She looked out the booth window and was surprised at how many visitors were in the room. With the tension in the prison, the inmates were only being allowed out a few at a time and the backlog of visitors was growing. All manner of husbands and wives slouched at tables, waiting. A gaggle of dwarf children chased a troll kit around. One of the prisoners, dressed like a harlequin, was juggling and failing to entertain them.

"Featherlight," the warden said. "Come on up. I want you to see something."

"I'm looking after Clankerbell."

"Remy's fine. Come on up."

"Sure." She hung up with misgivings and leaned down to her pixie partner. "Hey Remy, you got this?"

Remy nodded and flapped his wings. "If you gotta go, you gotta go. Odbottom will back me up. Besides, me and Clankerbell here are old friends, ain't we, Clank? She'll behave."

Featherlight hustled upstairs to the catwalks. As she headed in the direction of the warden's office, she took note of the dwarf entering Clank's small room. He wasn't someone she was familiar with, but then Clank rarely got visitors since her mother and grandmother were also incarcerated. Nothing looked out of the ordinary as he clambered up onto a stool and pulled down a phone receiver from the wall. Clankerbell lifted a tiny receiver in her birdcage. Guards in the booth monitored the conversation.

Featherlight pushed through an exterior door into late October sunshine and hurried down the catwalk, passing over the brownie basketball courts. Several elf-guards monitored from above, arrows half-drawn in their bows. She could feel the tension in the air. Yesterday's fight had been a bad one.

She nodded to the guards, glancing down at the heavily muscled, shirtless brownies scuffling below over bright orange, squeaky-balls. The brownies used toy basketballs, and the noise was always riotous. Today it was worse than ever, and she could barely hear herself think. They were dribbling as hard as they could. Featherlight had always thought using a dog's chew-toy was degrading, but the brownies, as tough as they were, loved the noise.

Next came the dwarf-yard on her right, if you could call it a yard. It was all concrete, elevated a few feet above the ground. There was no way the dwarfs were going to tunnel out through that, though they were constantly kicking and scuffing at it, and frowning. Looking for cracks, the guards used to say. Because of the lockdown, there were only four dwarves out today. One was bench pressing a massive weight. Two were braiding each other's beards. The fourth glared and shouted insults over at the adjacent faerie yard. He was new, came in with a number of faeries dressed like pirates a week before. He looked like all the other dwarves now in prison-orange.

The modestly-sized faerie yard on Featherlight's left was completely enclosed in a Kevlar, mesh cage. The faeries couldn't tolerate the usual steel chain link fences, and the prison had to box them in somehow.

A few blues were hanging from the west end of the cage, their wings drawn up tight. A few reds were clustered on the east end. They could hang there for hours, trading insults and hatred. Today they were joined together in common cause, shouting insults back at the dwarf. Below them on the ground of the yard stalked the pathetic non-fliers with broken or damaged wings. Faeries could be vicious when they fought, going after each others' wings first.

She passed through another security gate and into the Admin Wing. It was warmer here. She shook off the early season chill. She always got cold so fast.

"What's up?" she said as she opened the warden's door. He was on the phone, but he waved her in with a sasusage-fingered hand. He was a brownie, as fat as brownies came when they dined on too many cakes and bowls of milk a day.

"So? What do you think," he said when he hung up.

"About what?"

"Clankerbell."

"Did something happen?" Featherlight immediately thought of Remy. He was a fighting pixie, but Clankerbell was Clankerbell.

"Not yet. Take a look." He gestured to the bank of video screens along his wall. Several were trained on the Visitors' Rooms, on Clankerbell's in particular.

Featherlight dropped onto a seat. She hadn't created wings for this body, so she didn't need to use the wing-cutout at the seatback. "If you think Clank's up to something, I should be there."

"No, you should be out here because something *is* up. That fight yesterday was bigger than any I've seen in my thirty years here. And Clankerbell, who always fights, didn't fight. Then she gets a visitor today, her first in years. It's all tied together somehow."

"Did you send over more guards?"

"I've got four extra on the catwalks above the Visitors' Room, that's it. I don't want to drain my resources if trouble breaks out elsewhere."

A siren wailed. Featherlight scanned the screens. The brownies and redcaps were quiet. The ogres sat in their cells, staring at the stone walls, which always seemed to fascinate them. She pointed to the screen showing the dwarf and faerie yards.

"They're trying to rip through!" she said.

One of the insults must have hit home, because two of the four dwarfs were pressed up against the Kevlar mesh, trying to pull it apart. There was no sound, but it looked like they were screaming as they strained. Kevlar was strong, but an angry dwarf might be stronger. Blue and red faeries fluttered everywhere inside of the cage. Several were right up in the dwarves faces, yanking at their beards through the mesh and shouting back.

"I'm going out there," Featherlight said.

"Sit tight! The elves can handle it, and I'll call in a troll or two if need be. This might be a distraction, so keep an eye on Clankerbell."

Elves fired pixie-dust tipped arrows down into the dwarf-yard, but the dwarves were too worked up to go down easily. Nearby faeries began falling from the top of the cage like bugs from a hot lightbulb as the dust grew thick.

Suddenly the squawk-box on the warden's desk erupted in shouting and a cacophonous barking. It quickly clarified into Wheezer's voice. Wheezer was the head troll over the mess hall.

"Warden! We've got a situation!"

"What's going on?"

Both the warden and Featherlight stared at the security screens and the scrum of brown, furry bodies in the mess hall.

"The faeries all dumped their trays into the Selkie watering hole. I've got pissed off seals everywhere!"

"There she goes," Featherlight said, pointing up at Clankerbell's screen.

Clankerbell's dwarf visitor stood and smashed through the Plexiglas wall separating him from her birdcage with one powerful punch that must have broken his hand. Undeterred, he tore her cage from its anchors and charged out into the Visitors' Room. An elf guard jabbed him with an electric-stick but he shrugged it off and continued his bowlegged run for the front security door.

The two guards at the security station and the four additional guards that the warden had sent lined up at the door, while behind them the ogres pulled down the steel shields. Arrows were drawn and Featherlight looked to the warden, wanting permission to go.

In a blink, a table crashed into the guards. Then another. Featherlight stood. There were other dwarves amidst the visitors, helping Clankerbell. Guards sprawled and arrows sprang disjointedly from bows to land into the crowds of panicking civilians. People fainted from errant clouds of pixie dust. Three dwarves rushed forward. The two ogres at the door hunkered down at the ready. The dwarf carrying Clankerbell's cage hadn't slowed his run.

The Warden started slapping buttons.

"What are you doing?" Featherlight's head was spinning. Clankerbell was getting away. Conversely, Clank might get injured in her own riotous escape. Ogres were excitable, and pixies were squashable.

"I'm neutralizing the situation with pixie-dust bombs before someone gets hurt," he shouted. "We don't want a hostage situation, and I can't let Clankerbell escape. And I can't spare more guards for her or for the Mess Hall until that damned dwarf stops tearing up my Kevlar cage. If he gets it open, we'll have faeries flying for the hills."

The screens showing both the Visitors' Room and the Mess Hall blossomed into white like swirling snow, as pixie-bombs exploded *en masse*.

"You shouldn't have let her have visitors," Featherlight said.

"Just go out make sure everything's settled. I want everyone in full lockdown, in their cells with the doors closed."

"The brownies, too?"

"Yes, the brownies, too. But they're the least of my concern. What are they going to do, break out and clean my office?"

Featherlight stood. "Something's not right."

"Is it that obvious?"

"No, Clank had to know we'd gas her in the Visitors' Room. She's not stupid."

"So go check on her after you check on my Kevlar." He poured himself a quick shot of milk and tossed it back.

"I'm on it." Featherlight hustled back out to the catwalk.

There were eight elves above the dwarf yard now, dropping arrows like pennies into a wishing well. There was a thick cloud of pixie dust below them, and one dwarf was staggering. The other was still bellowing and madly trying to tear his way in at the faeries. The red and blue faeries who hadn't succumbed to the dust were pressed against the far side of the pen, as far away as possible. Still, there were probably thirty sleeping bodies stretched across their cage.

"He's going down!" someone crowed.

Featherlight leaned over the railing, studying the Kevlar. The dwarf had managed to stretch the weave big enough to get his arm through. They'd have to replace that section before the faeries could come out again. Faeries were like those octopi in the nature specials, they could wriggle out through anything. Cartilage for bones.

She wasn't needed here.

She hurried on, over the brownie pen where the small men watched the commotion with agitation, squeaky balls held at rest. They hated pixie-dustings. All that mess just upset them.

With barely a thought, she dropped down into the form of a huge black dog, loping along the catwalk. It hurt for a moment as her bones reconfigured themselves, and then it was done. Her shaggy fur ruffled in the breeze of her own swift passing. She wanted to be ready for anything.

She raced through the door at speed, stirring up clouds of recently settled pixie dust. She snorted and sniffed at the air, but couldn't smell anything over that dust. Her sharp eyes immediately discerned Clankerbell's open cage on the floor near the room's main door. Clank's dwarf accomplice was simultaneously trying to wedge the doors open a crack with a table leg and trying to breathe fresh air through that same crack. The rest of the dwarves who had been involved were unconscious amidst guards and children. Had Clank escaped?

No, Featherlight was certain of that. Clank was up to something. The open door had not yet been used. She raised herself back up into bipedal form and scooped a handful of pixie dust from a table-top. She walked to the frantically working dwarf and tapped him on the shoulder. When he turned, she blew the dust directly into his face. He shouted and leapt off-balance like a drunk. In a second, he was snoring.

She jogged up the stairs in the now terribly silent room and walked carefully through the vacant security gate. The guards were sprawled, asleep. No sign of

Clank. Also no sign of Remy.

Featherlight crushed herself down tight into pixie shape and walked into the pixie corridor. The door to the corridor was open and dust had drifted in. She reached the fourth floor of P-Wing and walked past cell after cell of sleeping or groggy inhabitants. She slowed as she approached the open door of Clankerbell's cell. The steel bars had been torn and bent open. Two doll-sized oven mitts lay on the floor, obviously Clank's protection when she ripped apart the steel.

"Is that you, Big Pig?" a muffled version of Clank's voice called. "Come on in."

Featherlight stepped into the door opening and took in the scene: Clankerbell sat on the edge of her bed wearing a gasmask; Remy and Odbottom out cold and in a pile on the bed next to her. She held a plastic dog tag like a guillotine blade over Remy's neck, ready to decapitate him. It wasn't sharp, but she was plenty strong enough to do it.

"Where did you get that?" Featherlight said, pointing to the gas mask. She took a step forward. If she could swell up, maybe she could knock Clank and her dogtags back up against the wall.

"You could search a dwarf's beard for three days and still not find everything he's hidden there," Clankerbell said. "How do you think we get our drugs?"

"We should shave the dwarves when we bring 'em in," Featherlight said softly.

Clankerbell actually laughed. "The bleeding hearts would scream about cruel and unusual punishment. So tell me, how is it you're breathing when all of the other pigs are down on the deck?"

"You were expecting me," Featherlight said, ignoring the question. She reached out and grabbed the bent bars of the door with her bare hands, showing Clankerbell that steel didn't bother her.

"My grandmother told me you were the Big Pig in her day, too. She said that if I ever tried to escape, I had to handle you or it would never work."

Clankerbell launched herself straight into Featherlight's stomach, tearing her hands from the bars and hurtling her over the railing and into the empty space over the common area four stories below. Featherlight felt the pain of her feet leaving the deck, the panic of not touching ground. She felt powerless for the first time in years. She flailed and struggled.

Clank laughed as they clipped one of the steel wires the prison had strung above the open area. Featherlight's hand was cut cleanly from her arm. She screamed in pain as they went spinning from the impact. A second wire chopped through both of her legs. Clank leapt clear, twisting out of the way as several more staggered wires cut greater and greater parts from Featherlight's body: her pelvis, then torso, then her head from what was left.

Blackness descended and she lost vision for a moment, until her head cracked and bounced across the floor. That woke her up. She could hear other parts of her body slapping wetly to earth. Clankerbell whistled and sang from behind her gas mask and swung back and forth from wire to wire on her way to the floor. Other pixies had ventured out into the common area, pixies far enough from the entry corridor to have missed the full dose of dust.

Featherlight shut her eyes. No use in broadcasting she was still here and in pain.

Clank landed in an awkward clatter as her one wing failed to keep her balanced at the last minute. The pixies cheered anyway.

"That, ladies and gentlemen, is how it's done," Clank crowed, pulling her gasmask off with steel-burned hands. "Big Pig is down. Separate the head from the body, and I dare you to find me anyone that can survive. Now who's with me? The front door's open and I've done all the hard work. You just have to hold your breath long enough to fly across the Visitor's Room."

Again the cheers. Featherlight had heard enough. Clankerbell's carefully laid plan was nothing more than brute force—arrange for the faeries to riot outside, arrange for dwarves to riot in the Visitor's Room, and wait for the warden to start dropping bombs. Featherlight had been hoping for something more. Clankerbell's grandmother had been a master of subtlety.

She formed a body out of the concrete floor below her head and climbed to her two, new feet. Her broken head wobbled a little on the neck until she could settle it and heal the broken skull. Silence fell and pixies rapidly backed away.

"Hey Clank," Featherlight rasped, then cleared her throat.

"What the hell?" Clankerbell was brought up short, her eyes wide. "I ripped your damned head off your body!"

"Whatever."

Clankerbell shrieked and charged again, but Featherlight was ready this time. She swelled up one of her hands until it was six inches tall and grabbed Clank roughly. The pixie struggled in vain, spewing curses and blasphemies.

"Anyone else want a piece of me?" Featherlight shouted. She almost laughed when she realized she was surrounded by pieces of her old body.

The pixies, shocked, shuffled back to their cells. Featherlight dragged her huge hand and Clankerbell up the winding stairs to the top, and out through the entrance corridor. She swelled her body size to match her hand, and waited for the cavalry to arrive. She *was* the Big Pig. She was the last defense; always had been.

"How did you survive?" Clank demanded as they took her away to a long stint in solitary confinement. "What kind of a faerie are you?"

Featherlight shrugged and returned to the catwalks. Elf guards passed her, slapping her on the back and congratulating her. Her new body ached with all of the wounds of the old one, so she escaped the crush of medical personnel helping visitors and guards gathering troublemakers, and climbed to the roof.

There, amidst the mushroom-shaped fans and air conditioners, she watched the sun set.

She was not a faerie. She had been once, but not for a long, long time. She was the prison Grim.

Formerly a prisoner in the old jail, over four hundred years ago now, she had been executed for her crimes. Lucky her, they had buried her under the foundations of the new prison as the guardian Grim. Forbidden to leave the prison, even to fly for a second, she would prowl the catwalks and corridors day and night, night and day, until they tore the prison down and released her.

But hey, at least she was free to climb up to the roof and smell the fresh air. After so long, she didn't want to leave the prison. She would protect it and keep the inmates as safe as she could, from each other and from the guards. Even Clankerbell, her great-great-great-great granddaughter.

Author Bios

James Chambers "writes stories that are paced fast enough to friction burn a reader's eyeballs," says Horror Reader.com. His tales of horror, fantasy, and science fiction have been published in numerous anthologies, including *Bad-Ass Faeries, Breach the Hull, Crypto-Critters* (Volume 1 and 2), *Dark Furies, The Dead Walk, The Dead Walk Again, Hardboiled Cthulhu, No Longer Dreams, Weird Trails,* and *Warfear,* as well as the magazines *Bare Bone, Cthulhu Sex,* and *Allen K's Inhuman.* His short story collection, with illustrator Jason Whitley, *The Midnight Hour: Saint Lawn Hill and Other Tales,* was published in 2005. His website is www.jameschambersonline.com.

Mostly, **Bernie Mojzes** has dabbled. In what? you ask. Well, let's see. He's fiddled with UNIX, he's framed pictures, he's taught college courses and karate classes, he's designed and built networks and generated propaganda for the technical elite masses. He has studied the Great Philosophers and mocked them all. And, apparently, he's also dabbled with writing. Loki disapproves of this last activity: she looks at the screen, then at Bernie's face, then sighs deeply and lays her adorably furry head across the keyboard. *Enough,* she says. And then: *Feed me.*

Trisha J. Wooldridge is a freelance writer and editor with experience ranging from *Dungeons & Dragons Online* to animal rescue public relations. She is also a columnist, ad rep, and proofreader for *Massachusetts Horse* magazine. Trish has written a YA science-fiction novel, *A Silent Starsong,* and isco-writing *Fae Sithein: Yesterday's Shadows,* with Christy Tohara. An active member of the Editorial Freelancers Association and Broad Universe, Trisha has published essays on writing and marketing in *TOTAL Funds for Writers* and *The Freelancer.* For more information, check out Trish's website and blog at www.anovelfriend.com.

Christy E. Tohara is a middle school English teacher from South Jordan, Utah. Graduated from Brigham Young University with a bachelor's degree in Secondary Education, she's currently working on her first novel with Trisha Wooldridge. She has also published a few poems in chapbooks. While writing and editing is a daily practice in the classroom, Christy extended her experience by administrating writers groups. She has taken part in orchestrating various genres of writing as well as coaching writers with different skill levels.

Christopher Sirmons Haviland is the author of the young adult fantasy novel *Faith & Fairies* (as C.S. Haviland) and the angel fantasy *Change,* a short story published in *Pronto! Writings from Rome.* He studied under Terry Brooks, Ben Bova, John Saul,

Dorothy Allison, and Lawrence Montaigne. He is the editor of *The Synopsis Treasury of Science Fiction and Fantasy: Actual Synopses, Outlines, and Story Ideas Submitted to Industry By Published Authors* (soon to be released), featuring never-before-published work by H.G. Wells, Robert A. Heinlein, Frank Herbert, Andre Norton, Terry Brooks, Ben Bova, Frederik Pohl, Orson Scott Card, Connie Willis, Piers Anthony, L.E. Modesitt, David Brin, and many more. He co-produced an award-winning motion picture in 1997 called *The First of May*, which aired on HBO and HBO-Asia in 2000-2003. He lives in East Longmeadow, MA with his wife whom he met on the internet.

L. Jagi Lamplighter is a fantasy author. She has published numerous articles on Japanese animation and appears in several short story anthologies, including *Best of Dreams of Decadence*, *No Longer Dreams*, *Bad-Ass Faeries*, and the Science Fiction Book Club's *Don't Open This Book*. She recently sold her first trilogy, *Prospero's Daughter*, to Tor. Volume One, *Prospero Lost*, is scheduled for the Winter of 2009. Her website is http://www.sff.net/people/lamplighter/.

Elaine Corvidae has been telling stories about faeries, elves, and dragons since she was a small child. Her dark fantasy novels include several award-winning novels set in the *Shadow Fae* universe. When she isn't wandering the worlds of her imagination, she lives in Harrisburg, NC, with her husband and several cats. You can visit her on the web at www.onecrow.net.

D.C. Wilson lives in Harrisburg, PA with his wife Maria and their dog Rosie. His fiction has appeared in such anthologies as *Bad-Ass Faeries*, *No Longer Dreams*, and *Fantasical Visions III*. He's also been the feature author in the periodical *Tales of Indiscretion*. He attend Penn State University from which he earned both his Bachelor's and Master's Degrees. Allegedly, he works for the Pennsylvania Department of Environmental Protection and teaches part-time at Harrisburg Area Community College, but these may be just rumors.

Award-winning author **Skyla Dawn Cameron** has been writing approximately forever. Her early storytelling days were spent acting out strange horror/fairy tales with the help of her many dolls, and little has changed except that she now keeps those stories on paper. Her first novel, *River*, a unique werewolf tale, won her the 2007 EPPIE Award for Best Fantasy. If she ever becomes a grown-up, she wants to run her own pub, as well as become world dictator. Visit her on the web at www.skyladawncameron.com.

In addition to the first volume of *Bad-Ass Faeries*, **Lorne Dixon's** fiction has appeared, or is scheduled to appear, in *+The Horror Library+ Volume 2*, *Strange Stories Of Sand And Sea*, *Bound Is The Bewitching Lilith*, *Dark Distortions*, *Bound For Evil: Curious Tales Of Books Gone Bad*, *Dark Wisdom Magazine*, and PS Press' wildly anticipated *Darkness On The Edge*. In 2006 he was awarded the Graverson Award, by the Garden State Horror Writers.

Steven Earl Yoder has been writing for nearly 30 years, but only recently began pursuing publication. Previously he has been just about everything, including the founder of two science-fiction conventions, HurriCon in Ft. Walton, FL and JerseyDevilCon in Edison, NJ. He lives in Virginia with his wife, artist Christina Yoder, and three cats. He dedicates this story to his Father and Mother, who always believed but didn't live to see it.

C.J. Henderson is the creator of the Teddy London supernatural detective series, author of such diverse yet fabulously interesting titles as *The Field Guide to Monsters, Baby's First Mythos, The Encyclopedia of Science Fiction Movies,* and some fifty other books and novels. He has had hundreds of short stories and comics published along with thousands of non-fiction pieces. The first novel in his latest series, *Brooklyn Knights,* will be coming out from Tor later this year. Published in some ten languages around the world, he is as beloved as he is rotund, which is saying a lot. For more on this happiest, and heaviest, of fellows, check out his website, www.cjhenderson.com. If you send him a pie, he will remember you in his prayers.

Brian Koscienski & Chris Pisano are fun guys who lurk the realms of south central Pennsylvania, spreading their warped minds through the likes of novels, stories, comics, articles and even bawdy haiku. In their insidious quest for world domination, they created Fortress Publishing, Inc, which can be visited at www.fortresspublishinginc.com.

Danielle Ackley-McPhail has worked both sides of the publishing industry for over a decade. Her novels are *Yesterday's Dreams* and *Tomorrow's Memories.* She has also co-edited and contributed to numerous anthologies, including *Dark Furies, Breach the Hull,* and the upcoming science fiction anthologies *Barbarians at the Jumpgate* and *Space Pirates.* Her non-fiction works include select chapters *The Complete Guide to Writing Fantasy: The Author's Grimoire,* the upcoming *Elements of Fantasy: Magic.* She is a member of Broad Universe, a writer's organization focusing on promoting the works of women authors in the speculative genres. To learn more about her work, visit www.sidhenadaire.com.

Lee C. Hillman considers herself primarily a fanfiction author and has become a fascinated informal scholar of both fan culture and transformative works. Known online as "GwendolynGrace," she is a founding administrator at FictionAlley, where she moderates discussion boards and records readings for their fanfiction podcast, "SpellCast." She ran the first Harry Potter Conference (Nimbus - 2003) for HP Education Fanon, Inc., http://www.hpef.net/, and although she is the outgoing President of their Board of Directors, she looks forward to their upcoming conferences. By day she is a Project Manager, on the weekends she is a Baroness and bard in the Society for Creative Anachronism, and at all times, but mostly in the evenings, she is an actor, singer, and dancer in Boston area theatre. Sleep is optional.

A native of Cincinnati, Ohio, **James Daniel Ross** has been an actor, computer tech support operator, historic infotainment tour guide, armed self defense retailer, automotive petrol attendant, youth entertainment stock replacement specialist, mass market Italian chef, low priority courier, monthly printed media retailer, automotive industry miscellaneous task facilitator, and ditch digger. The *Radiation Angels: The Chimerium Gambit* is his first novel. Most people are begging him to go back to ditch digging.

Jason Franks runs the small press comics imprint Blackglass Press. He has published a number of comics anthologies, *One More Bullet*, *Rockstar Pizza*, and *Hard Words*, featuring work in many genres by a variety of independent writers and artists. His prose and comics work has been published in *Deathlings*, *Tango*, and *Robots Are People, Too*. Franks currently resides in Melbourne, Australia.

Steven Mangold co-runs the small press comics imprint Blue Rose Studios. He has published various mini-comics including; *Neighbor Relations*, *Nature's Call*, and *Another Day*. His prose and comics work has been published in *Robots Are People, Too*, *One More Bullet*, and the upcoming *Sketch South* compilation. He currently resides in central Florida.

Phil "Satyrblade" Brucato "To write is to tell the Truth." Those words hang next to Phil's computer, and for almost 20 years they've defined both his writing and his life. From *Weird Tales Magazine* to *newWitch Magazine*, from *Pop! Goes the Witch* to *Deliria: Faerie Tales for a New Millennium*, "Satyr's" creations mix playful satire with passionate Romanticism. A recipient of various awards, Phil has published dozens of columns, short stories, essays, interviews, and comics, in addition to the role-playing games for which he's famous. This tale comes from a combination of his Sicilian heritage and some of the rougher elements of the starving artist life. "I have met the Money Ogre," Phil says, "and he is me." Satyr's blogs are at: http://satyrblade.livejournal.com and http://www.myspace.com/satyrblade.

John Passarella co-authored *Wither*, which won the Horror Writer Association's prestigious Bram Stoker Award for best first novel of 1999. Columbia Pictures purchased the feature film rights to *Wither* in a preemptive bid. Passarella's other novels include two standalone sequels: *Wither's Rain*, and *Wither's Legacy*, three media tie-in novels (*Buffy the Vampire Slayer: Ghoul Trouble*, *Angel: Avatar*, *Angel: Monolith*) and, most recently, *Kindred Spirit*, a paranormal thriller. He resides in southern New Jersey with his wife and three children. Please visit him online at www.passarella.com.

Jeffrey Lyman (www.jdlyman.com) is a 2004 graduate of the Odyssey Fantasy Writing Workshop. He has been published in various anthologies, including *No Longer Dreams* by Lite Circle Press, *Sails and Sorcery* by Fantasist Enterprises, and *Breach the Hull* by Marietta Publishing. He was involved in editing both *Bad Ass Faeries I* and *II*. He is currently finishing up a novel about some pretty rotten faeries.

Artists Bios

Thomas Nackid has been a professional artist and designer for over seventeen years. His artwork has graced the cover of *Space and Time Magazine* and he is currently working on several cover art commission, including the *Bad-Ass Faeries* series. He has worked as a staff artist for: a major university; a technical communications firm providing training materials for Fortune 500 companies; and the country's largest provider of legal graphics. To learn more about his work, please visit www..tomnackidart.com.

Christina Yoder is an award-winning fine artist and graphics designer who has worked in the commercial industry for over twelve years. In 2003, she went solo and opened up a freelance business, Dragon Graphics, and relocated to Bishop, VA. Her works for DVD covers, book covers, publications, corporate identity and packaging design have been widely distributed in Canada and the U.S. In addition, Christina has been branching out to sculpture and fine arts.

Bryan Prindiville is the creator of the monthly feature Frances & Friends, digitally published though the online distributor, Clickwheel.net. In between keeping up with his work as an illustrator, cartoonist, and graphic designer he sneaks in time to do daily sketches at his egotistically named blog, BryanPrindiville.com. He also wants to say hi to his Mom.

Matt Hawk, a Seattle-based artist enjoys Costello over Presley, thinks American cheese is not only an insult to America but to the entire Dairy Industry, and lastly feels everyone should try just a little stinkin harder on April Fools Day. You can see his work on his web site, www.greatscotproductions.homestead.com.

Ruth Lampi has been drawing bad-ass and well-armed faeries from the time she was a tree climbing pirate princess of five. As an illustrator and sculptor, Ruth loves nothing better than creating new worlds and realms of story. Her work can be found in *Children of Morpheus, Goblin Tales, No Longer Dreams, The Chronicles of Ramlar NPC Guide, Vampire Universe*, and the novel *Children of the Orcs*.

Bring it on!
Bad-Ass Faeries battle it out next in:

Bad-Ass Faeries 3:
In All Their Glory

Coming from Mundania Press in 2010

In the finest tradition of faerie folklore, transitioned into
the modern day, experience challenge and conflict
as seen through fae eyes.

Visit www.sidhenadaire.com/books/BAF3.htm for more details.